HOUSE OF Aries

BOOK I
The Ascendant Series

Whitney Estenson

Flint Hills Publishing
www.flinthillspublishing.com

ISBN-13:978-1537020860
ISBN-10:1537020862

For Josh and Avery: my rock and my inspiration.

"True it is, without falsehood, certain and most true. That which is above is like that which is below and that which is below is like that which is above, to accomplish the miracle of unity."

Hermes Trismegistus

1

I *hate* mornings.

I wasn't always that way. I used to be the first one up in the house, downstairs and cooking breakfast before my parents were dressed for work or my younger brother Chase dragged himself up from his room in the basement, eyes still bleary from sleep. When he reached the kitchen, his greeting was always the same, "What are you burning this morning, Kyndal?" I'd look up briefly from the skillet, raise my eyebrow at him, then return to what I was doing. Now all mornings do is remind me how much my life has gone to hell.

I lay in bed staring at the unfamiliar ceiling above me. I've lived with my Aunt Alessandra for two weeks now, and every time I wake up, I still expect to see my old room and every morning I am hit with how much I miss it. The purple walls, the back wall of my closet where my friends signed their names and wrote me messages, the mirror on my dresser covered with so many photos; I could barely even see my reflection. I even miss the orange stain on the carpet where I accidentally knocked over my nail polish when I was thirteen and was too scared to tell my mom about it. By the time she saw it, the stain had already set in. Everything about that room held a memory, told a story from my life. Now that room is gone. I look around this room and see nothing of that vibrancy. Just four beige walls and a wooden floor. No story, no life.

It's hard to imagine my dad living here. According to Alessandra, this is the house she and my dad, Mark, grew up in. When my dad was eighteen, he met my mom. She was a few years older, coming through town with some friends on a camping trip. According to my parents, it was love at first sight. My dad was sitting in a local cafe when my mom, Sofia, walked in and stole his heart. After that, they were inseparable. When my mom left, Dad followed, leaving behind his parents and a ten-year-old Alessandra. He never came back. Not long after, I arrived. Now, I'm living with a woman I don't know, all because she is the only family I have left.

I pushed back the covers and swung my legs off the side of the bed, stretching as I sat up. I knew that if I didn't make an appearance soon, Alessandra would be knocking on my door. I slowly wandered out of the room (I can't think of it as *my* room) and down the stairs into the kitchen. I found my aunt sitting at the kitchen table, dressed for the day in her heavy hiking boots, khaki shorts, and guide shirt. Her short, dark hair was still wet from her morning shower. She was drinking coffee and reading what looked like the weather report. In the short time I've lived here, I've come to recognize this as her routine.

Although her back was to me, she knew I was there. This house is so full of creaking boards, there's no such thing as a quiet entrance.

"Good morning," she said. Her smile was warm and her brown eyes were dark but gentle. "Did you sleep well?"

"Yes, thank you." I didn't mention waking up in tears. I had dreamt about my parents being alive, and I was so convinced it was real. She didn't need to know that.

"Glad to hear it. Look, I have an ATV tour this morning through Allegheny Park, but if you're ready in 30 minutes, I can give you a ride to school before I head to work."

I winced. "Ah, *no offense,* but I'm already going to be enough of a freak show to everyone there by being the new girl. I don't need to be the new girl who has to get a ride to school from her aunt. I'm seventeen, not seven."

"Well, *no offense,* but I know how much you don't want to go to this school, and I don't trust that you'll actually go. So, I'm taking you." With that, she turned back around, bringing the discussion to an abrupt end.

I turned on my heel and headed back up the stairs. I sighed. Time to get ready for my first day of school. Starting school with only nine weeks left until summer seemed like a waste of time, but Alessandra assured me it would be good for me; allow me to, "get involved in the community and make some friends." *Just kill me now.*

I took a quick shower and stood wrapped in a towel in front of my closet. My options of what to wear were limited.

3

Almost all of my wardrobe was designed to be worn in the near constant heat of Texas, not the cool air of a Pennsylvania April. I settled for a deep red sweater (my best color), skinny jeans, and nearly knee-high black boots. I got this outfit when I went to a cabin in Colorado on spring break last year with my family. I smiled slightly at the memory.

I had dragged Chase shopping with me, forcing him to give me his opinion on all the outfits I tried on. Chase hated shopping. His own fashion sense was limited to shorts, graphic tees, and sandals. He always looked like he was headed out to surf, even though we lived nowhere near the beach. The last shop we entered that day had the best pair of boots I had ever seen. The second I put them on, I knew I wanted them. They fit perfectly. Unfortunately, their price would have meant no gas for the next two weeks. So I took them off, waved goodbye, and left. Chase and I returned to the cabin, and I swear, that night—I dreamt about those boots. I woke up the next morning to a note on the table by the bed:

> *Happy early birthday. These made you look like you could kick some ass…You better wear them ALL THE TIME!*
>
>   *C.*

Confused, I looked around the room until I eventually found a box at the foot of the bed. I opened it up to find the same boots from the day before. How and when Chase went back for them, I didn't know. I put them on immediately, not caring that I was still in my pajamas, and headed to the kitchen to start making breakfast. Ten minutes into making scrambled eggs, Chase walked into the kitchen, smiling at me from the other side of the breakfast bar as he walked toward the kitchen table to sit down. "What are you burning this morning?" he asked. Rather than answer, I grabbed an empty glass, filled it with OJ and walked around the breakfast bar to hand him the drink. Hearing the noise of my steps on the wooden floor, Chase turned to look at me and burst out laughing as he saw me in my boots, zipped tightly over my Superman pajama bottoms. I joined him in his laughter, kissing him on the cheek as I handed him his OJ saying, "Well, you did say to wear them 'all the time'."

I jolted away from the bittersweet memory. I wiped the tears from my cheeks and shook my whole body quickly, trying to shake off the feelings that always came when I thought about my family. It's been seventeen days since they were stolen from me.

"No time for all that now," I whispered to the mirror. I hastily brushed my long brunette hair, then ran my fingers through it just enough to give it that "tousled, but not ratty" look. I figured it could dry on the way. I added very light makeup to my face, just enough to accent my green eyes. I've never been conceited, but I had to admit—I looked good. The combination of my dark hair and naturally tan skin brought out the jade in my eyes. The sweater hit me just right, accenting my curves in all the right places, not too tight, but enough for people to know what I was working with. I liked the added height the boots gave to my 5'9" frame. To an outsider, I bet I looked as if nothing was wrong, but as I looked closely, I could see the light shadows under my eyes, the haunting look of grief in the gaze that stared back at me. Sighing, I turned to brush my teeth and headed back downstairs.

As I hit the bottom step, Alessandra turned to me from the kitchen sink where she was rinsing out her coffee cup. "Ready?" she asked.

"Can't wait," I deadpanned.

Twenty minutes later, we pulled up out front of East Forest High School. Class didn't officially start for another 25 minutes, so many students were sitting on benches and in the grass, enjoying the cool weather until they were forced to go in. Alessandra thought it would be best for me to get there early so I could find my first class ahead of time. Breathing out deeply, I looked over, smiled at my aunt and mumbled, "Thanks for the ride." I opened the door. Just as I was about to exit, Alessandra gently grabbed my arm.

"Kyndal."

I turned and looked at her. "Yes?" I raised my eyebrows. I only pretended to care what she had to say.

She hesitated, looked down, then met my eyes. "Never mind, just have a good day. I'll see you out here after school."

I gave her a small nod and headed toward the building.

I tried my best to ignore the stares I got as I walked inside. At a school with a student population of 200, the new girl does not go unnoticed. Once in the building, I walked toward the office to return the registration papers Alessandra and I had filled out. As soon as I opened the office door, I was greeted by the secretary; an older woman whose name I don't know. She looked up from her desk, smiling at me from behind her glasses and tacky red lipstick. "Good morning, Kyndal! Are you excited for your first day?"

Thrilled.

I responded quietly. "Good morning," I ignored her question. "Here are the signed registration papers."

"Oh, thank you dear. Give me just a moment and I will print out your class schedule."

As she walked away, I turned and looked out the window toward the front of the school. The number of students hanging around had grown. As I scanned the area, two guys caught my attention. I don't know what it was, but something about them kept me from looking away. Maybe it was the fact that they had slightly separated themselves from the rest of the students, or that they were complete opposites. They stood facing each other, their profiles to me. The boy with dark skin and a shaved head moved around excitedly. His well-defined muscles flexed every time he moved his arms. The other was leaning against the school's brick wall. He was clearly the taller of the two, even though the first was far from short. He wasn't as obviously muscular and bulky, but his posture implied that he was well-built. His stance was relaxed, but his eyes would scan the area regularly. He missed nothing. His brown hair gave off a faint blonde tint in the morning sunlight. His mouth was raised slightly in a smirk as he listened to whatever story his friend was so enthusiastically telling him. I stood there frozen, staring at these two strangers. The brunette boy turned his head as if he heard his name called and looked through the window directly at me. I was so taken aback by the intensity of his blue eyes, I gasped. I looked away instinctively, but when I returned my gaze, the boy was still staring. His eyes were squinted, sizing me up. I wasn't surprised. Small town like this, there can't be a lot that happens. As the new girl, I doubted that this was the last time I'd be stared at, but it was still annoying.

I'm not a damn circus act.

"Here you are dear." The secretary had returned. The sound of her voice startled me away from the odd staring contest. I turned back toward her, grabbed my schedule, told her thanks, and left the office without glancing over my shoulder to see if the strange boy was still looking my way.

/|\

The first half of the day went by uneventfully. Only one of my first three teachers, Mr. Fulmer, my trigonometry teacher, forced me to stand up and introduce myself.

Hi, I'm Kyndal Davenport. I just moved here from Dayton, Texas.

I immediately decided that it was my least favorite class (as if I needed another reason to hate math.) Nobody attempted to talk to me, which I found surprising. I always thought small town people were supposed to be nosy.

By the time lunch rolled around, I was starving. Apparently there is an open lunch policy as I saw several students leaving school to eat elsewhere. I don't know where they went; it's not like this place has many options. I walked quietly to the cafeteria, grabbed a lunch tray of food, and headed outside to eat. I found a quiet, secluded table to sit at near the edge of the forest that flanks the school. Just as I was about to take a bite into my cheeseburger, I was interrupted by a blonde-headed girl plopping herself down unceremoniously next to me. She looked at me, smiling wide.

"Hi," she said. She bounced up and down on the bench, shaking the table. Her bubbly personality was bursting out of her.

"Hi," I responded warily.

"I'm Lydia Warner. You're Kyndal Davenport right? Sorry to just act like I know you when I really don't, but I was in the class where Mr. Fulmer forced you to introduce yourself. What a douchey move. Things like that are the reason no one really likes him, well that and sometimes he smells like cheese."

I just stared at her, wide eyed, overwhelmed by the flood of information that was spilling out of her.

"So, you're from Texas, huh? It's weird that you don't have a drawl. What brought you here? I bet you think the weather here is really cold. Is your first day going well?

Are people being nice to you?"

"Which question would you like me to answer first?"

"Sorry, I'm overwhelming you. Let me start over. Hi, my name is Lydia Warner, and you are?"

"Kyndal Davenport."

"Nice to meet you."

"You too, I think."

"I'm sorry, but I ramble when I'm nervous or excited and I really wanted to meet you because I thought you might need a friend, but now I can't seem to stop talking and you probably don't even want me to sit with you and..."

"It's fine." My interruption was stiff. She breathed out deeply, looking as if a huge weight was lifted off of her shoulders. I gave her a reluctant smirk and took a second to really get a good look at her. Lydia was a petite little thing. Her face was dainty, framed by her shoulder-length blonde hair and glasses. While her build seems to be average, her wardrobe is anything but. She sat next to me wearing bright pink skinny jeans with a grey screen-pressed shirt reading *Your Mom Goes to College* paired with black ankle boots. Both wrists were covered in bangles of various colors. She looked more like she belonged in a big city, not Marienville, Pennsylvania. I looked back up at her face to see her looking at me expectantly. I realized she asked me a question. "What?"

"I said, how are you liking East Forest High so far?"

"Honestly? It's pretty unremarkable. There were more people in my junior class in Texas than there are in this entire school."

"Yeah, it's a pretty small town, I know. Imagine being born and raised here. I've known the same people my entire life. I'm pretty sure I could give you the full name, birthdate, and social security number of everyone at this school."

She went on to give me complete details on the few students who were in our eyesight. She was explaining to me how a boy named Dylan tried to pull a prank on a teacher last year and accidentally ended up glued to his own chair, when we were interrupted by a football hitting our table. It landed a few feet away from us.

"Holy crapballs!" Lydia shouted. "Watch where you're throwing that thing!" I got up to throw the football back to its owner. But as I reached down for the ball, my fingers touched another hand. As soon as we made contact, heat shot up my arm followed by a cool breeze. The feeling was exquisite. It reminded me of going into an air conditioned house after a hot day in the sun. Pure relief. All too quickly, the hand pulled away. I looked up and found myself face-to-face with the same guy from earlier in the day. Again, I was completely struck by his piercing blue eyes. He held my gaze, the same bewildered look on his face as me. Up close, I noticed just how attractive he was. His skin was tanned and unmarred. His lips were thin, slanted in a smirk. He opened his mouth to talk, but was interrupted.

"Roman! Hurry up man, throw the ball." He kept eye contact, ignoring his friends. Did he feel the same thing as me when our hands touched? "Rome! Come on, man!" He cocked his head to the side quickly as if to apologize and turned to rejoin his friends.

Rubbing my arm, I sat back down next to Lydia. The feeling had faded too soon. "Who is *that?*"

"Roman Sands," she replied automatically. "Sexy, huh? Almost every girl is completely obsessed with him but he doesn't give any of them the time of day. That was the closest I have ever seen him come to flirting."

Really? A guy that hot doesn't give girls the time of day? I found that hard to believe. *Wonder if he's gay.*

"Nope," Lydia said.

"No, what?" I asked. "I didn't say anything."

"I know what you're thinking though. And no, he's not gay. Kellee Copeland asked him that exact question last year at a party after one too many jello shots."

I blushed a deep crimson. Lydia knew exactly what I was thinking. *But why do I care?*

Just then the bell rang. Back to class.

"So what do you have next?" Lydia asked as we walked toward the building.

"Umm," I fumbled in my book bag for my class schedule. "Chemistry, lit, and then gym."

"Well, crap! Maybe catch you after school?"

"Uh, yeah, sure," I replied. I was still rubbing my arm. The cool tingle lingered there.

"Cool. See ya later, Tex!"

I waved goodbye, but my response was late and I don't think she saw it. I shuffled back to the building, the odd encounter with Roman already forgotten. Maybe this school won't be so bad. Seems like I already made one friend and the day is only half over.

I should have known better.

2

Walking into Mr. Sykes' chemistry class, the first thing I noticed was Roman sitting at the back table. He was looking down, sketching something in his notebook. I turned away from him and introduced myself to the teacher. He directed me to an open stool at a lab table in the middle of the room on the opposite side from Roman. The stool next to me was empty, so I sat down and took the time before the bell to look around the room. The classroom looked like the standard American science room. High, black topped lab tables, two stools resting at each. Three of the walls were covered in a variety of posters. The fourth wall, the one to my left, was lined with windows that looked out into Allegheny National Forest.

Maples are common in Allegheny. Their green leaves contrasted with the charcoal bark of the black cherry trees. I wanted to get lost in them. The warning bell rang and I snapped out of my daydream. I looked toward the door to see three girls walk in, talking to each other in hushed tones. Almost simultaneously they stopped in their tracks, glaring directly at me. *I knew this day couldn't continue to go well.*

The trio sauntered over. Two of them sat in front of me: the tall, pretty girl with long, caramel hair, and a cheaper knockoff version of her. The third, a tan girl with dark hair and eyes, took her seat next to me. I kept my head down and popped my knuckles under the table, a nervous habit of mine when I'm stressed out.

The final bell rang and Mr. Sykes started class. He was trying to describe the lab we would be doing that day, but the three girls blatantly ignored him. The cheap twins in front turned around and whispered quietly to the one next to me. Although I couldn't hear everything they said, I caught words like *Texas, dead, her fault*. Their eyes darted my way quickly as they talked, but whenever I looked over, they averted their gaze.

"GIRLS!" Mr. Sykes hollered toward our tables. The two in front of me rolled their eyes before slowly turning to face the teacher.

"Yes, Mr. Sykes?" It was the caramel haired one who I have determined is their leader. Her voice was sickeningly sweet.

"If what you are saying to each other is so much more important than what I am teaching, do you care to share with the rest of us?"

"Well, I was just saying to Kellee and Jules," she nods to Mini-Me then to my table partner, "I think it is negligent of the school to allow a dangerous student into our classrooms."

Dangerous? What the hell? Was she talking about me? I was the only new kid there.

"That's enough Paige," Mr. Sykes warned.

"I'm just saying, if she killed her own family, what would she be willing to do to us?"

Shocked, I shot up, pushing back my stool as I went. "Excuse me?!" I bellowed at the paper-thin girl sitting in front of me. "What the hell is your problem? You don't even know what you're talking about."

"I know *all* about what brought you here," she turned in my direction, a plastic smile stuck to her face. "You're a killer."

I placed both hands on the lab table and leaned over it, getting as close as I could to Paige. I looked her square in the face and spoke, my voice steady, "If I was a killer, don't you think I would be the wrong person to piss off?"

Paige's eyes showed a brief moment of fear before she turned back toward the front of the room. "Mr. Sykes, didn't you hear her? She threatened me! Aren't you going to do anything about it?"

"That's plenty from you, Ms. Christensen. Ms. Davenport—report to the office immediately. I'll have someone show you where it is." I gathered my bag and headed toward the door. "No need, I remember," I threw the bag over my shoulder as I walked out of class.

I stomped, my boots echoing off the hallway floors. *How dare she—how DARE she bring up my family?* This girl knew nothing about me or what I had been through. I was ready to leave school. It hadn't even been one day and I already hated it. Unable to control my rage, I turned and punched a locker. I dropped to the floor, leaning against the locker that I had dented. I placed my head in my hands. My emotions spilled out in tears. I cried because of what Paige said, because of the reaction she was able to get from me, but mainly because she made me remember.

I couldn't control the images flooding my mind. *Driving home from my birthday celebration. Me behind the wheel, Mom in the passenger seat, Chase and Dad in the back. It's late. Our drive home should have taken only 15 minutes, but there was a detour that forced us to take an unfamiliar route. I remember Mom said something funny, I looked at her briefly—just one split second. When my eyes returned to the road, there was something standing out in the middle, I don't even remember what. I swerved, attempting to miss it. Our car flipped several times, landing upside down. I'm not sure how long we hung in that vehicle, trapped upside down by our seatbelts. I must have blacked out for awhile because when I came to, mom was screaming at Chase and Dad to wake up. The smell of smoke choked me. Somewhere the car was burning. It was difficult to see or think as the oxygen was stolen from inside the vehicle to feed the growing flames. I strained my eyes, coughing uncontrollably, and looked over at Mom desperately trying to escape her seat. The belt had latched her. It's harder to breathe now. The last thing I remember before everything went dark was Mom's typically dark eyes glowing a vibrant yellow.*

My memory was interrupted by someone placing a hand on my shoulder. I jumped up so quickly I knocked the intruder back. I looked up to see Roman standing there, his eyes a mix of concern and curiosity.

I looked deep into the eyes that had already captivated me twice, but I refused to be humiliated for being caught in a moment of weakness. "What do you want?" I spat.

"Your hand is bleeding," he said, pointing down. Sure enough, my knuckles were stained red.

I responded quickly. "I'm fine." He squinted his eyes, like he wanted to get a better look at me. I hastily wiped the tears from my cheeks. "Look, I know Sykes sent you to make sure I made it to the office, but I can get there just fine on my own, so run along." I made a shooing motion at him.

He smiled slightly, almost as if I amused him. He just stood there; quiet, unmoving. I rolled my eyes and turned away from him, continuing my trudge to the office.

Roman called after me. "What Paige said about your family—"

I stopped in my tracks, turned around, and glared back at the dark-haired boy rooted in the middle of the hallway. I pointed my finger at him, "is none of your damn business." Once again I turned toward the office, at this point welcoming any punishment they will give me just so I can get away.

"No, you don't understand," he tried to tell me.

"Leave me alone," I growled at him and continued on down the hallway. Thankfully, no footsteps followed.

I left the office over two hours later. Apparently, the punishment for threatening someone in class is an incredibly boring lecture, a call home, and a week of after school detention. Alessandra told me we would discuss what happened when I got home. I wondered if she'd care what Paige had said to begin with. The principal sure didn't. I headed toward the gym for my last class of the day. My time in the office had forced me to miss my entire literature class, the one subject I actually liked at my old school. By the time I had made it to gym, the class had already started.

The class was in the middle of a basketball game. On a typical day, I would jump right in. I've been an athlete my whole life. But on that day, I just wanted to go home and pretend like none of it happened. I handed my late pass to my teacher, who luckily gave me the option to join in the game or sit and watch. I opted for the latter. I moved toward the bleachers, had a seat, and waited for the wretched school day to end.

When the bell freed me at 3:00, I was out the gym doors into the fresh air. I saw Alessandra sitting in her car and I shuffled her way, my head down. I looked up briefly when I heard my name called. Lydia was headed toward me, a smile on her face. I kept walking without recognizing her. When I reached the car, I was so eager to get in I couldn't get the car door open. My fingers struggled to grab the latch. My hand fumbled with the handle. I growled in frustration. Any punishment Alessandra gave me at that point was preferable to staying there. I removed my hand, stopped, and took a breath before finally getting the thing to open. I plopped in the passenger seat and Alessandra looked over at me. "I think that girl was trying to get your attention."

"Can we just leave, please?"

"S-Sure." She hesitated, staring at me for a moment with concern and confusion in her eyes before she started the car and left the parking lot. I was clearly upset, and she could tell. Luckily, she didn't push it. I stared out the window at the unfamiliar town that was now my home. One grocery store, one gas station, a town library, a hotel, and more churches than there are houses. The town is so small it doesn't even have a stoplight—something the locals apparently take great pride in for reasons I don't understand.

Directly on Route 66, Marienville is a stop on the way to somewhere better, not a place someone wants to live. Unlike the town itself, though, the scenery is beautiful. Marienville is almost completely surrounded by Allegheny National Forest. Over 800 square miles of old growth forest, winding creeks and rivers, and breathtaking, sometimes steep cliffs. The Allegheny is the real life of this town. Tourists come here to ATV, kayak, hike, rock climb, and camp almost year-round. The Allegheny is where my aunt worked. She gave hiking and ATV tours through a local tourist group. She was still wearing her uniform in the car that day: khaki shorts and a shirt that read "Allegheny Explorers."

"Do you want to talk about it?" Alessandra asked quietly.

"I really don't," I replied. I kept staring out the window.

We rode the rest of the way home in silence.

When we reached the house, I jumped out of the car and immediately headed toward the front door.

"Where are you going?" Alessandra asked.

"Upstairs. I have homework to do," I lied. I really just wanted to go upstairs, curl up on the bed, and cry.

"It can wait." I turned around, expecting her to be standing right behind me. Instead she was reaching into the trunk of her car. "Here," she said. She threw a pair of outdoor boots at my feet. "Change into these."

"Why?"

"You'll see. Just do it." I grabbed the boots, sat down on the front porch, and changed my shoes.

"What am I supposed to do with the boots I was wearing?"

"Leave them on the porch."

"What if someone takes them?"

"Who?" she asked, gesturing around us. She had a point. We lived on a gravel road, and there wasn't another house for miles. "Braid your hair too."

"Why?" I asked again.

"I told you; you'll see. Now follow me." We headed around the house toward a large detached garage that Alessandra used to keep all of her gear for work. "Can you work a clutch?"

"Yes," I said warily. *Where is she going with this?* She opened the garage door, revealing a variety of outdoor gear. Carabiners and ropes for rock climbing, kayaks for the river and creeks, and finally, two ATVs.

"Put these on." She handed me a helmet, goggles, gloves, and a CamelBak. "You take this one," she said, patting the seat of the closest four-wheeler. "I'll take lead. You follow behind. Don't get too close. In case something happens to me, I want you far enough back that you don't get in trouble, too. We'll start out on the trail, but where we are going will require hitting some rough terrain. You up for it?" I looked up at her and grinned.

Alessandra wasn't kidding when she said we would hit some rough terrain. Twenty minutes into our ride, she abruptly turned off the trail, winding in and out of trees, over dead stumps, even through a low-running creek. We rode for so long I was beginning to wonder if she actually had a destination in mind, or if she just wanted to go for a ride so I could clear my head and forget about my day. If the latter was the case, it was working. I could already feel myself calming down, forgetting about the terrible things Paige said, or about yelling at Roman in the hallway.

All of a sudden, the forest opened up and I was in the most

beautiful place I had ever seen. In front of me was a large, treeless meadow. The grass was wild and knee high, highlighted by beautiful wildflowers that sprinkled the field with yellows, reds, and pinks. Just past the grass was a lake. As we brought our ATVs to a stop, I removed my helmet and marveled at the water. It was a gorgeous blue and perfectly still—the surface interrupted only by a small island in the middle. The water reflected the sky like a mirror. I walked to the water's edge and looked down. The water was so clear I could see the bottom even though it was several feet down. Except for the small clearing we were standing in, the lake was completely surrounded by dense forest. It was perfectly silent except for the occasional chirp of a passing bird.

Alessandra stood next to me, looking out over the lake. "What is this place?" I asked her. She must have heard the awe in my voice.

"My favorite place in the whole world, and not on the tourist's map," she said with a smile.

"It's unbelievable."

"Your father showed it to me, not long after he met your mom. Said it was his safe haven from all the evils in the world. I come here when I need to think, when the world gets to be too much for me."

"So that's why you brought me here, to help me calm down?" I was surprised. The gesture, along with the consideration behind it, were unexpected.

"Look, Kyndal. I know I can only begin to understand what you've been through in the past few weeks. I lost my brother, someone that I hadn't seen in 18 years, someone I didn't really even know. You lost your entire family." I turned and looked at her, wondering where she was going with this. "Your entire world was turned upside down. Forced to leave the only place you've ever known to live with an aunt you've never met. I know it's going to take some time, but I just want you to be happy here and know that I am here for you, whatever you need." Her smile was kind. It reminded me of my father. I smiled back. I saw her arm twitch, and I knew what she was going to do, but I was too slow to stop her. Next thing I knew, she had me wrapped up in a hug. My body stiffened. I hadn't had any real contact with anyone since my family died. She released me quickly. Although I don't mean it, my manners took over. "Thank you, Alessandra."

"I've been meaning to tell you—call me Allie. Please. Only my mom called me Alessandra, and only when I was in trouble," she said, laughing slightly. I nodded, and we both turned back to look at the lake. The silence was comfortable. I don't know how long we stood there.

Finally, I turned back to her and spoke quietly: "She told everyone that I killed my family."

"The girl from school?" Allie asked gently, turning toward me.

I nodded. "Paige. She said the school shouldn't have let me in because I was dangerous. Why would she do that? She doesn't even know anything about me."

"Some people are just naturally afraid of anything new. Rather than take the time to get to know you, she decided to attack."

"But how did she even know about the accident?"

"I don't know." Her voice was grim.

"I shouldn't have lost my temper and threatened her the way I did. I just got so angry. I couldn't believe the things she was saying, and the teacher didn't even stop her. Tomorrow everyone will know about what happened and think I'm some kind of lunatic."

Allie's eyes looked determined. "You are not to blame for your family's death. Tell me you believe that." Rather than answer her, I turned back to the lake. *Did I know that?* So much about that night was blurry, but on a few things I was crystal clear. I was the one driving. I was the one who looked away. I was the one who swerved. So why was I the one who survived?

By the time we returned home, the sun had dipped below the canopy of trees, casting the forest into alternating sections of light and shadows. We parked the ATVs in the garage. I was surprised to feel that even though I was drained from the emotional rollercoaster I had ridden that day, I felt physically rejuvenated by the ride through the forest—almost as if my body was replenished by being a part of nature. Once inside, I helped Allie make dinner. Cooking has always been something that relaxes me.

After we cleared the plates, I headed upstairs for the night. I took a shower, hoping the hot water would wash away the remainder of my worries about returning to school tomorrow.

After the shower, I laid in bed and put on my headphones. I scrolled through my music and chose a band that Chase loved. Heavy metal has never been my thing, but it made me feel close to him, and the screaming and deafening beat kept me from thinking. I laid that way until everything went black.

3

I am back at the lake. I lay on the island in the middle of the water, my body wet, and the sun on my face. There is movement on the edge of the water, and when I look, Roman is standing there. The sun makes his hair look more blonde than brown from this distance, but even as far away as we are, I can still see the intensity of his blue eyes. He shouts something to me, but it is lost in the wind. "What?" I yell back. "I can't hear you!" I can see he answers me, but again, no sound reaches my ears. Suddenly, the sun disappears and the world is thrown into shadow. Roman disappears and the earth underneath me begins to tremble. I look down to see a giant fissure split the small lake island in two. Frightened, I scramble backward on all fours, away from the growing crevice. My hand lands on something hot. I cry out in pain as it sizzles on the rock beneath me. I struggle to my feet, running toward the safety of the water as the island falls away. I dive into the water and swim furiously toward the shore. When I make it to solid ground, I turn to look at the island. Only a small piece remains. The outer edges fall into the water like a building being demolished piece by piece. I lay back on the grassy shore, breathing heavily, and examine my hand where the pain has suddenly reappeared. On my hand is a violent red burn running from my palm to my wrist.

I woke with a jolt, my alarm blaring. I was breathing heavily and my heart was racing. I looked at the clock. It was 6:30 in the morning. Time to get ready for another day of school. I pulled back the covers and staggered to the bathroom, hoping a drink of water would help shake me from the dream. When I reached the bathroom, I smacked my hand on the wall several times searching for the light switch. I finally found it and reached toward the sink to fill my cup. As my arm reached out, my eye caught a slice of color against my skin. I turned my hand over and saw three livid marks on my palm exactly where I had burnt my hand in the dream. They began at my wrist, moving toward my thumb. They were close together, wider at the bottom, each one narrowing as it moved outward. *What the hell? How did that happen?* I forgot the drink. I hurried back to my room and sat on the edge of the bed. *How is my hand hurt? Did I do that during the ride yesterday and not notice? Is it from the dream? That can't be. Dreams aren't real. They can't hurt you.* Even as I thought the words, I wasn't sure I believed them.

I sat there longer than I realized. When I looked back at the clock, it was 7:00. I needed to leave in 10 minutes if I wanted to get to school on time. I wasn't eager to go back to school, but I didn't want Paige and her friends to think I was scared to return. I quickly threw on a black hoodie, jeans, and tennis shoes then braided my hair. Just a little bit of mascara and lip gloss and I was ready to go.

Downstairs, my aunt was putting her dishes in the sink, already dressed for a day in the forest. "I have a meeting this morning with the County Sheriff's Department and Allegheny Park Rangers, so I won't be able to take you to school."

"That sounds serious."

"Some hikers went missing in the forest. They want my help navigating some of the lesser-known areas. These searches take some time. There's a good chance I won't be back until late tomorrow evening. You going to be alright on your own?"

I nodded. "How am I going to get to school?" Alessandra smiled and threw something at me. I caught it with my left hand, but kept my right hidden in my pocket. When I opened my hand, I saw her car keys. "Get there yourself."

I shook my head, "I—I can't." I hadn't driven since the accident.

Understanding lit in her eyes. "You'll be fine. Just take it easy on the gravel roads."

"How will you get to work?" I asked, looking for an excuse.

"I'm taking an ATV through the trails." Damn. *There goes my last out.* I breathed in deep. *Driving. I can do this.*

I walked outside to the driveway and looked at Alessandra's car—nothing special really. Just a four-door sedan. Practical. Just like her. You would think someone who works in the outdoors would have a four-wheel drive, but as she explained to me once, anywhere she went in the forest could only be reached by foot, kayak, or ATV. The paint on the car was supposed to be white, but driving it up and down the gravel roads had turned it more of a dusty grey color. I got in the driver's seat and buckled my seat belt. It took me a few tries before I heard the click. My hands were shaking. Before I could put the keys in the ignition, my breathing started to pick up. I closed my eyes and leaned my head back on the seat. "Come on, K. You can do this." I tried to steady my breathing, but it only seemed to get worse. I undid my seatbelt and got out of the car as quickly as possible, completely panicked. I just wasn't ready. No way. I looked toward the house, hoping I could somehow convince Alessandra to drive me, just as I heard her ATV start up out back. *Crap. Looks like I'm walking.*

I made it to school over half an hour later. I tried to use the time to create a plan of attack for school, but I didn't make it very far. By the time I hit the parking lot, my entire plan involved avoiding Roman and trying not to hit Paige.

The front of the school was already full of students. Several of them turned and looked at me as I walked into the courtyard, whispering to their friends in hushed tones. I readjusted my book bag over my shoulder and walked inside with the most neutral face I could manage. I was determined not to let people see how much their stares affected me. I went directly to my first class, choosing the silence of the classroom over the whispers of the hallways.

The good news—no one bothered me about what happened yesterday in class with Paige. The bad news—even if they did, I wouldn't have noticed. I was too busy thinking about all the freaky stuff happening to me. First; the feeling I got when Roman and I touched. Then; the vivid dream that may have left me with a burn on my hand. *Maybe I'm going insane.* I read once about people who got so overwhelmed with grief that their brains couldn't deal with it and they had a psychotic break. Seems like a definite possibility. God knows I've got enough grief going on to push me over the edge.

The whole day continued that way. People talked behind my back, but not directly to me. When the final bell rang at the end of the day, instead of heading for the front of the school to start the walk home, I headed to the office to report for my first day of detention. It had to be some sort of record—getting detention this quickly. The secretary pointed me in the right direction, not nearly as cheery and friendly as she was yesterday. Funny how quickly people change their minds about you.

Detention is held in the library. When I walked in the doors, I saw two other students already there. One was a grungy looking kid with long, dark hair. He was wearing headphones, his head down on the table. The second was the guy I saw Roman talking to the other morning. He sat leaned back in his chair, hands relaxed behind his head, feet up on the table. He was wearing jean shorts and a yellow shirt that looked great against his dark skin. He smiled at me and winked as I walked past. I plopped my book bag down on the table next to his and sat, looking around.

There was a teacher sitting at a counter across the library, but she paid us no attention—more interested in what was on her computer.

"You're her, aren't you?"

I glanced at the boy in the yellow shirt. "Who?"

"The one everyone is talking about. Kyndal. I'm Isaac." I glanced up at the teacher, waiting for her to tell him to be quiet. Nothing.

"Purposefully wrecked your car to off your family, right? You're supposed to be some big, bad, scary chick."

I turned in my chair to face him, eyes determined steel. "That's what everyone is saying, huh?"

"Ye-p," he replied, exaggerating the last letter to make a popping sound. "So, is it true?"

"Would you believe me if I said no?"

He raised his eyebrows at me and smiled slightly. "Maybe. Depends how convincing your truth is."

"It's not *my* truth; it's the only truth."

"No such thing. What people think is truth is only what they believe. It's impossible to have all the facts and know the *real* truth. There's always two sides for everything. Always."

"Not necessarily," I said defensively. "Lots of people dedicate their lives to finding indisputable answers:

scientists, scholars, lawyers."

"And for each one of them, there is someone else working just as hard to prove something that discredits them. Two sides," he said, holding up two fingers. "Always."

I rolled my eyes at him and turned away.

"To be honest, I'm kind of disappointed. You're not as scary as I expected."

"Huh," I huffed. "Sorry to let you down."

"That's alright. Something tells me you'll have plenty of opportunity to provide entertainment."

"Oh, really? What makes you—"

"What happened to your hand?" he interrupted, abruptly changing the subject. When I turned to look at him, I saw that he had abandoned his casual stance and was leaning forward, his eyes intense.

I moved to cover my palm with the sleeve of my hoodie. "I—I don't really know."

"Let me see it." He reached out his hand and grabbed at my fingers.

"No!" I yelled at him and pulled my hand away.

"Sorry, sorry. I didn't mean to scare you. Can I see your hand please?" His arm was still outstretched. *What is it with the people here?* Frustrated, I pulled the sleeve of my hoodie back, exposing the three burns on my hand.

Although still clearly visible, their color had faded from a livid red to a bright pink. They looked as if they happened days ago instead of last night. Isaac took hold of my wrist, almost pulling me out of my seat in his eagerness to see my hand. His hand was hot: not uncomfortable, but definitely above normal. He ran his thumb along the marks. I looked up at his face to see a small smirk pass his lips. "When did this happen?" he asked without looking away from my hand.

"I first noticed it this morning," I answered, confused by his fascination. "It's no big deal. I'll be fine." I tried to pull my hand away.

"When is your birthday?" he asked, ignoring my attempt to retrieve my hand.

"What? Why does that matter?" *What an odd thing to ask.*

"Just answer the question."

"March 23. Why?"

"Let's just say I was right," he replied, finally releasing my hand and looking at me. "You are definitely going to be entertaining." With that he stood up, collected his stuff, and walked out of the library. No one even attempted to stop him.

/|\

The next day I looked for Lydia. I wanted to tell her we couldn't be friends, that I didn't need friends. I saw her briefly during trig, but didn't have a chance to talk to her.

During lunch, I caught sight of her bright, blonde hair blowing in the breeze. She was sitting at the same table we shared my first day, her back to me, facing the forest with headphones covering her ears. There was someone else at the table, but they didn't seem to be talking to each other. Pushing my way past a group of kids, I headed toward her and sat down. She pulled her headphones down and looked at me.

"I—"

She held up her hand to stop me.

"No need."

"No need for what?"

"Apologies. Paige is a bitch. I don't care what she said. As far as I'm concerned she deserved everything you gave her and more." She shrugged one shoulder. I stared at her briefly in disbelief, then lunged at her, hugging her firmly. I pulled back, quickly, feeling awkward. When I looked at her, she was laughing. "What was that for?"

I shook my head, embarrassed. I glanced at the boy across from us. He was obviously looking anywhere but at us. "I'm sorry, I shouldn't have done that."

"Not a prob, babe," she replied, popping a grape from her lunch into her mouth. She pointed across the table. "Kyndal Davenport, this is Evan Dixon. Evan—Kyndal."

"Hey."

He looked at me with a polite smile, then went back to his

plate of food. I didn't take offense. His grey eyes were soft, kind. His ignorance of us seemed more of an attempt to give us privacy than be rude.

I turned my attention back to Lydia. "Can I ask you one question?" she asked. I cringed. I knew this was coming— she wanted to know if it was true—did I kill my family? This was exactly why I didn't want to get close with her. "What's that?" I asked, bracing myself.

"Why did you bite Roman's head off?"

Okay, not what I was expecting. "How did you know about that?"

"Small school. And you don't yell as quietly as you think you do." She gestured to the boy across from her. "Tell her, Evan."

I turned and looked at him again. Now he looked uncomfortable, clearly not enjoying getting dragged into my drama. Can't say I blame him. "Is that what people are saying? That I bit his head off?"

He dropped the fork he'd been holding and ran his fingers through his sandy blonde hair. "I—I don't know. I just heard you yelled at him."

Great. Just what I needed. I turned back to Lydia. "He followed me into the hallway after Sykes sent me to the office. Probably to finish off what Paige started."

"What did he say?" Lydia prodded.

"He brought up my family."

"But, what did he say *exactly*?"

"I don't know. I didn't exactly give him the chance to finish," I said matter-of-factly. "Why all the interest in what happened between Roman and me?"

"It's just that if you didn't give him the chance to finish what he was saying, how do you know what he was going to say would be bad?"

"I highly doubt he had anything polite to say, Lydia. Kindness hasn't been the theme of this place."

"That might be true, but you should probably know that first thing this morning, the principal had to pull Roman off of Jared Atchison. Apparently, Roman overheard him talking to his friends about how all that stuff about you was true, and that the school should kick you out. Roman had him up against the brick wall before anyone knew he was even listening. Got a couple good punches in, too."

What? Why would he do that?

"It's true," Evan interjected. I didn't realize he was still listening. "I saw it. Jared's nose was gushing blood. Roman has a wicked right."

"That doesn't make any sense," I responded, shaking my head.

"You're tellin me, Tex. I'm just saying—maybe you should talk to him, figure out what he was trying to say to you yesterday."

Great. There goes my Avoid-Roman-At-All-Costs plan.

I walked to chemistry class debating how to approach Roman. What do I say? *Hey, I heard you beat some kid up for talking about me. What's that about?* Yeah, I don't think so. When I made it to the classroom, my eyes immediately drifted to the back of the room where I saw him sitting the other day. The chair sat empty. My shoulders slumped with disappointment. *Of course he's not here.* You don't exactly get to stay at school the day you get in a fight. I took my seat right as Paige and her minions walked in. They sauntered over to their seats. Paige stopped right by me, leaning down and whispering in my ear.

"Not enough to destroy your own family? Now you get Roman in trouble, too?" I glared up at her. My fingers itched to scratch her eyes out. I clenched my hands under the table, but whether it was to calm myself down or swing at her, I didn't know yet. Kellee and Jules snickered behind her. "Keep your disgusting hands off him. He's mine."

I pushed the stool out from underneath me, meeting Paige eye-to-eye. Just as I was about to do something stupid, the bell rang, and Mr. Sykes walked in. Paige looked over at him, but didn't back down. She was taunting me. It was so tempting to hit her, but I really didn't want to get in anymore trouble. I took a deep breath, and with every ounce of self-control I possessed, sat back down in my chair.

Immediately after class, I tracked down Isaac. If anyone could tell me what Roman's deal was, it had to be him. I found him in the hallway, chatting up a redhead. I stood there awkwardly until he noticed me. Both he and the girl he was talking to turned in my direction. "Hi," I said stiffly. "Can I talk to you?" Isaac gave me an exasperated look, like I was interrupting his game, but he excused himself and walked with me down the hallway.

"What's up?" he asked.

Suddenly I was nervous. I cracked my knuckles. "Um— you're friends with Roman Sands, right?" Isaac looked at me with confused eyes. "I mean; I saw the two of you talking the other day before school."

He crossed his arms. "You want to know about the fight this morning."

"It's just—someone told me the fight had something to do with me. Is that true?"

Isaac looked at me silently, his chocolate eyes studying me as if deciding what to say. "Why don't you ask him?"

"They sent him home."

He nodded slightly. "Look, Roman has a temper. Who's to say why he does what he does?"

"What kind of answer is that?" I whined.

"The only kind I can give you right now. You want more than that, you're going to have to get it from him."

I rolled my eyes at him. "Thanks for nothing."

4

After school, Lydia offered to give me a ride home. Since I had already screwed up earlier by hugging her like a lunatic when I had planned to tell her we couldn't be friends, I gave in. There was no getting rid of her now. I asked her to take me to Allegheny Explorers. I walked in the front door and stepped up to the young man working the counter. "I'm looking for Alessandra Davenport, please."

"She's out back," he told me, pointing down a hallway. I smiled my thanks and headed that direction.

Behind the front store was a large shop holding all the outdoor gear, a much larger version of what Alessandra has at home. She was standing in the open garage door, talking with someone. The stranger wasn't dressed in the Allegheny Explorers khaki and polo uniform, so I assumed he was a customer. The man looked to be about 40-years-old, well built, with light brown hair and grey eyes. He was wearing a dress shirt, tie, and slacks. Strange attire, considering where he was. Not wanting to interfere with

40

her work, I hung back and waited for her to finish. Her eyes flickered my way and she quickly wrapped up the conversation. Soon, both of them headed toward me.

"Hi, Kyndal," Alessandra said. "Everything okay?"

"Sorry to interrupt, Alessandra."

"Allie," she corrected me.

The man spoke up, smiling at me. "Don't worry, we were just finishing up here."

"Kyndal, this is Deacon Matthews. He's a businessman visiting the area and I'm going to show him and some friends around."

Deacon extended his hand. I reached out and took it. Suddenly, I was filled with an intense heat and the smell of smoke filled my nose. I closed my eyes, momentarily overwhelmed. I stepped back, dropping his hand and instantly the sensations disappeared. Deacon smoothly returned his hand to his side. I watched as the skin weathered and the color drained away. The veins darkened, crawling up toward his wrist. When he noticed my gaze, he placed his hand casually in his pocket. *What was that?* My breath came out in ragged gasps. I looked over to Alessandra. She didn't seem to have seen anything strange.

"Are you alright?" Alessandra asked. She reached out and placed a hand on my shoulder.

I straightened myself up, trying to get my bearings. "I'm fine," I said, harshly. "I just wanted to see if I could borrow an ATV, maybe go on a little ride."

Deacon abruptly turned to Alessandra. "Thank you for your help. I look forward to seeing you soon." With one final glance at me, he left, hand still hidden.

Alessandra watched him go. She seemed surprised by his quick exit. I repeated my question. She turned back to me. Her eyes squinted with concern. "I don't know if that's a great idea. You know, we still haven't found those hikers. I'd feel more comfortable if you stayed out of the forest until we know what happened to them."

"I won't go very deep in, I promise. I'll stay on the biggest trails." I was lying. I wanted to go back to the lake she took me to—the one in my dreams.

Alessandra stayed quiet for a long time. "Fine," she relented. "Just drop it back at the house when you're finished."

"Thank you." I grabbed the keys and headed to the garage before she had a chance to change her mind.

The search for the lake didn't go well. I spent the entire evening looking for it without any luck. I was so frustrated. I was just positive that if I could get there, I'd find some answers. If the marks on my hand really did come from my dream, maybe the lake's island really fell apart. Finally, I gave up and returned home. The sun had set and the sky was lit up with stars. I parked the ATV in the back shop just as Alessandra wanted. It was late and the empty house felt eerie. I went directly upstairs and fell into bed. Luckily, sleep came quickly.

It's the night of the accident, but instead of being in the vehicle, I'm standing in the road. I can see the car upside down, the back half of it ablaze. The sound of my mother's voice yelling at Chase and my dad can barely be heard over the roar of the flames. I run to Chase's door, hoping to pull him free. When my hands touch the door, the fire grows, racing to consume the rest of the vehicle as if it just had a can of gasoline poured on it. I back away, scared to touch the car thinking I will only make it worse. I scream for help until my voice is hoarse but no one is around to hear. I stand there, frozen, as my family perishes.

I woke up screaming. I still felt the heat on my face. I ran my hands over my face, through my hair. They came away covered in sweat. This nightmare was different than the others. Used to be I dreamt of my family being alive—of happy times that left me crashing in the morning when I realized they weren't real. Now I dreamt of their deaths. Of it being my fault.

Refusing to wallow in my despair, I got out of bed and started to get ready for the day. I took a cold shower, hoping to erase the stickiness from my skin. I dressed in jeans, a green top that brought out my eyes, a black jacket, and my boots that my brother gave me. I left the house, turning to lock the door behind me. I passed the car in the driveway without even giving it a second glance and began the walk to school.

I only made it about a half-mile up the road when I heard a car pull over on to the gravel behind me. I turned toward the clunker just as a tall, familiar figure got out of the driver's side. Evan.

"What are you doing?" he asked.

"Walking to school."

"Why? Don't you have a car?"

"I don't drive," I snipped.

He shrugged, not pushing the issue. "Hop in. I'll give you a ride." I looked back toward the direction of school and briefly entertained the idea of turning him down. "Come on. It looks like rain. You don't want to get caught in that."

I gave in and slid into the passenger seat. At first we rode in uncomfortable silence, but Evan broke it. "I'm sorry about the other day."

I turned to look at him, puzzled. "For what?"

"I didn't know Lydia was going to talk about such personal stuff. I would have left the table if I had known." I sighed deeply. "Seriously," he continued, "I didn't mean to eavesdrop."

"It's okay," I told him. What else was there to say? He opened his mouth to say something, but then hesitated.

"Just spit it out, Evan."

"I don't think you should talk to Roman."

I'm taken aback. "Why?"

"I don't know how to explain it exactly, but he and his

friends are just—different." Right as he said that, we pulled into school and parked the car.

"Thanks for the ride." I got out and removed the jacket I had put on that morning. The morning air was brisk and I couldn't seem to cool down. Evan and I headed toward school together. I immediately noticed Roman sitting at a table out front. He sat by himself, head down, his hand scribbling furiously in the notebook I saw with him before. As his hand moved, I could see slight bruising on his knuckles. Wounds left over from the fight. He was wearing light-wash jeans and a blue shirt that made his eyes look even brighter. He seemed oblivious to the other students. I paused and looked at Evan. "I'll see you inside." He shook his head disapprovingly, but continued in. With a deep breath and a quick pop of my knuckles, I walked right toward Roman.

"Uh, hi. Roman?" *Good one, Kyndal.* He looked up at me from where he sat. His eyes were like deep pools.

"Hey."

"Mind if I sit?"

"That depends. You going to yell at me again?" he asked, a smile in his eyes. *Is he teasing me?*

"Yeeaah, about that. I wanted to apologize. I'm sure Mr. Sykes sent you to make sure I made it to the office and I shouldn't have bit your head off for doing what you were told. So—sorry." Having done what I was there to do, I turned and started to walk away.

"Sykes didn't send me."

"What?" I turned back, surprised by his answer. I sat down across from him, even though he had never actually responded when I asked if I could. "Then what were you doing?"

"Looking after a damsel in distress. It's a good thing I did. You were in the middle of a breakdown when I got to you in the hallway. I was too late to save the poor locker, though."

"Damsel in distress? You know, you have an unrealistic sense of self-worth. I can take care of myself just fine thank you, so next time, don't bother. I don't need some over-confident, gorgeous guy riding in to save me."

He responded with a smile that I would have found distracting if I wasn't so angry. "I thought you were here to apologize, not yell at me again."

"I was, but you pissed me off by acting like I needed someone to take care of me, and I *don't*. So just stop. Don't check on me, don't go around beating people up for me." With that, I got up and started to walk away. Before I made it five steps, Roman was there in front of me. I almost had to lean my head back to look him in the eye, he was so tall and so *close*.

"Beating people up? What makes you think that had anything to do with you?" he asked in a low voice. His eyes stared right into mine and I found myself unable to respond at first, transfixed by the blue sapphires staring at me.

"Didn't it?" I asked. My voice was much quieter. He reached out and grabbed my hand, turning it palm up. He looked down at the three dull scars that were bright red just yesterday. A pained look crossed his face as he ran his thumb across them. I looked down to where our hands were joined.

"And if it did?" His voice was close, personal. I could feel his breath on my cheek as he talked. At the touch of his hand, the feeling from two days ago returned. It traveled up my arm and through my body—a warm breeze coming off the ocean. I felt more relaxed than I had in weeks. I forgot the anger I felt just moments ago. "Kyndal, what if it did?" he repeated.

I finally looked at him. His eyes had changed. They held tiny flecks of yellow in them. "Then you would have some serious explaining to do." I tried to put some force behind my words, but they came out like a tease.

"Would I?" he asked, a small smile played at his lips. "How about I explain it to you at dinner?"

"Dinner?" That snapped me out of it quick. "You're asking me out?" Not what I expected when this conversation started.

"You catch on quick," he said, sarcastically.

I glared at him. "Why do you want to go to dinner with me? You don't even know me."

"But I want to."

I took a deep breath to steady my thoughts, but all I could manage to do was inhale his scent. He smelled amazing. Crisp and fresh like he spent a lot of time outdoors, but with an underlying hint of something else, something familiar. The smallest hint of oil. My dad always smelled that way after he finished working on a car. It was comforting.

"Fine. Dinner. Tomorrow. But you better have some answers for me." I felt like if I had closed my eyes, I would have been lost in the warm feeling thrumming through my body.

"Why not tonight?"

"My aunt comes home tonight; I need to be there."

"Tomorrow it is then." He let go of my hand and walked into school. I was left there, crashing from the wonderful high of his touch.

/|\

"How could you not tell me?!" I looked up from my lunch to see Lydia barrelling toward me, a five-foot, five-inch, blonde ball of rage.

"Tell you what?"

"Oh, you know exactly what," she said, pointing her finger at me dramatically. "You have a date with Ro—"

"Shh! Quiet down!" I don't know why I shushed her. No one else was out there. The rain Evan predicted started not long after school began. The benches outside were still a little damp.

"You have a date with Roman Sands," she mock whispered as she sat down across from me. "You have officially done the impossible."

I shook my head at her. "It's not really a date. It's the only way he would explain what the fight was about."

"Not really a date? Ha! Give me a break." She reached over and stole a carrot off of my tray. "That guy has not shown an ounce of interest in a girl since he moved here. You've been here what—three days—and he asks you out. It's a date—you know it, I know it, hell, the whole school knows it."

"How exactly does the whole school know?" I asked, giving her a pointed look.

"Tex, this school is tiny. Anytime something juicy happens, word travels fast. Not to mention, it's not like it happened in a particularly private location. Half the junior class saw you two on the front lawn today, including Paige. Word is you two were pretty intense." She waggled her eyebrows. *If they only knew.* Intense didn't cover it. Confusing—definitely. Exquisite—absolutely.

"Wait—why did you single out Paige? Who cares if she was there?"

"Personally? I don't. But you goin' out with Roman is definitely not going to help you with her. She's had a thing for him since he moved here. But like I said, he doesn't give anyone the time of day."

"Well, damn. I really felt like she and I were starting to be friends," I said, my voice dripping with sarcasm. Lydia and I made eye contact and burst out in laughter.

"Really though," Lydia asked as our laughter died down, "where is he taking you? What are you going to wear?"

"I have no clue. All he said was dinner."

"Well, that's not acceptable! Are you supposed to wear jeans? A dress? A girl needs to know these things." Now she was making me nervous. It's not like I'd never been on a date before. I'd always been interested in boys and they've always liked me. I dated several boys back home, but nothing overly serious. Since the accident, I hadn't even talked to the guy I was dating when my family died. He hadn't called and when I moved, I didn't tell anyone where I was going.

The bell rang. Lydia rolled her eyes and groaned in frustration.

"I'm coming over to your house after school and we are going to find you something HOT to wear."

"I have detention."

"Well, then afterward. I refuse to let you go on a date with Roman frickin' Sands and not look your best." I beamed at her, giving in. "Good," she said with a final nod, as she turned and skipped back into school.

I walked to chemistry, my body filled with nervous energy.

What am I supposed to do? How do I act toward Roman? Do I acknowledge him in some way, or just walk to my seat like normal? I tried to tell myself it wasn't really a date—I just need information. But I knew it was a lie the second I thought it. There's no denying he's attractive. Anyone could see that. But he had some power over me I didn't understand. His touch excited and calmed me in a way I'd never felt. It was addicting.

Walking into the classroom, I couldn't help but turn my gaze to Roman's seat. He sat there, his gaze already on me, as if he knew I was walking into the room. The intensity of his look stopped me in my tracks. His gaze inched leisurely down my body. By the time he reached my eyes again I knew I was blushing. *Ya, I'm in trouble.* He smiled knowingly and returned his attention to whatever he was doing in his notebook. I released a breath I didn't realize I was holding and started to move forward just as something hit the back of my shoulder. My book bag fell off my arm and onto the ground, spilling the contents everywhere. As I bent down to pick everything up, two lean, tan legs stepped over me.

"Oops, sorry about that. I didn't see you there." I looked up to see Paige staring down at me. "I'd help, but—I just don't want to," she said as she walked to her seat. I took a deep breath in, knowing I couldn't afford to get in any more trouble and returned to picking up my stuff.

"Bitch," I mumbled under my breath.

"Anyone ever tell you you have a dirty mouth?" I turned to see Roman kneeling next to me, one of my books in hand. I snatched it away from him and rose to my feet.

"I don't need your help."

"Clearly." He moved aside and opened up his arm as if presenting the path before me. "After you."

I rolled my eyes and walked to my seat. I could feel Roman's eyes on me as I sat and I swear I heard him chuckle. Thankfully Mr. Sykes entered the room and started class. *My life is turning into a soap opera.*

/|\

"I am not wearing this!" I shouted from the bathroom.

"Will you quit your whining and come out of there?" Lydia hollered from the bedroom. I sighed and trudged into my room stopping inside the doorway, hands on my hips. "Well?"

Lydia lifted her head from where she lay in the middle of my bed. She was surrounded by the outfits she forced me to try on and then decided were not good enough. "Now *that's* what I'm talking about!" I turned to look at myself in the full-length mirror. I was wearing a long, low-cut, red racerback tank, black leggings, and ankle boots. "I can't wear this. It shows way too much cleavage."

"Exactly."

"Lydia!" I glared at her in the mirror.

"Fine, fine. Here." She searched through the clothes on the bed and tossed a garment at me. "Put that on over it." It was a grey button-up jacket. I slipped it on and buttoned it part-way. "Much better."

"Prude," Lydia replied, giggling.

Just then I heard the front door open. "Hello? Kyndal?" my aunt called from downstairs, slamming the door behind her.

"Up here!" I hollered back at her. A few moments later, she peeked her head into the room and gave me a tight smile. She looked stressed, tired.

"Hi." She looked over at the bed, surprised to see Lydia sitting there. "Who's this?"

"Hi, Ms. Davenport. I'm Lydia. Kyndal's friend from school."

"Hi, Lydia. Please, call me Allie." She looked my way and raised her eyebrows as if to say, *Look—you made a friend.* "What are you girls up to?"

"Nothing," I replied quickly before Lydia could say anything. "Just trying on some outfits."

"She has a date." I glared at her and she poked her tongue out in return.

"A date? With who?"

"A boy from school. It's no big deal."

"It *is* a big deal," Lydia huffed, "his name is Roman and he is *the* most gorgeous guy at East Forest High."

"And what are you doing on this date? On a school night."

"Just going to dinner. Nothing big, I promise." I did my best to convince her. I needed to go to dinner with Roman to see if I could get some answers. It would be horrible if Allie decided to practice her parenting skills by telling me I couldn't go. "I'll be back home early, I promise."

She rubbed her eyes. "It's fine."

I smiled slightly and Lydia squealed from the bed in pure joy. You would think it was her going out. "Thank you," I told Allie. "Any luck finding those hikers?"

Allie's face dropped. "Sheriff recovered a body this morning. We haven't identified it yet, but the clothes it was wearing lead us to believe it was one of our missing hikers. The remains were in advanced decomposition. The skin was dried out, pulled tight across the bones."

"Gross," Lydia said, shivering with disgust.

"What about the other hikers?" I asked.

Her frown deepened. "No sign yet. Until we find them, stay out of the forest. No exceptions."

/|\

School the next day dragged on. No matter how hard I tried to focus on what the teachers were saying, I couldn't help but think of the upcoming date. Roman grabbed me first thing in the morning, told me he would pick me up at 5. I think I only managed to nod like a complete dork. I didn't know what my problem was around him. I was either completely mesmerized by his looks or I was so mad at him

I saw red. If I was going to get any answers out of him that night, I had to find a happy medium.

At lunch, Evan sat with Lydia and me. He made it perfectly clear he didn't approve of my going to dinner with Roman. I challenged him, asking why, but he never gave me a clear answer. He sulked and left the table when Lydia insinuated his only problem was that *he* wanted to take me to dinner.

I headed straight home after detention. There was a note on the front table from Allie.

> *Have fun tonight, but not too much fun.*
> *I'll be home late, probably around 11.*
> *I expect you to be here when I get home.*
>
> *-Allie*

I loved that she signed the note. *Who else would it be from? We're the only two that live here.*

I ran upstairs and jumped in the shower, turning the water on cold. Although I didn't want to admit it, my nerves must have been getting to me because I couldn't seem to cool myself down. Even my palms were sweating.

When I finally finished my shower, I threw on the outfit Lydia and I picked out last night, sans the jacket. I was showing more cleavage than I usually cared to, but the jacket made my already sticky skin worse. As an afterthought, I threw the jacket on my purse to take with me. You never know. I briefly blew-dry my hair, leaving it to dry in natural waves down my back. Just a light touch of makeup—mascara, minor eyeshadow, lip gloss—and I was done. Just as I gave myself a final once-over in the mirror, the front door bell rang.

I breathed out deeply. "Alright. Here we go."

5

I walked down the stairs slowly, an old piece of my mom's advice playing in my head. *Always make men wait. It's good for them.* When I opened the front door, Roman was leaning against the house, looking toward the driveway. Before he turned my way, I got a second to admire the view. Dark-washed jeans, black collared shirt fit just right to show off the muscles in his arms. *We match.* His hair was windblown and reckless. *Holy Moses, he really is hot.* He turned to look at me, his eyes traveling over me appreciatively. When our eyes finally met, I saw his were a dark blue, changed by his dark clothing.

"Hi," I managed to say in greeting. He chuckled in return. "What?" I asked him.

"We match," he said, echoing my earlier thoughts. "You ready to go?"

"Sure," I said, following him off the front porch. I made it three steps down the driveway and froze. Sitting there was a very sleek, very sexy looking motorcycle. The body of it was black, accented by streaks of yellow. This thing was obviously built for speed. *Glad I didn't wear a dress.* I looked at Roman who was leaning up against the bike, smiling at my obvious surprise. "This is yours?" I asked.

"Yep," he replied. "Just got her." I gave him a worried look. No way was I getting on the back of a bike with a novice.

Roman laughed. "I used to ride all the time, but I had to sell my last bike. Don't worry, you are perfectly safe." He held his arm out, a helmet in his hand. I walked toward him, grabbing the helmet. "Where's yours?" I asked.

"Don't need one."

"What, your head is thick enough to withstand any damage?"

He laughed. "Something like that."

He swung his leg over the bike, lifting it off the kickstand so that it was balanced only by him. I strapped my purse across my body and put my foot on the peg, hand on his shoulder. I swung my leg around to sit on the slightly raised seat, and sat there awkwardly. I had never been on a motorcycle before. What was I supposed to do with my hands? "You are going to have to put your arms around me," Roman said, reading my mind yet again. *Oh, no.* If I reacted the same way to his touch as I had before, there was no way I could hang on. I hesitantly leaned down and wrapped my arms around him. No reaction. I was touching only clothes, no skin. That seemed to be safe. My body relaxed. "Hang on," Roman said as he started the bike. I could almost feel him smile.

We turned out of the driveway, taking it slow on the gravel. As soon as we hit pavement, he opened up the bike. I gripped him tighter as the bike shot down the road, hugging curves like it had the roads memorized. The further we went, the less I was afraid. *This is amazing.* We were moving so fast, the scenery had blurred into a giant, green wall. The cool evening air hit my exposed arms, giving my skin a reprieve from the heat within.

Just as my body started to relax, I saw the town up ahead. Roman slowed the bike and we cruised until he pulled up in front of a building on the opposite end of town that could only be described as a shack. Surrounded, as many things are around here, by three sides of forest, it was a small, one-story wooden building in desperate need of a paint job. Above the door was a sign reading *Sandra's.* There were only four vehicles in the gravel parking lot besides the bike. I could hear music coming from inside. I couldn't make out the words, but it sounded like country.

I dismounted the bike and took off the helmet. I looked at Roman nervously. "*This* is where you're taking me?"

"Have a little faith. This place has the best burger around. Trust me." When I didn't respond he looked at me worriedly. "What, are you a vegetarian?" I continued to stare blankly. "Vegan? Fruitarian? Raw foodist? We can find somewhere else to go."

I smiled, happy to see I could ruffle his feathers. "I'm from Texas," I said as if that explained it. "I'm a carnivore." He let out a breath, obviously relieved I didn't have any strange eating habits. He reached for the helmet, setting it on the seat of the bike. He took my hand, lacing his index and middle finger with mine. He did it gracefully, naturally. As if we held hands all the time. That time I was prepared for the feeling. The second we made contact, I felt the warmth. Like putting my hands in front of a bonfire. It made me feel safe. Protected. The wind came next. A chilling gust that did nothing to cool my heated skin. I looked up at him, searching for any reaction, but his eyes were focused ahead.

Walking into *Sandra's* was exactly what I expected. Handful of tables right in front, two pool tables on one side, a small dance floor on the other, a full service bar along the back wall. A country singer on the jukebox singing about his lost love. It's not too far off from some of the places I had been to in Dayton. It felt like *home*. Roman led me to a table, waving at the woman behind the bar with his free hand. She returned his greeting with a warm smile. Her smile quickly faded though when she saw me. Her eyes narrowed and her mouth grew tight in disgust. Even as I looked away, I felt her eyes stay on us until we reached our table. Once seated, a waitress immediately took our orders. After ordering a burger and fries (he did say it was the best) I turned toward Roman, giving him a serious look. "Alright, spill."

He looked back at me, his blue eyes feigning surprise. "Spill what?"

"You know exactly what. You promised to explain the fight over dinner. Well, it's dinner. Talk."

He shook his head, laughing. "You're very direct, you know that?"

"Yes, I've been told. Don't change the subject."

"I'm not explaining right away. What's to keep you from walking out the second you get your answers?" *Your smile, your eyes, the way you look in that shirt.* "Anyways, I have some questions of my own I want answered first."

"What? That wasn't part of the deal."

"Too bad, deals change." He leaned back in his chair, immensely pleased with himself. We stared at each other for a while, his eyes challenging. Finally, reluctantly, I gave in.

"You get three questions but only *after* you talk."

"Promise to answer honestly?" He tilted his head to the side as if he didn't think I'd agree to it.

I looked at him confidently, although I felt anything but. "Only if you do."

"Okay. You have a deal."

Right then our food arrived. Apparently service is pretty quick when there's only a handful of people here. Roman dug into his meal. I ate slowly, refusing to speak. He promised to talk; I planned to wait until he did. Finally, he set down his half-eaten burger and took a swig of Coke. "It's not that easy to explain."

"Try."

He held my eyes. I refused to look down. I could see him waging an internal war, deciding exactly what to say and how to say it. He ran his fingers through his hair, ruffling the already tousled locks. "What Paige said to you was out of line, regardless if it's founded in truth or not. No one was standing up for you and I just felt like someone should."

"Like I said—you don't even know me—"

"It doesn't matter," he interrupted, his tone fierce. "I know what's right and wrong and what they were saying to you, *about you*, wasn't right." I was taken aback by the ferocity and emotion in his voice. I had never met someone with a sense of justice intense enough to act on behalf of a stranger.

I reached forward and grabbed my drink, stalling as I watched the storm calm within him.

"So, how does that equal you hitting Jared?" I asked, softly.

"Jared is part of the group Paige runs with. He might have been the one saying them, but those were Paige's words."

"And it's not like you could hit Paige, so you went for the next best thing," I finished for him. He waved his hand in front of him as if to say *exactly*.

"Isaac was right. You do have a temper."

He laughed without humor. "Yeah, well Isaac needs to learn to keep his mouth shut."

"I thought you two were friends?"

He cocked his head to the side; clearly a habit of his. "More like teammates. He's good in a pinch, but you won't find us braiding each other's hair and spilling our deep, dark secrets."

Just as I was about to ask what he meant by *in a pinch*, the waitress returned. *Worst timing ever, lady.* When she left, Roman's demeanor had changed and I could tell he wouldn't be answering any more questions. His eyes were on me—penetrating, as if he was trying to see into my very soul. I steeled myself. A deal's a deal. It was his turn to ask. I shifted uncomfortably in my chair, waiting for the interrogation. Abruptly, he scooted his chair back, stood, and held out his hand. "Come with me."

I willingly gave him mine, desperate to avoid any of his questions. He led me past the bar, through a door I hadn't noticed before. The same woman watched us silently, her eyes on us until the last possible second.

Out back was a covered porch jutting out from the building toward the forest. The roof was covered in small twinkle lights wrapping the porch in a soft glow. We could still hear the same, slow song inside, but out here it was softer, more intimate. We were completely alone. Roman gently tugged on my hand, pulling me flush to his body. "Dance with me." His voice was silk, there was no way I could refuse. I smiled shyly and placed my hand on his shoulder, careful not to touch his skin. His free hand came around to my waist, applying just enough pressure to lead me.

My dancing experience was limited to awkward swaying and line dancing. This was neither of those. This was close contact. Roman pushed and pulled me around the dance floor skillfully. Our bodies fit together perfectly, regardless of the fact that he was several inches taller than me. We didn't talk for a while, both enjoying the company. Then, my curiosity got the best of me. "Who is that woman?"

"Hmm?" he responded, his voice lazy.

"The woman behind the bar. Who is she?"

"Sandra, the owner," he answered evasively. He knew that was not why I was asking.

"She seemed like she knew you."

He shrugged. "Small town."

"Looked like more than that," I pushed. "She didn't seem happy to see me with you."

"She's an old family friend. She and my brother used to date a long time ago, back when I was younger. Now she's like the protective older sister. I wouldn't worry about her, she's just—" he sighed deeply, looking away.

"She's just what?"

"Not used to seeing me with anyone."

He looked back at me, his eyes piercing. I tried to hold his gaze, but the intensity proved too much and almost unwillingly, my eyes traveled to his mouth. His lips were perfect. Totally kissable. *Kissable? Seriously? That's not what you're here for K. Get a grip.*

"Lydia told me you don't date much," I blurted, trying to distract myself.

He chuckled slightly. We were so close I could feel it thrum through my body. "Is that what she said?"

My cheeks reddened. "Actually, she said you don't date at all. I was just trying to be polite."

"Well, she's right."

"Which time?" I asked, confused. "You don't date much, or not at all?"

"What do you think?"

"I don't know. Honestly, I have trouble believing either one."

He cocked his head to the side, smiling. "Really? Why's that?" *Crap. I've said too much.*

I pulled away, embarrassed. *There is no way I'm going to explain why.* I only managed to escape partially before he tightened the grip on my hand and pulled me back to him.

"Kyndal? Why?"

"You know why. Don't be dense," I retorted, refusing to explain.

"I want *you* to tell me."

I groaned in frustration. "I mean—it's obvious. Look at you. A guy that looks like you doesn't not date. It just doesn't happen."

"Maybe I wasn't ever interested in anyone before."

"But you are now?" I asked sarcastically.

"Now who's being dense?" His hand slid to the side of my face. He gently tucked a piece of loose hair behind my ear. My breath halted. His hand lingered just a moment before he smiled slightly and returned his hand to my hip.

"What about Paige?" I asked. "Seems like she's got a thing for you."

"Jealous?" he asked, chuckling slightly.

"You wish," I replied with a huff. I noticed that he didn't answer my question.

Eventually we returned to dancing, and as one song led into another, I found myself relaxing into his embrace. My head leaned lightly against his chest. I didn't stop to think about what I was doing or how I barely knew the guy I was dancing so closely with. All I could think about was how I felt safe. Protected. Cared for. After the weeks of grief and loneliness, I welcomed the change. I clung to it. Roman's hand moved from my waist to my bare shoulder, moving in rhythmic circles, but never breaking contact. A trail of fire and ice followed his fingers. It was absolute bliss.

Suddenly, he stopped dancing and pulled away, keeping hold of my hand. I looked at him through hooded eyes. I could see the flecks of yellow had returned to his typically pure blue.

"Why did you move here?" he asked. Softly. Sincerely.

Suddenly, I wanted to tell him everything. Not because of how he looked, or how his touch felt, but because he had *asked*. Few people had shown genuine caring toward me since I came here. None of them had asked me about that night. Everyone heard the stories and made their own conclusions. I was overwhelmed by the need for a cathartic release, to tell someone what I had been through, for someone to understand.

I led him over to the railing of the porch and sat, letting go of his hand. If I was going to talk about this, I was going to need a clear head. Roman sat next to me, waiting patiently. "I had a brother named Chase," I began quietly. I closed my eyes, opening myself up to the memories. "We were less than a year apart and damn near inseparable. Everyone always thought it was strange, how close we were. Siblings are supposed to hate each other, right? But we never did. Mom said we'd been that way even as babies."

"What happened to him?" Roman asked softly.

"We were coming home from my birthday dinner. Not just Chase and me, but our parents, too. He and Dad were in the back bickering about which was better: foreign or American made cars." I looked over at Roman. "Dad was a mechanic and owned his own garage. Chase shared his love of all things automobile, but they never agreed on which type was best. When he turned 16, Chase wanted a Nissan. Dad wanted him to drive a Ford." I smiled slightly and remembered the two of them working on cars in the garage together. "Mom and I would have to force them to quit working so they could come in for dinner. Sometimes they stayed out until the early hours of the morning, refusing to quit until they got the vehicle exactly how they wanted it." My eyes stung with unshed tears thinking about the happier times that I would never get back.

"Mom turned in her seat toward me, joking about hearing this debate *again*. I took my eyes off the road for a second—*a split second*—to look over and smile at her. When I looked back, something was in the road. To this day I still don't remember what. I swerved the car to miss it."

At that point, the tears had spilled from my eyes. Before I could think to move and cover them, Roman reached over and gently wiped them from my cheek. The gesture was so sweet it made me cry harder.

"The car flipped. Somehow it lit on fire while we were all stuck inside. I don't remember a lot after that. What I do remember is my mom yelling at Chase and my dad to wake up. I must've blacked out or something. When I came to I was in the hospital. The doctor told me no one knew how I survived. My lungs were clear; no smoke inhalation. No burns. Not even a scratch."

Roman moved to stand in front of me, the tips of his fingers lightly grazing my knees. "So, why Marienville?"

I shrugged sadly. "My father grew up here. His sister, Alessandra, is the only family I have left. I'm still a minor so it was either live with her or go into foster care until I turn eighteen."

"Can I ask you one more question?" His voice was low, wrought with emotion.

"You've already asked your three."

He reached out again to brush the remaining tears from my cheeks. Rather than dropping his hands, he left them on either side of my face. "Just one more." I looked up at him, his face blurry through my tears. He leaned in, our foreheads almost touching. He barely whispered, "Can I kiss you?" I looked into his eyes, searching. Searching for judgement or condemnation for what I'd done. All I saw was compassion, understanding, and yes—desire. I tilted my chin up slightly, aligning my mouth at a better angle to his, giving him permission. He brought my mouth to his slowly. Our lips touched and instantly his mouth was searing, igniting a blaze inside me so much more powerful than any other time he had touched me. The kiss started out innocent, but then he parted my lips with his tongue. As he deepened the kiss, my internal blaze strengthened as if given fresh oxygen. It was a wildfire. I wrapped my arms around his neck, pulling him closer. His hands were posted on the railing on either side of me, effectively trapping me where I sat.

Abruptly, he pulled away. I had to brace my hands on my knees to combat the storm of emotions raging inside me. That kiss was amazing. I've been kissed before, but never like *that*. Roman stood on the other side of the porch. He looked toward the forest, avoiding my gaze. Tension radiated from his shoulders—the only sign he was as affected by the kiss as I was.

I took several deep breaths, working to calm the heat inside me. Finally, the flames diminished, leaving me able to speak. "Tell me you felt that."

Roman turned and finally looked at me. His eyes were luminous and full of anguish. He started to walk toward me but stopped himself, thinking better of it. Speaking in a whisper, he said the last words I expected to hear.

"We should go."

He re-entered the bar without waiting for a response. Looking toward the door to the bar, I couldn't help but feel rejected. Did I imagine the spark between us? I thought it was pretty amazing as far as kisses go, but obviously he felt different. He couldn't escape quickly enough. Wiping my face and trying to save what was left of my dignity, I stood and followed Roman inside.

When he dropped me off at the house, he barely waited for me to hand him the helmet before peeling out of the driveway. No goodbye, just the dust left behind from the bike. I didn't even make the porch before the tears fell unbidden down my face. I hate crying and that was the second time it had happened that day. Crying made me feel weak, broken. Allie wasn't home yet and I could avoid questioning; my only luck that night. I climbed the stairs and fell into bed hoping to forget the horrible evening.

That night I was haunted by searing lips and yellow-blue eyes.

6

"**T**hat bastard!"

I lifted my head from my hands, looking up at Lydia from where I sat at our lunch table. She wore a path in the grass, pacing back and forth as I explained the disastrous date the night before. "Can you keep it down, please?" I whined.

"That bastard."

"You already said that."

"And he didn't say anything else after you had this big, epic kiss?"

"Nothing."

"Bastard," she whispered, plopping down on the bench across from me. I couldn't help but smile a little at her. As much as I tried not to let her, Lydia wormed her way into my life. "Well, screw him. You know what you need? A distraction. A little music, a little dancing, a little—" she made a drinking motion with her hand. "There's a party tonight at The Ridge and we are going."

"What's The Ridge?"

Another voice piped up. Evan walked toward us, lunch tray in hand. "It's a place in the forest that high school kids always go to·party. It's deep enough so the cops don't bother us." He sat down next to Lydia, immediately digging into his food.

Lydia looked over at him, disgusted by his lack of table manners. "Tell me, Evan. You're a guy, right?"

"Last time I checked," he said around the food in his mouth.

"Would you ever kiss a girl then dump her on her porch without any more than a word?"

"Lydia!" I hissed.

"What?!" she responded. "Totally hypothetical, of course."

Evan's eyes popped up, looking directly at me. "I take it things didn't go well with Roman?"

"That's putting it mildly." I was mortified. *I can't believe Lydia just said that.* "Go ahead, say, 'I told you so.' "

"I wasn't going to," he replied. "I would never do that."

Lydia turned to me. "See how mature he is?" She looked back at Evan. "So tell us, wise one, wouldn't it be totally appropriate to get over said rejection with a night of alcohol-induced shenanigans?"

"Absolutely. As all mature people would." Evan smiled.

Lydia turned and stared at me. "See? It's settled. You are going to The Ridge."

Parties had never really been my thing, but you know what? They were right. I did need a distraction. After a week of snotty girls with caramel highlights, detention, mystery burns, disturbing dreams, and the icing-on-the-cake rejection from a gorgeous classmate, I needed to blow off some steam. I looked at Lydia with a devious smile, "Alright. I'm in." She smiled back. Oh ya, this was going to be fun.

/ǀ\

When I walked into chemistry class, I immediately noticed Roman's absence. That put the last nail in the rejection coffin. *Not only did our kiss run him off from our date, apparently it was so bad he couldn't even face me at school.* Mr. Sykes gave us new lab partners. I was paired with a nice girl I hadn't met yet. I tried to focus on our experiment but my thoughts kept wandering to Roman. Every time that happened, I closed the lid on the train of thought and tried to think ahead to the party. *Forget him. Who needs him.* The bell rang before I knew it and I thanked my partner for her help with the lab. She smiled politely—I could tell I wasn't much help by the look on her face. *Way to go, K.*

After school I headed to the library for detention. Taped to the door was a handwritten sign:

DETENTION CANCELLED FOR TODAY.
GO HOME.

I burst out laughing. I didn't know people actually cancelled detention—seemed counterproductive. I hustled out the main door hoping to catch Lydia before she left. I spotted her bright blonde hair across the parking lot. "Lydia!" I yelled. She turned, searching for the source of her name. When she saw me, she smiled, confused. I jogged over to her. "Shouldn't you be in detention?" she asked.

"Cancelled," I shrugged.

"Cancelled? That seems to defeat the purpose," she responded, echoing my sentiment. "So, you have a day-pass from jail. I suggest we take advantage."

Lydia wasted no time dragging me back to her place to spend my free hours getting ready for the party. When we walked into her house, a standard two-story, I was instantly bombarded with noise. Two boys ran past us in the main hall—one chasing the other with a Nerf gun—and both screaming. Lydia pushed her way past an athletic bag to keep from getting knocked over. A pretty woman with a baby on her hip poked her head in the hallway and yelled, "Boys! Slow down!" She retreated back out of view, but Lydia and I followed her. We ended up in the kitchen where the woman was cooking. "Mom."

"Ya, honey?" the woman replied without turning around.

"This is my friend Kyndal. We're going to go downstairs

73

and hang out." Lydia's mom glanced briefly back at us and flashed a smile before returning to what she was doing.

"Hi Kyndal. Nice to meet you."

Lydia looked at me and rolled her eyes. "Oh, and later—we're going out. I'm staying at Kyndal's overnight." I gave her a meaningful look that said *you are?* She held up one finger to keep me quiet.

"Fine, honey. Have fun," her mom said dismissively.

Lydia smiled at me and motioned toward the basement stairs. At the bottom, I was met by multi-colored walls plastered with posters of bands—most of which I had never heard of. Mismatched furniture: a wooden desk, black metal framed bed, and a pink futon, all screamed Lydia. One thing I have learned about her is that she has eclectic taste. We both sat; her on the bed, me on the futon. "How many of you are there?" I asked.

She laughed. "Of me? Only one. The original. But if you are asking how many siblings I have, I am one of six. Seventeen, fifteen, ten, three, three, and 10 months." My eyes bugged out. She laughed again. "Trust me. I know how you feel."

"So, you're staying at my house tonight, huh?"

"Ya, sorry about that. Thought of it spur of the moment. Sounds like a good time though, doesn't it?"

"Sounds great."

"Good. Now that that's out of the way, let's get you ready."

We spent the next several hours painting our nails, picking out outfits, and doing our hair and makeup. Although I wasn't usually one for all the girly stuff, it was fun. I had time to ask Lydia about her life and I got to forget about my own for awhile. Turned out her dad left six months ago, after 20 years of marriage. Just up and left her mom in charge of six kids. Lydia hadn't even heard from him since he split.

"Do you miss him?" I asked, watching her closely in her vanity mirror.

She shrugged. Her eyes stayed focused on my hair where she was adding in random curls. "I'm too mad at him to miss him." My heart clenched at the pain in her voice. While I understood the pain of losing a parent, mine were ripped from me. They didn't leave by choice.

By 8:00 we were primped and ready to go. "The party starts this early?" I asked while adjusting the top I had borrowed from her closet. Lydia is smaller than me. The red shirt fit me snugly, showing off my curves. "Oh honey, no. I don't know about you, but I for one need some grub before we hit the party." I nodded in understanding. "But before we go," she walked behind a small partition in the back of the room, "there is one thing left to do," she said from behind the screen. I heard the clinking of glasses and she emerged holding two shot glasses full of clear liquid.

I gave her a surprised look. "What is that?"

"Pre-game," she responded.

"Aren't you driving us? You can't drink then drive." She gave me a look that said *no kiddin', idiot.*

"That's why they're both for you." She smiled, handing me both glasses. "Bottoms up, Tex."

I looked at the shot glasses indecisively. I grabbed them. "Screw it." I downed them both.

/|\

It turned out The Ridge wasn't a ridge at all. It was a plateau. And Lydia was right; although we drove in on a clearly worn dirt road, this place was deep in the forest. It was nearly impossible to see through the dense trees, especially at night. As we got out of the car, I took a look around. A large circular area had been cleared and in the middle of it stood a raging bonfire. The flames lit up the area, showing fallen trees lying all around it. The party-goers sat on them like benches. Those that weren't sitting were dancing to music coming from someone's car—drinks in hand.

"Rangers don't worry about such a big fire in the forest?" I asked Lydia as we walked toward the action. I thought about Alessandra. She definitely would not approve. I was glad I took Lydia's advice and lied to her about where I was going tonight. I didn't think she would let me go, not after finding one of the missing hikers dead. I called her before we left and told her Lydia and I were going to eat and that I would be staying the night at her house. She seemed so excited I was out doing something, I had a brief moment of guilt over the lie. I didn't realize how much she worried about me.

"People have been partying here for years and no one's burnt the forest down yet," Lydia responded. "Come on, let's get you a drink. I want to introduce you to some people." After the two shots of vodka, I wasn't too eager for another drink, but as Lydia dragged me toward the keg, I noticed a familiar outline on the other side of the fire. Roman. He was talking to Isaac and a woman I didn't know. She seemed a few years older, definitely not a high school student. Her hair was vibrantly red, a color so distinct I could see it through the dark from where I stood several feet away. It was pulled back in a slick ponytail. She was built like an athlete. As I watched, the woman laughed and reached over to place her hand on his shoulder. It was a familiar gesture. Instantly, I was consumed with jealousy. A touch like that and giggling? *She is definitely flirting and he is letting her. How can he kiss me yesterday and flirt with her today?*

"Here you go," Lydia handed me a cup. When I didn't acknowledge her, she followed my line of sight. She gasped dramatically. "That bastard!" Just then, Roman looked over, his blue eyes pointed directly at mine. I held his gaze for just a moment, one that I knew would cost me. Then I broke the trance, grabbed the cup from Lydia, and downed it. "Atta girl, way to take the high road," she joked.

"Let's get another," I responded. We headed back to the keg but someone grabbed my hand. I didn't have to turn to know it was him. I could feel the familiar pull. The heat sparked in my fingertips. Lydia gave me an apologetic look, then turned away from me. *Traitor*. I masked my feelings as best as I could and turned to face him.

"I need to talk to you," he said immediately. I tore my hand from his.

"Now you want to talk? Really? Because that's not the vibe I got when you practically dumped me on my front porch last night, or today when you avoided me altogether by not even showing up to school. I got the message. No need for further explanation." I tried to turn away but he grabbed my hand again, practically dragging me into the cover of the trees.

"Let go of me," I growled, ripping my hand back. The heat in my hand had grown to what felt like a living flame. I swear if I had touched a tree, I would have burned the whole forest down.

"Look," Roman rumbled. His tone commanded my attention. "This isn't about us. You need to leave. It isn't safe for you here."

"What are you—" I tried to ask, but he interrupted.

"I'm serious Kyndal. Grab Lydia and go home. I promise I'll explain everything later."

I rolled my eyes and barked out a frustrated laugh. "Heard that before, Roman." With one last glare, I walked away from him, ignoring his pleas for me to leave.

An hour and two beers later, I was tipsy. Lydia and I stood with a group of classmates she had introduced me to. For the life of me I couldn't remember all of their names. Luckily, Evan was among them. Next to Lydia, he had been the most welcoming of anyone. He effortlessly entertained the others while simultaneously keeping me included and my Solo cup full. But I was still distracted. I tried to keep up with the conversation but I couldn't stop thinking about my frustrating encounter with Roman. I think Evan was talking to me about an upcoming dance, but I was only half-listening. *Dammit, Roman! He is just so aggravating! What makes him think he can kiss me, ignore me, then tell me what to do?*

Evan interrupted my internal rant. "Kyndal, did you hear me?"

"What? Yeah, I did. Sorry." I hadn't actually heard a word he said.

"So," he looked at me with expectant eyes, "what do you think?"

I tried to think back. *What was he talking about? Crap, I have no idea.* I felt bad for not paying attention.

"Uh, sounds great."

His eyes lit up. He was happy about something. I smiled uneasily in response.

Just as I was about to admit that I didn't know what I had just agreed to, I felt heat on my back. It wasn't from the bonfire. The feeling snaked up my spine, filling me with dread. I turned, searching for the source of the feeling. On the tree line I could just make out Roman, Isaac, and the mystery woman. They weren't enjoying the party. In fact, they looked deadly serious. All three looked around suspiciously then disappeared into the timber. My curiosity got the best of me and I decided to follow. I excused myself from the conversation with Evan and headed to the opening I saw them disappear through. It was difficult to keep up. It was dark. The only light came from the moon and stars above. They were moving quickly, but were impressively quiet. They moved like they had known the terrain for years. I followed them for so long, the sounds of the party had disappeared behind me. Just as I thought I had lost them, I saw a flash of orange through the trees and heard what sounded like a fight.

I broke through the tree line and froze in my tracks. Whatever I expected to find when I followed them, it definitely was not this. It was all-out war. The mystery woman was up against a tree, trading blows with what looked like a 30-year-old man. I caught a glimpse of his face and was shocked when I noticed his veins. They were dark and protruding, weaving through his face like a spider web. The girl took a particularly nasty blow to the face, but she lashed out with her leg, kicking the man in the gut. He faltered and she took the opportunity to jump on him, knocking him to the ground. I looked away from her just in time to see Isaac throw another man with inhuman strength across the clearing. Isaac reached into his pocket and pulled out a lighter. Lighting it with one hand, he reached over with his other, holding it above the flame. When he pulled his hand away, he held a fireball the size of a softball. The flames licked over his fingers, but he showed no signs of pain. With a twisted smile on his face, he launched the fireball at the man he had thrown. Right before my eyes, he went up in flame, screaming. Then—nothing. Only a faint trace of ash floated in the air where the man had stood just moments ago. Searching for Roman, I found him in all-out battle with two men, his back to me. He was holding his own, but I could see that his opponents were starting to get the upper hand. Isaac joined the fight, distracting one of them. Fully focused on his opponent, Roman pulled something shiny from behind his back. It looked like a large knife, or dagger. It gave him the upper hand. Before I knew it, he had shoved the dagger into the man, up to the hilt. Just like before, the man disappeared as if he was never there.

Roman ran to check on the red-haired woman who was lying unconscious on the ground. I didn't see what happened to her. As he leaned over to check her pulse, I saw the man she had been fighting earlier get up and head toward Roman. He had no idea there was someone behind him. I looked over at Isaac, but he was still locked in battle, lashing out at his opponent with a dagger similar to the one I saw Roman use, absolutely oblivious to what was going on around him. He wouldn't be able to help Roman in time. Before I knew what I was doing, I yelled Roman's name. His head snapped up, zeroing in on me instantly, his eyes a luminous gold. Without thinking, I threw my arm out toward the man. I didn't even register the flash of intense heat until after the ball of fire left my hand. It struck the man square in the chest. He was gone before he could hit the ground. Roman looked behind him at where the man would have landed, then back to me. I held his eyes for just a moment, then turned my gaze to my hand.

What the hell did I just do?

7

"**K**yndal." I heard my name through the fog. "Kyndal, wake up." Someone was shaking me, trying to get me to open my eyes. I tried, but all I could see was fire flying through the air, bodies disappearing before they hit the ground, a boy with gold eyes. "Kyndal, god dammit, open your eyes!" I broke through the fog framed by the starry night and saw a pair of icy blue eyes staring at me. *What happened? How did I end up on the ground?*

"Roman?"

"Are you alright?" He looked at me as if he thought I might pass out again.

"I think I drank too much." I started to sit up. "I must've passed out. I dreamt that you and Isaac were in a fight and get this—I saved you by throwing fire at someone." I shook my head in embarrassment, letting out a slightly insane giggle. Roman gave me an unsure look. Before he could say anything, I saw movement over his shoulder. I looked toward it and saw Isaac helping the redhead from the party up from the ground. Her cheek was bruised and her lip was bleeding. I laid back on the ground, putting my hands over my face. "Shit. It wasn't a dream, was it?" I uncovered my face and looked up at Roman.

He shook his head. "Afraid not."

I jumped to my feet, panicked. Roman followed, standing much slower. I started to yell, "What the hell was—How—What—" I was so freaked out, I couldn't even form a sentence. I took a deep breath then lowered my voice. "I shot *fire* out of my hand. How did I do that?"

Roman looked over his shoulder. Isaac and the girl were making their way toward us. He took a step into my personal space, speaking in hushed tones. "I don't know. But for now, don't mention it to anyone else. Even them." He nodded toward the others. I lowered my eyebrows, confused by his secrecy. "Please, trust me." He looked right into my eyes, imploring me. I just barely nodded before the others joined us.

"Hey, man. You alright?" Isaac clasped his hand on Roman's shoulder.

He looked at them both in turn, "Yeah, I'm good. You? Cassie?" They both nodded.

"That big one packed a hell of a punch," Cassie said. She lifted her hand to her lip, anger showing on her face as she saw it come away red. "You bring a date on a hunt, Roman? Smooth."

Isaac laughed, but Roman's face was completely serious.

"Not exactly," Roman replied. He pointed to me then her. "Kyndal Davenport, this is Cassandra White. Cassie— Kyndal." She held out the hand without blood on it and I took it. She gripped my hand firmly, turning it over, exposing the burn on the edge of my palm. Her eyebrows shot up, and although she looked at me, she spoke to the boys.

"You didn't tell me she was one of us."

"One of you? What does she mean?" My eyes darted between Roman and Isaac. While Isaac was smiling, Roman refused to meet my eyes. "Roman! What is she talking about?"

He finally looked at me. His eyes seemed sad, defeated. "Follow me. We need to talk."

/|\

Cassie and Isaac headed straight to their vehicle. Covered in blood, they were both a little too suspicious. Roman and I headed back to the party. "Find Lydia, I'll wait here." I spotted her sitting on one of the fallen logs, laughing with one of the guys we were standing with earlier. When she saw me, her smile grew. "Hey! There you are! Where did you go?"

I ignored the question. "Can I talk to you for a second?" I looked at the boy next to her. "She'll be right back, I promise."

She was confused, but she followed me anyway. I led her a few feet away so we could talk privately. "Hey, Evan told me the news. Good for you, rebounding right away."

I gave her a puzzled look. "What are you talking about?"

"The dance. Evan said you agreed to go with him."

Crap. That must have been what he asked me. I rolled my eyes in frustration. *No time to deal with it now. Right now I have to get out of here.*

"Look, I need to leave."

"Okay, let me get my purse." She started to turn away but I stopped her.

"No. I, um—kind of have another ride."

She crossed her arms. "Oh, really? And who exactly are you bailing on me for?"

I cringed. She was totally going to get the wrong idea. "Roman."

Her mouth dropped open. "Seriously?"

"It's not like that."

"Oh, suurre it's not," she replied with amusement, winking at me.

"I'll call you tomorrow?" I asked, hoping she wouldn't press for more details.

"You better." I reached out and hugged her before turning

to rejoin Roman.

"Alright," I said when I reached him. "Let's go."

We wound through the roads on the edge of the forest, the wind blowing against my face, my arms firmly wrapped around Roman's waist. He turned toward the trees, down a one-lane road so well hidden I barely noticed it. We followed the road until we reached a house that seemed to grow out of the earth itself. Two stories with the roof coming to several peaks, it was made completely of natural wood. There was a covered porch held up by pillars, each one wrapped tightly in dried vines. Roman surprised me when he didn't stop out front. Instead, he pulled around the side and continued toward a guest house camouflaged in the trees. He stopped the bike next to a Jeep. I followed him in silently.

The house was beautiful. After a small entryway, the main floor was completely open. In it was a kitchen, a living room behind it, and an open stairway to the right leading to what I thought might be a bedroom loft. The living room contained a cozy looking couch facing a fireplace. No TV. Behind the couch was a well-used punching bag and a weight bench. As impressive as it all was, that's not what held my attention. The entire back wall was glass. Standing where I was, the forest was in clear view. It was breathtaking.

"Would you like something to drink?" Roman whispered, breaking the silence. I shook my head.

"Do you live here all by yourself?" I asked, awed at the

house, but confused. *Why does a teenage boy live alone?*

"Ezekiel owns the property. I used to live in the big house, but I moved out here about a year ago." He moved into the living area, switching on lights as he went. He sat on the end of the couch and gestured for me to sit on the opposite side. *How could he be so calm? My whole world just turned upside down!* I sat down, my hands shaking, my mind reeling. Roman watched intently. "I'm assuming you have questions."

I barked a laugh. "Yeah, one or two."

Roman took my sarcasm in stride. "You can ask anything you want."

I started with the most obvious. "Who's Ezekiel?"

"To the outside world, he's my older brother and legal guardian. In reality, he sits on the Council as one of twelve Nomarchs."

"A No-what?"

"Nomarch," he repeated. "Think of him like a local governor or leader."

"Leader of who?" I asked, confused.

"The Kindred."

"What does that mean?"

"It means to share a commonality, or be related—"

"I know what the word means," I interrupted. "What does it

mean to *be* Kindred?"

"The short version—we're warriors. We hunt down and kill wraiths." I pinned him with an annoyed look. "Demons," he clarified.

"Demons," I repeated. "Like from hell?"

He shook his head. "Not exactly. Wraiths used to be human. When their mortal life ended, their spirit refused to move on to the afterlife. What exactly the afterlife *is*, well," he shrugged. "They can only survive on our plane inside a living body. Since their original one isn't available, they steal someone else's."

I cut to the chase. "You're talking about possession." He nodded. "What happens to the people they possess?"

"Dead." His jaw clenched in anger. "Humans never survive the possession. It's too much raw power. Once a wraith is inside someone, they latch onto the human's soul as an energy source. They slowly consume the soul, using the energy to keep the human's body working. But as the soul depletes, the body wears down. Shadows form under their eyes, they lose weight, and their skin pales. Inevitably, the soul is consumed, and the body dies. Then the wraith has to find someone else to jump into."

Wow. I took a deep breath. Instinctively, I popped my knuckles.

"And you—you fight these things?"

Roman got up from where he sat and moved into the

kitchen, grabbing himself a bottle of water from the fridge. My eyes never left him. "Thousands of years ago, wraiths were running rampant. They would move from village to village, city to city, possessing people and causing strife and discord. You'd be shocked if you knew how many famous battles in history were actually wraiths. They would tear through the citizens, leaving no survivors. Thousands of people were dying. Then they would move on. No one was able to stop them. It wasn't until a group of twelve devoted followers prayed to the god Hermes Trismegistus for help."

"Wait," I interrupted. "Hermes? Like the guy with the winged feet?"

One side of his mouth lifted in a smirk. "No. Hermes Trismegistus is the god of magic and the afterlife. He is both Greek and Egyptian. He is the one responsible for collecting the spirits that have avoided the afterlife. He answered the prayers of the twelve and created the first Kindred to hunt them down and kill them."

"So, Kindred are basically bounty hunters, searching for demons that skipped bail."

"That's one way to look at it."

I nodded, processing. "And that's what I saw earlier, in the forest? Those were wraiths you killed?"

Roman didn't miss a beat. "We had received reports of missing hikers in the Allegheny. The rangers couldn't find their bodies, which isn't completely unheard of around here. Yet because no bodies were found, that left a strong possibility of possession. With the party at The Ridge, we knew that if the hikers had been turned, they would more than likely show up there. Wraiths can't resist parties like that. All those young bodies ripe for feeding."

"What do you mean, 'feeding'?" I hesitated, afraid of the answer. "Do they *eat* people?"

Roman chuckled. *Glad I'm amusing.* "No. Although their teeth are sharp, they only bite as a means of offense. Think of wraiths like parasites. When their host's body can no longer sustain itself, they must feed on an outside source in order to avoid finding a new host." He placed his hand over my heart. "They can pull energy from other people and absorb it in their host's body. It temporarily reverses the wear on the body."

My brain flashed to Alessandra's description of the dead hiker. Dried out. Skin pulled tight. "What happens to the person that was fed on?"

"It depends. When a wraith feeds, it's excruciatingly painful for the victim. It feels like your heart is being ripped from your chest. But, if the wraith doesn't pull too much energy, the person will eventually recover."

"Alessandra was a part of the team looking for those hikers. There were four of them. One was found dead a few days ago. She said the body was unidentifiable. The skin was dried out, taught against the bones. Was he—was he fed on?"

Again, Roman nodded. "Yes."

I shuddered.

I took a deep breath in and looked down. My hands were shaking. I stared at them in fascination, remembering what they did in the forest. I clenched them together, doing my best not to completely freak out. Roman reached out and touched my knee. "I'm sorry, Kyndal. I know this is a lot to take in." The contact broke what little self-control I had left. I stood up, my voice rising in panic. "I shot fire out of my hand. How did I do that?"

His expression stayed impassive. It irritated me even more that he was not as panicked as I was. "The Kindred were created as a counterpoint to the wraiths. But where wraiths consume and destroy everything around them, Kindred have to maintain balance. Our powers work on an order of duality. Where there is light, there is dark. Male, female. yin, yang. life, death." I thought back to my first conversation with Isaac. *There are always two sides for everything. Always.* "When Hermes Trismegistus answered the prayers of the Original 12, he told them their powers would not come without sacrifice. On their next birthday, he took from each of them a family member. The duality of their deaths on a day meant to celebrate life created an opening for their powers. When your family died on your birthday, your powers burst forth."

My shoulders slumped. *It all goes back to the wreck.*

"All Kindred have lost someone close to them?"

"Yes," he replied, his tone sad. "On their birthday. Part of the reason you won't find any of us celebrating getting older." I looked at him. *I wonder who he lost.*

"This happens automatically to all those people?"

He shook his head, following my train of thought. "No. Losing someone is only the first step of the process. Duality creates the opening, but the powers have to be cemented by the time your House falls out of rotation. Without that second step, the power dissipates and can never be called up again."

"I don't understand. What do you mean House? And what powers?"

"Earth, water, air," he held his hand out to me, "fire. Each Kindred has powers based upon one of the elements."

"How is it decided which element you possess?" I paced back and forth, replaying all the run-ins with fire this week.

"Are you familiar with the Zodiac?"

"Vaguely," I replied, still pacing. My brain was moving so fast, I felt the need for my body to match it.

"The Zodiac is separated into 12 houses, each house, or sign as you have probably heard them called, is assigned to a specific part of the calendar year. Every house is attached to an element. Three for earth, three for water, three for air, and three for fire. Whichever element is attached to the house you were born in is the element you develop. You are an Aries. Fire."

I stopped pacing briefly. "Twelve houses? One for each of the people who prayed to Hermes Trismegistus." He nodded. "And you, what are you?"

"Libra. Air." I resumed pacing, my brain processing. Roman sat there silently, allowing me to work through all the information he dumped on me. I don't know how long he waited, but he never broke the silence. Finally, I stopped and sat down on the couch next to him. He turned to look at me, his piercing blue eyes locked on to me, reminding me that earlier they were not blue at all. "Why were your eyes a different color earlier?" Roman grinned.

"Most of the time, our powers lie dormant within us. When we use them, it leaves a signifier on the outside. For Kindred, it's eye color. Your element determines the color. When you threw that fireball, your eyes were bright red." For some reason, this startled me the most. I tried to imagine myself with bright red eyes. I shook off the image, uncomfortable.

"How *did* I throw the fireball tonight?"

He turned his body toward me. "That I don't know. The Kindred can wield the elements, but we can't create them. All other fire users I've met—Isaac for instance—have to reach out to existing fire." I thought of Isaac and the lighter.

I looked down at my hand, running my fingers over the burn on my palm. Isaac had noticed it earlier in the week. When Cassie saw it, she called me "one of them."

"It's our brand," Roman said softly. I looked up at him. He lifted the side of his shirt up revealing an impressive set of abs. Along his ribs was a mark identical to the one on my hand. "When our powers manifest, we are branded. It makes it easier for us to identify each other, but it also works as a ward against wraiths. Keeps them from possessing our mind or bodies." *Even the brand has dual purpose.*

He reached out and gently took my hand. A comforting heat followed his fingers. "The middle line," he said, running his finger over it, "represents nature in its steadfastness. It is constant, always moving straight ahead. The two outside lines are mirror images of each other as are all things in life. Masculine and feminine. Good and evil."

"Duality," I whispered.

"Exactly." He continued to trace the brand, almost absentmindedly. "As above, so below. As within, so without. As the universe, so the soul." I looked down at our hands. I moved mine slowly, interlocking our fingers. "And this?" I asked, hesitating slightly. "What is this?" He looked at our hands, and then met my eyes. His gaze was heated, showing me for the first time the effect I had on him. His thumb moved in small circles on the back of my hand, causing my breath to catch.

"I don't know," he responded, his voice as quiet as my own. "It's nothing I've ever experienced before." His hand stilled. His gaze flickered down to my lips. The desire in his eyes made me stop breathing completely. He leaned closer, and just as his lips brushed mine, a phone rang. Roman paused, making a frustrated noise. Reluctantly he pulled back and released my hand to reach into his pocket. He stood and walked to the wall of windows to answer it.

The moment broken, I leaned back on the couch, my mind flooded with information. I tried to put the pieces together. My family's wreck. The car on fire. The doctors that couldn't understand how I survived. The dreams since I came here. The mark—brand, whatever—on my hand, and the feeling I got when Roman held it, brushing his thumb over the lines. *Wait.* My mind stopped, stuck on a detail that had been lost in the confusion of the last several days. I looked at Roman accusingly. As he ended his phone call and walked back to me, I stood up.

"You knew." He looked confused, but it didn't slow me down. "You saw my hand days ago. You touched the brand. I remember. You knew then what I was and you didn't say *anything.*"

He breathed out deeply, a look of sorrow on his face. "Yes," he admitted. "Isaac saw it first, in detention, but then he told me."

I shook my head, feeling foolish and betrayed. "Why didn't you tell me?"

"I wanted to. I meant to." He ran his hand through his hair, ruffling it. "I was going to tell you at dinner. I just couldn't. After what Paige did to you and—"

"Oh, come off it," I snapped at him. "Stop acting like you were trying to spare me. Truth is—you lied to me. And then you couldn't even face me because of your own shame. You asked about my family and I trusted you with that information. You *kissed* me—" I broke off, running my fingers through my hair. "You told me you stood up for me because you know the difference between what is right and wrong. But that's not why you did it. It's because you thought I was some sort of freak like you. You thought what Paige did was bad? It doesn't even compare. She may be horrible, but at least she's honest." I pointed directly at him. "But what you did? Lying to me, keeping something this big to yourself? *That* is wrong." At my final word a look of great pain crossed his face. Any other time I might have apologized, but not tonight, not after what I had seen. He opened his mouth to speak but I cut him off. "No. Take me home."

"There's more you should know. You're not safe."

"I don't care," I responded icily. "Take me home. Now." Reluctantly, he conceded.

We took the Jeep. I don't think I could have handled close contact with him on the bike after all I learned tonight. The drive took less than ten minutes. Still unfamiliar with the area, I didn't realize we were so close to my house. When he pulled in the driveway, I opened the door immediately.

"Kyndal." His voice was a razored edge. I paused to listen, although I refused to turn and look at him. "You have a choice to make, but know—even if you choose to reject this world, it doesn't always care. The power that runs through our veins, through *your veins*, can't be ignored. It's satisfied for now, but it will come back and you'll need to be ready. You need to learn to control it. It serves a purpose and it will demand that purpose be met."

I slammed the door.

8

A knock at the door woke me up the next day. I shoved my head under the pillow hoping that if I ignored it, the person would go away. No such luck. The knocking only got more persistent. Letting out a frustrated groan, I sat up in bed. The clock read 12:47. It was after one in the morning when Roman brought me home. I didn't fall asleep until after four. With everything I learned, I couldn't exactly sleep.

By the time I made it to the door, whoever was out there had started pounding with their fist. I ripped the door open and was surprised by who stood there.

"You look like crap," Cassie said bluntly.

She, on the other hand, looked perfect. Red hair braided, green shirt, and jeans. No sign of the bruises or split lip I saw her sporting the night before. I tried to run my fingers through my hair, but they got stuck in the tangles. "Hi to you, too."

She pushed past me, walking into the house.

"Come on in," I said sarcastically. I followed her down the hall, into the kitchen. She looked around appreciatively.

"You live here alone?" she asked.

"With my aunt," I replied. *Where was Alessandra? Why hadn't she answered the door?* I spotted a note on the kitchen counter.

Day tour today. Be back in time for dinner.
                                                    -Allie

I shook my head. Most people would take the weekend off, but not my aunt. She was married to her work.

"What are you doing here, Cassie? Did Roman send you?"

She gave me an exasperated look. "He's worried about you. I was up with him all night." I tried not to think about that. Roman and Cassie alone. Her comforting him.

I sat down at the kitchen table, crossing my arms defensively. "Yeah, well, he should have thought of that before he decided to lie to me."

"Look, I get it," she replied, leaning against the kitchen counter and facing me. "He screwed up. He should have been straightforward with you from the beginning. But come on—he's a guy. They're not exactly known for their amazing decision making skills." I glared at her. She stared back smiling, a hopeful look in her eyes. I could tell she was waiting to see if she cracked me. I didn't smile back.

"So, he explained everything to you?" I asked, my anger and jealousy seeping through my words. *Why would he be so honest with her about everything and lie to me since the moment we met?*

She nodded. "Everything."

"You two must be pretty close for him to just spill his guts to you." I tried to be nonchalant, but from the look on Cassie's face, she could see right through me.

"Easy there, green eyes. It's not like that. Rome is like my annoying little brother. Trust me—he's not my type."

I rolled my eyes. "Why not? Is it because you're older than him? You can't be more than 23. Not that big of a gap."

She threw her head back in a laugh. Her eyes were playful, but they also held a secret.

"What?" I was missing something.

She shook her head. "Don't worry about it for now. But, about Roman—" I groaned in frustration. "Fine. Don't forgive him, whatever. But here's something you need to think about—maybe there's a reason he did what he did. There's a lot you need to learn and only a handful of people who can teach it to you. Regardless of how you feel toward Roman, you need to start training."

"I didn't ask to be a part of this," I told her indignantly.

"None of us did. Doesn't change the facts though. When you're ready, give me a call." She reached into her pocket and handed me a piece of paper with what I assumed was her phone number. "Think about it." With that she got up and left.

After a quick shower, I detangled the bird's nest my hair had turned into, dressed in some comfy sweats, and laid on the bed to call Lydia. My cell phone burned in the car accident so I was relegated to the house phone. She picked up after the first ring.

"Y-ello?"

"Hey, it's Kyndal."

"Tex! How's it going? You get lucky last night?" I rolled my eyes. I knew she would get the wrong idea when I left with Roman.

I laughed humorlessly. "Definitely not. What about you? Anything interesting happen with that guy I saw you talking to last night?"

She sighed dramatically. I heard her flop onto her bed. "Wes? God, don't I wish. He is scrumptious!"

I laughed. This was the life I wanted. Normal. Girl talk on the phone. Not fights to the death in the woods and fireballs flying out of my hand. After talking for a while longer, I promised to go to lunch with her the next day.

I spent the rest of the afternoon cleaning, doing laundry, and working on homework—anything to avoid thinking about what happened at The Ridge. I studied for a test coming up in chemistry. Even though I'd only been here for one week of the four-week unit, Sykes was making me take the exam. *I really hate that guy.* I thought about unpacking some boxes, but decided against it. Not only did I move with all my stuff, but also a lot of my mom, dad, and brother's belongings, too. At least what Allie and I didn't sell. While we got rid of the mundane items, there were a lot of sentimental things I wasn't ready to part with. They sat in boxes in the corner of my room. Around 5:00 I started dinner. Alessandra rolled in an hour later, just as I was finishing up. She didn't seem to know that I came home last night. I cringed when she brought up the search for the hikers. They had called off the rescue, now officially declaring it a recovery mission. They were looking for the bodies. I knew they wouldn't find them. The bodies didn't exist. What was left of the hikers was ash on the forest floor.

By the end of the weekend, I'd almost forgotten all about The Kindred. After Cassie left, no one else checked up on me. I hung out with Alessandra Saturday night, watching old movies until we both fell asleep on the couch. Lunch with Lydia on Sunday was spent listening to her gush over Wes and all the things she wished happened but actually didn't. Even my dreams were free of all things supernatural. While it was nice to have some normalcy, I knew it wouldn't last. Come Monday I would have to return to school and face Roman.

/|\

Dressing for school Monday felt like preparing for battle. Maybe I was overreacting, but I felt the need to arm myself against Roman. I put on a dark-grey thermal, one of my favorite shirts. I chose it purposefully because of its thumb holes. I deluded myself into thinking if I covered up the brand it would disappear. I knew the effort was pointless, but it didn't stop me from doing it. Paired with a set of dark-wash jeans, I was ready. I left my hair down and wild.

I opened the front door to walk to school. My fingers fumbled with my keys. I knew Alessandra never locked the door, but I couldn't bring myself not to, not after everything I had learned recently. Finally successful, I turned to the road and yelped in surprise. Evan was standing on my porch steps.

"What are you doing here?" I accused. I had thought he was a wraith. "You scared the crap out of me."

"Sorry! You said you didn't have a car. I figured you could use a ride," he replied. I got my breathing under control and then walked to his car. We barely made it out of the driveway before the questions started. "So, what happened to you at The Ridge? You just disappeared."

Besides Lydia, Evan was the only person who would have noticed my absence that night. Luckily, I was prepared. "Yeah, sorry about that. I drank too much and ended up puking in the trees. Not my finest moment."

"How'd you get home? Lydia was still there when I left."

I cringed. I hated lying to him. "Ana Garcia gave me a ride."

He furrowed his brow. "I didn't know you two knew each other."

I nodded. "We have chemistry together." I stole a glance at him. He looked unconvinced, but thankfully he dropped it.

When we arrived at school, I immediately noticed Roman sitting on the same bench out front where I first talked to him. He was writing in his notebook, but he looked up often. I could tell he was searching for me. A nervous tingle ran up my spine. As much as I didn't want to see him, I knew he was unavoidable. Rather than wait for him to find me, I decided to do this on my own time. I walked straight for him.

Before I could reach him, he looked up and our eyes locked. I tried to hide my emotions, but I doubt I succeeded. Those eyes belonged to the one person in this town, in the *world*, that knew the most about me. In a week, he had taken me on an emotional rollercoaster that left me flipped inside out. Even looking at him then, as mad as I was, part of me wanted to return to the night we danced at *Sandra's*. That night there was no Kindred, no death, no betrayal. Just safety, warmth. He looked past me to where I was sure Evan was standing guard. His face turned cold, unfriendly. He stood when I reached him although his eyes never left Evan.

"You two seem to be spending a lot of time together," he said, quiet enough for only me to hear. *What was that? Jealousy? It couldn't be.*

I looked back at Evan who stood with his arms crossed. Others had joined him, openly gawking at Roman and me. In the back of my mind I noticed Paige and her minions were among them. Annoyed with the audience, I reached out and grabbed his hand, knowing the contact would cost me. Trying to ignore my body's instant reaction, I dragged him around to the side of the building. It wasn't completely private but it would have to do. I dropped his hand quickly, scalded by his touch.

Roman spoke first. "I've been worried about you."

"I don't want you to do that." I said the words without anger, just steely determination. I decided to get it all out before I lost my nerve. "Look—I believe everything you said Friday, about The Kindred—me being a part of it. I even believe what you said about not meaning to lie to me. But that doesn't change that you did. You lied. Big time." He tried to interrupt but I stopped him. "No. There's no changing it. I just wanted to let you know that I believe you. That being said," I took a deep breath, "I can't be a part of it."

"What? No!" His voice thundered, echoing off the side of the school. I'd never seen him so unhinged. He walked away a few steps, running his fingers through his hair. When he returned, he took a deep breath, steadying himself after his outburst. When he spoke again, his voice was tense. "This isn't something you can just blow off. Please, Kyndal. Think about this."

"I have thought about it," I said quickly, my temper responding to his surge of emotion. "And what I know is that I don't want to be a part of any club that requires the death of a family member as payment."

Roman shook his head in disbelief. "You're making a

mistake." He sounded defeated.

I ignored him. "Tell Isaac and Cassie not to worry. I'll keep it secret."

"You can't do this alone, Kyndal. It's not safe. You need to learn to control your powers," he insisted.

"Goodbye, Roman."

/|\

I walked along the gravel road. The sky was overcast and the clouds produced a light mist. My running shoes were wet from puddles. I lifted my face to the sky, allowing the rain to stick my hair to my face. The water was cold but it felt more refreshing than anything. My skin was hot and clammy to the touch, like a fire was burning its way through my veins. It had been over a week since I talked to Roman. Almost two weeks since that night in the forest when the rules of the world went sideways. Even though we hadn't spoken since, I still heard Roman's voice every day. *You're making a mistake.*

Was I?

I had no desire to be involved in Kindred business. The only thing I wanted was to focus on finishing the school year with as little trouble as possible. But even I couldn't deny that things seemed to be getting stranger.

Just as Roman said it would, the power inside me was stirring. I tried to ignore it, but it spread through me like wildfire and every inch of my skin was sensitive, exposed.

It was as if my veins were being charred and replaced with liquid fire. That fire begged to be released, a weakness I could never allow. The physical turmoil left me ragged. I was like a raw nerve, snapping at the slightest pressure. Every person was a potential wraith in my eyes. Determined to overcome my feelings by sheer force of will, I relied on caffeine and exercise to keep me level. The caffeine took the edge off just enough to get me through the school day. I did my best to ignore the blue eyes I could feel on me; but I was always aware of him. I swear sometimes I could sense when he was close. I would get this tingle of cool heat up my spine. The few times he tried to talk to me I managed to avoid him, usually by surrounding myself with Evan or Lydia. I knew he wouldn't bring the Kindred up if they were around. Lydia, bless her heart, did her best to hold up a conversation with me. I would smile and nod at the appropriate times, but didn't offer much more than that. She'd asked several times what was wrong, but I didn't exactly know how to explain that my body was being taken over by supernatural fire powers. She hadn't pushed harder for answers, but I knew it was only a matter of time.

I ran every day after school. Through town. Down the gravel roads. Or my favorite—the forest. It was the only place I let some of my power out. I ran full speed down the trails, leaping over fallen trees, and splashing through the creeks. Each day my stamina increased. The rush of it was exhilarating. I started pushing myself farther, faster, never quitting until my legs gave out and I had to drag myself home. I fell into bed, exhausted, grasping at a few precious moments of sleep before the dreams began.

They started small. A high fever, night sweats. I took to sleeping with my window open even though the nights got down close to freezing. No matter what I did, I couldn't cool down. When I did manage to fall asleep, my rest was short-lived. My dreams were haunted by what happened in the clearing. Anytime I shut my eyes all I saw were men with red eyes, Isaac's bloody sneer as he threw the fireball, Roman's dagger up to the hilt in flesh. I would bolt up in bed, covered in sweat, hair stuck to my neck, the scent of smoke in the air. And just when I thought my nightmares couldn't get worse, they did.

I'm in the clearing, alone. It's daytime. Suddenly, a man appears at the edge of the trees. I can see his face but he is no one I recognize. He smiles at me and I feel we are familiar. Friends even. I walk toward him, but before I go far, the clouds move over the sun and the whole place is shrouded in darkness. I hurry toward the man, concerned for his safety. Just as I reach him, the man's face begins to change, morph. His eyes turn bloodshot, the veins around his eyes darken to a blood red, leaving a dark spider web of lines. He smiles, and his teeth lengthen, sharpening into fine tips. They remind me of small shark teeth. I turn and run but I trip over a tree root and fall. The man grabs my ankle, pulling me back to him. He leans over me, pinning my arms down on either side. Just as he leans in, I scream.

That's always where it ended. Even asleep, my powers reacted to the wraiths. Usually, when I woke up, the room would smell like smoke. Once, after a particularly vivid nightmare, I woke up to the corner of my bed on fire. Luckily I had a cup of water on my nightstand and was able

to put it out. There was no going back to sle
literally charred my bedding. I knew I should
could have gone to Cassie, Isaac, even *
refused. Going to them for help would just p
world I wanted no part of. So instead, I chose an
alternative.

The crunch of gravel under car tires pulled me away from
my thoughts. I moved over to the side of the road and
waited for the car to stop. I knew exactly who it was.

I hugged Evan hello. "Ready for a workout?" he asked.
Evan was a stud player on all our school sports teams. I had
asked him to go running with me. I wanted to see what I
could really do. That, and I suppose I enjoyed his company.

I smiled at him. "Let's do it."

He wasted no time, taking off down the trail. I followed,
twisting and turning through the trees, the area more
familiar after my recent exploration. Evan didn't hold back,
something I appreciated. I stayed right on him the whole
time, thrilled to find that I was able to do so without too
much effort. When he noticed I was following closely, he
turned into rougher terrain. Everything was going well until
I planted my foot on top of a fallen tree and jumped. My
ankle turned wrong. I heard something snap and I fell to my
knees, crying out in pain.

I laid there for a moment before I managed to sit up. I
brushed the dirt off my knees and carefully lifted the leg of
my sweats. My ankle was already starting to swell. I
touched it gingerly and winced in pain.

an shouted through the trees. "Kyndal? Kyndal?! Where'd you go?"

"Evan!" I hollered back.

I heard the rustling of leaves. "Kyndal, where are you?" he repeated.

"Over here!" I shouted from the ground. When he found me laying on the ground, he laughed. His hair was wet, a mixture of rain and sweat. "What are you doing on the ground?"

"Taking a nap," I quipped. "What do you think? I fell. Help me up."

He reached down and grabbed my arm, helping me to my feet. At the first point of pressure on my ankle, my leg collapsed under me and I grimaced in pain.

"You're hurt," he said, looking down at my ankle. "Let me see."

"No," I replied quickly, hobbling away from him. "I'm fine."

He rolled his eyes but didn't try to look at it again. Slowly, we headed back toward the vehicle. "Come on. I'll give you a ride home."

"No, I'm fine," I started to protest, but he cut me off.

"Kyndal, stop playing the tough chick. You can barely walk." Reluctantly, I gave a small nod and limped back toward the road. "I shouldn't have taken you down such a rough trail."

Now it was my turn to roll my eyes. "Evan, stop. This isn't your fault. I rolled my ankle. It's not that big of a deal."

"Still, I feel bad. I promise to make it up to you Saturday."

"Saturday? What's Saturday?"

He looked at me with wide eyes, mock pain in his voice. "You forgot? I'm wounded, really I am. Honestly, I don't see how you could, there are signs up all over school."

Realization set in. "The dance. Evan, I'm sorry. I completely forgot. I've been—distracted."

He gave me another genuine smile. "It's fine. Really it is. If you don't want to go I understand." He sighed dramatically. "I can find another date—"

"No. No, I want to go." As I said the words, I realized how true they were. This was my perfect chance at doing something normal. Evan looked back at me, delight evident in his eyes.

"Good," he said, smiling before he returned his eyes to the trail. He put his arm around my waist when we reached a fallen log and helped me get over it. My cheeks flushed at the contact. The rest of the slow walk we talked comfortably about a variety of topics: movies, favorite foods, sports. Evan was sweet and easy to talk to. So much in fact that I felt guilty for not treating him better before. With him, I laughed more than I had all week. In particular, I cracked up at his surprise when I told him I was a jock at my old school.

"Sorry," he said laughing, "but I just have a hard time picturing it." He eyed my freshly injured ankle.

"Well, believe it, bub. Volleyball, basketball, track. My whole life."

"Quite the stud," he responded, eyeing me appreciatively.

"Darn right."

"I'll have to remember that." He gave me a sly smile.

I smiled back, the pain of my ankle forgotten. Maybe there was still hope for a normal life.

9

The next day, I immediately went searching for Lydia but I didn't find her until lunch. Everyone was eating in the cafeteria due to the rainy weather. "Well, if it isn't my best friend in the whole world," I said. I only limped slightly as I sat at her table. I did my best to ignore the blue eyes I could feel boring into me from across the room. I only looked up once. Roman was staring at my injured foot and he did not look happy. Although still swollen and tender, my ankle had made remarkable improvement overnight. More than was normal, actually. At this rate, it would be completely healed in a few days. Chalk it up as something else freaky about me.

Lydia shot me a confused look, obviously taking note of my improved mood. "I'm going to choose to ignore the fact that I'm your only friend, therefore by default your best friend. So what's with the good mood all of a sudden?"

"I need a favor."

Lydia set down her fork, pushed her blonde tresses out of her face, and folded her hands in front of her. Her eyes were locked on me, completely serious. "You have my attention."

"You know Evan, right?" She glared at me. "Sorry, stupid question. Well, we talked a little at The Ridge and—"

She interrupted. "Before you blew him off and left with Roman."

It took every ounce of willpower not to look over at him. "You know he asked me to the dance this weekend."

"And then you blew him off and left with Roman," she repeated.

I huffed at her. "Yes. Okay. I blew him off. I'm a horrible person. But we talked yesterday in his car and—"

"What were you doing in his car?" Lydia interrupted again, raising an eyebrow.

"Are you going to keep interrupting or are you going to let me tell the story?"

"That depends. You going to keep leaving out the juicy bits?"

I rolled my eyes at her. "We went running together yesterday. He gave me a ride home. That's all. No juicy bits."

Lydia shrugged her shoulders before returning to her lunch tray. "Too bad. What does any of this have to do with me?"

"Well," I started again. "I don't have anything to wear to the dance."

Her eyes popped up, her delight obvious. "One condition," she responded. I sucked in a nervous breath. *What if she asks questions I can't answer?* I hated lying to her. I had lied enough by omission.

"What's the condition?"

"You relinquish full control. I'm in charge. Dress, hair, makeup, jewelry, shoes. Everything."

I released the breath I didn't realize I was holding. "Not a problem," I promised.

The squeal that escaped her reminded me of a child on Christmas morning. I giggled as she started to bounce up and down in her chair with excitement. "This is going to be So. Much. Fun!"

/|\

I stared in the bathroom mirror, completely mesmerized. For the past three hours, I had been buffed, polished, and hair sprayed within an inch of my life. Lydia adamantly refused to let me see myself until she was done, claiming the wait would "add to the effect." She was absolutely right. I barely recognized the girl staring back at me. My hair was pulled partway up, the majority of it left to fall down my back in soft curls. My makeup was expertly done, highlighting my best features while simultaneously hiding my flaws. *Lydia has mad skills.*

My eyes dropped to the dress. It was floor length, strapless, with a heart-shaped neckline. The bodice fit tight, accenting my curves. At my waist, the material billowed out in soft chiffon, barely kissing the floor as I stood in tasteful heels. But that's not what had me frozen in my tracks. It was the color. There was no way she could have known, no way she did it on purpose. The dress was a perfect royal blue. Exactly like *his* eyes.

"What do you think?" Lydia asked, walking up behind me. I turned toward her. Her blonde hair was slicked back, her almond eyes highlighted by dramatic, colorful eyeliner. Her multi-colored dress was a mixture of pastel pinks, blues, yellows, and purple. It plunged dangerously low until it cinched across her waist, flowing freely from there until it hit the floor. On anyone else, it would have looked horrible. But on Lydia, it worked. When it came to fashion, she was fearless.

"It's perfect."

She gave a little twirl, giggling as she did so. "The boys should be here anytime now."

Almost on cue, the doorbell rang. We headed down the stairs, rounding the corner into the main living room. Wes and Evan stood there in their tuxes, talking with Alessandra. As we entered the room, they both turned. Evan looked me up and down appreciatively before walking toward me, hugging and then kissing me on the cheek. "You look beautiful," he whispered.

My cheeks reddened. "Thanks," I replied, allowing him to

put the corsage on my wrist. My eyes glanced quickly to Alessandra who stood quietly to the side, her eyes glistening. She walked my way, giving me a hug of her own. "Stunning," she whispered. "Look just like her."

I pulled away slightly and looked at my aunt, this woman who took me in that I'm still getting to know. "Who?"

She smiled sadly. "Your mother."

My eyes blurred. I would have given anything for Mom to be there. I swallowed back the tears. "Thank you, Alessandra."

"Allie," she corrected quietly. I nodded my head and turned away, discreetly wiping a tear.

After a round of pictures, we managed to finally escape the house. The dance was in the gym. Dodging the streamers, I walked through the school doors and took in the scene. The hallway leading into the gym was lined with small candles. In the gym, a DJ was working on the far wall. I could feel the beat pounding in my chest. A table filled with snacks and punch was off to the left. If East Forest High was anything like my old school, I could guarantee that the punch was spiked. At the back were tables lined-up behind the dance floor. It was dark. The only light came from the hundreds of twinkle lights strung from the ceiling and the small candles lit at each table.

As I scanned the room, I felt a cool, familiar tingle up my spine. I knew exactly what it meant. As much I tried not to, my eyes instantly found him. Roman sat at the back table. Isaac was there, along with a few people I didn't know. But he paid them no attention. His eyes were glued to mine. I told myself to look away, but I couldn't. The tux he wore reminded me of why they were made in the first place. Even from this distance, I could tell he was trying—*desperately trying*—to hold my gaze. But as if against his will, his eyes traveled south. When they returned, his gaze was intense. *Hungry.*

My power flared far greater than the little I released during my runs. The heat traveled down my arms, toward my hands, begging to burst forward. I looked away, breaking the trance.

He lied to you, I reminded myself, trying to get my emotions in check. *You're not here for him. You walked away.*

Evan grabbed my hand and the heat disappeared. "Want to dance?"

I forced a smile and shoved my feelings for Roman away. "Sure."

I lost track of how long we were on the dance floor. Evan was a horrible dancer but that didn't stop us. We danced to every song. Joined by Lydia and Wes, we made absolute fools of ourselves, getting lost in the beat. But I didn't care. It was exactly what I needed. Senseless. Thoughtless. *Fun.* Only when I was covered in sweat did I excuse myself to get some fresh air. I rounded the corner into the dimly lit hallway and froze in my tracks.

Leaning against the wall was Roman. He wasn't alone. His head was down, allowing the girl with him to talk quietly in his ear. I couldn't see her face but I knew instantly who it was, dressed in a skin-tight, pink dress plastered to her fake, baked skin. It could only be one person. No one else would wear a dress that tacky. *Paige.* Whatever she was saying, he liked. I heard him chuckle softly. Paige pulled away slightly, catching my eye. She moved her hand up his arm to the side of his face. He looked up at her. She smiled at me before leaning in and kissing him square on the lips.

Oh, hell no.

Suddenly, I was consumed with jealousy. The rush of it was so intense I didn't even register my power building. My brain told me to leave, but I was rooted to the floor. It was like a train wreck. I couldn't look away no matter how much I wanted to.

The candles lining the hallway flared, but my brain didn't acknowledge it. The first thing I noticed were her screams. Paige jumped back from Roman as if her hair were on fire. Then I realized, her hair actually *was* on fire. Small licks of flame crawled slowly up her caramel locks, inching toward the root. Before they got too far, the side door swung open and a stiff wind blew through, extinguishing the flames. Paige took off running, still screaming even though she was no longer on fire. Frozen in my tracks, Roman glared at me, his eyes a brilliant gold. Frightened by my actions, but even more angry at Roman for his, I did the only thing I could. I ran.

/|\

I leaned up against the brick wall of the school, hands on

my knees; bent over and breathing hard. I closed my eyes and tried to control my breathing, but every time I did, all I saw was the two of them.

Together. Kissing.

I had no right to feel this way. I had no rights to him. So why couldn't I make this ugly feeling go away? I clenched my fists. Heat rushed down my arms. I could feel it in my veins. Every time I replayed it in my head, the intensity of the flames inside grew. All the power I'd kept hidden was rearing its head, begging to come out. I looked down at my hands. Small flames flickered in each palm. I stared at them, fascinated. I raised my hands and the fire adjusted, the tongues of the flames rising up, licking over my fingers. I didn't feel an ounce of heat. I was mesmerized by the beauty of it.

Suddenly, the door ripped open. I closed my fists quickly, extinguishing the flames. Roman burst through, his eyes pinning me where I stood, the blue almost luminescent under the moonlight.

He's pissed.

"I warned you," he growled, his tone as angry as his stance.

"I'm sorry, okay?" I answered defensively.

"No, it's not okay!" he roared, continuing to invade my personal space. "You could have really hurt Paige."

I laughed before firing back sarcastically. "You know, I find it interesting that not too long ago, you beat a guy bloody for repeating something *she* said, and now you're in the hallway making out with her. Pick a side, would ya?"

"You're going to judge me? You just threw a fireball at a classmate."

I groaned, frustrated. He didn't understand. "I didn't throw a fireball at her! I would never do that. I just—"

"You just what? Lost control?" he taunted, not backing down.

I pushed myself off the wall and raised my voice to match his, eager to defend myself. "I know!" I sighed. "I don't—I don't know what happened. I just saw you guys together, talking and—" I cut off, unable to finish. I couldn't bring myself to tell him. My shoulders slumped and I looked away briefly. "I just lost it."

I watched as realization set in. Now he knew. Even after the lies, even after the fight, I still cared about him. *Stupid, stupid girl.*

His body language changed, the anger draining out of him, replaced by something different but just as intense. "Kyndal," he began, his tone noticeably softer. He took a step toward me and grabbed my hand. Instantly, the cool heat stirred in my fingertips, swirling up my hand. I felt my power relax. I backed up, trying to create some distance between us, but he followed me until my back was up against the wall. He leaned in close, his breath tickling my cheek.

"There is nothing going on between me and Paige." It

surprised me how happy I was to hear that.

"That's not what it looked like a minute ago," I told him. "You kissed her."

"She kissed me," he corrected. "Why do you care? You're here with another boy."

He had a point. "Evan and I are just friends."

He laughed ruefully. "That's not what he thinks."

That got my attention. I looked up at him, studying the flecks of yellow that had appeared in his eyes. A hint to his inner power. I couldn't look away. I threw his words back at him. "Why do you care?"

His eyes moved down, wandering over my dress for the second time tonight. My breathing picked up. "Why were you limping a few days ago?" he whispered. The question surprised me.

"I sprained my ankle running in the forest." His fingers slid up my bare arm until his hand came to rest on my shoulder.

"It's healed now." It wasn't a question but I answered anyway.

"Yes."

He nodded. His thumb teased my collarbone. The trail of power that followed his hand forced me to close my eyes briefly. It was intoxicating.

Before I could think too much about it, I sprung off the

wall and closed the distance between us, slamming my lips into his. Lips that just minutes ago were kissing another girl. He responded instantly, parting my lips with his own. His body pressed into me, pinning us together. I reached for him, running my fingers through his hair. He made a small sound in the back of his throat and my power lit up. But unlike before, this time I could feel it happening, control it. His hand snaked around my waist, fingers splayed against my lower back, pulling me even closer.

I don't know how long we stayed that way, but eventually, he pulled away from me, just as he did the first time we kissed. His eyes were like golden honey and I knew if I could see my own, they would shine a bright red. I expected him to close off, lock himself down, just like he did before. Instead, he leaned forward, pressing one more gentle kiss on my lips. I smiled at him. The moment was perfect. Suddenly he pushed me back against the wall and turned his back to me. Through his tuxedo jacket I could see his arms were tense, his hands in tight fists.

"Roman, what's wrong?" I asked, out of breath.

He turned his head only slightly my way and said the last word I expected to hear, his voice a growl.

"Wraiths."

10

They came from the woods. Three of them. They were too far away for me to see their features in the dark, but I knew what I'd see if I could. Bloodshot eyes. Veins spreading through their faces. Small, sharp teeth, twisted in a demented smile. Death had found me. Just like in my dreams.

"Kyndal, run," Roman spit out through gritted teeth. But I couldn't. I was frozen in fear.

"Kyndal," Roman repeated. "Run. Find Isaac." His voice was a distant echo. I still didn't move. Roman turned to face me. He grabbed hold of my shoulders, shaking me violently. "NOW!" he shouted.

The trance broke and I took off running toward the door. I turned and paused just long enough to look behind me. One of the wraiths had broken rank and was coming after me. The other two moved in on Roman, swords in hand. Roman pulled his dagger out from beneath his jacket, squaring up with the wraith in front of him; the larger of the two. The other moved around behind him, forcing him to split his attention.

Just as I reached the door, the wraith grabbed my arm. Without thinking, I reared back with my free arm. My elbow connected with his nose and I heard a satisfying crunch. I ripped the door open to the empty hallway. I yelled for Isaac, but before I took a step onto the tile, my feet were taken out from under me. The wraith had grabbed my ankle, pulling me back outside. I kicked out as violently as I could, forcing him to release me. I crawled on all fours, but I knew I couldn't escape. The wraith landed a kick to my stomach and I doubled over in pain. He followed up with two more swift kicks to my midsection. I heard a crack in my ribcage. His fingers dug into my arm. He yanked me up and threw me against a tree. I took the brunt of the hit on my shoulder and the bark scraped into my skin, drawing blood. I landed in a bloodied, beaten heap. I tried to call up my powers, but I couldn't reach them. They were blocked. Buried under a mountain of fear.

The wraith sauntered toward me, surprising me when he spoke. "I'm disappointed, Kyndal." I sat up straighter against the tree, my arm clutching my injured ribs.

"How do you know my name?"

"You don't recognize me?" he asked, a satisfied chuckle in his voice. I squinted through blurred vision. His face changed from his true form to the one the world sees. His veins faded. His bloodshot eyes cleared, replaced with a dark grey. His face teased my memory. He looked like someone I'd met before, only thinner, paler. I gasped in recognition.

The strange man from Allegheny Explorers! "Deacon?" I managed. It hurt to talk.

"That's right. I thought your aunt would be useful, I had no idea how much." Faster than I could follow, his arm snapped out, grabbing me by the throat and lifting me off the ground. He might have looked frail, but his strength was impressive. He pinned me against the tree, my feet dangling helplessly in the air. His face contorted, returning to its true, twisted form. He placed his hand over my heart. I knew what came next. Desperately, I looked at Roman. He was locked in battle with one wraith, looking worse for wear. I didn't know what happened to the other; Roman must have killed him. He had a large gash on his forehead and blood dripped down the side of his face. From the way he bounced on one leg, I could tell he was injured. Regardless of his injuries, he stood strong. Fearless. He managed to beat the wraith to the ground, using the quick reprieve to look my way.

"Hang on, Kyndal!" he shouted.

His voice was lost in the sound of my own screams. An icy coldness bloomed in my chest. So cold it burnt. It felt as if Deacon was ripping my heart out of my chest. The cold spread through my body, consuming my power. I could feel it leave. As the cold spread, Deacon's features changed. Color returned to his face, his cheeks became fuller. I reached a hand up and scratched weakly at his face, desperate to push him off me, even as the cold took over. He continued to feed from me. Again, I reached for my power. I dug as deep as I could. I didn't know what I was doing but I followed my instincts. I put all my fear and anger into the action. I thought of everything I'd been through.

The loss of my family.

Moving to Marienville and leaving my friends behind.

Paige and the bitch brigade.

Meeting Roman...kissing Roman.

Kindred.

Betrayal.

Wraiths.

The heat began in my stomach. It moved toward my heart, burning the cold away and gaining strength. Finally, it reached my arm, traveling down toward my hand. When it reached my palm, it exploded. I pressed my hand to Deacon's cheek. I felt his skin sizzle and boil. He screamed in pain, dropping me in the process. I crouched down, breathing hard. The world started to blur. Black spots played at the edge of my vision. I knew I didn't have long before I passed out. Then Deacon would finish me off.

I tried to crawl away, but Deacon's demented cackle stopped me. "A Descendant?! Oh, Kyndal. This is better than I could have ever hoped!"

He lunged for me again. I was powerless to fight back. Just as he reached me, his fingers inches from my throat, he was ripped backwards, as if pushed by invisible hands. Roman ran toward me, faster than humanly possible. With him came the wind. Deacon stood and charged again. Roman wasted no time. He threw a punch, although he was nowhere near Deacon. The wind, like an extension of Roman's arm, hit Deacon underneath the jaw, throwing him back several feet into the brick wall of the school building. I struggled to stand as Roman reached me, his posture defensive, daring Deacon to attack again. Deacon stood, squaring off with Roman. The left side of his face was a livid red. I could see the outline of a few of my fingers from where I burnt him.

Just then the side door ripped open. I expected it to be Isaac, but my gut wrenched when I saw who stood there.

Evan.

His eyes moved frantically from me, to Roman, to Deacon, and back again. Driven by his own protective instincts, he lunged at Deacon.

"Evan, no!" I screamed. Half a second later, Roman charged in. He was too late. In a move too fast for my eyes to follow, Deacon was suddenly directly behind Evan, his hands on either side of his head. He looked squarely at me, his mouth curved in a twisted grimace made worse by the grisly burn that pulled at his lip. I could see the moment he'd made his decision, and yet, I was unable to stop him.

Too slow.

Too weak.

I screamed.

His hands twisted.

The snap rang through the clearing, bouncing off the trees.

Roman reached Evan just in time to catch his lifeless body before it hit the ground.

I screamed again. A keening wail that pierced the night. Exhausted and beaten bloody, I slumped to the ground. My vision blurred, the world faded, and suddenly, the ground came up to meet me and my world went black.

/|\

I woke in an unfamiliar bed. Soft sunlight streamed in from the window, the only light in the room apart from the few candles lit on the bedside table. I looked around, trying to get my bearings. The room had three walls. Where the fourth should have been was a banister that looked down on the main floor. Over it, I saw a familiar wall of windows. *Am I in Roman's room?*

My brain was fuzzy and it took a while for the events of last night to break through. When they did, they came all at once in a torrent of sensation I couldn't stop. I wished I could forget them, pretend they didn't happen. Evan was dead. Deacon killed him and I couldn't stop him. I should've been faster, stronger. Better. *Someone else is dead because of me.*

I struggled to sit up, grimacing as pain shot through my injured ribs. I looked down and noticed I was no longer in my dress. Instead, I was wearing a grey sweatshirt and black sweatpants, both a size too big. I heard voices downstairs, murmuring in soft tones. Trying not to make the pain worse, I inched across the bedroom into the attached bath. I surveyed the damage in the mirror. My hair was a mess and I had serious racoon eyes. Other than that, my face was damage free. I lifted my chin, exposing my neck. Blue and purple marks circled it, creating a violent necklace. I lifted my shirt next, baring my stomach. A deep purple bruise dominated my left side. I touched my fingers to it. I sucked in a breath on contact. *God, that hurts.* The other side wasn't as bad, speckled with greens and yellows. The bruising there wasn't as deep. I twisted carefully to see my shoulder. There were deep scratches down my shoulder blade from where I hit the tree, although I was surprised by the lack of blood. Obviously, someone had cleaned my wounds.

I fixed my shirt and wandered back into the bedroom, pausing at the dresser. On it was a framed picture of two young children. A boy and a girl. They had an arm around each other, their heads together and were smiling widely. The two looked nothing alike, except for one startling feature: their eyes. They both had brilliant, sapphire eyes.

"Her name was Diana."

I turned to find Roman standing just inside his room, at the top of the stairs. He'd changed his clothes, dressed now in casual jeans and a long sleeve thermal. The gash on his forehead was still visible, but he seemed to be in better shape than the last time I saw him.

"Who was she?" I asked, picking up on his use of the past tense. My voice came out scratchy. *Hopefully Deacon didn't do any permanent damage.*

"My sister," he responded. "Twin, actually."

"What happened to her?" I asked quietly.

He gave me a sad smile. *Oh.* I don't know how I had missed it before. It was so obvious now. The look on his face was one I saw in the mirror every day. The mark of losing a sibling was something that could not be removed. It seemed Roman and I were more similar than I knew. "How are you feeling?" he asked, changing topics.

I shrugged, unable to meet his eyes. "Exhausted." I knew he was asking how I felt *emotionally*, but I couldn't allow myself to think about that right now.

Roman nodded. "That makes sense. You've been out for several hours," he replied. "It's two o'clock in the afternoon." My eyes widened. *Lydia must be freaking out.* "Cassie and Isaac are checking in with Ezekiel. Updating him on what happened last night. Seeing if he has any answers for us."

I nodded and my mind clicked on. *Answers.*

"Let's go." I walked slowly toward the stairs.

Roman stepped in front of me, blocking my way. He reached up toward my bruised neck. I cringed. *If I could have just left him alone, Evan would still be alive.*

Roman pretended not to notice my reaction, but he dropped

his hand. "You should be lying down," he said quietly, then paused as if he meant to say one thing, but changed his mind. "You took quite a beating last night."

I dropped my head. His words were a reminder of my guilt. *I should've been faster, stronger, better. I should've saved him.* Hot tears fell from my cheeks.

Roman reached out to me again, but I backed away. I didn't deserve his pity.

"I don't see you resting," I retorted, attitude dripping from every word. A weak attempt to cover up my true feelings.

Anger flashed in his eyes, but he covered it quickly. "I don't need to. You do." His voice was tight, restrained.

I didn't back down. "The man-wraith, whatever—that attacked last night—*killed* my friend. If Ezekiel has answers, I want to hear them. Now move."

In the living room, Cassie and Isaac were sitting on the couch, mid-discussion with someone on speaker phone. The male voice, Ezekiel I'm assuming, came through, his tone stern and angry. It reminded me of how my dad used to sound when I did something particularly stupid. I sat on the edge of a chair and listened in.

"The bottom line is, you should not have engaged the wraiths so close to a public venue, those were not your orders. And now a local is dead." I flinched at his callousness.

Isaac rolled his eyes. "It's not like we meant to."

"It couldn't be avoided," Roman interjected from where he stood against the wall. "We were on site, strictly for recon purposes as ordered. Kyndal and I were outside," his eyes flicked up to mine, "discussing her training, when we were attacked."

"Kyndal? The girl from the House of Aries?" His voice was formal. He spoke as if he belonged in a different era.

"Yes, sir," Roman replied. "Three of them came from the woods. Two attacked me, and the third, the one we now know is named Deacon, went for Kyndal."

"And what of her? Was she injured?"

Cassie responded. "Minor injuries, sir. But she will heal." *Minor? My throat burns when I swallow, my stomach is riddled with bruises, and I'm almost positive I have a broken rib. That's minor?*

"That's good to hear," he replied, relief in his voice. It was the first hint of emotion I'd heard from him. "It seems this Deacon was aware of her status as Kindred. Any ideas as to how?"

All eyes looked to me. I took a deep breath, then cleared my throat, trying to disguise the rasp. "I met him before. Deacon. At my aunt's work, my first week here. She said he hired her to show him and some friends around the forest."

"I see," he replied, tersely. "Kyndal, it's my understanding that you have chosen to reject your powers and refuse to train to become Kindred."

"Yes—yes sir," I stuttered. It's weird to call someone sir when you've never met them. "But I think it no longer matters what I want." Deacon knew who I was, my life was in danger no matter what I wanted. Had I trained from the start, I wouldn't be so useless. My stubbornness cost Evan his life. I would never let that happen again. "I'm in." Roman took a deep, relieved breath and stood a bit taller.

"I'm happy to hear it, Kyndal. Know that you are in good hands." His words suggested excitement, but his tone was flat. This man left a lot to be desired in the range-of-emotions department.

"There's more," Roman added. "He called her something. A Descendant." I didn't know he had heard that part.

The line was quiet.

"Sir?" Roman prompted.

"Roman, take me off speaker."

With a confused look, Roman promptly grabbed the phone and walked to the other side of the room. I looked at Isaac and Cassie inquisitively, but they wore the same bewildered look I did. A few moments later, Roman returned to the group, the phone silent in his hand. His face was troubled, strained.

"He's coming home."

"Ezekiel?!" Isaac exclaimed at the same time Cassie yelled, "Why?"

"Is—is that not normal?" I asked, feeling stupid for even

saying it. "I mean, he lives here, right?"

It was Roman who answered me. "Ezekiel hasn't been home in two years."

/|\

The next morning I stood outside the house, slowly tying my running shoes. It was well before sunrise and the sky was just beginning to turn a light purple. Cassie insisted we train early. I didn't object.

Alessandra was pissed at me for not telling her where I was the day before, especially as news of Evan's death spread through the town. I hadn't talked to Lydia either since the dance. I didn't know what to say to her. Roman explained to me that after he took me to his house last night, Cassie called the sheriff and made an anonymous tip that led them to Evan's body. No one knew Roman and I were involved. Even so, knowing the truth, I just couldn't face anyone. Instead, I buried myself in training.

As Cassie explained it, there were three aspects to my training: mental, physical, and elemental. She was in charge of the mental, although I failed to see how a run through the forest was supposed to help me mentally. When I voiced this opinion, she promptly told me she would "explain it when we got there."

We took off through the trees, Cassie in the lead. Despite my natural athleticism and my recent independent training, she made me feel like I'd never run a day in my life. My injuries throbbed and I barely kept up with her. Common sense suggested I should wait until I healed to train, but one thing I'd already learned was that if I was going to do this, there was no time to pause for pain.

Cassie never slowed down and never looked back to see if I could keep up. As we wound through the terrain, I almost lost her twice. As she changed direction, I caught glimpses of her red ponytail that keep me on course. Just as I was about to drop from exhaustion, she stopped by the edge of a creek. Digging for any remaining energy, I caught up with her. I found her sitting cross-legged on a large rock next to the water's edge. I leaned over and placed my hands on my knees, trying to catch my breath. Cassie wasn't even breathing hard. In fact, she seemed completely relaxed and fresh. Before she could notice how pitifully I had performed, I stood up straight, trying to pretend like my lungs weren't on fire.

"You alright?" she asked. Although the words suggested concern, her tone was mocking, competitive. She knew I struggled.

"Fine," I said, but I was betrayed by my ragged breathing.

"Kyndal, why do you think I brought you here?"

"I don't know," I huffed, shaking my head, "so you could kick my ass?"

She laughed. "No. I mean, don't get me wrong, that was fun. But why through the forest? I could've kicked your ass on a track."

I stopped and thought but only came up blank. I shrugged.

"Nature," she explained. "You're Kindred now. Your powers come from nature. Along with that comes increased senses. You will be able to hear, see, smell, feel, and taste more than any normal human. Also, it gives you a heightened level of speed and strength. We are at our best when we are surrounded by the elements." I looked down at my sweat-soaked shirt. *This is my best?*

She took note of my less-than-impressive condition. "You have to learn to draw from the elements around you, allow them to feed you. Sit down." She gestured to the rock across from her. I sat down slowly, mindful of my throbbing ribs. I faced her, mirroring her position. "Close your eyes," she instructed.

"Are we meditating? Because that's not really my thing."

She gave me a stern look. "Just do it." I did as she said. "Take a deep breath. Now, focus your senses. You need to use them to draw energy from the natural elements. What do you hear? Feel? Smell? Draw all that into your body and let it replenish you."

I giggled, which quickly turned into a cough. *Ow, that hurt.* Cassie sounded like a New Age massage therapist offering to realign my chakras. "Kyndal," she admonished. "Take this seriously."

"Alright, alright. Sorry," I replied. I shook my shoulders out, focusing. Breathing in deeply, I sat for a few minutes, trying my hardest to focus on everything nature, but nothing happened.

I groaned in frustration. "This is pointless! I don't feel

anything. How am I supposed to pull energy from nature? I'm a fire sign." I waved my hand around us. "I don't see any fire here, do you?"

Unfazed by my outburst, Cassie explained, "Fire is your element. It responds to you and does as you ask. It is where you are strongest. But all Kindred can pull energy from every element. Watch."

Before I knew what happened, Cassie reached out and grabbed a sharp rock near her. She slashed it across her open palm. Blood gushed from the wound.

"Cassie!" I screamed, lunging for her. "What are you doing?"

"Watch," she said again. Keeping her palm open, Cassie closed her eyes. At first nothing happened, but then I noticed the bleeding started to slow. Then, before my very eyes, the wound completely closed up. There was no remnant of it, not even a scar. My mouth dropped open in astonishment.

"You healed yourself. How did you do that?"

"It's simple. I used the elements. You need to start thinking of nature as a living thing, with never-ending energy. Kindred can borrow some of that energy to heal ourselves when necessary." I almost argued, I mean there was no way I had super healing powers, but I stopped myself. After everything I had seen, why couldn't this be true? Why couldn't something good, something beautiful, come out of these powers?

"That's why you weren't bruised and cut when I saw you the morning after the fight." She nodded, pleased I was catching on.

"I want you to try again. This time, think of a peaceful place. Somewhere you feel safe, cherished. When your mind gets there, reach out and pull the elements to you."

I closed my eyes and took a deep breath. I searched through my memories for a safe place. My mind immediately went to my family, but then I moved away. All of those memories were shadowed with grief. As I worked to steady my breathing, I tried to remember the last time I felt at peace. The first thing I heard was the soft lull of a country song. Then in my mind's eye, I saw the glow of the porch lights, felt his touch on my shoulder, his fingers leaving a trail of embers in their wake.

Working to stay in the memory, I reached my senses out to my surroundings. I could feel it now; the connection. It was like a million different fibers attaching me to everything. The water in the creek, the earth under me, the trees, even the wind. I pulled gently on the connection, willing it to lend me strength. The change was small at first. My breathing steadied, the burn in my lungs disappeared, small lashes from the trees sealed up. I pulled harder on the little chords. The pain in my ribs lessened and the scratch in my throat disappeared.

I slowly opened my eyes. Cassie was looking at me, smiling. "How do you feel?"

I took a deep, pain-free breath. "Better." That wasn't the

full truth, but I kept that to myself. My body may have been refreshed, but my mind was a storm of confusion. I was elated that I used the elements, but I couldn't help but feel guilty about how I did it. I didn't want to think of Roman. If I could have just left him alone I never would have been outside the dance. Evan never would have chased me. He would still be alive.

"It will be easier next time. As you improve, you will be able to pull from any natural element around you, no matter how small." She cupped her hands in front of her. Her eyes flashed blue and a fountain of water jumped from the creek into her waiting hands. She used the fresh water to clean the remains of blood from her hands.

"How does this work? Can I heal anything?"

She shook her head, answering me quickly. "No, no. There are limitations. Nature sustains us, allowing us to heal quicker than non-Kindred, but we are still susceptible to injury, obviously. The more severe the injury, the more power you must draw to heal it. If you are too weak from injury to use the power, you will die just like anyone else."

"Well, couldn't another Kindred heal me?"

She shook her head again. "No. The healing comes from the internal relationship between you and nature. It cannot be transferred to anyone else. The more your power is used, the stronger the connection between you and nature. Eventually, typically a few years after branding, the power will attach to your life force, allowing you to not only heal externally caused injuries, but also correct internal wear on the body." I gave her a confused look. She took a deep breath, hesitating. I started to get nervous. What information could possibly be crazier than everything else I had learned?

When she still didn't speak, I prompted her. "Cassie—spell it out. What does that mean?"

"It keeps you from aging."

11

Hidden in the stacks of the library, I stared at a blank computer screen. The school was buzzing about Evan's death and I just couldn't handle it. First thing that morning, I heard people talking about his pending funeral. I almost broke down right in the middle of class. Instead, I excused myself to the restroom and never returned. I ran to the library, choosing to have my breakdown in private. All day, the same thought played through my head. Evan was dead and I would probably never die. *Because apparently, I'm frickin' immortal.*

As if that wasn't enough of a bomb, Cassie had gone on to explain exactly how it worked. The more I used my powers, the tighter they would bind themselves to my life-force, until eventually I stopped aging. I could live hundreds of lifetimes. If I quit using them for an extended period of time, I would start to age again. At least that explained how the Kindred I met all appeared to be different ages. I leaned my head back on the chair and closed my eyes. I breathed slowly, in and out, trying to clear my head.

"You alive, Davenport?"

I chanced a peek and was met by a set of deep brown eyes. Isaac. I closed my eyes again, hoping he would disappear. I heard the sound of a chair moving. *No such luck.*

"Let me ask you something. Exactly how old are you Isaac?"

"Eighteen," he replied. At that I opened my eyes and gave him a disapproving look.

"No, I mean how old are you *really?*" He smiled at my obvious disbelief.

"Ah ha, I see someone has been busy studying their Kindred textbooks. Sorry to disappoint but I really am eighteen."

"And your parents? Do they know about your magical side?"

"My mother died on my sixteenth birthday. Ever since then, Dad drinks himself into a stupor every night. He pays no attention to what I do."

"That's horrible," I responded.

"Yeah, well," he crossed his arms, "is what it is, I guess. We all have a sob story."

I nodded. *He's not wrong.* "Do you know how old Cassie and Roman are?"

"Well, that," he said emphasizing the final t, "is something you will have to ask them. The elderly get so touchy about their age."

Elderly? Exactly how old was Roman? "I know you're a fire sign. Are you an Aries like me?"

He laughed. "You wish. I," he held his arms out, "am a Sagittarius." I looked at him stone faced and clearly unimpressed. He lowered his arms. "Anyways. I'm actually not here for your rousing conversational skills."

"Then why exactly are you here?"

He smiled again. It seemed impossible to bruise his ego for long. It was almost endearing. "To kidnap you." I raised my eyebrows as he jumped to his feet. "It's time to start the next part of your training."

"Now?" I asked, "What about school?"

"You spent the entire morning hiding in the library."

"Touché." Begrudgingly, I followed him. Just as we reached the front door, I heard my name called.

"Kyndal Davenport."

I turned and saw Principal Gibson standing outside the office. *Busted.* He beckoned me with one finger. I looked up briefly at Isaac. The principal held the office door open for me and followed me through.

"This way, please."

He moved toward his office. I started to follow, but through the window, I saw the sheriff waiting inside. I froze in my tracks. *What is he doing here?* My breathing picked up. I took a step back toward the exit. I hated running away, but there was no way that my talking to the cops would end up well. Just as I prepared to bolt, another deputy walked in behind me, cutting off any retreat. Left with no other option, I kept moving.

As I walked in, the sheriff stood and introduced himself. The pounding in my ears was so loud I didn't hear his name. Gibson sat at his desk. The sheriff in the chair next to mine turned to face me. He was nothing like what I imagined a small town sheriff to be. I expected someone short and pudgy, maybe with doughnut glaze on his moustache. Instead, the man before me was tall and trim, his dark hair buzzed close to his head, his brown eyes caring but sharp. He looked like a man who missed nothing.

Gibson began. "Kyndal, we need to ask you some questions about Saturday night." I swallowed, my throat suddenly thick. "You're aware one of our students, Evan Dixon, was found dead outside the school on the night of the dance."

I looked down at my hands and nodded slowly, unable to form words.

"Did you know him?" the sheriff asked, taking over.

I nodded again. I could feel the tears forming at the back of my throat. I cleared it and found my voice. "He was a friend of mine."

"From what we've been told, you were more than that."

At that, the tears fell. Roman's words played in my head. *That's not what he thinks.* He liked me and I had spent his last night kissing another guy.

The sheriff was waiting for a response. "No. Just friends." My voice caught at the end.

"But you were his date to the dance?"

"I just moved here. I don't have a lot of friends. Evan offered to take me."

He reached out, placing his hand on my knee. "I know it's difficult. But I need you to take me through what happened that night."

And I did.

I gave him the edited version. Cassie warned me I could be questioned. She had created a story that had enough truth to be believable but also kept me out of trouble. As far as the sheriff knew, I had attended the dance with Evan, Wes, and Lydia. We danced most of the night until the spiked punch made me sick and Alessandra had to come pick me up.

The sheriff clarified, "Alessandra Davenport?" I nodded. "That's your aunt?"

"And guardian," I replied. He nodded, writing furiously on a notepad in front of him. He remained silent. Long enough to make me nervous.

"Is that all?" I asked, my voice shaking. "I'd like to return to class."

"Absolutely, Kyndal. Thank you for your help," Gibson answered, smiling encouragingly.

I got up to leave but the sheriff interrupted my exit. "Actually, I have one more question."

I looked at him expectantly.

"If you were sick that night, why was it that you were seen with another student after the time you allegedly left? A boy named Roman Sands?"

My eyes widened at his words and the accompanying accusation. If someone saw Roman and me together, that meant he knew I lied. *Who could have seen us?* I looked at the sheriff's name badge for the first time and gasped.

Christensen.

The sheriff was Paige's father.

I am so screwed.

/|\

I stood in a clearing behind Roman's house, my heart still racing after my encounter with the sheriff. Isaac paced in front of me. He removed his jacket to reveal a muscle tank underneath. Standing in my sweatpants, I was suddenly happy I dressed for a workout. Isaac reached into his pocket, producing a lighter. "Cassie explained to you how to heal yourself?"

"Yes," I responded warily, "but I'm not very good at it." He nodded in response, satisfied. My breathing quickened. Isaac's posture took on a new stance. He was more defined, sharper. This was not the joking Isaac I had met in school. Now he was a dangerous warrior. He flicked the lighter open using it to light a nearby torch stuck in the ground. He looked up at me, his eyes a lively red. "As a member of the Kindred, you have instincts you didn't have before. Your strength and speed are powered by nature, but until you can access them willingly, you have to use your emotions as a pathway."

This was the same as what Cassie told me. While I managed to access my power through my emotions that morning, I highly doubted I would be able to do it now. That took focus and relaxation and I hadn't been able to calm my nerves since my encounter with Sheriff Christensen.

My eyes moved from his face to the lighter. I could feel my adrenaline surging. While my first thought was to run, the will to fight was there as well. "Today, we are going to test your instincts and see if you can reach your power in a more high-stress situation." My eyes darted from Isaac to the torch. "You have to find an emotion to channel into your power. To begin, the easiest one for you to access will be fear. If you are staring down a wraith, your fear of death is your best asset."

I thought back to my fight with Deacon. Fear didn't help me access my power. It blocked it.

"How exactly do you plan on testing this?" I asked,

although I thought I already knew. Rather than respond, he reached his arm out toward the torch. Next thing I knew, a fireball was hurtling toward my head.

I dove to the side, the fireball barely missing me. I could feel the heat of it on my face. I stood up quickly, wheeling around on Isaac. "What the hell, man?!" He remained silent and methodically created another fireball. It too, came flying at my head. I dove out of the way again, landing face-first in the grass. Our deadly game of dodgeball continued, Isaac throwing, me moving out of the way just fast enough. I could feel my strength waning, but Isaac showed no signs of slowing down. "Use your fear, Kyndal. Find the well of power inside you," he commanded. "You're an Aries. The fire won't burn you. Block the fireball!" He threw another one. This time I didn't try to dodge it. Instead, I threw my arms up as a shield, hoping to block it. I misjudged where the fireball was headed and instead of it hitting my arms, it glanced off my shoulder. I spun around, hitting the grass hard. Just as Isaac said, the heat of the flames didn't hurt me, but the impact sure did. It was like getting hit with a sledgehammer. I cried out in pain.

"Isaac, stop! She's had enough." Roman's voice rang through the clearing. I sat up and saw Roman running toward the training ring. Isaac ignored him completely. Instead he prepared another fireball and launched it. Before I could react, a gust of wind blew through, forcing the fireball the opposite direction. It hit the ground, lighting small pieces of grass on fire.

Roman now stood in the middle of the ring. "Isaac, I said ENOUGH!"

"Stay out of it, Roman," I yelled at him.

He wheeled around, giving me a dangerous look. His eyes were bright gold. "No. This is stupid. You're not ready for this." Hearing his words, anger boiled up in me. Suddenly, the pain in my shoulder was gone.

"Is he right, Princess?" Isaac taunted, another fireball rolling around in his hand. "Is this too much for you to handle? Maybe you're not tough enough to be one of us. Have to have Roman step in and protect you? Can't take care of yourself?"

I stood up, nothing but rage and determination in my veins. Ignoring Roman, I looked right at Isaac. "Again."

Roman begrudgingly backed out of the way. Isaac pulled his arm back preparing to throw. When he fired, instead of diving to the side, I rolled toward him, under the fireball. I swept my leg underneath him, knocking him down. I straddled him, then swung, punching him cleanly in the nose. Before I could think about it, I reached my right arm out to the nearby torch. I pulled the fire into my hand and held my arm up by my head and aimed directly at Isaac. I could see the flames dancing in his eyes. "Tough enough for you?" I growled at him.

He smiled, blood staining his teeth. "Not bad, Princess."

I leapt off Isaac and moved quickly toward Roman's house. While the fireball had evaporated, I could still feel the rage pumping through my veins. Isaac wanted me to focus on my fear to access my powers, but there was one problem. I wasn't afraid when he was throwing those fireballs at me; I was *angry*. Just like when I went up against Deacon, it was my anger that allowed me access to my power. This time, every leap toward the ground built the rage inside of me; a building pressure that was released when I attacked. Now I couldn't seem to shut it off.

I paced on the back porch, unable to calm the raging storm inside me. I looked at the wall of windows that had turned to mirrors in the daylight. I froze. I'd never seen my new eyes before. It was so unexpected—all the anger and hate inside me bled out. As I watched, my eyes changed from livid red to rusty brown to pale green and finally, my normal jade. Mesmerized, I didn't immediately notice the stormy blue eyes that had joined my own in the reflection.

Roman followed me.

I held his eyes for a moment, then turned around slowly, suddenly self-conscious about being caught gawking at myself.

"How's the shoulder?" He sounded concerned. Renewed guilt immediately twisted in my gut. *If I had just left him alone, Evan would still be alive.* I glanced at my shoulder. I saw nothing but smooth skin through the burnt hole in my shirt. "I had a nice conversation with the sheriff today."

"Did he buy your story?"

"No, because his *daughter* saw us together."

His eyes widened.

"You didn't think it was important to mention that the sheriff was Paige frickin' Christensen's father?"

"I didn't think it would be a problem."

I couldn't help it. I laughed. "Of course you didn't." He and Paige were so close he was probably over there for Sunday dinners. It all made sense now. How Paige knew who I was the moment I showed up. How she knew about what happened to my family. Her dad would have access to all that information.

"What's your issue, anyways?" he asked, obviously frustrated.

Wrong question. I lashed out—my grief transforming into anger. "You are my issue. You were the one who wanted me to train. You practically begged me to become Kindred. And now that I have, you're interfering with my training!"

He ran his hand through his hair in frustration, turning away from me. He didn't say anything for a while, but suddenly he wheeled around, his eyes steely. "What am I supposed to do, huh? Just sit back and watch while you're in danger?"

I laughed without humor. "Danger? It's training. Isaac wasn't going to hurt me, not really."

"You know that for a fact, do you?" he challenged. "You have zero control over your powers and here you are, letting Isaac throw fireballs at your head. There's a difference between being brave and just plain stupid, Kyndal."

"Stupid?" I roared. I could feel the rage building in me again, my power surging forward. Before I could stop them, the words erupted from me like wildfire. "Stupid was agreeing to go on that date with you. Stupid was dancing with you, telling you about my family, kissing you, the whole time thinking it was because you cared about me as a person, when really you just wanted to find out if I was a member of your warrior club."

"Is that what you think?" he hollered back. "That I don't *care*?"

"You made it pretty obvious how you feel. You got the answers you were looking for then you couldn't ditch me fast enough. So excuse me if I don't quite buy the whole protective act. Maybe you should go protect your girlfriend Paige." I was being petty and jealous, but I didn't care. I wanted him to hurt as much as me.

"That's such bullshit," he responded, taking a challenging step toward me. "You know I care. And so do you. Let's not forget that it was *you* who kissed *me* the other night."

"A momentary lapse of sanity, I promise you. It won't happen again." I let out a frustrated sigh. I didn't have time for this. Ezekiel would arrive in less than two weeks. I wanted to make a good impression and I couldn't do that if was busy arguing with Roman instead of training. Aggravated, I stomped past him, slamming my shoulder into his as I passed.

"Where are you going?" he hollered after me.

"Training. Alone!"

/|\

With Ezekiel arriving soon and Deacon's threat hanging over my head, my life fell into a strict routine. I woke up before dawn and ran through the forest with Cassie. She used the time to not only condition my body, but to teach me about Kindred politics. The Kindred around the world are governed by a council of 12 Nomarchs, one from each of the Zodiac houses. The oldest living member of a particular house sits on The Council, located on The Island. Originally settled by the first Kindred as a safe haven from wraiths, The Island is a mysterious place inhabited only by Kindred and hidden from the outside world. Supposedly it moves around the world and can be accessed only with permission from The Council. It is there The Council monitors wraith activity and sends Kindred out to hunt them. Ezekiel—Roman's "brother"—sits on The Council as the representative for Capricorn.

While my studies of the Kindred culture were going well, my school studies were not. In fact, school was the worst part of the day. Roman and I hadn't spoken since I yelled at him, an act I deeply regretted but was too proud to admit. He didn't seem to mind the distance. Paige, and her now shorter hair, was still determined to get his attention. From what I could see, she succeeded. I saw them together everywhere. They sat at the same table at lunch and were lab partners in chemistry. It seemed he didn't mean a single word he had said to me just a few short days ago. I hadn't spoken to Lydia either. She had taken Evan's death particularly hard. I wanted to be there for her, but I couldn't look her in the eye. I couldn't look at her and pretend that his death wasn't my fault.

I'm a coward.

After school, I trained with Isaac. Since accessing my powers on that first day with him, I had graduated to hand-to-hand sparring. We spent our afternoons trading blows—physical and elemental. I was a quick study. I learned to harness my emotions and channel them into my powers. I could make a fireball with barely a thought, but only by pulling it from fire. I hadn't created the element since the dance.

Although he hadn't interfered again, Roman watched me train every day, arms crossed and silent. He always showed up a little late, after taking *her* home. I think he watched just to see if I was going to crumble under the weight of recent events. He treated me like a china doll, ready to break at any moment. His always watchful eyes put me on edge. One day, I finally snapped.

"Are you just going to stand there like a statue?" I glared at him, pausing to wipe the sweat from my brow. Isaac and I had been going at it long enough that the sun was beginning to set behind the trees.

His face stayed impassive. "What am I supposed to do?"

I threw my arms out, frustrated. "I don't know. All you do is stand there and watch me kick Isaac's ass."

"Hey!" Isaac interrupted. I rolled my eyes. *Boys and their egos.*

I looked back at Roman. "You could help. Do *something.*"

He raised his eyebrows at my tone. I expected him to say something snarky, but instead he reached up and lifted his grey shirt over his head, revealing a white tank underneath. As if they had a mind of their own, my eyes wandered over his body. Starting at his now exposed, muscular arms then to his chiseled abs clearly defined through the tank, it was easy to appreciate the man standing in front of me.

"Problem?" Roman asked, his voice dripping with suggestion. He knew exactly what he was doing.

I cleared my throat. "Wha—what are you doing?" I stammered. I could feel my cheeks burning.

Isaac snickered from where he'd moved to the sidelines. I glared his direction.

"You wanted me to help," Roman said, as he took position inside the fighting ring.

Yeah, but this is so not what I had in mind. "Scared?"

"No," I responded defiantly. "I'm just surprised you have time to actually participate. Figured you had a hot date later."

"Jealous?" he taunted. My power stirred, angry.

"Just tell me how you want to do this."

"One round. First one to go for the kill shot wins."

Perfect.

12

I'd seen Roman fight twice before. The first time I was shell-shocked by what was happening, and the second, I was busy fighting for my life. So, it's not like I exactly took the time to watch his form and study his fighting habits.

"Let's get this over with." I closed my eyes and took a deep breath, calling my power. It rose up quickly, filling me with strength. When I opened my eyes, the world around me was sharper. I could see the smallest detail, hear the tiniest noise. I could sense the life of the trees, the flow of the nearby stream, the power in every stone and patch of earth. I felt unstoppable.

I looked at Roman, expecting him to be in the same fighting stance I was. Instead, I found him standing completely still, knees locked, arms crossed, eyes a fierce blue.

"You sure about this?" he asked. I glared in return.

I wasted no time, immediately going on the attack. I struck

out at Roman with my right hand, a move he easily dodged. I followed it with a series of kicks, only one of which I manage to land. Roman was unfazed by the contact and responded with a straight right of his own. The punch connected, landing soundly under my eye, whipping my head back.

Before I could think about healing, Roman was on me again. He advanced with a combination of hits and kicks. I moved into a defensive position, managing to deflect the majority of the strikes, but he was relentless and his final kick hit home, spinning me around and knocking me to the ground.

"Had enough?" His voice was dead. Empty. I stood up, grimacing. His last kick threw me right next to the ever-burning torch on the edge of the training ring. I reached toward it, pulling a fireball into my hand.

Roman looked down at my hand then up to me. "I wouldn't if I were you."

Too late.

I launched the fireball at his head. He dodged it easily, but I was prepared for that. A second one ready, I threw again. He ducked underneath, barely breaking a sweat. The third and fourth attempts were misses too, but I didn't stop. Roman dodged each one easily, but he never attacked. I had never tried to use this much power before and I could feel my strength wane. I took a moment to catch my breath. I wanted to rest, but I refused to show Roman any weakness. Only then did I notice the wind had picked up.

Desperate, I dug as deep as I could into my power. With barely any strength left, I focused on the heat of the eternal flame at the edge of the ring. Pulling power from my own element was easier than the others and I managed to pull just enough to muster one more fireball. I hurled it toward Roman with every ounce of force I had left. The flame neither hit home nor passed by Roman. Instead, it seemed to stop mid-air, as if caught by some invisible force. It paused momentarily, then reversed its course and headed directly back at me. I ducked under it and rolled toward Roman, hoping to use the same move I'd used on Isaac. I took Roman's legs out from under him and straddled his hips. Just as I lifted my hand to deliver the final punch—the deciding kill shot—I was yanked off of him. It felt as if someone grabbed the back of my shirt and pulled with superhuman strength, landing me unceremoniously on my ass. The move was so startling it knocked the breath out of me. I laid on the ground coughing. Before I had a chance to recover, a knee pressed on my chest and a fist pushed on my heart.

"Kill shot."

His words rang in my ears even as he moved off me. He took several steps back, his eyes returning to normal and his power receding. Humiliated, I stood slowly. I could feel the tears build, but I defiantly held them back. Finally, I dragged my head up and looked at Roman. He was standing there, seemingly unaffected, but when our eyes met, I could see the twinge of regret in them.

Good, you should feel bad.

Refusing to stand in embarrassment any longer, I walked past Roman, toward the forest. During one of my early morning runs, I had discovered an old path that could be used to get from Roman's house to mine. Several miles long and mainly overgrown, you could follow it if you knew what to look for. I walked that path slowly now, stewing in my defeat. I didn't even have the energy to pull on the elements and repair the damage from the fight. By the time I reached the house, my throat burned and my vision was blurry from unshed tears. I fumbled through the back door, slamming it behind me. I walked up the stairs and through my bedroom door. Curling up on the bed, not even bothering to take off my fighting gear, I finally let the tears fall.

/|\

The next day, I refused to face the world. I blew off my early-morning training with Cassie. When I didn't get up for school, Alessandra came into my room to check on me. I dismissed her by telling her I didn't feel well and needed to stay home. She insisted on staying home with me, but I eventually convinced her that I was old enough to take care of myself and there was no need for her to stay.

I spent the day in bed, sleeping some, but mostly wallowing. I cried off and on. The fight with Roman left me not only physically exhausted, but also emotionally drained. My defenses down, all the events I had been refusing to deal with came surging forward, demanding attention.

I replayed it in my head. His determined eyes. The coldness

with which he delivered my beating. *How could I have been so wrong about him?* How could he go from defending and protecting me against emotional bruises to being the deliverer of very real ones? Thinking about Roman, I was unable to come up with any answers, just more questions. As my confusion grew, I realized I missed my mom. The tears returned, now for a completely different reason.

My mom and I had always been extremely close. Whenever I had an issue, I was able to go to her. She had this uncanny ability to give the perfect piece of advice and you knew you wouldn't be judged for anything you said. We were so close, I even told her when I lost my virginity just after Christmas last year to my then-boyfriend, Colt. He dumped me not long after. My first lesson that being physically close with someone didn't equal loyalty.

Should have paid closer attention to that one.

It wasn't until the sun rays were beaming through my western window that I dragged myself from bed. While I didn't feel any better, my growling stomach simply could not be ignored any longer. I trudged to the kitchen, passing by the table where my lit books lay open and untouched. I rolled my eyes when I remembered I had a test in that class today that I would have to make up. I opened up the fridge, staring blankly. I settled on some ice cream, grabbed a spoon, and proceeded to eat it directly from the carton. Half-way through, the doorbell rang. I wasn't expecting anyone, so I treaded lightly to the door and looked through the peephole. Lydia stood on my front porch. I froze.

"Kyndal, open the door!" she yelled, banging her fist on the door. "Come on Kyndal, I know you're here!" I remained silent. I knew it was cowardly, but how was I supposed to explain everything to her? Finally, the pounding stopped, and I breathed a sigh of relief. I tiptoed silently back to the kitchen. When I got there, I nearly jumped out of my skin.

"How did you get in here?" I shrieked. Lydia sat at my kitchen table, arms crossed.

"Back door was open," she replied. "This place isn't exactly Fort Knox, you know."

"Look," I began, trying to come up with an excuse for why I didn't answer the door.

Lydia interrupted. "Don't you dare give me some excuse, Kyndal Davenport." I instantly shut up. I'd never seen her angry before. "I stood up for you when other people said horrible things. I ignored you when you said something mean or callous because I know what you've been through. I've always been nice to you, and if I'm being honest, you are sometimes not all that likeable. You owe it to me. What is your problem?"

I looked away from her, trying to inconspicuously wipe a fresh tear. "I—I don't know what you mean."

She raised her eyebrows in disbelief. "Oh, really? You move here—" she paused, swallowing, "under tragic circumstances."

As if I forgot.

"You go on a date with Roman, with whom you have this *amazing* moment, but then he promptly dumps you. You have a great time with Evan at the dance until—" her voice broke and she was unable to finish the sentence. "You avoid me like the plague."

I thought about interrupting her, but I didn't. I had no defense. Everything she said was true.

"You've skipped school, refuse to answer the door, and when I barge my way in, I find you eating ice cream straight from the carton. And don't think I don't notice the bruise on your face either." *Crap.* During my pity party, I only had enough energy to remove the worst of the injuries. My left eye still showed the effects of Roman's straight right.

Hearing all my problems listed so bluntly, I couldn't help the fresh tears from falling. "Evan is dead," Lydia said bluntly. "And it's like you're too busy to even care." I shook my head violently at her words. *It's my fault. It's my fault.* "You didn't even go to his funeral."

"I couldn't," I whispered. My voice was thick with tears.

"Talk to me," she begged.

"I can't," I managed between sobs.

"Why?" Lydia shouted.

"Because!" I yelled back.

"Tell me," Lydia demanded. "Tell me why not!"

"Because it's my fault!" I screamed.

Lydia froze.

"It's my fault," I repeated, my voice much quieter now.

"I don't understand." I nodded, knowing that truly, she didn't. "But maybe I would if you explained it to me."

I took a deep breath. No one had ever told me I couldn't tell anyone about the Kindred, I just never did, thinking no one would believe me. I wanted to tell Lydia everything so badly I could taste it. *What would she think? That I'm a freak? A killer?* I looked at her now. Arms crossed, jaw clenched. She was clearly upset. But when I looked in her eyes, all I saw was concern. *Concern for me.* Like she said, she'd always been a friend. Hell, she broke into my house to see what was wrong with me. That's loyalty.

"Okay," I relented. I told her everything. I told her about my family's crash, how that had allowed my powers to emerge. Going on the date with Roman, how he knew what I was becoming. Using my powers for the first time. Wraiths. Deacon's attack at the dance and his impending return. The truth about Evan's death. Training with Cassie and Isaac. The fight with Roman.

To her credit, Lydia sat and listened quietly the whole time. Most sane people would have gotten up and ran, but she didn't. Somehow we ended up on the floor, me crying, her arm around me as I explained it all. As I finished the story, I felt lighter—like a burden had been lifted. It was nice to have someone know all my secrets.

"Look at me," she said, speaking for the first time since I started my story. "What happened to Evan was horrible. But it was not your fault." I shook my head in disbelief. "I mean it, Kyndal. There was nothing you could have done. Grieve him, but don't punish yourself. You deserve to be happy. That's what Evan would want. Blaming yourself for his death and punishing yourself by avoiding Roman are not."

"How are you taking this so well?" I asked her, wiping away more tears.

She shrugged. "When I was twelve, I went on a camping trip in the forest with my Girl Scout troop. We were out hiking and I could have sworn I saw something. Like a Windigo or Big Foot. This isn't much different."

A laugh burst out of me. Before I knew it, we were both giggling.

"Can I ask a question?" Lydia said, between giggles. I nodded. "Can I see?"

I rolled my eyes at her, "Seriously?"

She jumped up, her smile huge now. "Ya! Come on, Johnny Storm. Flame on!"

I gave her a confused look. "What?"

She dropped her arms down. "Human Torch?" When the confused look didn't move from my face, she groaned. "You're telling me you've never heard of the Fantastic Four?" I shook my head at her. "You're hopeless!" she responded, laughing.

By the time Alessandra got home that night, Lydia was long gone. I had spent most of the evening giving Lydia demonstrations of my elemental powers, much to her delight. She was fascinated by my ability to hold fire in the palm of my hand without pain, although she did admit she found my red eyes "freaky." I also showed her my ability to heal myself, erasing the remainder of the shiner from the fight the previous day. After that, my body felt pretty good. She begged me to go out this weekend for a girl's night. I reminded her of Ezekiel's arrival and told her I would try my best, but made no promises. She left only after I forced her to promise to never tell anyone about the Kindred. It was dangerous enough with her knowing. I didn't need to risk anyone else.

I felt completely rejuvenated. Whether it was an after effect of healing myself, or just the release of exposing my secrets to a friend, I wasn't really sure. Either way, I felt ready to face Ezekiel in three days.

Alessandra took immediate notice of my improved condition when she walked in the door. We ate a late dinner together, enjoying casual conversation. She shared that she had spent her day scouting trails and streams for a group coming in this weekend.

"They want to kayak down the river, but only in areas with limited traffic," she explained. "So basically, this means I have to take them through the forest by Jeep, camp overnight, hike to the river with the kayaks, make the trip down river, camp, then hike back out."

I listened intently and when I responded, I tried to keep my tone casual. "Is it that same guy I saw you with before? What was his name? Damon or something—"

She searched her brain. "Deacon?"

"Yeah, that's it. Deacon. Is it his group?"

"Funny you should ask," she responded. "I never saw him again after that day at the shop. He called the next day and cancelled his outing. It was the strangest thing."

I tried my hardest to keep from jumping for joy. No one had seen Deacon since the night he killed Evan, but after the intense interest he showed in me, I was worried he might come after Alessandra.

"The whole thing will take at least three days. Will you be alright at the house by yourself?" she asked, turning the focus on me.

I took a bite of my spaghetti and nodded. "Lydia invited me over this weekend, so I'll probably just stay at her house."

"Good. I like Lydia, she's a nice girl. Shame what happened to her family though, dad leaving like that." It didn't surprise me Allie knew the Warner family story. "Sorry," she said, "in a small town like this, there isn't much room for secrets."

Except when it involves wraiths and the super-humans that fight them.

13

"**S**top fidgeting."

"Sorry," I replied, forcing myself to stop popping my knuckles. "I'm nervous. How am I supposed to act? Do I bow or something?" Cassie looked at me from behind the steering wheel and smiled, chuckling slightly. She picked me up early in the morning for the meeting I had been anxiously awaiting—and dreading—for weeks. Ezekiel.

"He isn't royalty, you know." I breathed in deeply. "He'll want to see your abilities. Probably put you through a series of exercises that test both your fighting and elemental skills. I've known Ezekiel for more years than you've been alive, Kyndal. He's a good man, a good leader. You have nothing to worry about."

Known him more years than I've been alive? I looked at Cassie again, wondering, not for the first time, exactly how old she was. Once, when I was jealous of her and Roman's relationship, she alluded to the fact that she was too old for him, a statement I didn't believe at the time. But that was before I knew Kindred didn't age. Although Cassie looked to be 22-23 years old, she could actually be old enough to be my mom. Or grandma!

"Are you ever going to tell me how old you are?" I asked her, desperately curious. I knew it was rude to ask, but I couldn't help it. I wanted to know!

She laughed at my eagerness. "One day," she said as she parked the car at the end of Roman's driveway, "I'll tell you my story."

"But not today," I finished for her.

"Not today," she agreed.

I got out of the vehicle and followed Cassie toward the main house. I'd never been in it before. Every other time I had been here, this house had been deserted. Lights off, doors shut, gardens overgrown. It was a building that was built from the earth and was slowly being reclaimed by it. Moving toward it now, the difference in its appearance was astonishing. The front pillars were wrapped in vines; beautiful red, purple, and pink flowers burst through the green to form a colorful mosaic. The bushes along the porch were a rich green, and I swear, they looked *taller*. A bird's song broke through the silence of the forest. The scene was all-around *peaceful*. I turned, tipped my head back, and breathed in deeply through my nose.

"Kyndal!"

Cassie's voice ripped through the moment with all the finesse of a bulldozer.

I turned and found her waiting on the porch with her arms crossed. "You coming in, or are you going to stay out here all day literally smelling the roses?"

The walls inside were made of the same light wood as the exterior. When I walked in, I was immediately greeted with a staircase. Voices and the din of movement echoed down the stairs. I craned my neck trying to see who they belonged to, but I came up empty. Cassie led me down the hall. As we entered the kitchen, decorated in the same motif, a cool breeze danced up my spine. Roman was near. I'm wasn't surprised. I quickly tied down my emotions. I hadn't forgotten what Lydia said about punishing myself, but I couldn't deal with it yet. Cassie took me through a swinging door off the side of the kitchen. The tingling grew and I prepared myself.

The new room I entered was an office of some sort. Even though I promised myself I wouldn't, my eyes went to Roman first. He stood at the back of the room, arms behind his back, face a blank mask. On the other side of the room was someone else, standing in almost a mirror image of Roman. The stranger's hair was buzzed into a close cropped Mohawk, his wide shoulders and muscular arms were a caramel brown. His eyes were unnerving. Deep and laser focused, everything about this man screamed danger. I looked away, uncomfortable, toward the man sitting behind the mahogany desk. His light brown hair was long, probably shoulder length. It was pulled back in a short ponytail at the back of his neck. He looked up and smiled at me when I entered, his hazel eyes kind. He stood and rounded his desk. He was dressed in a white dress shirt, the sleeves rolled up to his elbows, and slacks. He appeared to be in his late twenties, but I knew better. As the oldest living Capricorn on the planet, Isaac told me he was well over 500-years-old.

"Kyndal Davenport," he said, shaking my hand. "It's an honor to meet you."

"Hello, sir," I responded, nowhere near his eloquence.

"Sit, sit," he said eagerly.

I followed his instructions, sitting in one of the plush chairs in front of the desk. He sat next to me; his back perfectly straight, his posture rigid. Cassie had discreetly left the room, but Roman and the scary guy remained posted along the wall.

"Let me begin by offering my condolences on the passing of your family. We have all lost someone, but to lose everyone so unnecessarily—" he let the end of the sentence linger. Everyone always tried to apologize for their deaths, or give me some sort of silver lining. I appreciated that Ezekiel did neither. "And let us not forget your friend, as well."

"Evan," I interjected. I refused to let his death be glossed over. Brushed under the rug as collateral damage.

"Of course," Ezekiel smiled slightly, "I apologize. Roman was just updating me on the status of your training." My eyes flicked to his. "He tells me you are making remarkable strides in not only your fighting, but especially in your elemental control."

I smiled weakly, "I've been working hard." *Remarkable strides? Wonder if he mentioned how he unceremoniously handed me my ass just a few days ago.*

"And it shows!" he said enthusiastically. "Although, one would say it's to be expected from someone with your pedigree." *Pedigree? What the hell does that mean?* Suddenly my head was filled with images of the pet food commercials with the dancing dogs, but I couldn't see how that related.

"Excuse me," I interrupted again, forgetting to call him sir, "I don't understand what you mean. My pedigree?"

"A question for a later time," he replied, brushing me off. "Tell me; exactly what elemental control are you experiencing?"

"I've gotten pretty good at making fireballs," I responded. I thought back to the candles in the school hallway. "Sometimes I can pull from several flames at once." Ezekiel nodded in agreement. "The cold doesn't seem to bother me anymore," I added, "like my internal temperature is higher, and—" I looked up at Roman before continuing, his warning from so many weeks ago still ringing in my ears. *Don't mention it to anyone else. Even them.* He was the only one who knew what I could do. That I could not only manipulate fire, but create it. He gave me a small nod, encouraging me to continue. "I can also create fire, without needing to reach out to an existing source." Ezekiel's eyebrows shot up in surprise. Even the scary Mohawk man reacted. "Well—sometimes," I added. Being Kindred was weird enough. I didn't need to be a freak among the freaks.

"Impressive," Ezekiel said. "But again, not entirely surprising for someone like you."

"What does that mean?" I asked again, growing increasingly agitated. "Does this have something to do with what Deacon said? With me being a—Descendant, or whatever?"

"The answers you seek will be given in due time." I rolled my eyes at his cryptic answer. "First, let us move to the training ring. I am eager to see you in action." With that, he stood and left the room. The silent guard followed him out. I glared over at Roman, still standing frozen at his post. "Do you know what he's talking about?"

"You can trust him," he responded. *Doesn't answer my question.* Frustrated that Roman seemed to be keeping things from me *again*, I got up and followed Ezekiel out of the room.

/|\

Three hours later, I'd gone through what felt like every physical and elemental drill possible. Some I performed well, others—not so much. I sparred with Isaac and Cassie. I did well against Isaac. We had sparred so much in the last few weeks we knew each other's entire playbooks and anticipated each other's moves. Our fight ended with him on the ground and me standing triumphant. I tried to help him up, but he slapped my hand away. Instead, he stalked off and didn't watch the rest of my testing. My fight against Cassie didn't go so well. She was lightning quick and I couldn't follow her moves. Every time I created a fireball, she would douse it with water from the nearby stream. I didn't have anywhere near the stamina she did and my powers waned, leaving me defenseless. She took advantage with full-force. By the time she was done with me, I was limping out of the training ring.

After the hand-to-hand sparring, Ezekiel had me practice with weapons. I'd never touched a dagger before. I'd only seen the others use them. So, that obviously didn't go well. I squared off against one of the visiting Kindred; I think her name was Mallory. She was a tall, thin woman with cocoa skin. She had long arms and legs, like a ballerina. She didn't look especially intimidating, but she wielded her dagger with deadly accuracy. In less than a minute, she had cut me twice. Once on my shoulder, and the other, a deep cut across my thigh. I could feel the blood dripping down my leg and pooling in my shoe. On the second round I managed to avoid being cut, but it ended just as quickly when she disarmed me, leaving me empty-handed and her wielding twice the weapons. When Ezekiel called an end to our fight, she threw down my practice dagger and stomped out of the ring. "Like fighting a baby," she told Ezekiel as she walked past.

Those that had not taken me on directly, gathered to watch. It seemed Ezekiel had traveled with quite the posse. Attracted by the promise of a fight and testing the new girl, there were at least fifteen new faces standing around the training ring. Throughout every drill, Ezekiel stood and watched in intense silence, speaking only to bark out orders for the next drill. Mohawk man was always slightly behind him, standing stoically while Roman was at his left, leaning over to whisper in his ear occasionally. Even with my enhanced hearing, I couldn't pick up what they were saying. The only thing I could make out was that Ezekiel seemed to be growing increasingly frustrated with each passing moment. Regardless, I completed every drill dutifully. Ezekiel promised answers, and the sooner I jumped through these hoops, the sooner I could get what I wanted.

After what seemed like forever, Ezekiel ended it. "That's enough for today."

My shoulders slumped forward in relief. *Finally.*

Without another word, the crowd dispersed. The entertainment was over. All that remained was Roman, Ezekiel, and myself. Ezekiel looked at me. "It was nice to have met you. Roman will take you home."

"I thought you were going to give me answers," I shrieked. Jogging up to him, I winced when my leg protested. *Mallory really is good. I should practice with her again.*

"I hardly see why I should," he answered.

"You—you promised," I stuttered, stunned by his response. My words sounded stupid and childish.

"I did no such thing. The secret of the Descendants is something that has been entrusted to very few throughout the centuries, and from the display I just witnessed, you have done nothing to convince me that you are either a Descendant yourself or worthy of such trust. Unless you can show me something that proves otherwise—" He crossed his arms behind his back, waiting.

I stood there, frozen. My temper flared and I felt fire run down my arm. I was dying to give this guy a piece of my mind but I knew that would get me nowhere. Ezekiel stared at me impassively, waiting for me to do *something*. The longer he stared at me, the more my anger built, but I kept my body frozen.

He squinted at me, as if he could see the fire inside me. He knew I was on the verge of exploding. When I didn't, he smiled slightly. "As expected." He turned his back and headed toward the house. That did it. I had reached my boiling point, heat rolling off me in waves. After all I put myself through today trying to impress him, I couldn't stand to be brushed off so carelessly. I acted without thinking, creating a fireball from thin air. I launched it at the back of Ezekiel's head. Before it could reach him, Roman stepped in, using his power to brush the fireball aside, just past Ezekiel's head. The heat whipped past him fast enough to ruffle some of the hair out of his neatly kept ponytail.

Still seeing red, another fireball grew from my palm. Ezekiel turned to face me, but I didn't care. He looked from my face to the fireball that was still gaining size. I expected him to yell at me. Maybe even use his own power against me, but instead; he clapped, and for the first time, I felt like he laughed with genuine pleasure.

Stunned, the fireball extinguished in my grasp. "Well done," he said. "Follow me."

I expected us to go back to the house, but instead, Ezekiel led me into the forest, down an old, forgotten path covered in brush. I worried about having the energy to climb over the brush that had fallen in the path, but that turned out not to be an issue. With one small wave of his hand, Ezekiel moved a fallen tree to the side. *Right. Earth-user.* I glanced behind me, expecting to see Roman. He had been Ezekiel's constant shadow all day, and I could still feel his presence. To my surprise, he wasn't there.

After several more minutes of walking, Ezekiel finally stopped in the middle of the path. "Why here?" I asked.

He pointed to his ear. "No eavesdroppers. The information I am going to tell you is known by precious few. Even Kindred centuries-old have never heard a whisper of what I am about to tell you."

I looked back the way we came. I couldn't see the house anymore. We must have been at least a mile away. Could Kindred really hear that far?

"What do you know about me, Kyndal?" Ezekiel asked. I looked back at him. It took a minute to get my bearings before I could answer. The cut in my leg was throbbing and my foot was wet with blood. I wanted nothing more than to go home and rest up until I could heal myself, but I knew I needed to hear what Ezekiel had to say.

"Not much," I answered honestly. "I know you're an earth sign. A Capricorn, specifically. The oldest Kindred in your House. You sit on the Council of Nomarchs and you haven't been in Pennsylvania in over two years."

"And what is the job of the Council?"

I huffed, getting annoyed with the twenty questions. "I have no frickin' clue." He chuckled. "I'm glad I amuse you," I quipped.

"The Council works as a governing body for the Kindred. Each member, or Nomarch, as we are known, is in charge of a different part of the world. A general to the Kindred army, if you will. The Eastern section of the United States is my region."

"How can you protect a region you don't even live in?"

"Through soldiers like Roman. Experienced, good fighters, who are loyal to a fault. I have several like him, spread throughout the region in areas where wraith activity is high. They run the coast, allowing me to fulfill my duties on The Island."

"You use them," I said, cutting through the fancy talk. I was too tired to play nice.

"I delegate," he amended.

My injured leg could no longer handle my weight, so I flopped down on a nearby fallen tree. "What does all this have to do with the Descendants?" I asked.

"In addition to being the ruling body of the Kindred, we are also the keepers of its secrets. You see, most believe that when Hermes Trismegistus first blessed the original twelve, he gave them the ability to reach out to nature and pull it into themselves."

"And that's not what happened?" I asked.

"That did happen, but there's a whole lot more to the story." He sat down next to me on the log. "Each element has what is called a Cardinal sign. Some say it's the strongest of the four houses within each element on the Zodiac. When The Thrice Great Hermes, as he was known then, blessed the original 12 with their elements, he bestowed upon the four Cardinals an additional gift. Hermes *infused* the elements in each of them. It ran in their veins like blood. Each was able to manifest their element with no assistance from the outside world. A Cancer could pull water in the middle of the desert. An Aries could create fire in the cold depths of winter. With their natural superiority, they were appointed as leaders. Hermes also bestowed upon them *The Book of Breathings*. It contained a number of useful incantations, including one that bound the powers of the four Cardinals with the rest of the Kindred, allowing them to share their gifts."

I held up my hand to interrupt, "My brain hurts. Kiddie version, please."

"Imagine if you will, all Kindred being able to generate the elements. With no need for a pre-existing source to feed them."

"That's what this book did?" I asked, still confused. The story Ezekiel was telling sounded like something out of a mythology book. I was having trouble putting these events in reality.

He nodded. "With these abilities, the Kindred were almost

unstoppable. Their power easily outmatched the wraiths. For hundreds of years the wraiths were kept on the other side, scared of the power of the Kindred. The world was at peace. Unfortunately, as it always goes with peace, the Kindred became lazy. They didn't realize that the wraiths were organizing, planning an assault. They came in force and The Great War began. It's a battle we still fight today."

I was genuinely fascinated, but still frustrated. "Where do I fit into all this?" So far I felt like I was just the punching bag—there to be hit, stabbed, and knocked down.

"Kindred are immortal, but not invulnerable to death. Through the centuries, each of the original Cardinals was lost, despite best efforts to protect them. When a Cardinal dies, it breaks the spell that binds them to the other Kindred within their element."

"They lose their ability to create their element," I translated.

"Precisely," he responded. "However, it was written in *The Book of Breathings* that an element can be rebound if an heir to the Original Cardinal is branded within the same house. These heirs are to be known as—"

"The Descendants," I finished for him. "And that's what you think I am?"

"Your abilities would suggest so."

I laughed ruefully. Ezekiel's earlier behavior now made sense. "You baited me. You wanted me to get angry enough to throw a fireball at you."

"I needed to make sure you were what I hoped. Roman suggested that getting you angry might help you access it."

Roman. Figures.

He looked me square in the eye. "You need to understand how important you are, Kyndal. You are the only Descendant in existence. You must be protected at any cost."

"So, you want me to read some spell out of a thousands-of-years-old book so all fire users can create their element?" I asked, desperately trying to understand his end-game.

"I wish it was that simple. *The Book of Breathings* was stolen. Hidden away several years ago. Both sides, Kindred and wraiths, have been searching for it ever since."

"How do we find it?"

"I believe you can help with that as well."

I looked at him, confused. "How?"

"It was your mother who stole it."

14

The next night, I found myself standing in the middle of a dark field two towns over, surrounded by cars. Lydia and I were both wearing old, ripped jeans and white T-shirts. She told me the matching outfits were required, although she refused to explain why.

Her shirt was cut to bare her midriff. When she tried to make me do the same, I swiftly declined. Insisting I show a little skin, she ripped off my sleeves and used her scissors to make cut-outs up the sides. I had to give her credit. The shirt looked good. It was tight in all the right places and showed just enough skin. I looked hot.

Lydia's blonde hair was curled, highlighting her pixie face and her makeup was dramatic. She wore dark eyeliner, framed by bright eyeshadow and her eyelashes were tipped with glitter. On anyone else, it would look ridiculous. But on Lydia—it was perfect.

"What are we doing here?" I whined at her.

"What part of surprise do you not understand?" she asked, hands on her hips. This was not the first time I'd asked this question. I'd had enough surprises in the last three months and wasn't eager for another one. But how could I not indulge her? She stuck by me after learning everything. The least I could do was play along.

I hadn't told Lydia what had happened yesterday with Ezekiel, at least not all of it. I talked about the physical trials, but I left out all the information about the Descendants. She demanded that I take a night off and have some fun.

We walked for a while, then I started to hear it: pounding bass. I reached inward, grabbing just enough power to increase my eyesight. I hadn't fully recovered from yesterday and I didn't want to deplete what little magic I had left. I looked toward the direction of the beat. Sure enough, far enough away that my eyes couldn't have seen it, sat a large brick barn. As we got closer, I could see the details. At least three-stories-tall, old and run down, the building was made entirely of red brick. Chunks of the stuff were missing, leaving gaping holes of efflorescence behind. The roof was a dark wood, faded and blending in with the trees behind it. On the near side of the structure was a large, wooden double door, probably originally used for moving large equipment in and out. Next to it was a door painted black.

"This place is creepy," I told Lydia.

She ignored me and knocked loudly. I didn't know who was inside, but I doubted they could hear her over the music. I was proven wrong when the door swung open without hesitation. House music came blaring out the doorway. The man behind it looked us over once. Apparently we passed his test, because he let us in.

Two steps inside, I froze.

The inside of the barn looked like a scene right out of a big city club. The room was completely dark save for black light, strobe lights, and flashing lasers. A DJ was posted at the other end of the barn, his music blaring. Everywhere I looked, people were dancing. I was surrounded by fluorescent shirts, neon hair, glow-in-the-dark necklaces and bracelets, even luminescent body paint. Everyone was glowing. *It was awesome.*

I looked at Lydia, my smile beaming. "Good surprise?" she asked, returning my smile. I nodded enthusiastically. "Want to go get painted?" she gestured to a station in the corner filled with glow-in-the-dark paint.

"Absolutely," I responded.

Fifteen minutes later, my arms were painted with spiral flames in a variety of reds, yellows, and oranges. My clothes were splattered with a rainbow of colors. The only part of me that didn't glow was my face. Lydia's clothes were similarly splattered, but she opted to leave her arms bare, choosing instead to decorate her stomach in delicate purple flowers.

We headed directly to the dance floor, losing ourselves among the throngs of people and surrendering to the beat. We only left to gets drinks—the bartender wasn't carding.

Once I was buzzed, I abandoned myself to the music, relishing in the fact that besides Lydia, no one here knew me. I wasn't the new girl that killed her family. I wasn't Kindred. I was no one. And that was fine with me.

Hours later, while at the bar for another drink, I heard someone call my name. I expected to see Lydia, but when I turned, she was nowhere to be seen. I saw a guy walking directly toward me. The first thing I noticed was his height. He was well over six feet. His arms were well-built, clearly exposed in the neon tank he wore. His dark skin contrasted beautifully with the fluorescent tribal paint that decorated one side of his face and wrapped itself around his arms. I squinted, trying hard to see through my alcohol-fueled buzz. "Isaac?"

He leaned against the bar. "Look who it is. Ezekiel's new favorite warrior."

I ignored his jab. "What are *you* doing here?" I demanded. *Oh no. Did I just slur?*

He reached over and stole my drink, tossing it back. "We always patrol places like this. Young, impressionable kids drinking and dancing—it's a regular buffet for wraiths." Roman had told me something similar after The Ridge. "I'm surprised you're here, though. I would have thought you'd be training. Trying your best to be a perfect little soldier."

I squared my body with his. "What is your deal?"

He eyes skittered around the room. "No deal, Princess. We peasants will be out of your way soon."

I sobered slightly. Isaac had never talked this way to me before. Something was definitely wrong with him. Right now though, only one word sunk in.

"What do you mean *we*?"

Before Isaac could answer, my eyes searched the area for him. It was hard to see any specific person, especially on the dance floor. Everyone was just a large, glowing mass of bodies. Finally, I spotted him on the other side of the room. He was standing up against the wall, his dark shirt blending in with the shadows. I only noticed him because he was the one person that wasn't glowing. The sight of him immediately twisted my gut.

"I—I need some air," I pushed past him, desperate to escape. I headed back out the main door and turned toward the forest. As soon as I reached the trees, I closed my eyes and inhaled. The night had turned cool and crisp, but it didn't affect me. I pressed my hand to the trunk of the tree nearest to me. I centered myself and pulled the tree's power into me. The good news: I managed to heal the soreness in my legs that had returned from all the dancing. The bad news: it totally killed my buzz.

I knew he was there. Even if I hadn't heard the crunching of his feet on the grass, I would've known. I felt him. The now familiar cool tingle of his presence danced up my spine. Earlier, I had been too preoccupied to notice it. Now with him so close, it was hard to focus on anything else.

"Go away, Roman."

"I can't do that."

I still didn't open my eyes. "I don't want to fight."

"That's not why I'm here," he responded.

Resigned to the fact that he wasn't leaving no matter what I did, I opened my eyes and turned to face him. "Did Ezekiel send you?" It wouldn't surprise me if his idea of protecting me at all costs included a babysitter.

"He's a good man, Kyndal," was his only response. *No wonder Isaac is getting pissy with me. I'd be mad too, if I was being used as a glorified babysitter.*

"He's keeping things from you."

"He'll tell me when I need to know."

I huffed at him, annoyed at his assuredness. "You have such blind faith in him."

He shook his head at me and paused a moment before speaking. "I'm not from here, did you know that?"

"What are you talking about?"

"My sister, Diana, and I grew up in South Philadelphia. We never knew our father and the only memory I have of our mother is that she was blonde, like Diana was. I imagine she looked a lot like our mother, actually. Our whole lives we were in and out of foster care. Some situations were better than others. No matter how bad it was though, Diana and I always had each other."

As annoyed as I was at Roman for being here, I couldn't help but listen to his story. Roman didn't share often and an opportunity to see into his past was a rare chance I wouldn't pass up.

"So, what happened?" I asked tentatively. I already knew this story didn't have a happy ending.

"A few days after our 12th birthday, something changed. I awoke in the middle of the night with an intense pain in my chest. Like my lungs were on fire. I rushed to Diana's room, for some reason more concerned for her, even though I was in excruciating pain. I found her doubled over on the floor."

"You were being branded."

He nodded. "Obviously, we had no idea what was going on. Not long after, my powers manifested. Diana was always sensitive and one day our foster dad was mad at her for accidentally breaking a dish. I can still remember him, standing over her in the kitchen, screaming. She was just standing there, bawling. A poor, defenseless child." My eyes started to tear up as his voice got thick with emotion. "I screamed at him to get away from her, and before I knew it, the back door flew open and this huge burst of air flew in. Knocked him clear into the other wall. We knew we couldn't stay there, not after that, so we ran. For almost a year, we lived on our own. Squatting in houses, sleeping on benches, whatever it took. Until one day, a wraith found us. To this day I don't know if he sensed me, or if it was just dumb luck. Diana's powers never manifested and mine were in no way developed. I tried my best to fight him, but I was no match. He killed Diana first, but not before draining all the energy out of her. He was about to kill me when someone stopped him."

"Ezekiel," I said, finally understanding.

He nodded. "He saved my life. Took me in and taught me to be a warrior. He gave my life purpose. So, you see. It's not faith that makes me follow him. It's gratitude."

It wasn't hard to imagine the scenario Roman described. Two kids living on their own. Starving, scared, and trying to adjust to powers they were too young to understand or control. It explained Roman's loyalty to Ezekiel. If he raised him, of course he would look up to him. I could even see how his past influenced the way he treated me. Loss of someone close to you can make you zealous in protecting those you still have.

"How long ago was this?" I still didn't know Roman's real age.

"Fifteen years." I couldn't help it, my eyes bugged out, and my mouth popped open. Roman was 27. That made him ten years older than me. If he was branded at twelve, he had already been fighting wraiths for over half his life.

"What are you doing in high school?" I asked incredulously. I couldn't think of anything worse than repeating school over and over.

"Ezekiel and I didn't move here until a few years ago. Before that, we were living in a town on the other side of the Allegheny. I had graduated years before, but I still look young enough to be of school-age. Part of our cover story involved me repeating high school."

"That's miserable," I said. Then, I found myself saying the words I had always hated hearing. "I'm sorry about your sister."

"I wasn't able to protect her." He paused, considering his words carefully. "But I made a promise to myself that I would never let a wraith take someone close to me again."

Even though he didn't say it, I knew he was talking about me. "You have an interesting way of going about it." I might understand the reasons behind why he acted the way he did, but that didn't mean I was ready to forgive him.

"I know, and—"

"You really hurt me. And I'm not just talking literally," I interrupted.

"That's why—" he began again.

"I trusted you, and you kept information from me. You kissed me, then blew me off. Begged me to train, then interfered when I did. I can't—" I didn't get to finish my sentence. It's kind of hard to when someone is kissing you. The kiss was innocent and brief. When he pulled away, I looked back at him, stunned.

"Why did you do that?" I asked, taken aback.

He smiled at my confusion. "I've been trying to apologize this whole time, but you have a bad habit of interrupting. It seemed like the best way to shut you up."

I glared at him, momentarily rendered speechless. "You can't just kiss me whenever you want."

He smiled again. "Why not? You've seemed to enjoy it each time I have."

"That's beside the point," I told him. "It's not your right."

"And if I want it to be? I told you before, I want to get to know you better."

"Is that what you were doing in the training ring the other day? Getting to know me better?"

"I treated you like an equal in the ring, just like you wanted. When you're up against a wraith, they aren't going to pull any punches or go easy on you. You're being stubborn by refusing to train with anyone but Isaac. You're not going to improve that way. Not like you could if you trained with me."

Point taken.

"What about Paige?" I asked.

He exhaled loudly. "Paige doesn't mean anything. She never has. She only has an issue with you because of me. After what happened at the dance, she was the one person who could place you at the school when Evan died. I thought the best way to keep her quiet was to let her think she was getting what she wanted."

I shook my head, looking back toward the trees. "Meaning you."

I saw him nod out of the corner of my eye. "Paige is more concerned with what everyone thinks is happening than what really is. I talked to her a couple times in the hallway at school, gave her a few rides home. But nothing ever happened."

I swallowed sharply, trying to conceal how thrilled I was at his admission.

"Look," he continued, "can we just forget about Paige? I want to talk about us."

"Us?" I asked, turning to look at him.

"Obviously there is something between us. You can't deny that. We can barely keep our hands off each other."

I chuckled, even though nothing was funny right now. Everything he was saying was true. There was *something* between us. But it was nothing I deserved.

"I can't."

"Why not?" he asked desperately. "I messed up. I should have told you the truth from the beginning. I planned to at *Sandra's* that first night, but I just couldn't. Your powers hadn't manifested yet and I kept thinking that maybe you would make it. Maybe your House would come and go and you could be spared from this world of demons and death. And then you show up at The Ridge. The one place it was most dangerous for you to be. And I was so mad at you, like all my efforts to protect you were for nothing."

"But, you don't—" I started, interrupting again. But I didn't care. He needed to know that protecting me was not his job.

He continued as if I hadn't said anything. "I tried to get you to leave, but you're so damn stubborn. Then, you save my life. I can't tell you how guilty I feel that saving me is what solidified your gifts. But it wasn't until after the dance that I knew I'd lost you. I could see it in your eyes then. I still can. You blame yourself for what happened to Evan."

He reached up and wiped a tear I didn't realize had formed. "Why should I get the happily-ever-after when he didn't?"

"Evan didn't deserve to die. He was a great guy; nobody would dispute that. But you can't sacrifice your own happiness. It won't bring him back. You honor him by *living*."

His words echoed Lydia's. I was stunned silent. There was more emotion and truth in his tiny speech than I had seen the whole time I'd known him. It didn't excuse all of the missteps we had taken with one another, but it was a start. Unsure of what to say, and really not wanting to screw it up, I changed topic.

"I think my mom was Kindred."

He put both hands up. "I didn't know, I swear. Did Ezekiel tell you that?"

I breathed a sigh of relief. If he had known this and not told me, I don't think I could have recovered. "Not directly, but it's the only thing that makes sense. He said she took something valuable and now Ezekiel wants me to help find it. Problem is, I have no idea where to even start."

"Alessandra. Start with her."

I shook my head. "She was only a kid when my dad ran

away with my mom."

"We'll figure it out, I promise."

I stared at him. "We?"

"Yes, we. I'm not letting you do this alone."

I nodded, suddenly completely exhausted. "Will you take me home?"

He didn't hesitate. "I'll have Isaac tell Lydia." Too tired to argue, I followed him back to the makeshift parking lot where his bike waited. When we reached it, a small giggle escaped my lips. Roman turned to me, an amused look on his face. "What's so funny?"

"Nothing," I replied, my laughter growing. "I'm just thinking about Lydia's reaction when she hears I left a party with you. *Again.*"

We shared a moment of quiet laughter before we took off into the night.

15

It was almost noon by the time I woke up. It was a Monday, but we didn't have school. Teachers were using the day to prepare grades before our final three weeks.

I rolled sluggishly out of bed, noticing that the body paint I had been too lazy to wash off last night was now smeared all over my sheets. "Perfect," I mumbled. I collected the sheets, trudged down the steps and put them in the wash. When I returned to my room, I eyed the boxes in the corner. It was all that remained of my family's belongings. It occurred to me late last night that the answers about my mom might lie in there, but I was too chicken to find out. Now, in the daylight, I couldn't seem to avoid them anymore.

Shower first, I decided.

Shower then coffee, I amended.

Freshly clean, and now paint free, I sat in front of the boxes, my wet hair dripping down the back of my T-shirt, warm mug in-hand. I grabbed the closest box and opened it. On top was an old sweatshirt of my dad's. He wore it almost every time he worked in the garage. It was covered in stains and holes. It smelled of gasoline and oil. The scents were so much stronger now. I set it lovingly in my lap.

Three hours later almost all the boxes were open, their contents covering the floor. I paused when I felt a familiar cool breeze dance up my spine. Roman was here. I took a deep breath. Shortly after, he stood in the doorway to my room.

"You can come in," I told him. He didn't ask me how I knew he was here, which made me wonder if he felt something when I was near as well. I was too afraid to ask.

The floorboards creaked as he stepped in the room. He sat precariously on the edge of my bed. "What's all this?" he asked.

"My parents' stuff," I replied without looking up from what I was doing. "At least what we didn't sell. I thought a lot about what you said last night—that I should honor Evan by living. I'm going to start by finding what my mother stole." I handed him the small notebook in front of me.

"What's this?"

I shrugged. Nervous, I turned to look at him. "I think it's a journal of some sort. It's my mother's handwriting."

"What does it say?" he asked, searching my face for unspoken answers.

"I only read the first page."

"What about the rest?"

"Will you do it?" I asked, my voice timid. It wasn't easy for me to ask for help.

"Me?" he responded, clearly surprised. "I don't know what I'm looking for."

"Anything that mentions *The Book of Breathings*."

Shock registered on his face. He obviously knew the importance of the book. I cringed. I knew I wasn't the one who took it, but I was ashamed just the same. "Please, don't ask," I begged. I could tell he was dying to say something, but thankfully he didn't. Instead, he opened the journal and began reading.

I returned to the boxes, hoping to distract myself. Over an hour later, Roman was still reading and hadn't said a word about what he'd learned. The anticipation and fear was piling up and I needed a way to take the edge off. Deciding a run was the best option, I headed outside.

As soon as I hit the trees, I took off. The sun was below the tree line, casting the forest into opposing shadows and light. Months ago, I would have had trouble seeing and probably would have lost my footing, but now I didn't even think about it. I opened up my powers, letting them push me, reveling in the release. I ran faster than humanly possible. At this time of day, I wasn't worried about people spotting me.

I didn't stop until my lungs burnt. My route took me to a small clearing with an open view of the sky. The sun was below the horizon now and the stars were out to play. I laid back in the dewy grass and stared up at them. When I was younger, I used to lay outside with my mom for hours looking at the stars. Texas has such an open sky, I sometimes thought we could see every star in the universe. Now, I laid here, naming the constellations she taught me. I found Orion first. The belt's three bright stars were always mom's favorite. From there I traveled to Taurus, Pegasus, past Cancer to Leo the proud Lion. As I was searching for the Hydra, one of my childhood favorites, the sounds of the forest stopped. The springtime animals had been busy chirping and stirring the landscape, excited about the rising temperatures. But now there was nothing. Only silence. Even the trees had stopped rustling in the wind. I sat up quickly, my instincts kicking in. I looked around the clearing. I didn't see anyone, but I knew someone was there. I could feel their eyes on me.

"I know you're there!" I yelled. "I don't want any trouble!"

I dipped into my power while I listened for a response. My hand started to warm at what I knew were the beginnings of a fireball, but I didn't fully create it. The possibility was slim, but it could be an innocent person out for an evening hike. This forest was occupied by hunters, fishermen, hikers, and nature enthusiasts of all kinds, and I'd hate to see what happened if I ran into one of them while holding a living flame in my hand. *That would just be awkward.*

I started to think I was imagining things when I saw

movement to my left. Some sort of dark shape was leaning against a tree. I focused my eyes and jumped to my feet at what, or rather—who—I saw there.

Definitely not an innocent hiker, Deacon leaned against the tree, oozing arrogance and danger. The half-formed fireball jumped to life in my hand and I launched it at him. He sidestepped lazily as the fireball ricocheted off the tree behind him, leaving embers smoldering in the bark.

"Don't be rude," he said.

Ignoring him, I threw another fireball, but it missed too. I noticed that while he was avoiding being hit, he wasn't making any move to attack.

"I just came to talk," he tried again.

Literally seeing red, I threw again. Another miss. "I have no interest in *anything* you have to say." Last time I saw Deacon, he had fed from me and killed Evan. *Now he wants to talk?* "You murdered my friend!" I screamed at him.

"The boy interfered," he responded without remorse. "He had no business being there and you know it. If you could have left him alone in the first place, he'd still be alive."

His words hit home. The ever-present guilt rushed forward and I lost my grip on my powers. The heat from my hand dissipated. My shoulders slumped forward and my eyes welled up. *He's right. Evan is dead because of me.*

"What do you want, Deacon?"

"I simply came for a closer look. I've heard about your kind for years, but there's never been one in existence, at least not in my lifetime. And last time we were together, we were *interrupted.*" He looked me up and down now, assessing me. "Can't say I'm impressed. If you weren't the key to all this, I'd kill you where you stand."

I looked up at him, surprised. "You're not going to kill me?" At our last encounter, he had no issues with killing me and anyone else in his way. *Now all of a sudden he wants to keep me alive?*

He laughed. The sound was deranged. It was cruel, hungry, insane. "Oh, Kyndal. I have every intention of killing you, just not until you've played your role. And when I am done with you, you will beg me to end your life."

His words sent a chill through my bones. "Did you know what I was when we met?"

"I was told your aunt was familiar with the terrain, that she was the best at finding hidden places. Her relation to you is just an added bonus."

His words clicked something in place. "You're looking for the book, aren't you? And if you need Alessandra's help, it must mean it's in the Allegheny."

The smile vanished from his face and his eyes turned bloodshot, showing me, however briefly, a glimpse of his real self. "Clever girl."

Emboldened by getting one-up on him, I pressed on. "You won't get it. And whatever plans you have for me, I'd forget about them. I'm not very good at following orders. How's your cheek by the way?" I asked, referencing the still vivid outline of my hand on his face. It reminded me of the damage I was capable of. My strength. *My power.*

His lip twitched, causing the scars to raise. "Careful, Kindred," he sneered, his tone murderous, "before I forget your necessity and kill you now. Better yet, your blue-eyed lover."

Unconsciously, my power rushed forward. A fireball now sat in my hand. My voice came out a growl. "You will not *touch* him."

Deacon laughed, but wisely backed away farther into the trees. Even from that distance, I could see his black veins pulsing. "See you soon, child of Aries." Then, he vanished.

/|\

By the time I made it back to the house, Roman was waiting for me where the forest met the yard.

"Where have you been?" he asked hastily. *Man, he really does have a temper.* I decided not to tell him about Deacon until after he calmed down. Instead, I went for my usual tactic—distraction.

"Did you learn anything from the journal?"

"Mostly it's just stories. About your father, your brother," he paused, "you." I nodded, trying not to think about it too much. Memories of my past were still too difficult to think about. "You guys seemed close," he added. I turned my face away.

"Yea—yeah" I said, after pausing to clear the emotion from my throat. "We were."

"I did find one thing," Roman said. He dug in his back pocket and pulled out an old picture that was folded over many times. It was obviously from several years ago judging by the quality and weariness of it. Someone had held this picture many times and worried over it. According to the writing on the back, it was taken in June 1980. Four people stood in the picture. Three women and one man. They were all smiling, their arms around each other.

I pointed at the one on the end. "That's my mom." From what I could tell she was about twenty, which didn't make sense considering she should have been six years old in 1980. It did play into my theory that she was Kindred, just like me. They stood outside, the forest at their back, sand at their feet. "Is that a training ring?" I asked Roman, who was watching me carefully.

"I think so," he answered, "but that's not the most interesting part." He pointed at the woman directly next to my mother in the picture. "Recognize her?" he asked. I studied the picture closely. Her features seemed vaguely familiar, but I couldn't come up with a name.

"Should I?" I asked, coming up empty.

"Her name is Sandra."

The name instantly registered. *Sandra's* was where Roman took me on our date. They seemed familiar at the time, but

I had no clue she was a part of our world.

"I didn't know she was Kindred," I said.

"She's not. Well—not really. She's—You see—" I gave him a funny look at his obvious loss of words. "It's—it's tough to explain. Just think of her as retired."

"Do you think she'd help us?" I asked, hopeful. He nodded.

"Then what are we waiting for?"

/|\

Sandra's at near midnight on a Monday was completely dead. As we walked in, there was no one in sight, not even Sandra. The lights were on and music was playing, though. The bell over the door rang as we walked in.

"Sorry! We're closed!" A voice yelled. Sandra rounded the corner moments later, carrying pallets of glasses. She glanced over, smiling when she saw Roman, her face lighting up with genuine joy. She set the glasses on the bar. "Roman! Hi. What's going on?" Her joy was short-lived however, because as soon as she saw me, her face dropped into a cold, unfriendly mask. *What did I do to her?*

"I need your help," he said. Without further ado, he handed her the picture. She took it, gasping when she unfolded it.

"No," she said forcefully, shoving the picture back into Roman's hands. "Anything but this. You two need to leave." She turned us both around, pushing us toward the door. Seeing my chance at answers slipping away, I moved out of her grasp.

"Please," I begged. "The woman in the picture next to you, Sofia, what do you know about her?"

"I will not discuss her," Sandra responded icily.

"I'm begging you. It's life or death."

Her eyes flared with anger. "Do you think I don't know who you are?" Her voice was accusatory. "You stand here, a spitting image of that woman and demand answers. From me?" she shook her head vigorously. "No. I have given enough of my life to that traitorous woman. I will not help her again. I will not give anymore." Her tone left no room for discussion.

Roman walked over and whispered in my ear, suggesting that I wait outside. With one last death-glare at Sandra, I headed to the door. I paused when I reached it. "She's dead, you know." I turned back around. "My mother. She died a horrible, painful, fiery death, while I watched helplessly. So whatever your issue is with her, maybe you could at the very least, show an *ounce* of respect." I slammed the door, allowing it to echo behind me.

/|\

Roman and I drove home in silence. He wasn't any more successful with Sandra by himself. She obviously knew something about my mom, but she wasn't talking. I kept replaying her reaction in my head. Her outburst when she saw the picture was violent and there was pure hatred in her voice. My whole life, my mom was the sweetest, most caring person I'd ever met. But now, I was beginning to wonder how much of that was true. According to Sandra, I was the daughter of a traitor.

When we pulled into my driveway, the house was pitch dark. Allie wouldn't return from her excursion until tomorrow. I got out of the Jeep quietly. Roman followed me to the door.

"I'm sorry we didn't get the answers you were looking for."

I smiled sadly. "It's not your fault. At least you tried though, right?" I wanted to be uplifting, but I knew I failed. A soft breeze moved through the porch, pushing my hair in my eyes. Before I could fix it, Roman's eyes changed color, a luminescent blue to a liquid gold, and the wind changed direction. It caressed my face, gently moving my hair back in place. My stomach tightened and my breathing picked up. Roman searched my face, studying every inch as if committing it to memory. I knew he wanted to kiss me. I took a small step toward him. He surprised me when he stepped back. "Good night, Kyndal."

I stupidly watched him walk away. He made it to his Jeep door before I found my voice. "Stay!" I yelled. He turned to look at me.

He took a deep, unsteady breath. "I don't think that's a good idea." I understood why he said it. He was trying to respect my wishes and stay away. But I wasn't sure that's what I wanted anymore. Something had changed between us. Whatever this *thing* we had was, it was getting harder to ignore.

"I know, but do it anyway." I was begging, but I didn't care. "My aunt is gone until tomorrow and I don't want to be alone. Please. At least until I fall asleep."

We stared at each other for a while. I could see his internal battle. After almost a full minute of silence, I folded. I opened the door and walked inside. I didn't hear his footsteps follow. His rejection stung. I headed to the upstairs bathroom, washed my face, brushed my teeth, and changed into the tank and boy shorts I typically wear to bed. I walked into my bedroom and gasped. Roman was sitting on the edge of the bed, his eyes glued to me. I really didn't think he'd stay. His eyes took a lazy stroll from my toes all the way up, slower in some places than others. The expression on his face said it all. Suddenly aware of how little I was wearing, I blushed head to toe.

"I can't promise I'll stay," he said quietly.

"I know." And I did. I understood that what I was asking wasn't fair—not that it kept me from asking it. Selfishly, I rounded the bed before he could change his mind. I pulled back the covers and slid into bed. Once I was situated, Roman stood, his back to me. He kicked off his shoes then reached for his shirt. I watched quietly until he went for his pants button.

"What are you doing?" I asked quickly.

He turned and looked at me, confused. "Going to bed."

"With your pants off?"

"I'm wearing boxers," he said as if that explained everything. I just stared at him. "You expect me to sleep in my jeans?"

"Yes!" I answered definitively. He rolled his eyes, but kept his pants on. He turned off the bedside lamp before climbing into bed next to me. The room was dark except for the moonlight shining through my thin window curtains. It didn't provide much, but it was enough for us to see each other.

My bed was small, but he somehow managed to fit his large frame onto the mattress without touching me. We both laid there silently, not moving for what felt like forever. Finally, I broke the silence.

"Well, this is awkward."

The bed shook with his quiet laughter. "Get some sleep. You have school tomorrow."

"So do you," I pointed out.

"I'm not going. I'm gonna take another run at Sandra."

"You really think she'll talk? She didn't seem too helpful tonight."

I felt him shrug. "Sandra's history with the Kindred is a sordid one. They aren't exactly on the best of terms, to put it lightly. That being said, it doesn't hurt to try again. If she's going to help anyone, it would be me."

"What makes you so special?"

He turned on his side, facing me. "Several things make me special," he teased. "I could show you a few, if you like."

My eyebrows shot up at his thinly veiled innuendo and my cheeks flushed red. "You know that's not what I mean."

He smiled at me, reveling in my embarrassment. Then, taking a deep breath, he got back to the issue. "Sandra was branded in the last century. She was well-revered until she, along with a few others, broke Kindred law nearly 20 years ago."

I threw my arms up, fully exasperated. "We have *laws*? Every time I turn around, there is something new with you people!"

Roman smirked at my frustration. "Not many. And it's not like they're written down anywhere."

"No," I said sarcastically, "that would make it too simple. So what did she do?"

"She's never told me. All I know is, she didn't act alone. She, along with two others, were put on trial in front of the Council. All three were found guilty of conspiracy to commit treason. They were forbidden to ever use their powers again."

My eyes bulged. "They can do that?"

He reached out and grabbed my hand. He turned it over, exposing my brand. "Remember I told you the brand works as protection against wraith possession?" I nodded. "Damaging, disfiguring or removing the mark negates that protection. The Council ordered Sandra and the others to remain near an active group of Kindred. If they tried to leave, or were caught practicing, their brand would be removed, leaving them vulnerable."

His story brought a sick feeling to my stomach. "You think she helped my mom steal the book."

"It seems the most logical conclusion," he responded, rubbing his thumb on the back of my hand, something I wasn't sure he was aware he was still doing.

"So, she's a prisoner?" I asked. "Wouldn't know it from the way she acts toward you."

"Being stripped of your powers is the worst punishment a Kindred can receive, apart from death. Add on to that the suffocating feeling of being the ward of the Kindred, Sandra isn't exactly a fan of us."

"But she talks to you, likes you even. What changed?"

He cracked a genuine smile. "Me. I've already told you that Ezekiel took me in when I was young. Well, he might have known how to train me, but he had no idea what to do with me outside of that. I was a young, angry kid, mad at the world. Sandra stepped in. For several years she taught me, fed me, bought me clothes, yelled at me when I screwed up. When Ezekiel and I moved to Marienville, she followed. I was old enough to be on my own, so she opened the bar as an escape."

"She raised you?" I asked. "If she hates the Kindred so much, why would she be willing to do that?"

"Many Kindred never have a family. I mean, we're capable of it, but with the constant danger, and lack of aging, most consider it to be unrealistic. Given the chance to raise a child within our world, without being forced to hide the impossible things we are capable of—it's not an easy thing to pass up."

"But she can never leave. Never have a life of her own."

He shook his head. "I like to think those years with me made it better for her."

There was really nothing to say to that, so I stayed quiet.

"Now, sleep Kyndal."

"So bossy," I pouted playfully. But I closed my eyes anyway. The bed shook again with his laughter. With only our hands touching, and the cooling feel of Roman's powers dancing up my arm, I fell into a deep, blissful sleep.

16

The next morning, I was rudely awoken by my alarm clock. I tried to reach it, desperate to stop the insistent noise, but I couldn't move. When I figured out why, I blushed a deep crimson. Not only did Roman stay, but we had moved positions sometime during the night. We were now a tangle of arms and legs. His left arm was around me, pinning me to his side, while my arm was draped over his bare chest. I managed to untangle myself from him long enough to turn off the alarm, but when I moved, he followed me, pulling me back down to him and nuzzling my neck in the process, effectively pinning me on my back.

Dear, sweet, holy Moses.

I stayed as still as possible, afraid to make any sudden movements. Instead, I focused on my breathing.

In.

Out.

In.

Out.

I could tell the moment he woke up. His breathing stopped and he became very still. His eyes opened and looked around slowly. He looked at me and I held my breath, waiting for the inevitable. I knew at any moment he would pull away. But he didn't. Instead, he sat up, leaning on one elbow. His other hand reached out, moving smoothly across my stomach, landing tightly on my hip. Sweet shivers of power I still didn't understand followed his touch, making the hairs on my arms stand up.

His fingers kneaded my skin and his gaze dropped to my lips. He leaned toward me, and my lips parted instinctively. Just as his lips touched mine, the silence was shattered by the screech of a buzzer.

The trance broken, Roman pulled back, sitting up quickly on the opposite edge of the bed. I scrambled to my alarm clock, making sure to turn it off this time, not just snooze. Embarrassed, I ran to my dresser, grabbed my clothes for the day and ducked into my bathroom. By the time I emerged, Roman was standing at the window, fully dressed.

I opened my mouth to apologize, but he spoke before I got a chance.

"I'll give you a ride to school."

It was a quiet ride. Roman and I both seemed to be lost in our own thoughts. He kept his eyes on the road the whole time, making sure to never look at me. I should have used the time to tell him about Deacon's visit yesterday, but

213

instead, my mind was stuck in an endless loop, replaying the events of this morning.

When we reached the school, Roman parked toward the back. Getting seen together in the morning wasn't a good idea. "I'll come by tonight after I've talked to Sandra. Hopefully, I'll have some answers for you." His voice was quiet, reserved. I could tell the moment between us this morning was affecting him, too.

I nodded and opened my door. I didn't feel right leaving him to talk to Sandra without me. This was my battle, too. "Be careful," I told him. I started to say something about this morning, but at the last second, I chickened out. Instead, I said the lamest thing possible. "Thanks for the ride."

/|\

By late that evening, I still hadn't heard from Roman. I tried my hardest to focus on my chemistry book in front of me, but I looked up every few seconds, waiting for headlights to pull into my driveway, but they never came. The unease that began the moment I left Roman's car that morning had festered all day. It started with me just wanting to know what was going on. I attempted to make up my missed lit exam, but I spent most of the time wondering if Roman was successful. It was made worse when I tried to find Isaac to see if he had heard anything. I couldn't find him anywhere, even though I knew he had been at school that morning. Lydia told me he had gone home sick during lunch. I knew full well that Isaac wasn't sick. Something was going on, and I needed to know what.

I had half-a-mind to go directly to Roman's after school, but Alessandra was coming home, and she would expect me. We spent the evening making small talk. For the most part I just listened to her tell me about her latest excursion. I tried my hardest to pay attention, but every little noise I heard made me jump, wondering if it was Roman at my door with answers.

Allie was finally asleep upstairs, exhausted from her trip. Unable to wait any longer, I pulled the phone out of my pocket. Ezekiel had given me a cell phone a few days ago, insistent that I be reachable at any time. I texted Roman. *Where r u?* I waited as long as I could for a response, but none came. Moving as quietly as possible, I snuck out the back door, taking special care to keep the door from squeaking.

I took the trail to Roman's as fast as possible. When I broke into the clearing behind his house, it was completely deserted. I focused my energy and tried to tap into the strange connection Roman and I shared, using it to look for him. I pushed it as far as I could, but I came up empty. The familiar cool breeze wasn't there. And if he wasn't here, something must have gone wrong.

There was movement at the main house. When I reached the front door I was almost plowed over by someone running out. He didn't stop, not even to apologize. He threw a bag into the back of a truck and climbed in. He honked the horn several times impatiently. "Come on! Let's move!" he yelled.

I ran over to the stranger. His skin was dark like Isaac's.

His eyes were sharp, focused, and a beautiful caramel brown. "What's going on?" He ignored me.

"Let's go! Move it!" he yelled again. Two people piled out of the house at inhuman speed, so fast I couldn't track them until they reached the truck. I recognized one as Mallory, the woman from my testing. All of them seemed to be in a hurry. *Something* was going on. Finally, the driver looked at me.

"Wraiths attacked just outside of town. Some of our people were there. Not all of them made it. Some are still trapped."

My heart dropped. *Roman.* Even though he didn't say it, I knew it had to be him. "I'm coming with you," I told him, already reaching for the door.

"We don't have time to babysit newborn Kindred," Mallory sneered from the backseat. *Wow. She really doesn't like me.* My anger rose at her condescending comment. My hands began to heat up, turning the truck's door a molten orange. I didn't care that they were seeing me create my element. I didn't care that it was supposed to be a secret. All I cared about was getting to Roman. I stared right at Mallory. "I'm not asking," I shot back, speaking slowly and punctuating each word. The driver looked down at my hands.

"We don't have time for this," he said to Mallory. To me, "Get in. But stay out of the way."

I nodded, pulling my powers back before getting in the back and piling in next to Mallory. She gave me a dirty look, but I didn't care. If she didn't like me, it was her problem, not mine.

The driver, who I learned was named Darius, drove like a bat out of hell. He didn't even slow down as he went through town, though luckily traffic was almost non-existent. We went unnoticed. Just as I had feared, Darius brought the truck to a roaring stop not far from *Sandra's*. As we jumped out of the truck, I noticed there was already a handful of Kindred on scene. Ezekiel, Cassie, and Isaac were there, as well as three others I didn't recognize. With the four of us from the truck, our numbers sat at ten. Roman was nowhere to be seen. When we reached the group, they were in the middle of a strategy meeting. I stood toward the back. I was able to hear what was being said and I wouldn't draw any attention to myself there.

Ezekiel was mid-sentence. "—minimum of five wraiths. We know that Roman went in there with two others, although we do not know the status of any of them, or of any patrons that might have been in the establishment." I continued to listen even as I pushed my power out. It moved toward *Sandra's*, searching for Roman. I concentrated, pulling from the surrounding elements to amplify my range. I kept searching, not stopping until finally I could barely, *just barely*, feel a soft, cool breeze on my back.

I interrupted Ezekiel. "Roman is alive." The whole group turned to look at me.

"You're sure of it?" he asked.

I nodded. "He's weak. Most likely injured. But he's alive."

"You can't possibly know that!" Mallory shouted at me.

She is really getting annoying.

I glared at her across the group. "You're just going to have to accept that I do." Before she could say something else snotty, Ezekiel spoke up.

"What of the others? Are they alive?"

I shook my head, my eyes darting around to all the Kindred looking to me for answers, for hope.

"I—I don't know. I'm sorry. I just know that Roman is."

Ezekiel nodded quickly, accepting the limits of my powers. Then, he wasted no time creating a plan of attack. I listened carefully. He placed the air and fire users at the front, their powers being the most helpful getting in the bar and disabling the wraiths. I was surprised to find he included me in the plan. The earth and water users were the second wave, focusing on hand-to-hand combat in case it was necessary. His plan was smart. It was obvious he was much more than just a bureaucrat.

We were separated into two groups. Ezekiel ordered the first group to go through the main entrance and the second through the back door accessed through the porch. Isaac and I were the only fire users in the group, so we were split up. My group, comprised of Cassie, two earth users, and much to my chagrin—Mallory, were sent around back. As an Aries, my role was key. Our orders were to wait until we heard the first group breach the door, then I would throw a fireball through the back one. Mallory was set to move in first, using her air powers to push any wraiths away from the Kindred and others trapped inside. The earth and water users would handle anyone she missed.

We crouched on the back porch, hidden in darkness, waiting for the signal. Nervous, I continuously flicked the lighter Isaac gave me. Even though it wasn't a necessity, I was happy he gave it to me. Last thing I needed was my powers stalling.

"Don't screw this up," Mallory whispered in my ear. *Thanks for the pep talk.*

Luckily, we didn't have to wait long. The sound of an explosion rang from the front of the building and I knew Isaac had breached the front door. I didn't hesitate. I flicked the lighter, calling forth my powers at the same time. They came to me quickly, fast tracked by my adrenaline. I threw the fireball, exploding the door into a million splinters. Mallory leapt inside, her feet landing before parts of the shattered door.

As soon as she landed, she splayed her arms out in either direction. The wind picked up out of nowhere, eager to do her bidding. She pinned two wraiths to opposite walls. A third wraith appeared from Sandra's office, noticed her vulnerable state and ran for her, blood lust written on his face. Before he could reach her, a streak of red crossed the room. Cassie had joined the fight. Spinning and flipping, they were stuck in a deadly dance. Members of the first team had also engaged. It seemed we had underestimated their original numbers. There were at least seven wraiths here. While the fight raged on, I searched for Roman. I moved through the room, stopping only when I reached a felled body. I felt for a pulse on each one I encountered, but every time, I found nothing. I avoided looking at their faces. Kindred or not, I couldn't know yet. I didn't want to know. I couldn't help but notice other details: the stab wounds in the stomach, the pool of blood surrounding the body. One was completely desiccated. The skin was pulled taut, all color leached from it. It reminded me of how Alessandra described the dead hiker. All that remained was a shallow husk of the former person. I had crossed at least five on the floor. Five dead.

As I moved across the room, I stayed low to the ground. The summoned fire and wind filled the room with a smoky haze, turning visibility to almost zero. As I neared the pool tables, the feeling on my spine increased and I knew I must be getting closer. Finally, I spotted him, thrown in a bloody, unconscious heap in the corner of the room. I dropped to my knees as I reached him. His tall frame was twisted to the side and I couldn't see his face. Delicately, I turned him to his back, my fingers checking for a pulse. I couldn't help but exhale when I found it. My senses told me he was alive, but I still needed the confirmation. I started checking him for wounds, beginning at the top. His head was bleeding and he had multiple bruises along his cheeks and jaws. It looked like someone had pummeled the crap out of him. There was a pool of blood on his shirt. I took a deep breath, preparing myself for what I might find, and lifted up his shirt. Just below his rib cage, on his left side, was a deep stab wound. Blood was seeping out of it slowly. I didn't think he had much left of it to lose. I pushed both my hands down on the wound, trying to stop the bleeding, when suddenly a backhand whipped across my face.

I was thrown back, my head knocking into the nearby pool table. My vision went blurry for a second, but I could still make out the dark shape moving my direction. I got to my feet despite the dizziness. Just as I did, the wraith struck out again and the fight was on. Acting on instinct, and thankful for the little training I'd been given, I managed to hold my own. We traded blows back and forth, and while I was taking several hits, I managed to give as good as I got. My confidence started to rise and I thought I might win—until he reached behind his back and pulled out a long dagger.

Crap.

The wraith smiled at me, his sharp teeth bright in contrast with the dark veins that dominated his face. Weaponless, I went strictly on the defense, managing to dodge his main attacks. He managed to cut me once on the arm, but luckily it was superficial. I heard my name yelled across the room. I threw a hard kick, briefly knocking down the wraith, allowing me to look away. I locked eyes with Cassie.

Her arm moved quickly and something shiny came flying my direction. Luckily I realized what it was. I snatched the dagger from the air by the hilt. The metal was cool and unfamiliar in my hand. Other than the brief, disastrous sparring incident with Mallory, I'd never handled a weapon before.

"Help Roman!" I shouted back at her, right as the wraith I was fighting got back up. I managed to keep the wraith busy long enough to see Cassie get to Roman. Eventually though, my inexperience showed through, and I made a mistake. I pushed the wraith with both hands. He slid back, leaving his torso exposed. I lunged with the dagger. The movement was sloppy. He easily deflected it and his right arm thrust forward, hitting me in the nose with the hilt of his dagger. My own dagger flew from my hand with the force of the blow as I dropped to the ground. I vaguely heard it clatter nearby along the ground. The wraith pinned me down, straddling my hips. He placed a hand over my heart just as his mouth twisted in a bloody smile. My experience with Deacon told me what was coming next. If I didn't do something, I would end up a dried up husk like the one laying on the other side of the room.

I reached my right hand out, blindly searching for the dagger, even as I felt the wraith start to pull on my powers. Finally, my fingers touched cool metal and I wrapped them around the hilt. Without thinking, I raised my arm, bringing it down hard into the back of the wraith. As the dagger sliced through him, his face froze in surprise. I was sure my own expression matched his. It was only seconds before his body started to crumble, breaking apart until there was nothing left but a thin sheet of dust on my skin. I laid there, breathing hard, the dagger still in my hand. Only two thoughts entered my brain.

I killed him.

But more importantly—

I survived.

17

It was chaos.

The fight was over, but there was still a lot to do. All ten of the Kindred that stormed the place survived, although some were injured. Cassie and Isaac took Roman out through the newly made front door, driving off in a hurry. I wanted nothing more than to go with them, but I knew I was needed here. I never saw Sandra in the melee, and she was not among the dead on the floor. *She must be here somewhere.*

I made my way over the rubble, toward her office. I found her right inside the door, tied to a chair. Her back was to me and her head was slumped forward. I cautiously walked around to her front, fearing the worst. Blood dripped from her fingers. Most of her fingernails had been ripped off, presumably with the pliers I saw laying on the floor. I knelt down in front of her. I noticed the shallow rise and fall of her chest and I slumped with relief.

She's alive.

I slowly lifted her head. I had to hold back the bile in my throat at what I saw. She was soaked in blood. Her face was almost completely covered with bruises. Both her eyes were swollen shut and her lip was cut and bleeding. I pulled at the ropes, but they didn't budge. Frantically, I searched the room for something to cut the ropes with. I found a kitchen knife on the floor. It must have been thrown there in the chaos of the fight. Her arms now free, I carefully picked Sandra up, cradling her in my arms. I struggled to make it out to the main area without dropping her.

"Help!" I called out. Several Kindred rushed my way. The closest one, a serious looking man, took Sandra from me. "She needs medical attention."

I sat down on a broken piece of the bar and put my head in my hands to catch my breath.

The two Kindred that came to Sandra's with Roman didn't make it. The others wrapped their bodies reverently in different colored material. One in blue, the other green. I wondered about the color choice, but didn't ask anyone. Now was not the time. The one wrapped in green was the desiccated body I had seen earlier. Everyone stopped moving and stood silently as they were taken from the building, so I did the same.

The bodies were placed carefully in the back of a waiting van. Everyone else loaded up. I got back in the truck with Darius, although this time Mallory had no snide comments. She sat in the back, cradling her left arm. "What about the others?" I asked quietly. We left three dead people behind. People who had done nothing wrong other than choose the wrong place to eat that evening.

Darius answered, "Once we're clear, someone will call the sheriff. Make an anonymous tip of suspicious activity. He'll handle it from there."

"That's horrible." To just leave those poor people behind, as if their deaths didn't matter felt wrong.

"There is nothing we can do for them now," Mallory said bluntly, but it lacked her usual bitchiness. She wasn't any happier about the situation than I was.

When we made it back to the house, I immediately looked for Cassie and Isaac. I didn't find either of them in the main house, so I headed next door. When I walked in, all the lights were turned on. In the kitchen, Cassie and Isaac were a flurry of activity. Roman's still unconscious form was laid out on the counter, his tall frame barely fitting.

"What can I do to help?" I asked.

Neither of them stopped moving, but Cassie did respond.

"Grab those scissors." She pointed to the pair sitting next to Roman. "Cut his shirt off. I need access to the wound."

I did what she said without argument.

"Isaac, apply pressure to the wound. We'll need to move quickly. If he wakes up in the middle of this, he won't be happy. We need to clean the wound and close it to stop the bleeding. If we can do that, he has a chance."

"Can't he heal himself?" I asked her.

She shook her head furiously. When she responded, her tone was frustrated. "His wound is too severe. We're going to have to help him out. Kyndal, do exactly as I tell you."

I followed every direction she gave me. She cleaned the wound vigorously and thoroughly, first using wet washcloths and then some antiseptic scrub that I knew would sting like hell if Roman was awake to feel it. The wound sterilized, she grabbed a needle and thread and began stitching him up. About half way through it, Roman started to come around.

"Hold him down," Cassie ordered. Her eyes never left his wound and her hands never faltered. Isaac reached over, pushing down on Roman's shoulders, keeping him pinned to the counter even as he started to thrash around. Trying to help, I moved to Roman's head. I placed my hands on either side of his face and whispered quietly to him that everything would be okay. His eyes opened briefly, searching the room wildly before passing out again.

Cassie finished the stitches. "We need to get him upstairs and comfortable."

Isaac picked him up, cradling him in his arms; no small feat. I followed him up and turned the covers down so he could get him in bed. I sat on the edge of the bed and took his hand.

"I'll stay with him," I told the others.

"You look pretty beat up yourself. I should take a look at your wounds," Cassie replied.

"I'm fine!" I snapped at her. I took a deep breath. "I'm sorry. But I'll be fine, thank you."

Isaac stood with his arms crossed, eyes narrowed. Cassie took a step back into the room. I could tell she wanted to say something, but was holding back. I was too tired to be patient.

"Just ask, Cassie."

"Outside *Sandra's* you told Ezekiel that you knew Roman was alive. How?"

"I didn't know for sure," I lied.

"Ezekiel believed you. And he doesn't listen to many people. Were you in communication with him?"

I spun around and faced her, dragging my hands through my greasy, bloodied hair. "We weren't in contact. I just said what I had to so Ezekiel would let me in on the rescue."

"She lying," Isaac said to Cassie.

I ignored him and focused on Cassie. "How I knew he was alive doesn't matter. All that matters is that he gets better. Now, if you don't mind, I'd like to focus on Roman."

She gave me one final disapproving look before heading back down the stairs, pushing Isaac along with her. I was finally alone with Roman. It was the middle of the night. I was dirty, sweaty, covered in blood—both mine and other's—and my energy level was running on E, but I refused to fall asleep. Instead, I alternated between running my thumb back and forth over Roman's hand and watching his chest rise and fall steadily.

I never should have let him go to Sandra's without me. If I had been there, I could've helped protect him. It was thoughts like these that occupied my mind through the night. I only left Roman's side once, to take a quick shower. I didn't want to leave him, but Isaac forced me to, pointing out that Roman wouldn't want to see my dirty, bloody face first thing when he opened his eyes. I stepped quickly into Roman's attached bathroom, stopping to open the window in his loft. I did it in the hopes that exposure to the outdoor breeze would bring him strength.

I took a look at myself in the mirror and cringed. My face was covered in dried blood and wraith dust. I was also sporting a pretty impressive shiner on my left cheek. My hair was an absolute rat's nest. I showered quickly. With no change of clothes, I was forced to put back on my dirty jeans and T-shirt.

I immediately returned to Roman's side, stroking his hand and counting his breaths. I must have fallen asleep at some point, because one moment it was silent and dark, and the next—there was light streaming through the window and Roman was moving.

The unexpected movement pulled me up from where I had laid my head on the edge of the bed. I anxiously looked at his face, waiting for him to open his eyes. I started to pull my hand out of his, but his fingers tightened. I didn't want him to strain more than necessary, so I kept my hand where it was. Finally, his eyes opened. Beautiful blue looking right at me.

"Hey," I said soothingly. "How are you feeling?"

"This is starting to become a habit," he replied.

I didn't understand. "What's becoming a habit?"

"Waking up next to you."

I flushed a deep red. I tried to pull my hand away again. This time he let me.

"What time is it?" he asked. *Good question.* I looked at the clock on his dresser across the room.

"It's early still."

"You should be at school."

A small, humorless laugh escaped before I could stop it. "I'm not worried about school right now." That wasn't exactly true. By now, Alessandra knew I had snuck out last night and learning that I didn't go to school either would make her flip. And then there was Lydia. I hadn't talked to her since the rave and she didn't handle being ignored well. As if on cue, the phone in my pocket buzzed. I glanced at it and sure enough, it was Lydia.

> **There are 3 ppl dead at Sandra's bar and you are MIA.
> CALL ME!!! I AM FREAKING OUT HERE!!!**

Given her use of exclamation marks, she really meant it. I shot her a quick reply.

I'm fine. Call u when I can.

I felt my phone buzz again, but I ignored it. Roman was trying to sit up. Knowing it was pointless to stop him, I helped him sit back against the headboard. Just that small action put a light sheen of sweat on his brow.

"You're hurt," he said. Unconsciously, I touched the tips of my fingers to my bruised cheek. Leave it to him to be laid up with a stab wound and he's worried about my shiner.

"I'll be fine," I told him.

He shook his head and even laughed a little. "So stubborn."

I smiled. I knew I should probably wait, but I couldn't help it. "What happened, Roman?"

He didn't seem to take offense to my question, as he immediately answered. "I went to talk to Sandra, just like I told you. I took Lauren and Adelle with me, just in case." He didn't ask me what happened to them, so I assumed he knew. Selfishly, I was glad he did. I did not want to have to break that news. "I was in Sandra's back office with her when we heard sounds of a fight in the main bar. When we made it out there, a group of wraiths were surrounding everyone. Lauren was already dead and Adelle was unconscious on the floor. Deacon was there."

At the mention of Deacon's name, my stomach twisted with guilt. Deacon had threatened to go after Roman and I didn't warn him. My naivety cost five people their lives and almost cost Roman his.

Roman continued his story, oblivious to my internal lashing. "They were looking for something. Deacon must think Sandra has the book. We fought as hard as we could, Sandra and I both, but there were just too many. Is she okay?"

I reached out and grabbed his hand, hoping to provide some comfort. His eyes moved to our now joined fingers, then quickly back up to my eyes, concern etched on his face. "I found her in her office. She was pretty beat up. It looked like—" The images of her torn hands and swollen face entered my head. I had to swallow them down before I could finish. "Roman, it looked like she'd been tortured."

Before I could even finish talking, Roman was moving. He unceremoniously dropped my hand and pushed the covers back, trying to get out of bed. I stood quickly, gently pressing him back toward the bed. "What do you think you're doing?"

"I have to see her," he said, a determined look on his face.

"You—" I began, pushing him a little harder, until finally he laid back. It was a sign of how weak he was that I was even able to do so. "—need to stay in bed. You lost a lot of blood."

"I'm fine," he told me.

"Now who's being stubborn?" I asked him. Before he could stop me, I reached out and poked him in his wound. I knew it was a low blow, but I had a point to make. He immediately cried out in pain, his hand moving to cover his stitches. "That's what I thought," I said, matching his bullheadedness with my own. "You're not going anywhere. Stay put. You need your strength so you can heal yourself. You are no help to her like this. I'll go find out what I can. Promise me you'll stay put until I return."

Walking out of Roman's house, I passed Isaac. "Make sure he doesn't move."

"You giving orders now, Davenport?"

"Just do it!" I hollered back.

"Aries," I heard him mumble. "What a pain in the ass."

It took me a while to find Sandra. Eventually, I found her in an upstairs room of the main house. She was resting comfortably in a bed, being attended to by a woman I hadn't seen before. Her wounds had been cleaned, her hands wrapped, and all the dried blood had been washed from her face. While she looked better, she was still in pretty bad shape.

"Has she woken up?" I asked.

The woman shook her head. "It will be some time before she does, if she is ever able to."

"But she should heal quickly," I said, "I mean, she is still Kindred, right?"

"She has not used her powers in many years. Even if she is still able to touch her magic, it is forbidden for her to do so."

My eyes bulged. "They won't allow her to heal herself?"

"It is our law," she replied, firmly. I shook my head in disbelief.

"May I sit with her awhile?"

The woman nodded. "I will return soon to rewrap her hands."

I pulled up a chair next to the bed. For a while I just sat and stared, watching her breathe steadily. Then, even though I didn't think I ever made the conscious decision to do so, I started talking.

"He'll be okay, you know," I began. "Roman. He's in pretty bad shape, but he'll be okay. Cassie stitched him up, and as we speak, he's getting stronger. He's so worried about you. I literally had to force him to stay in bed because he wanted to come check on you." I popped my knuckles. "Look, I know you hate me, and I know you and I don't see eye to eye on much of anything, but I want you to know I hope you recover. Not because I need your help, but for him. He's had so much taken from him; I don't want him to lose you, too. From the way he tells it, you are the closest thing he's had to a mother. And speaking from experience, that's the worst thing you can ever go through. Losing your mother. But if you can raise someone to be as strong and brave and beautiful as him, you can't be all bad. So, just come back. Come back for him."

/|\

I didn't go back to Roman. Not yet. Instead, I went home. When I got there, the house was dark and Alessandra's car was gone. Hopefully, she was at work. Knowing I was on borrowed time, I ran upstairs to shower—again—and put on new shorts and a T-shirt. Finally clean, I gorged myself on whatever I could find in the fridge, completely famished from the last twenty four hours.

Once full, I grabbed the house phone to make the call. She answered on the first ring.

"He-hello?" I could hear the concern in her voice. "Kyndal, is that you?"

"It's me."

I could almost feel her relief. "Where have you been? Are you hurt?"

"I'm fine." I began to explain, but she interrupted me.

"Do you have any idea how worried I was? There was some sort of attack at *Sandra's* last night and people are dead. Then you weren't in your bed this morning. Where were you?" she asked again.

"You wouldn't believe me if I told you," I responded. *Completely the truth.*

"Try," she said blankly. Her concern was wearing off now that she knew I was safe. Now she just wanted answers.

I took a deep breath and closed my eyes. "I couldn't sleep last night, so I went for a walk in the forest. I couldn't see where I was going and I slipped. I hit my head on something. It was either a rock or a log, I don't know for sure, but I was knocked unconscious. I just woke up on the forest floor and found my way home."

I cringed as the lie left my lips. It wasn't the strongest story, but it was believable. A Southern girl like myself, new to the forest and unaware of its dangers, falls prey to her own stupidity. *Can't be the first time it's happened.*

I held my breath, waiting for Alessandra to respond. "Well, I'm glad you're home now." I released the breath. She bought it. "Do you need me to come home?"

"No!" I responded quickly. Too quickly. "No," I repeated, calmer. "I feel fine. I just want to go to school."

"Are you sure?" she asked. "I can leave here."

"I'm fine. Trust me. And anyways, I don't want to have to make up any missing work."

"Okay. Well, I'll see you tonight."

"Actually, I was planning on staying at Lydia's. We have a big test tomorrow we need to cram for." The lies just kept pouring out of me. My aunt rearranged her life for me and I was repaying her with deception. "I'll see you after school tomorrow, okay?"

It took a moment for her to answer. "Fine. And Kyndal—"

"Yes?"

"—no more late night trips to the forest."

/|\

I took a deep breath. Confession time.

"It's my fault Deacon went to *Sandra's*." I said the words quickly, afraid I might chicken out.

Roman stared at me, guarded and confused. Isaac and Cassie were also in the room, with similar looks on their faces. I looked down at my hands, unable to face them. I returned this afternoon to tell Roman about Sandra's condition, but once I saw all of them together, I decided it was time to come clean. Secrets had caused enough confusion, heartache, and death.

"I saw Deacon two days ago, in the forest. On my run while you were looking through my mom's journal. He found me. I expected him to attack, but he didn't. It was more like he was taunting me. He said something that reminded me of what Ezekiel told me, and I put two and two together. He's looking for the same thing we are. *The Book of Breathings.*"

"The book?" Cassie asked. "Like *The Book*? As far as I know, only a select few have ever laid eyes on it. It contains spells that only those highly trained could pull off. Anyone else who tried, died in the attempt."

I nodded, then gave Cassie and Isaac the short version. None of this was new for Roman, but this was the first time the others were hearing any of it. "According to Ezekiel, my mother stole *The Book of Breathings*. Roman and I have been trying to find it."

"Wow," Isaac said. *Understatement of the century.*

"There's more," I added before anyone could say anything else. "I mouthed off to Deacon about it and he told me that if I didn't play my role right, he would come after someone I care about. That he would come after *you*." I said, my eyes glued to Roman.

His eyes softened at my last words.

"What exactly is your role?" Cassie asked, breaking the trance between Roman and me.

"The book contains a spell that when read by a Descendant, a.k.a. me, allows all Kindred within the same element the power of creation."

Her eyebrows raised. "So all fire signs would be able to make fire out of nowhere? Can you do that?"

I nodded.

"Wow," Isaac said again. He huffed, "Why would your mother want to keep that from us?"

I shook my head, unable to give him an answer that I didn't know myself.

"When Deacon showed up at *Sandra's,* it was not a coincidence," I explained, returning my gaze toward Roman. "He doesn't want us to find the book, so he's trying to get to it first. He followed you there and left you as a reminder. For me." Tears formed in my eyes, but I blinked them away before they could fall. I didn't deserve to cry.

"So, this is all your fault," Isaac accused.

"Isaac—" Cassie admonished.

"What?" he responded indignantly. "I'm just saying what we're all thinking. She knew what Deacon would do and she still didn't say anything. If she had told someone what she knew, Lauren and Adelle would still be alive, and Roman and Sandra wouldn't be laid up in bed."

Surprisingly, Cassie jumped to my defense again and the two of them started bickering. I put my head down and tried my best to tune them out, the tears falling freely now. Their bickering was interrupted when Roman finally spoke.

"Get out."

I snapped my head up at his tone. The sound was forceful, full of authority. He didn't want me here and I couldn't blame him. I stood immediately and turned for the door.

"Not you," he said to me. He looked at the other two. "You two. Out. Now."

Isaac looked like he was going to argue, but one look at Roman's face and he wisely shut up. He cast me a glare as he and Cassie walked past me toward the stairs.

"Isaac hates me," I told Roman once we were alone. "He's been that way for weeks now." He held his arm out, gesturing for me to come sit on the edge of the bed. Reluctantly, wiping my tears as I went, I came to sit next to him.

"He doesn't hate you," he began. "He's just jealous. You're advancing faster than he is. He doesn't know how to deal with it."

"Yeah, well it's turning him into a real asshat."

Roman chuckled. Something he'd taken to doing quite a bit around me lately. It seemed my bad attitude amused him.

"Cassie told me you fought well. She said you were brave. She also told me you made your first kill." I thought about the dagger in my hand, slicing through the wraith. The ash of the wraith covering my face. "You alright?"

I shrugged, really not wanting to talk about it. "I'm sorry, Roman. I should have told you about Deacon. I really messed up," I whispered. The words felt small and useless, but they were all I had.

"Yes, you did." He didn't say it cruelly, just with a sense of certainty. The truth of his statement bit at my flesh. "The question now is, what are you going to do about it?"

"What do you mean?" I asked him.

"I've been Kindred over half my life now. One thing I've learned is that the tough decisions don't go away. You're always going to be faced with a choice that holds another person's life in the balance. Sometimes you'll choose correctly and sometimes you won't. The real test comes with how you react when you choose wrong."

"What do you do," I asked, hoping he had some sage advice, "when you choose wrong?"

He shrugged. "Apologize. Beg for forgiveness. Whatever it takes—and just hope. Hope that maybe," he took a deep breath, "maybe one day she'll forgive me."

I blushed. I'd been so hard on him, so angry. I blamed him for things that were beyond his control. After all the mistakes I had made, it wasn't fair to condemn him for his.

I moved up the bed, sitting closer to him. I reached across his waist, putting my hand down on the other side of the bed, careful not to touch his wound. Again. At my proximity, his eyes danced.

"And if she forgives you?" I asked quietly, my eyes moving between his eyes and his lips. I moved closer. "What then?"

I was already close enough to feel his breath on my lips. Slowly, I closed the gap and our lips touched. This kiss was different than the others. It was tender, deliberate. Every other time we'd kissed, it seemed to be more of a primal connection forcing us together than a conscious choice. When we finally broke apart, we were both grinning like fools.

His hand reached up and cupped the side of my cheek. "We have to trust each other, Kyndal. Without trust, we have nothing." I nodded. "No more secrets?"

I kissed him again. "No more secrets."

18

Late that night, I woke to the soft touch of Roman brushing the hair from my forehead. I was tucked snugly into his uninjured side, his arm draped over me. We had fallen asleep not long after Cassie and Isaac left us. We were both exhausted, sleep deprived, worn down.

"How are you feeling?" he asked.

I sat up. Roman pouted when I moved away a little. I put my arms up over my head and stretched. "Much better," I replied.

"Your bruise is gone." My fingers touched the once tender skin.

"What about you?" I asked, diverting the attention from me to him. "How are you?"

"100 percent." I glared at him, not believing him in the slightest. I reached over and uncovered his wound. I peeled the protective gauze away. While the wound had improved remarkably, it wasn't done healing by any means. I ran my

241

fingers gently over the stitches, as if I could make his pain go away with just a touch.

"Roman, look—" I began. While something had definitely shifted between us, we still had a lot to talk about. But before I could get too far, he shook his head.

"Don't. I know what you're thinking and it's okay. You are allowed to be happy." He leaned over slowly and gave me a light kiss. I didn't stop him. "Anyways, it's almost midnight." I looked up at him, confused. "We have somewhere we have to be."

Against my better judgement, I watched as he climbed out of bed. He was still moving slowly, but I had to admit it was good to see him back on his feet. He moved to his dresser and pulled out a clean shirt.

He led me outside. I didn't know what we were doing until we broke through the first tree line into an open field. Then it made sense. The field was almost perfectly circular and rimmed with evenly spaced torches, casting an eerie glow over the grove. In the center of the field were two wooden funeral pyres. Atop each sat the bodies of Lauren and Adelle, still wrapped in their colorful shrouds. I realized then that the colors represented their elements: earth and air. The other Kindred stood between the torches in silence. Roman and I took our place within the circle. I spotted Isaac standing near Darius. Across from us, Cassie stood with Mallory, whose arm was in a sling. The one familiar face I didn't see was Ezekiel.

As if on cue, Ezekiel emerged from the trees. He stood

before a wooden bench I hadn't noticed before. Without a word, he reached toward the bench and picked something up. He moved first to Lauren's pyre, then to Adelle's, sprinkling whatever was in his hands on the bodies. Just as I was about to ask what was happening, I felt Roman's hand on the small of my back.

He whispered in my ear. "Funerals always take place at midnight. At the joining of the previous day and the new."

Duality.

He continued as Ezekiel dusted the bodies in some sort of ritual. "When a Kindred dies, their body is blessed with all four elements. First, earth. The body is powdered with dirt and adorned with flowers. Symbolizing where we all come from and where we one day return. Water is next. The body is sprinkled with water from a local stream, cleansing the soul of the departed. Preventing its return." As Roman spoke, my eyes stayed glued to Ezekiel as he now moved to one of the torches, using it to light the one he held in his hand. He moved back to the pyres. "Lastly, fire and air. The bodies are burnt and the wind carries the ashes back to the natural world that sustains us."

"What about families? What if a Kindred wants to be buried by their loved ones?" I whispered back.

I felt him shrug. "Most have outlived their families and have no one to bury them. Others leave their families in favor of us. And only if a Kindred is blessed by all four elements can their soul truly rest. Without the blessing, their soul is at risk of becoming a wraith."

I watched as Ezekiel completed the ritual. Both bodies were burning, the smoke rising up into the starry night sky. I stood there in silence, Roman at my side, surrounded by our people. I watched two of our own burn for my mistake. It was in that moment that I decided I would succeed. *I must succeed.*

I will find the book.

I will make my people strong again.

/|\

School the next day was miserable. Roman, while up and around, wasn't returning for a couple more days, so I was forced to endure Paige on my own. To make matters worse, Sykes kept me after class, coming down on me hard about my grade and how if I planned on passing his class, I would need to do well on the final next week.

The only positive was Lydia. I gave her the full rundown on what had happened the last few days. I told her about Descendants, what really happened at *Sandra's*, as well as the shift in my relationship with Roman. I even included my early morning chit-chat with Sheriff Christensen. He had been waiting for me outside the school when I arrived. While he didn't accuse me of anything, he made it perfectly clear he was making connections between my arrival in Marienville and the sudden string of deaths. An "unfortunate coincidence" he had called it. His interest in me was going to make it very difficult to make any moves without him noticing.

"So, it sounds like you need to find out what Sandra told Deacon," Lydia said. I looked at her again, still impressed with how well she'd handled this whole situation. Honestly, she had handled it better than me. Most people would go running for the hills at the idea of demons and supernatural powers, but Lydia took it all in stride.

"That's problematic. She's been unconscious ever since the attack."

"Okay, take a different tactic. Where does this all begin?"

"With my mother," I replied.

"Then start there."

"It's not exactly like I can ask her, Lydia. And I've already gone through her stuff once."

"No, from what you've said, it sounds like you half-assed your way through her stuff and pushed off the most personal possession for Roman to look through." Lydia definitely had a way of cutting through the crap. She didn't stop there. "No one knows your mom like you did. It's possible you'll find something important in her journal that Roman didn't notice. Just need to put on your big-girl-panties and read it."

I felt ashamed, but she was right. I watched Lydia walk away toward class at the sound of the bell. The phone in my pocket buzzed. It was a message from Roman.

Come over after school.
It's important.

When I made it to Roman's, I found him out back in the sparring ring. He was going head-to-head with scary Mohawk man, whose name I finally learned was Xavier. He was a fire user, like me. I took a moment to watch the action. From what I could gather, Xavier was some sort of bodyguard for Ezekiel, so I imagined he was a good fighter. The men traded several blows back and forth. Roman seemed to be doing well. That was, until Xavier landed a kick in his stomach, right on his stab wound. It was a dirty move. Roman folded forward, his arm going protectively to his stomach. When he raised his head, the look on his face was murderous. He went on the attack. He landed hit after hit, kick after kick, absolutely relentless. After a roundhouse kick so fast I could barely follow it, Xavier was down and he was not getting back up. Bodyguard or not, the poor guy never stood a chance.

"This doesn't exactly look like taking it easy," I hollered.

Roman's head snapped toward me. He obviously didn't know I was there. His eyes were a vibrant yellow, showing how much power he was pulling on in the fight. He'd gone overboard.

"What'd he do to you?" I asked, nodding at Xavier who was still out cold. Roman looked back at him, his chest heaving from the exertion of the fight.

"He'll recover," he said simply.

He walked over to me, grabbed my hand and kissed my cheek. "You look nice," he said. Considering I was dressed in simple jeans and T-shirt, he was obviously dodging my earlier question.

"And you," I said smiling, allowing him to distract me, "look sweaty and smelly. What's so important you needed me here?"

He pulled on my hand, dragging me toward the main house.

"Sandra is awake. She wants to speak with you."

/|\

The change in Sandra was obvious. She was sitting up in bed while her caretaker spooned her sips of soup. Her hands were still wrapped tightly, but her face looked better. The swelling had gone down enough for her to open her eyes and the blood had been cleared away.

Roman spoke first. "Tessa, can we have some privacy please?"

Tessa stood, nodded at Roman and left the room, shutting the door tightly behind her.

I expected Roman to move to Sandra's side immediately, but instead he stood back, hands in pockets, eyes cast down.

"I'm glad you're here," Sandra said, looking at her adopted son. "After Deacon's attack, I was worried you had been injured. Or worse."

Roman didn't mention his brush with death. I wasn't surprised. When he didn't respond to Sandra, I stepped in.

"You asked for me?"

Her eyes lingered on Roman, traveling over him worriedly, before she looked at me. "Yes. I have a message for you. From Deacon."

"What'd he say?" Roman asked, speaking directly to Sandra for the first time. His tone was hard and his gaze was steel. This was not the soft, loving Roman. This was the warrior.

"Before I get to that, I want to emphasize something. I will take no part in any of this. I spent close to 100 years protecting this world from the wraiths and I hate them with all I have. And I love you Roman, but after what they did to me, I will not help the Kindred either."

"Sandra," I said exasperated, "just give us the damn message."

She took a deep breath and turned her swollen eyes directly to me. "Deacon knows you're searching for *The Book of Breathings*. He demands that when you retrieve it, you surrender it to him."

An incredulous laugh escaped my throat. "I'll never give him anything."

"He thought you would say that, so—" she paused, and an icy knot of fear twisted in my stomach. "He took some insurance."

Roman voiced my fear just as I thought it.

"Alessandra."

I turned around and tore out the room, down the stairs, and out the door. I knocked into someone, but I didn't stop to see who it was or to apologize. As soon as I hit the tree line, I reached deep into my power. Calling on it faster than ever before, my senses immediately sharpened. I could feel my connection to nature open up, fueling my body with increased strength and reflexes. My legs pumped as I sprinted toward the house. My feet barely touched the ground. I hurdled over the brush, the hidden path between Roman's house and mine, so familiar now I could run it blindfolded. I could hear someone running behind me, but I didn't stop. My thoughts were consumed.

She'll be okay.

No. She is *okay.*

She has to be okay.

I repeated it over and over in my mind like a mantra. As if thinking it hard enough would make it so. I just spoke to her the night before; there was no way she could be gone.

When I reached the house I went directly for the sliding glass back door. The lock broke as I hurled it open.

"Alessandra!" I called out to the dark house. "Allie!"

"Alessandra!" Roman called behind me. I wasn't surprised that he was the one who followed me. Even injured, he wouldn't leave me alone. The silent house gave no answer to either of us. He looked at me briefly, reached behind his back and produced two daggers. He handed one to me. "I'll look down here, you go upstairs."

I hesitated, looking at the dagger. All I could think about was the one time I used it to kill. It didn't matter that he was a wraith. Before that he had been someone. His body belonged to a very real person and I killed him.

"Kyndal," Roman said determinedly, "we need to find your aunt." I took the dagger and headed upstairs.

I searched each room thoroughly. Each time I came up empty. Every room was undisturbed, left exactly as I expected it to be, so I held onto hope. Hope that she was safe and Deacon hadn't reached her. When I finished my sweep of the upstairs, I met up with Roman in the kitchen.

"Anything?" I asked.

He shook his head. "Empty. But nothing seems to be disturbed either. Try calling her."

I did as he said. I called her cell phone first. No answer. I called her work next. Nothing.

"Nobody answered at the store. She wasn't scheduled to be on a tour today, but maybe something came up and she went out last minute."

"Maybe," Roman replied, but his tone fell flat. He was humoring me.

"You don't think something came up, do you?"

"I think we need to find her. Now."

Before we could go to Allegheny Explorers, we headed back to Roman's to get his bike. Allie's store was too far away for us to run, especially with Roman still hurt. We needed to conserve energy in case there was a fight.

The bike flew down the streets, hugging the curves of the road as our speed continued to climb. When we reached the secluded store, I was off the bike before Roman could even put the kickstand down. The gravel parking lot held two cars, neither of which were Allie's. I spotted her vehicle out back, parked near a storage garage.

"She's here," I said, relieved. I ran toward the building, eager to see my aunt.

"Kyndal, wait!" Roman yelled. I looked at him briefly, confused. Finally, I noticed what he must have already seen. The glass on the front door was broken. Shards of glass covered the floor, some of them tipped in blood.

Roman walked past me, dagger in hand. "Stay behind me," he said. I pulled out the dagger he gave me earlier and stepped inside.

The lobby of Allegheny Explorers was in ruins. An assortment of helmets, riding gear, kayak paddles, water bottles, and other outdoor gear were scattered over the floor. I almost tripped over it as Roman and I searched the room. Roman headed toward the back offices and I continued sweeping the front. I stepped quietly through the room. I moved around the counter and my foot slipped on something slick. I looked down and a small shriek escaped my lips. I was standing in a pool of blood. There was nobody to accompany it, but I knew whoever it belonged to was dead. No one could lose that much blood and survive.

Before I was able to dwell too long on the thought, I heard Roman call my name from the back.

I moved through the hallway, trying to ignore the destruction until I reached the back door. Roman was standing out back, looking down at something in the grass. I followed his gaze reluctantly, knowing what I would find. Three bodies laid there. Each had clearly had their life force drained from them—dried up like husks. They were just barely recognizable. I could see enough to know that none of them were Allie. A wave of relief washed through me, but the feeling was quickly followed by guilt. I should care more that these people were dead.

"What do we do?" I asked Roman. But it wasn't his voice that answered.

"I guess I shouldn't be surprised to find the two of you together." The voice came from the doorway behind us. Roman and I wheeled around simultaneously, still armed. The person standing there was young, attractive, and no one I had ever seen before. He was tall, not as tall as Roman, but still a good size. His hair was platinum blonde. It was so light in fact, it almost looked white. His eyes were a beautiful green, set off by his pale skin.

"Who the hell are you?" I asked, suspiciously. This boy was obviously unaffected by the bloody scene around him. A creeping, itching feeling crawled up my spine. Something was definitely off with this kid.

"I see you got Deacon's message," he replied, avoiding my earlier question.

Wraith.

I took a threatening step forward. "What did you do with my aunt?" Roman reached out and put his hand on my arm to hold me back.

"She's safe. Well—" he moved his head back and forth in a show of mock concern, "—safe-ish." I lunged forward, hell bent on beating answers out of him, but Roman grabbed me around the waist and pulled me back.

The blonde stranger held his ground. His eyes turned bloodshot and his veins darkened. I saw the bloodlust rise in him, but he reigned it in. "All Deacon wants is the book. Deliver it to him and your aunt will be returned safely to you. No harm, no foul." His flippant tone just pissed me off more. A fireball warmed my hand. The wraith smiled at me before turning to Roman. "I suggest you keep her in check and make sure she plays her part. We both know she has a tendency to make rash decisions. Any deviation short of Deacon receiving the book and her aunt will pay the price. And I think we can all agree, she's left enough bodies in her wake."

"Who are you?" Roman asked, echoing my earlier question. He released me and now stood at my side. I could tell he had the same sinking feeling I did. Something was not right. He was no ordinary wraith.

"I'm surprised you don't recognize me," he replied, pure evil dripping from every word. "I looked so different last time the three of us were together, but I have to say I'm disappointed you would forget me so quickly." Recognition creeped up on me, but remained just out of reach. "But then, you did spend what was meant to be our special night kissing him—" he nodded toward Roman and let the sentence drop. I gasped. His mouth twisted into a demented smile as the pieces finally fell into place.

"Holy shit," I whispered.

Evan was a wraith.

19

It was raining.

I was sitting on the edge of the fireplace in Ezekiel's great room, surrounded by Kindred. My eyes were cast down, tracing a pattern in the wood-grained floor, just like they had been for the past half hour. When Roman and I had returned from Allegheny Explorers, he immediately called a meeting. Even with Ezekiel here, who was officially the leader of these parts, everyone responded. Including Ezekiel.

Roman wasted no time briefing everyone on the situation surrounding my aunt's capture. Ezekiel listened intently, interfering only when Roman tried to discuss details surrounding the book. All he allowed Roman to say was that Deacon was interested in an important Kindred artifact. Each time he interrupted, Roman allowed it, playing the good little soldier. But I could see the signs of annoyance. The tense set to his mouth, the pulsing of the muscle in his jaw. Ezekiel was still keeping secrets from those he swore to protect, and Roman, now that he knew what those secrets were, was none too happy about it. Little did Ezekiel know Roman and I already let that cat out of the bag with Cassie and Isaac.

"The next step is to decide how to proceed with the rescue," Roman continued, when he was interrupted *again*, but this time it wasn't Ezekiel. It was Xavier.

"Who says there even needs to be a rescue?"

My head snapped up. "You're joking. It shouldn't even be a question as to whether or not we rescue my aunt. She's an innocent. It's our job."

I couldn't see Xavier from where I sat, but when I spoke, the group parted, and I was given a clear view of him. I expected to find him standing behind Ezekiel, much as he had been since he arrived, but instead I found them side by side.

"Strange words," he replied, "coming from the daughter of a traitor."

I jumped to my feet, livid. Roman stepped in, keeping me from doing something stupid. Ezekiel looked at me, his face pained. "Let's look at this rationally, Kyndal. No, we cannot simply allow an innocent to be killed. But I think we both know what is at stake here. An artifact of this magnitude cannot be turned over to the wraiths. The results would be catastrophic for our people. In some situations, a sacrifice is necessary for the greater good."

My mouth dropped open in shock.

It seemed I was not the only one surprised by Ezekiel's choice. A debate erupted in the room. Before I could stop them, angry tears formed in my eyes. The din of voices grew until one rose above the rest.

"What if there was a third option?" Cassie shouted.

"What would that be?" Xavier countered sarcastically. I glared up at him, no longer feeling bad about Roman beating him to a bloody pulp in training.

"Hunt Deacon," Mallory said, supporting Cassie. "You say he's holding Kyndal's aunt ransom, I say we hunt him down and kill the bastard." For once I agreed with her.

"And what if it's a trap?" Xavier challenged. "What happens when we go after Deacon, putting our lives at risk, and he kills her anyway?"

Mallory stepped toward him. She was now shoulder to shoulder with Cassie. "If you're too much of a coward to risk your life to save an innocent, then I suggest you find a different line of work." She pulled a short knife from behind her back with her good arm and held it out toward Xavier. "Just one quick swipe across your brand, and you can find yourself a nice, quiet, *safe* life."

Mallory's obvious challenge of Xavier's courage sent the group into bickering chaos again. Unable to take it, I quietly slipped outside.

"Kyndal?" Roman's voice cut through the quiet.

I turned toward him slowly. My eyes burned with unshed

tears and I tried to discreetly wipe my cheek where one had fallen unbidden. "What?" I asked him, my voice a hoarse whisper.

"Where are you going?" he asked.

"Home," I told him emphatically. "I can't take it anymore. I can't listen to them argue about whether Allie's life is worth saving. Tell Ezekiel that if they don't want to help, I'll do it my damn self. And he can find himself a new Descendant. I'm done."

"I'll fix this, I promise," he said. I turned toward the forest. The sun hadn't set yet, but the rain clouds had thrown the evening into early darkness. Oblivious to the rain, I walked into the trees, past the clearing where we paid tribute to Lauren and Adelle. The forest was quiet except for the rain hitting the leaves and splashing in the water of a nearby creek. All the animals were hidden away, waiting for the storm to pass. I breathed in deeply as I walked, trying to center myself and draw the elements to me. I willed them to calm me, to hold in my emotions.

By the time I reached the house, the skies had fully opened. I was drenched head to toe and shivering, but the cold didn't come from the rain. It came from within. It was a hard shell of guilt, grief, and truth—that I was responsible for the inevitable death of my last family member. I had no way of recovering the book or finding Deacon on my own. Without either of those, she was as good as gone.

I trudged up the steps and fell into bed, hoping for the merciful release of sleep. It eluded me, and instead, the dam I worked so hard to hold together broke, and my body was racked with soft sobs, the tears hitting my pillow in tune with the rain on the window.

/|\

"Honey. Honey, wake up." The voice pulls me from my dream and my eyes flutter open slowly. The curtains are pulled back and my room is filled with soft light, turning the purple walls a pale lilac.

A face appears in my doorway. A beautiful woman with long auburn hair, dark eyes, and an easy smile.

Mom.

"Come on, Kyndal. You're going to be late."

I sit up in bed and look at my mother. My mother.

I stare at her for too long before finally finding my voice. "What are you doing here?"

Her eyebrows knit together and she steps into the room, sitting on the edge of my bed. Without thinking, I reach out and pull her into a suffocating hug. "Are you feeling okay?" she asks. She manages to pull away and raises her hand to my forehead, just as she has a hundred times. "Honey, you feel warm."

She reaches down and grabs my hand. On contact, a searing pain ignites in my palm and I can't help but cry out. I look down and three livid marks now run the length of my hand. My brand. The pain brings me back to reality.

"This—this isn't my room," I whisper.

"What are you talking about, honey? Of course this is your room."

I shake my head back and forth violently, then jump from the bed. "No. No! You left me."

My mother gives me a hurt look. "Kyndal, you're acting crazy. What's gotten into you?"

"This has gotten into me, mother." I thrust my palm toward her, baring the Kindred brand for her to see. Her posture changes, her body becomes more rigid. She knows I know her secret. "You left me. You, Dad, and Chase. You all left me, and now I have no one." Angry tears form in my eyes. Before I know it, I'm screaming. "How could you all leave me?"

My mother stands and reaches out to me, trying to comfort me, but I pull away. "No," I spit. "Don't touch me. You're a liar. You lied to me, to Dad, to Chase, for years. You betrayed your people. You took the book and left them vulnerable." I slam my hands against my chest. "Left me vulnerable. You're a liar, and a thief, and a traitor. And now I have to clean up after you."

I try to leave the room, my old room, to look for a way out of this dream, but my mother grabs my arm and spins me around. "Kyndal, listen very carefully to me. You cannot look for the book. Do you hear me?"

"Leave me alone!" I yell at her, but she doesn't let go.

"The book is dangerous—"

"Wake up!" I scream, desperately trying to tune her out. I want out, I can't take this dream anymore. "Wake up!"

"It has so much more power than you realize, you have to—"

I take a deep breath and reach as far into myself as possible before screaming at the top of my lungs. "Kyndal, wake up!"

The room begins to shake and lose focus. I hear a pounding noise in the distance. I focus on the sound. As it gets louder, the room fades, until eventually I sit straight up in bed.

Gasping for air and covered in sweat, I looked around the room. Four beige walls, wood floor. I was back, but the pounding hadn't stopped. Someone was at the door.

I scrambled out of bed and down the stairs, still slightly disoriented from my strange dream. I had just about reached the door when the person on the other side spoke.

"Kyndal Davenport! This is Sheriff Christensen with the Forest County Sheriff's Department. Open up!"

I froze mid-step. I briefly entertained the idea of hiding away and refusing to answer.

"Kyndal Davenport. I have important information regarding your Aunt Alessandra. Open the door."

Hope fluttered in my chest. Maybe he found her. Maybe

Deacon let her go and she was safe now. I ran the rest of the way to the door and eagerly pulled it open.

The moment I laid eyes on the Sheriff, my hope shattered. He stood flanked by two deputies, a piece of paper in one hand and a set of handcuffs in the other.

"Kyndal Davenport, you are under arrest for the disappearance and suspected murder of Alessandra Davenport."

Panic rippled up my body like shockwaves. I started to back up, trying to retreat inside, but the two deputies grabbed me. Before I knew it, I was handcuffed and being read my rights as they walked me to the back of the squad car. Just before they placed me in the car, I saw movement in the trees across the street and glimpsed a boy with a shock of white hair.

/|\

The Sheriff's Department of Forest County was located in the center of Marienville, right next to Town Hall and across the street from a frequented restaurant. So being dragged out of a cop car during the lunchtime rush with my hair a tangled mess, barefoot, and in yesterday's clothes, did not go unnoticed. I spotted several people I recognized from school, including Jules—Paige's disciple—standing and gawking on the sidewalk as I was pushed inside.

After I was processed, they moved me into their interrogation room. In a town this small, that meant a tiny room with a table, chairs on either side, and a mirror embedded in the wall—one I assumed was double sided. The most important detail I noticed was a camera in the corner of the room pointed directly at me.

I expected the Sheriff to immediately come in and start badgering me with questions, but he didn't. Instead, he made me wait for what felt like hours, which was so much worse. They took off my handcuffs and I paced the room frantically. Five steps to the mirror, five steps to the wall. Repeat.

How do I get out of this? What do I do if they put me in jail? What do I do if my powers slip? How will I save Allie now?

Seconds turned into minutes and I still had no answers. My emotions slipped further from my grasp, and with them, my control over my powers. I could feel them start to heat up and I knew if I didn't get a handle on myself quickly, I'd soon be holding a living fireball in my hand. Then I'd *really* have some explaining to do.

I closed my eyes and focused on taking deep breaths in and out. It didn't work. I looked down at my hands, making sure my back was to the camera. Sure enough—both were lit up like torches. Just then the door opened.

"Have a seat, Ms. Davenport." It was the Sheriff. I didn't budge.

Breathe in.

Breathe out.

"Sit down, Ms. Davenport, or I will be forced to sit you down." His challenge stirred my instinct to fight and gave fresh oxygen to the fire. Knowing the danger of exposure, I took one more deep breath in before I turned around and reminded myself that he wasn't the enemy. I kept my eyes cast down to hide their color and clenched my hands closed. Once I was seated, I heard the chair across from me scrape the floor and the Sheriff take up residence.

"Kyndal Davenport. Daughter of Mark and Sofia Davenport—both deceased," he began. Hearing the names of my parents cut at the already open wound their deaths left behind. But he didn't stop there.

"Sister to Chase Davenport, also deceased."

I barely gained enough control over my powers to pull them back before I glared up at him, anger coming off me in waves. My hands remained clenched as a precaution. "I know they're dead. I don't need the reminder."

Unfazed by my reaction, he continued. "That's right. Because you were there when they died, weren't you?"

I pointed at the file sitting in-between us on the table. "You know I was. So, why don't you cut the crap," I challenged.

He smiled. "Alright. Kyndal—did you kill your family?"

"No," I responded immediately.

He leaned back in his chair and crossed his arms. "See, I've gone over this file several times and I can't quite make it add up. Roll-over accident, car catches fire," he pointed at me, "you behind the wheel. All three of your family members perish but you come out unscathed. Not even a scratch. How do you explain that?"

I shook my head back and forth. "I didn't kill them. It was an accident."

"I want to believe you Kyndal, but you don't make it easy. You moved here almost nine weeks ago, and in that time span, I have seven dead bodies and a missing person on my hands."

"I didn't kill anyone!" I screamed. That wasn't exactly the truth, but he didn't need to know that. Wraiths didn't leave any evidence behind.

"Let's review the evidence, shall we?" He pushed the folder with my family's pictures to the side, making sure it stayed open and in plain view. He opened the next folder and turned it toward me. I couldn't stop the whimper when I saw the picture of the smiling, grey-eyed boy looking back at me. "Evan Dixon. Seventeen-years-old. Found dead five weeks ago outside East Forest High, the night of the school dance. Neck broken." Tears ran down my cheeks as the memory invaded my mind. If he only knew what *really* became of Evan. "Evan was your date that night. An eyewitness places the two of you together less than an hour before time of death. Yet, you claim you left early that night. Picked up by your aunt."

The Sheriff opened two more folders, completely relentless. Each contained three pictures. He pointed at the first folder. "Three found dead inside *Sandra's Bar* just four days ago. One with their neck broken in a similar fashion to Evan, the others bled out and dehydrated." He pointed at the last folder. "And just yesterday. Three more found dead in the same manner at Allegheny Explorers. The same place your aunt works. Her car was found out back, behind the store. There was evidence of a struggle, but she is nowhere to be found. We've been through A.E.'s schedule. Your aunt wasn't scheduled to be in the field until the beginning of next week."

I sat back in my chair, mimicking his posture. I ignored the traitorous tears. "Is there a question in any of this?"

The Sheriff gave me a hard look. "My question, Kyndal, is where is your aunt?" I looked back defiantly and gave no response. "If you've done something with her, it may not be too late to help. Just tell me where she is."

How I wished I could. I wished it were that easy. I could just tell the Sheriff about Deacon, and he and his deputies, the ones who were supposed to be protecting the people of this town, would burst in, save my aunt, and bust the bad guys. Freshly reunited, we would hug, go home, and live happily ever after.

But that isn't my life.

This life is where evil reigns and good people are killed through senseless acts of brutality at the whims of those more powerful than them.

I broke eye contact with the Sheriff and wiped the tears from my cheeks. Just then, I heard a commotion outside the interrogation room. It came closer until the door ripped open and Ezekiel stepped inside.

Dressed in a three-piece suit, his ponytail pulled neatly back, he immediately commanded the room. "This interview is over."

The Sheriff stood up, turning toward Ezekiel. The moment he laid eyes on him, his whole demeanor changed. His back straightened, his feet came together. "Sir, what are you doing here?"

Ezekiel glared at him then produced a set of official looking papers. The Sheriff read over them. Her shook his head, confused. "Her legal guardian is missing. I wasn't aware she had another." *That makes two of us.*

"Well, she does. And you are in violation of Ms. Davenport's rights." He turned to me. "Let's go."

I glanced at the Sheriff, fully expecting him to shut Ezekiel down and force me to stay, but he didn't say anything. He just stood there, silent.

Not needing to be told twice, I left.

20

I jumped into Ezekiel's car, keeping my head down until we made it out of town. Once clear, I turned to look at him. He was focused on the road ahead, not paying me any special attention. "Thank you."

He turned my way and gave me a soft smile. His eyes were kind and held a touch of pity. "You're welcome, Kyndal."

"How did you get the Sheriff to let me go?"

Ezekiel kept his eyes firmly on the road, but I noticed a slight tension in his wrists where he gripped the wheel. "The Sheriff won't bother you again."

I squinted at him, fully confused. I waited for a while, but it became obvious Ezekiel wouldn't provide any more explanation. I ran my fingers through my hair, trying to push the tangles away from my face. That was when I noticed we weren't headed home. "Where are we going?" I asked.

"I have something I want to show you."

We drove on for a while. I knew we were on the opposite side of the Allegheny than my house. Nothing here was familiar. The roads changed from pavement to gravel, then finally to dirt, when Ezekiel pulled up to an old farmhouse. It was two-stories tall. The paint was chipped and faded, but I could tell it used to be white with blue shutters. It was clearly abandoned. "Follow me," he said. I got out of the car and followed him up to the front steps of the old house. I moved slower than him since I had to watch my step. I didn't want to cut my bare feet.

"What is this place?" I asked.

"The first house built in Marienville. It has stood since 1833. The founding fathers of this town built it."

"Did you know them?"

He turned and looked at me. "I was one of them."

I was shocked. "You founded Marienville?"

Ezekiel nodded. "Along with a few other Kindred, yes. Our people are strongest when surrounded by nature, something I'm sure you've learned by now. We needed somewhere that provided unlimited access to the elements. The Allegheny was perfect. At the time it was unsettled. We were able to hunt wraiths and practice our elemental magic without fear of exposure. However, over time, people invaded and we had to move into the shadows. We were forced to assimilate into the mainstream culture. We had to find ourselves roles within their society. For me, that meant being mayor of this town for several years until I was forced to leave."

"People noticed you weren't aging."

He nodded again. "Nothing definitive, but we couldn't risk causing a panic. I was furious we had to leave. I had grown quite fond of the little town we'd built. Even after we moved away, I've always kept some level of involvement in the town. In fact, I'm still an active member of the city council. I rejoin when I can, whenever the locals won't recognize me from the previous time I lived here." I could hear the regret in his voice. He sat there silent for a moment, lost in his memories.

"Why did you bring me here?" I asked.

"I'm very old, Kyndal. Sometimes I forget the zeal of youth. When I started this town, I was nowhere near the man I am today. I hadn't taken my seat on the Council yet. I was ambitious, daring, and outspoken." He nudged me with his shoulder. "Much like someone else I know." I smiled a little, just to be polite. *Where was he going with this?* "When you aren't a leader, it's easy to act without consideration for the consequences. I don't have that luxury now. I have to do what is best for the majority. No matter how difficult that decision is to make."

I popped my knuckles, aggravated. "This is your way of justifying why you're letting my aunt rot in Deacon's hands? You're just doing what's best?"

Ezekiel stayed calm. "Quite the opposite actually. This is my way of apologizing. You were right. Protecting innocents is our job. That's why I've organized a hunting party to find Deacon and rescue your aunt."

My head snapped up. I looked at him, my heart in my throat. "Are you serious?" I asked. "Don't tease me, Ezekiel."

"The team leaves tonight at dark."

I jumped up. "Then we should head back. I need to shower and change before I go."

"Kyndal, stop." I turned around. Ezekiel hadn't moved from the step. "You will not be in the hunting party."

My mouth dropped open. "She's my aunt. I have to help find her!" I yelled.

Ezekiel stood. "No, you don't. While your skills are remarkable, you are not ready for an assignment of this magnitude. Not to mention, the Sheriff has taken an obvious interest in you. It will not be easy for you to move about without being seen. Your presence could compromise the safety of the mission, something I will not allow."

"Then what am I supposed to do? Sit at home?"

"No. You will go to school just as you always would. When you are not at school, you will continue your training and search for the book. That is where you are most useful. Naturally, a trainer will be provided for you."

I crossed my arms. "You can't stop me from searching for Allie."

Ezekiel pulled on the edge of his finely pressed shirt, straightening out an imaginary wrinkle. When he spoke, his voice was stern. "Not only can I stop you, I promise you I will do just that. I am your legal guardian now. I was not bluffing earlier. I still have many connections in this town. It was not difficult to get the required documentation. More importantly than that, I am your Nomarch, and I am giving you a direct order. You will not pursue the wraith Deacon or any of his men. Furthermore, you are not to return to your aunt's home. You will stay at the compound where I can keep an eye on you. Do you understand me?"

I stared back at him; stubborn and silent.

"Kyndal, I said, am I understood?"

I spoke through gritted teeth. "Understood."

/|\

Pop, pop. Bang!

Pop, pop. Bang!

I continued the relentless pounding on the punching bag, the Sheriff's words mixing with Ezekiel's in my head.

Mark and Sofia Davenport—both deceased.

Pop, pop. Bang!

Direct order.

Pop, pop. Bang!

Signs of a struggle.

Bang! Bang!

As soon as we returned to the compound, I made a beeline for the empty training ring. I knew Roman and the others would find me soon and I needed to work some stuff out before I could answer any questions.

Soon enough, I heard several sets of footsteps approaching me from behind. I knew one was Roman, the familiar cool tingle was present on my spine, but for the first time, I didn't find it comforting. There were three others with him. Two of them were walking quickly, assertively. No doubt Isaac and Cassie. But the third set was slower, unsure and light-footed. It sounded oddly familiar, but I couldn't place it. I turned around.

Isaac and Cassie were there as expected, both dressed in fighting gear. But I didn't expect Lydia.

"What are you doing here?" I blurted out.

Lydia put her hands on her hips. "Is that anyway to greet the person who got you out of *jail*?"

Totally confused, I looked to the others.

Isaac explained, "When you took off last night, we didn't want to crowd. Figured you just went home. You know, sleep off the depression of recent events. So imagine our surprise when My-Size-Barbie over here comes tearing into our driveway today, demanding to talk to Roman. No sooner did he get outside then she goes into a tirade, yelling and screaming about how he got you arrested."

I raised my eyebrows in surprise and looked to Lydia, "You did that for me?"

"Yeah, girl," she said smiling, "I got your back. They tried to act like they didn't understand why I came to them, especially that one guy with the killer ponytail. But, I eventually convinced them I knew what I was talking about."

I smiled back at her and heard Isaac mumble, "That's putting it mildly."

A small giggle escaped my lips, but when it faded, I was left staring awkwardly as silence fell over the group. I looked to Isaac and Cassie. "You two are in the hunting party?"

Cassie answered. "Ezekiel has Xavier leading the crew. We're going to start at Allegheny Explorers, see if we can pick up some sort of trail."

Isaac piped up. "Too bad you aren't coming with us." His tone dripped with sarcasm.

I glared at him. I was really tired of his attitude. "If you have a problem Isaac, we can take care of it now. I've got five minutes."

"I only need three, Descendant."

"You know; I've heard that about you." Isaac stepped toward me. I straightened my back. Before it went any further, Roman stepped in.

"Both of you knock it off." Everyone stood silently while Isaac and I glared at each other.

Lydia, never a master of subtlety, broke the silence. "Soo,

obviously I'm no longer needed here. I'll just leave you supernatural warriors to it, while I go home and do my laundry or fry my brain watching mindless reality TV. You know, normal teenager stuff." She hooked her arm through Isaac's. It was a pretty gutsy move since he looked like he was ready to attack me at any moment. "Walk me to my car, handsome?" I didn't know if it was her natural charm or the small pat on the ass she gave him, but he turned and followed.

I watched them go for a moment, then turned to the others. Cassie looked me up and down with a scrutinizing gaze, paying extra attention to my face. I put my chin up in a useless gesture of strength, but I'm sure she saw just how broken I truly was. She pursed her lips, nodded slightly, then left. One thing I love about her, she never pushed. I guess when you live forever, patience comes easier.

Left alone with Roman and unable to face him, I cowardly returned to the workout bag. I wasn't surprised when he followed, standing off to the side, watching me work. I tried to focus solely on the bag, but I kept fumbling under his gaze.

"What?" I snapped out at him defensively.

He ignored my misplaced anger and spoke softly. "Breathe in quickly between punches, and blow out when you strike. You'll get more power that way." I followed his direction, pleased with the results. Roman stayed with me the whole time, holding the bag in place for me while I released my anger. He never spoke, except to give me a pointer on my form, or make a suggestion on technique. I worked the bag until my knuckles bled and the sky went black.

When I finally gave up, Roman grabbed my hands and led me inside. He sat me down on his couch and retreated into the kitchen. He returned with a towel and bowl of water. He sat on the coffee table across from me and started cleaning the blood from my hands. The gesture was unnecessary considering they would be healed within a day, but I didn't stop him. His touch was soothing.

He was meticulous. Once my left hand was completely cleaned, he moved on to the right. "Why aren't you hunting Deacon?" I asked quietly.

He didn't look up at me or stop his work. "Ezekiel wanted me to go. I thought I would be needed more here."

I hung my head as tears formed in my eyes. It seemed all I did recently was cry. I swallowed the lump that had formed in my throat, trying to take my words with it, but they escaped anyway. "I can't do this," I whispered. "I'm not strong enough."

Roman placed the bloodied towel on the table, but didn't release my hand. He was silent for a long time before he finally spoke. "Kyndal, look at me." I slowly raised my head to look at him, wiping away the ugly tears. Even in the dimly lit room his eyes were a brilliant blue. I saw a small sliver of yellow peeking through them. "You are strong enough. You can do this."

I shook my head. "The Sheriff was right. All I've done is screw things up, get people hurt—killed. It would be better for everyone if I had never come here."

He moved so quickly I barely saw it. One minute he was sitting on the coffee table, the next he was kneeling in front of me, his hand cupping my cheek. His eyes were feverish, determined. "I don't want to ever hear you say those words again. You coming here was not a mistake."

I wasn't buying it. I was on the self-pity train and I refused to get off. "Name one person I've helped."

He gave a low, frustrated growl before jumping to his feet and pacing the room. "God dammit Kyndal. You Aries are so stubborn. You refuse to hear what I've been telling you the whole time. Me! You've helped me! All I've known my whole life is survival. Kill the enemy, live to fight another day. And then you show up. And you're strong, and beautiful, with this mouth on you that refuses to take shit from anyone. You challenge me in ways I've never experienced before."

I jumped to my feet, "So what?" I yelled. "Seven people are dead because of me." I could see he was going to argue with me, but I held up my hand to stop him. "No. You can't deny it, or argue your way out of it. I may not have killed them, but their deaths are still on my hands. Deacon killed them because of me. Because of what I am. The price is too high."

Roman took a deep breath and stared at me from across the room. "What do you feel around me?"

The question took me completely by surprise, "I—I don't know what you mean," I lied.

"Bullshit," he responded immediately. "You know exactly

what I mean." When I didn't respond, he continued.
"Whenever you're near, a heat dances up my spine that
draws me to you, like a moth to a flame. As if I'd been
living in the freezing cold and your warmth is the only fire.
I have to be near you. Talk to you. Touch you." He started
to walk toward me. As he did, his voice changed. It became
softer, seductive. I watched him approach, but made no
move to retreat. He finally reached me and placed a hand
firmly on my hip, kneading at the skin there. "I'm so
acutely aware of you that I can tell what room you're in,
whether you're awake or asleep. You're the last thing I
think about before I go to bed, and the first thing I think
about when I wake up." He moved in even closer. I could
feel his breath on my lips. "Tell me that's not worth it. That
we're not worth it."

I couldn't.

He closed the last remaining space between us. I
completely melted into the kiss, desperate to lose myself in
him. What started out chaste quickly turned the opposite as
he led me over to the couch. He gently guided me down
onto my back. Holding himself over me, we took our time
exploring each other. My hands traveled up his back and
over the contours of his stomach, the muscles clearly felt
through his shirt.

One hand in my hair, Roman's other hand gripped tightly
on my hip, right at the edge of my shirt. He only strayed
slightly to wander to the sensitive skin around my navel, a
move that elicited a breathy moan from me. I returned the
favor, my fingers teasing the small patch of skin exposed

above his waistline before I grabbed the edge of his shirt and begin to lift. Roman swiftly sat back on his knees and pulled his shirt the rest of the way off. I looked at him through hooded eyes and reached up to touch his naked chest. I took my time, my fingers lazily exploring his body. I paid particular attention to where he was stabbed such a short time ago; the stitches still there. I sat up and kissed it lovingly before meeting him eye to eye.

"I felt this, you know."

His eyes darkened with worry. "You felt when I was stabbed?"

"Not exactly," I explained, my eyes following my fingers. "That night, the second I got to *Sandra's*, I could feel you—but it wasn't the same. It usually comes through so strong, but I only felt short glimpses of it. I don't know exactly how to describe it. It was like the connection was blocked or short circuiting. I knew something had to be wrong."

He took a couple of sharp breaths. "So, you do feel something?"

My hand continued across his chest as I moved to his ribs. There, on his right side, I found three linear scars. A brand that matched my own. I caressed it reverently, the mark of what made us different from everyone else, but the same as each other. Roman shuddered at my touch.

I looked back up at him and nodded. The change in him was instantaneous. He captured my lips again in a fiery kiss. "It doesn't scare you?" I asked.

He shook his head. "I'm not going to pretend I understand it, but no. It doesn't scare me."

I smiled to myself. "Your eyes are glowing," I whispered to him.

He kissed me sweetly. "That makes two of us."

I kissed him back, pulling away only slightly. "So apparently I'm not allowed to go home. Ezekiel says I have to stay at the compound."

Roman kissed my cheek, then moved lower, planting tiny butterfly kisses along my neck. "Here," he whispered. "You'll stay here with me, if you want."

I bit my lip to keep from grinning. "Okay." I could feel him smile against my neck. "Now, if you don't mind, I haven't showered in days."

"I wasn't going to say anything, but you are a little ripe."

I sat back and smacked his arm playfully. "That is not nice!"

He smiled at me adoringly, "You brought it up."

Still smiling, I reached up and gave him a steamy kiss before standing up and walking toward the stairs, "I'll be out soon."

His eyes watched me retreat. "Sure you don't need some help? I'm great with a loofah."

A giggle escaped my lips. "Maybe next time."

"I'll hold you to it."

I paused at the bottom of the stairs and looked back at him, still kneeling on the couch, shirtless. I seriously second guessed his offer to help, but I knew I wasn't ready to go that far. Yet. "Did Lydia really yell at you?" I asked.

Roman's face turned sour. "I didn't realize you had told her all about us. She demanded to know what I had done to get you in trouble. Called me an air wielding asshole of supernatural proportions."

I tried to keep a straight face, show some sort of sympathy for Roman, but I couldn't do it. A hysterical laugh broke free and I laughed all the way up the stairs.

/|\

I woke the next morning to the most intoxicating smell. I sat up in bed, well—Roman's bed, and stretched lazily, deeply inhaling a scent I hadn't smelled in months.

Bacon.

I snuck down the steps and quietly slipped myself onto a stool at the bar. I watched Roman juggle several different pans on the stove, his back to me. He was dressed in black sweats and a grey V-neck. His hair was still wet from the shower. *The view doesn't suck.*

"It's not polite to stare." His voice startled me. He hadn't even turned around. He really was aware of me at all times.

I snapped out of my trance. "You can cook, too? That

makes you almost obnoxiously perfect."

He smiled at me over his shoulder, pausing to stare at my sleeping attire. Since I wasn't allowed to go back home, all I had to sleep in was a shirt of his. "I had Cassie go to your house and pick up some things. Clothes and the like. They're over there." He nodded toward the couch.

I jumped up. "Nice!" I grabbed the bag and ducked into the bathroom to do a quick change. As I grabbed the workout clothes out of the bag, I heard something thump onto the floor. It was my mother's journal. I picked it up and shoved it back in the bag. I changed clothes before I threw my hair up into a ponytail. Back in the kitchen, bacon, eggs, and hash browns were waiting. I instantly dug in.

"This is delicious," I said between bites. He smiled as he sat next to me. "So, what's the plan for the day?"

His eyes lingered on my lips for a moment before answering. "I'm headed out. Cassie and the others found a wraith last night. They took it to one of our safe houses for interrogation. I'm going to assist."

"And if I insisted I go with you?"

"Then I'd remind you that you are under orders not to go anywhere near Deacon and his men."

"This sucks. I want to help."

"You are helping. You have to find the book. If we can't find Allie, the book is the only chance we have of getting her back."

I nodded. I hated to admit it, but he was right. "How long will you be gone?"

"Just the day. I'll see you back here tonight." He leaned over and kissed my forehead. "I'm sorry you can't go with us, Kyndal. I know this is difficult for you, but Ezekiel is a good man. He doesn't do anything without a reason. Trust in him. We will find your aunt."

"I barely know Ezekiel; how can I trust him?"

"Then forget Ezekiel. Trust me."

I stared at him. "You'll tell me everything you learn?"

"Absolutely everything," he promised. "Until I come back, you have other things to worry about."

"Like what?" I asked sarcastically. "A Sheriff who thinks I killed almost a dozen people, four of which were family members?"

He gave me a quick, disapproving look, apparently not finding my sarcasm funny. "Ezekiel told me this morning that he found you a trainer," he responded. "He wants you to practice weapons."

That's not too bad.

"With Mallory," he finished.

Crap.

When I entered the training ring, Mallory was waiting impatiently. A plethora of weapons were on the nearby table, their steel glinting in the sunlight. They were beautiful and deadly, just like the woman standing before me.

"Let's get one thing straight. The only reason I'm doing this is because Cassie asked me to. I'm not your babysitter and I'm definitely not your friend. I don't care that you are new to this and I will not go easy on you. You'll do exactly as I say, when I say to do it. No arguments. If you have a question, that means you weren't paying close enough attention the first time around. You got me?"

A sarcastic comment was on the tip of my tongue, but then I remembered my first encounter with Mallory, and how easily she put me down. She knew what she was doing and I could learn a lot from her. I swallowed the comment.

"Got it."

"Good," she said, her tone ringing with finality. She moved over to the weapons display. "Not just any blade can kill a wraith. Man-made weapons will injure the body of the host, but not touch its demonic parasite. The wraith can just jump into another body. The weapons we use, a true Kindred blade, are hand-forged on The Island. Each one etched with the brand of our people."

I ran my fingers over the hilts of the blades in front of me. Mallory reached over me and grabbed the dagger on the end. She held it out to me. "For you."

Hesitantly, I reached out and took the dagger. I looked at it in awe while Mallory continued her lesson. "Protect it at all costs. Get caught without it, or let someone take it from you, and you could pay with your life."

I nodded.

Suddenly, like a snake's strike, Mallory reached out and slapped the bottom of my hand, knocking my dagger into the air. Her other hand came up and grabbed the hilt. She took one step in and suddenly the blade was pressed to my neck. My eyes bulged at the speed and force of her skill.

She gave me a disapproving look. "Looks like someone wasn't listening." She kept the blade pressed a moment longer, just to punctuate her point before stepping back and handing the blade back to me, hilt forward.

I took a deep breath in. It was going to be a long day.

21

The bed dipped low and the covers pulled back, exposing my bare legs. I knew it was him without even opening my eyes. A cool breeze skittered up my spine and I could smell the scent of burnt leaves. Still sleepy, I turned toward him, flung an arm over his waist and buried my face in his side.

"You're late," I mumbled.

He reached around, twirling a piece of my hair. "Miss me?"

I took a deep breath, fully inhaling him. As I exhaled, my whole body relaxed. "Nope," I said playfully. "Not at all."

I felt him chuckle.

"What took so long?" I asked.

He didn't answer. I opened my eyes and waited for a response, but still nothing. His silence worried me. I propped myself up on my arm and got my first good look at him.

There was a cut on his right cheekbone and a deepening bruise along his jaw. "You're hurt." I sat up on my knees and gave the rest of him a quick glance. Thankfully, I didn't see any other obvious injuries. "What happened?"

"The safe house was attacked. We were outnumbered and they escaped with our prisoner."

"Is everyone alright?"

He nodded. "Nothing we can't heal. I recognized two of the wraiths as Deacon's men. They were a part of the attack on *Sandra's*."

"How did they know where the safe house was?"

He shook his head. "It's possible one of us was followed. Dammit, we were so close. The fact that Deacon attacked shows we were on the right track."

"Did you get any information about where Deacon is keeping Allie?"

He shook his head. "No. But one of the wraiths did say something that could be useful. Cassie thinks we might have a beat on where some of Deacon's men are hiding. The others are at the main house looking at a map now. If we can find their den, we might get lucky and be able to interrogate another one of Deacon's men."

"Why aren't you over there with the others?"

"I promised I would tell you everything I knew. I didn't want to make you wait. Not to mention, the idea of you alone in my bed was too appealing to pass up." His eyes traveled south, over my sleepwear. "I thought Cassie brought you clothes."

I gave him an ornery grin. "She did," I replied. "I like your shirt better."

"No argument here."

I bit my lip and took a deep breath in, meeting his eyes. We seemed to have the same thought, but Roman was quicker than me. Next thing I knew, I was lying on my back, Roman hovering over me, his mouth molded to mine. His right hand pulled at the borrowed T-shirt, twisting it in his hand. I gripped both his arms, pinning him to me. My fingers were itching to comb through his hair, but I resisted. I didn't want to go anywhere near his injuries. We stayed that way for a while, kissing and groping, lost in each other. Eventually we detangled and laid there, catching our breath.

"What did I miss?" he asked.

I shook my head. "Just Mallory kicking my ass." I held up my arm, showing off my battle scars from the day. My arm was decorated in tiny cuts from Mallory's blade. "That girl is wicked." He ran his fingers over the shallow cuts. "Can I ask you a question?"

"Mm hmm," he mumbled. I looked at him. His eyes were closed, but his fingers still played along my skin.

"Do you think there's something going on with Cassie and Mallory?"

He opened his eyes and looked at me. "What do you mean?"

"Like, do you think they're a couple?"

He smiled at me. "They've been together as long as I've known Cassie. Why? Does that bother you?"

"No, not at all. They just seem like an odd pairing. Cassie is always looking out for others. She's such a kind soul. While Mallory, just—isn't."

"There's more to Mallory than you realize. You just haven't had a chance to get to know her yet."

I leaned up on my elbow, looking down at Roman. "You always see the best in people. I don't know how you do it."

He reached up and tucked my hair behind my ear. "Focusing on the beautiful things in life is the only way to keep the dark from taking over. Without those things, life is just one endless battle."

"Do you ever worry that trying so hard to find the good in people makes you ignore things you shouldn't?"

He shook his head. "No one is perfect. We all have darkness in us. But I choose to believe that most people are good."

I hoped he was right.

/↑\

I returned to school the next day. It was my first time being seen in public since my arrest. I really wanted Roman with me, but Ezekiel made him stay at the compound to help the others locate the wraith den. Instead, Isaac was assigned as my official Ezekiel-approved bodyguard. The assignment made sense. Isaac was already a student at the school; it wouldn't be odd for us to be seen together. Neither of us was happy about it though. Wherever I went, he followed. Behind us both, whispers stuck like shadows.

There goes the girl that killed her family. Did you hear her aunt is missing? What do you think she did with her body?

Even the teachers had decided I was guilty. At lunch, I overheard Paige bragging in detail to the people at her lunch table about all the things she and Roman had done. Even knowing that none of it was true, and that he was with me, I still couldn't stop myself from turning around and glaring at the entire table. Before I even knew what happened, Jules, second-in-command of Paige's bitch brigade, threw an apple at me.

A friggin' apple.

It was in plain view of all the people in the lunchroom. I stood up, determined to rip her head off, when Isaac intervened. We made a huge scene and yet the teachers did nothing. They just watched as Isaac dragged me out of the room and Jules, Kellee, and Paige left cackling.

After that, I worked through my lunches in the library. I followed Ezekiel's command and started putting in extra effort to improve my grades. Although I was reluctant at first, I started to see his point. I wasn't going to help anyone by failing school. Days passed, and slowly, people forgot about me.

Every day after school I trained with Mallory. When we finished, I holed myself up in Roman's house doing either homework or reading my mom's journal until I fell asleep.

Now, the sun was shining and there was a light breeze in the air. I was enjoying one of my few moments of freedom. I was posted up against the trunk of a giant tree outside school, reading over my mom's journal. Again. Isaac had ducked inside to flirt with some blonde chick. "Anything?" Lydia asked from beside me.

I shook my head and groaned in frustration. "I have read over this three times, and the only thing I've managed to figure out is that the book must be here, in Marienville. Which I already knew, thanks to Deacon. Beyond that, there is not a single clue as to where that stupid book is." I slammed the journal shut and threw it on the ground. The stress was getting to me and my temper flared. "How the hell am I supposed to save Allie if I can't even find where my mother hid the goddamn thing?"

"It's okay," Lydia said reassuringly. "We'll figure it out. I promise. Just calm down."

I whipped my head toward her. "I am calm," I gritted through my teeth.

Lydia was completely unfazed by my attitude. "Really?" she retorted. "Then why are your eyes red?"

I jumped to my feet. I looked down and pointed my finger

at Lydia. "You want to know why? Because I am tired of all this shit. I'm tired of everything bad happening to me. I never asked to turn into this—this—" I gestured down at myself, "—this *freak*. But no one asked me what I wanted. Not the universe. Sure as hell not my mom."

Lydia hopped up, her voice strong and steady. "Seriously, Tex. I don't know what your problem is, but your eyes are full-on glowing now. So unless you feel like burning down the school, which in your current mood is probably an option, I suggest you take a chill pill. You are seriously over reacting."

I opened my mouth to argue, but promptly shut it. She was right. All of the things I said were true. And yeah, I was royally pissed off about the sharp right turn my life had taken into Crapsville. But it's not like any of this was new. So why was I suddenly so upset?

"Is this because Ezekiel doesn't let Roman come to school anymore?" Lydia asked.

"I'm not—" I stumbled. "I don't—This has nothing to do with Roman."

Lydia laughed at me, "Ya. Okay. Aren't you living at his house? It's not like you don't get to see him. You can tell him all about your day when you're having your naked snuggle time."

"Lydia!" I shouted.

"What?"

"It's not like that."

"Seriously?" she asked. "Because if I was with him, there would be a lot of naked snuggle time."

I chose not to respond to that comment. Instead, I closed my eyes and took a deep breath in, trying to calm my flaring temper. It'd been almost a week since Roman and the others started looking for that wraith den. So far, nothing. I took another deep breath, focusing on the trees surrounding the school. I pulled on their energy to help me calm down. That was when I felt it. It started with a tingling feeling creeping up my arms, like when an insect crawls on your skin. It only meant one thing.

"There's a wraith here."

Lydia took a sharp breath. "Seriously? Where?"

I scanned the area. At first I didn't see anything and started to doubt my intuition. But then I caught a glimpse of shockingly white hair among the milling student body coming out of the building. It was the same thing I saw outside my house when the Sheriff hauled me in. The boy with the white hair looked up and gave me a wicked smile before disappearing around the back of the building.

Evan.

Instinctively, I stepped in front of my best friend. "Lydia, go to class."

"What? No—" she started to protest from behind me, but I turned around quickly and gripped her shoulders, cutting her off.

"Do not argue with me. Go. Now. I can't deal with this if I'm worried about you." I was begging. I hadn't told her about Evan coming back as a wraith and I planned to keep it that way.

Reluctantly, she listened and headed toward the building. I pulled out my phone, briefly entertaining the idea of doing the right thing and texting Isaac. At the last second I decided not to. He would just stop me from doing what I was about to do. And even if he didn't, he would definitely report back to Roman. And *that* was the last thing I needed right now.

I put my phone back in my pocket and took a deep breath. I needed a moment alone with Evan. I had some questions for him, and I was not stopping until he answered.

/|\

I found him outside the gym. He was leaned up against the brick wall, one foot up, his head back, eyes closed. I had a brief sense of Deja vu. The last time Evan and I were here, Deacon had killed him. I could still see the bloodlust on Deacon's face, the swiftness with which he moved, the horrible crack of Evan's neck.

"Weird, right?" His words tore me back from the painful memory. "Not many people get to visit where they died."

"What are you doing here, Evan?" I asked. I stood with my arms at the ready. I had no idea what he was prepared to do.

He kept his eyes closed, but a twisted smile crossed his face. "I missed school. Thought I'd come back to pick up the homework I missed since I've been, you know—dead."

The sarcasm dripped from his voice, but the words still hit home. "I'm sorry," I said. Surprise registered on his face, but he quickly covered it with a scoff. "I never meant for you to get hurt. If I had just left you alone, none of this would have happened."

He laughed but there was no humor in the action. "You look real sorry. You and Roman are quite cozy together. Anyway, I don't want your pity. If anything, I should be thanking you. The old me, the one when I was alive, was disgusting. He was soft, weak, *nice*." He visibly shuddered on the last word.

"Then what are you now?" I asked.

His head snapped up and for a moment he dropped the facade. His eyes turned bloodshot. The veins traveled down his face in dark lines. "Powerful."

I felt my power stir deep in my belly, begging to be set loose. And from Evan I could sense a darkness, a thickness in the air that promised violence. Both of us were itching for a fight, but neither was willing to make the first move. Regardless of the responsibility I felt for Evan's death, I wasn't going to forget what he really was.

"You've been following me," I said. It was a statement, not a question.

"Yes," he responded with no remorse. "Deacon wants to

make sure you don't do something stupid. Like find the book and give it to someone like Ezekiel."

"You had me arrested," I accused.

He laughed. A deep, genuine, belly laugh. "As entertaining as that was, and as much as I would love to take credit for it, I can't."

I narrowed my eyes, annoyed. "Deacon, then."

"Nope," he replied quickly.

My nostrils flared in irritation. "Liar. It had to be him."

He pushed off the wall and walked in my direction. He stopped just out of arm's reach. "Think about it, sweetheart. Deacon needs you to find the book. You can't exactly do that from a jail cell."

Crap. He had a point.

"We'll have it soon," I lied. Then I asked the question that had been eating away at me for days. "What does Deacon want with it anyway?"

Evan shrugged nonchalantly. "No clue. But I'm sure he has his reasons."

I cocked my head in his direction. "And not knowing doesn't bother you? You just do what he says? What a good little bitch-boy."

Apparently, that struck a nerve. His veins returned and he let out a low growl, showing a hint of his serrated teeth.

The power in my gut moved excitedly up my arms, heating them along the way. "Give me my aunt," I demanded, dropping all pretenses.

Evan took a long, hard look at my red eyes. "You really want to do this here?" he growled.

I answered him with fire. Both hands were bright and burning. Thank God there were no windows on this side of the building. "We don't have to. Just tell me where Allie is and you get to walk away."

"What are you going to do?" he taunted, taking a step closer. "Kill me? Seems redundant."

I was itching to attack, but I held off. I just needed him to take one more step. "You will release her, one way or the other."

"Go to hell," he sneered, but I barely heard it. He took that last step I was waiting for. I launched the fireball from my left hand at him. He feinted right, exactly as I hoped. Just as he moved, I spun into a killer round kick. It caught him across the jaw, knocking him back several feet. Right hand still aflame, I threw it where he laid sprawled on the ground, but he was too quick. He rolled left. I felt the heat rushing back down my arms, preparing to ignite, but it wasn't fast enough. Evan hopped up and lunged for me. His hands wrapped tightly around my neck. He pushed me backward until I hit a tree. With no time to call on fire, it looked like it was going to be hand-to-hand.

Fine by me.

I lifted both arms up and brought my elbows down sharply on his arms, breaking his hold. I kicked out with my right leg, catching him in the gut. He leaned forward, his arms moving to protect his stomach. Wasting no time, I brought my other leg straight up. My knee connected with his nose and I heard a satisfying crunch. He fell back to the ground. I straddled his hips This time it was my turn to grab his throat. With my free hand, I reached behind me, grabbing the dagger hidden in my waistband. I swiftly moved the blade to his neck, replacing my hand with its sharp edge.

"Tell me where Allie is," I demanded.

A demented cackle cut through his blood-stained teeth. "You won't kill me."

I punched him once in the face and raised the dagger behind my head, ready to strike. "I wouldn't be too sure about that."

"If you kill me," he coughed, choking on blood, "you'll never get your aunt back."

Before I had time to ponder his words, the door to the school ripped open. Through it ran Isaac, and two steps behind him, Lydia. Distracted by the fact that Lydia did not listen to me *at all*, Evan took the opportunity to escape. He punched me once, squarely in the face. The force was enough to knock me back on my ass. He got to his feet and ran, putting significant distance between us, but stayed close enough for me to hear him.

"Time is running out for your aunt. Find the book and give it to us," he commanded. "Fail to retrieve it and—" he looked at Lydia, still standing frozen at the door. "I suggest you put your precious friends in a place safe from all the evils in this world. Because I will kill you and everyone in my path." Then he disappeared.

I lifted my dagger hand up to my nose and it came away red. *That was a hell of a hit.* I kept my hand pressed there, trying to stop the bleeding. I replayed Evan's parting words. Although intended as a threat, it jarred loose the tendrils of a memory. I repeated his words like a mantra until finally it clicked. A smile broke across my face. Isaac and Lydia ran up to me, both ranting and raving. I didn't hear a word they said. My smile would have made the Cheshire Cat blush.

"This hardly seems like a time to be grinning like an idiot," Lydia admonished. I didn't respond. Instead, I started to giggle.

Isaac looked from me to Lydia. "She's lost it."

Finally, after my laughs became hysterical, Lydia snapped me out of it, and not in the nicest way. She pinched my arm. Hard.

"Ow!" I yelled.

"Kyndal, what is wrong with you? What's so funny?"

I quieted down, but I still couldn't wipe the grin off my face. "He told me," I said.

"Told you what?" Isaac demanded.

"He told me where to find the book."

22

I paced in front of Ezekiel's house. It was early, the sun barely shining above the horizon. School didn't start for hours. "Let me go in and talk to him first," Roman said.

"Why can't I go with you?" I asked, offended.

"Honestly?" Roman responded. "Convincing Ezekiel is going to take some finesse. That's not exactly your strong suit."

I pouted at him. "I have finesse. Other people are just stupid."

He chuckled. "I'll be right back."

As he headed inside, I turned and plopped down on the front step. The compound was quiet. Almost everyone was still sleeping.

After several minutes of waiting, I grew restless. I got up and started to wander about the yard. I walked along the tree line, studying the flowers there. I only recognized a few. Wild ginger, indigo, and plain old dandelions. Moving back toward the house, I paused at the columns holding up the porch. Each was now wrapped with beautiful vines of pink flowers. I moved closer to smell them.

"Bleeding heart." The voice made me jump. I whipped my head toward the doorway, where Roman now stood.

"What?" I asked.

"The flower," he said, stepping out onto the porch. "It's called the Wild Bleeding Heart. Ezekiel's favorite. He cultivates it wherever he goes."

"Oh," I responded quietly. "How'd it go?" I asked.

"He wants to see you," he replied.

Walking into Ezekiel's office, I had to admit I was nervous. I hadn't spoken with Ezekiel directly since the night he bailed me out of jail. Now, here I was, groveling at his feet.

Awesome.

When we walked into his office, I found him exactly where he was the first time I was in this room; standing behind his desk, looking at papers. Xavier stood behind him, as always.

"Have a seat, Kyndal," Ezekiel said without looking up.

"No thanks, I'll stand," I responded.

Ezekiel looked up from his work, his eyes shifting between Roman and myself. Only turning his head slightly my way,

Roman muttered under his breath, "Finesse." Then, he went and took a seat in front of Ezekiel's desk. I rolled my eyes but joined Roman anyway.

"Roman tells me you have located *The Book of Breathings*. That it is here, in the Allegheny."

"That's correct," I told him. "At least I think so, sir."

"That's great," he said eagerly. "Where is it?"

"There's a lake, perfectly circular with a small island in the middle. The trees are dense and you can only access it through one side. I went there with Allie not long after I moved here. There's a couple of entries in my mom's journal about her and my dad going there. He called it his safe haven from all the evils in the world. That has to be where she hid it. My guess is on the island."

"This is good news," he said. "Well done, Kyndal. I will arrange a search party immediately."

I stood up. "I want to go."

He looked at me. "No. I won't allow it."

"With all due respect sir, I'm not asking. I've done everything you told me. I deserve to go. And besides, you won't find it without me. I'm the only one that's been there before."

Neither of us moved, locked in a staring contest. I knew I was pushing him, saying all the wrong things, challenging his authority—pretty much doing all the things Roman was worried I would do. But I refused to sit this one out.

"Very well, Kyndal. You can go."

I looked at Roman, shock written all over my face. "Well, I did not see that coming."

"Good. Now that that's settled, I'm assuming you have a plan."

Roman smiled. "Yes sir, I do."

/|\

The next morning, I crawled out of bed at the promise of coffee and now stood on the back porch, thermos in hand, staring at the still-dark sky.

"Why are we up? It's dark out," I whined.

"Sunrise is in ten minutes."

"Exactly. That's ten more minutes I could be sleeping."

"We're going to be running full speed through the forest. The earlier we go, the less likely we are to be spotted."

Ignoring his logic, I turned toward a chair, fully intending on napping, when I heard a door open at the big house.

Shortly after, Cassie, Mallory, and Isaac jogged onto the lawn.

Looks like I can forget nap time.

"Let's do this," Isaac said. Always eager. Even at the butt-crack of dawn.

Mallory produced a map from her back pocket and spread it out over the table near the training ring.

"The areas marked in red are populated areas. Those are out. The parts in black are well established waterways or areas we've been to before. Also, not possibilities. These highlighted areas indicate places that the lake could exist."

My eyes bugged out. "That is a lot," I said, stating the obvious.

Roman stepped up to the map. "You can eliminate these waterways also," he said, pointing at several larger rivers and creeks. "Based on Kyndal's description of it, there is no large direct water source feeding it. Whatever is connected to it is small enough it's not named."

"These areas, too." I piped up, indicating locations on the map with high topography. "There were no large rock formations surrounding it either. We should focus more on low-lying areas surrounded by heavy forestation." Mallory struck out the areas Roman and I suggested.

"That's much better," Cassie said.

Roman took control. "Split into two groups. Cassie, Mallory, and Isaac—you take the eastern half of this area. Kyndal and I will take the western. If you find anything, call. Otherwise, reconvene here when your area has been covered."

Cassie's group turned and immediately took off into the forest where the sun was just starting to peek through the trees.

Roman looked at me. "Let's go."

We wasted no time, heading full-speed down the western trails. Roman was so fast, I was forced to draw on all of my power just to keep up. We started out on the more populated paths, eliminating those areas first. Then, we moved toward the center of the forest, where the trees grew closer together and the paths disappeared. Before I knew it, the sun was straight above us. We reached the thickest part of the forest and were forced to slow our pace when the foliage became too entangled for us to pass through quickly. I was just about ready to give up when I spied a glimpse of reds and pinks in the sunlight to my left. Following my instinct, I immediately turned and began to climb over a particularly large fallen tree.

"Kyndal! Where are you going?" Roman yelled from where he had stopped, several paces past where I'd been.

"I think I see something!" I hollered back. I pushed on, wading through the thick brush. As the trees thinned out, I saw the reflection of the sun off the water. Excitement coursed through my veins. I finally broke out of the foliage and into the meadow filled with pinks, yellows, and reds. Roman came to a stop beside me.

Before us was a lake. Perfectly circular and still, its surface only disturbed by the island that stood in the middle.

"This is it," I said. "We found it."

We immediately called the others. Within minutes, they cut through the brush on the other side of the meadow, close to where Allie and I came last time. We met at the edge of the water.

"So, this is it, huh?" Isaac said. "It's smaller than I expected."

"It's beautiful," Cassie added. As a Pisces, it was no surprise she would be drawn to the beauty of the water.

"What do we do now?" Mallory asked.

"Find the book," Roman responded.

"Um, ya. How exactly do we do that?" Isaac inquired.

"Kyndal, this was your idea. Where do we look?" Cassie asked. She, Mallory, and Isaac all looked at me with expectant eyes.

I shrugged my shoulders. "Hell if I know."

Mallory huffed. "Perfect."

I glared at her. "You know, I don't exactly know what I'm doing here, and your shitty attitude isn't helping. So, maybe less sarcasm, more helpful ideas."

"I think it's perfectly clear you have no idea what you're doing," Mallory retorted. "Should have known better than to trust a wraith," she mumbled under her breath.

"What'd you just say?" Roman asked her. *Shit.*

"Shut up, Mallory!" I yelled.

She ignored me completely. Instead she answered Roman. "She didn't tell you, did she?" She gave a wicked grin.

"Your girlfriend got into a brawl with a wraith yesterday at school. Claims he gave her the key to where the book is. Now here we are. A dead-end."

That flipped my bitch switch.

My power surged forward, ignited by my anger. "At least I'm trying to do something helpful. The only time you do something remotely nice is when Cassie makes you." Mallory's eyes instantly turned yellow. Roman tried to step in. He placed a firm hand on my arm, but the cooling effect of his power did nothing to douse the fire burning inside me. Cassie also stepped up. I didn't spare either of them a glance. My eyes were locked on Mallory. "Without her, you're nothing but a hateful bitch."

I had no time to react. A huge gust of wind burst forth from Mallory, aimed directly at me. The gust hit me square in the chest, knocking me down. But I came up throwing. Mallory easily dodged the fireball and the fight was on. She lunged for me, tackling me to the ground. We exchanged a handful of punches until Mallory was ripped off me by a very angry Roman. Gripping her around the waist, he tried to haul her away. She refused to go quietly. She elbowed him in the face.

"Screw this," Roman growled and released her.

The fight back on, we continued to exchange blows until finally I got fed up. Mallory had been kicking my ass for days. I decided to fight dirty. I yanked on her injured arm, causing her to cry out in pain. Then, I kicked her square in the stomach, forcing her to lean forward a little. I reached up and grabbed her by her ponytail as my other hand reached for her belt. Holding tight to both, I dug deep into my power and threw her with as much strength as I could muster into the nearby lake.

Or at least that was the plan.

Mallory's body went hurtling toward the lake, but the second she crossed the threshold of the water, she stopped mid-air and dropped to the ground, like a bird running into a window. Instantly, we all froze.

"What the hell?" Isaac exclaimed.

Cassie ran to Mallory's side, helping her get up slowly. Our feud forgotten, I joined them near the edge of the water. Tentatively, I reached my hand out to break the shoreline. Like hitting a wall, my hand splayed out against an invisible shield.

I turned and looked at the others. "It's some sort of barrier. I can't get through it."

Everyone joined me, testing different areas of the shoreline, all with the same result. Not far to my right, Cassie took a step back and raised her arms. The water in the lake started to break and small white caps formed on the tops of tiny waves. She lowered her arms.

"There's something blocking my powers," Cassie said. "The amount of power I just pulled should have split that lake like the Red Sea."

I turned and looked at Roman who was standing at my side

again. "Don't ask me," he said.

"Well, I'd say we're definitely in the right place," Isaac quipped, shaking his head in disbelief. "Now what, Princess?"

Good question.

/|\

We were forced to leave the lake without answers. We spent hours out there, trying everything in our collective powers to break the barrier, but nothing worked. Finally, we returned to the compound to regroup. Roman immediately went to Ezekiel and debriefed him. I wanted to go with him, but Roman blew me off. He hadn't said much to me since my fight with Mallory. The others spread out. Isaac disappeared inside the main house, no doubt in search of food. Cassie and Mallory sat on the back porch, whispering quietly. Their backs were to me. It was obvious I wasn't welcome there. Left alone, I wandered over to Roman's house and grabbed my mom's journal. Now that we found where the book was, maybe I could find a clue about how to break the barrier.

I hadn't been reading long when my phone buzzed. I reached over to Roman's bedside table and grabbed it.

"Hey, Lydia."

"Kyndal, where are you?" She sounded worried.

"I'm at Roman's. Why? What's wrong?"

I heard her sigh in relief. "I was worried about you. You said Ezekiel wouldn't let you miss any more school, and then you were gone today. I thought something happened."

"Something did happen," I told her. "We found the book."

"What?" she shrieked. "That's awesome! I want to see it. I'm coming over."

"Lydia, no," I stopped her. "We don't actually have it. It's—it's hard to explain."

"Well, you can explain it in person."

"I don't want to get you wrapped up into any more of this. It's not safe."

I heard her huff. I could picture her standing there, hand on her hip. "A wraith showed up at school. It doesn't get any more dangerous than that. And frankly, I'd rather spend my time with the people who have supernatural powers and can kick ass if necessary. I'll see you in ten." The line went dead.

Well. I guess that settles that.

Nine minutes later, I wandered outside to meet Lydia. I was surprised when I saw Roman in the training ring. I assumed he was still talking to Ezekiel. *Why didn't he come find me?* I stood there for a few minutes and watched him spar with Darius. Even though I knew Darius was several decades older than Roman, he handled him easily. He moved with impressive speed, handling the dagger as if it were an extension of his arm. I heard Lydia join me at the edge of the ring.

"Wow," Lydia said. "Hubba hubba."

I snorted at her reaction. "You're ridiculous."

She looked up at me. "And you are ridiculously lucky to be with that."

No argument there. I just wish I knew if he was mad at me.

Roman stepped out of the ring and picked up a towel, wiping the sweat off his face.

"I thought you were talking to Ezekiel," I hollered across the ring. "I expected you to be in there for a while."

He threw the towel down, but didn't turn my way. "I was, but there wasn't much to tell him."

"He have any ideas about how to break the boundary?"

He finally looked at me. His eyes held none of the usual affection. "He had one idea. It's a bad one though."

I looked at him warily. "I don't understand."

He walked over to me in order to speak quietly, waiting until Darius was out of hearing range. "He wants me to convince Sandra to help us."

I scowled at him. "Why does he think she would suddenly help?"

"I don't think she will, but we have to try."

"I don't want her help," I retorted.

"It doesn't matter what you want," he said roughly. I flinched at his tone. "Ezekiel gave us an order. That's the end of it."

I frowned at him. "Okay. Well, I'll do what I can to help you."

'No," he said quickly. "I'll do it myself." Then, he walked away.

"Woah," Lydia said. "What's his problem?"

Me. I'm his problem.

23

It was just before sundown. Lydia and I wound through the country roads, headed toward town. Roman never returned after brushing me off to find Sandra. Apparently, he was successful. The only thing I had heard from him was a brief text.

Meet at *Sandra's* at dark.

I looked out the window nervously. I popped my knuckles out of habit. "Would you chill out?" Lydia asked for the third time.

"You don't understand," I told her. "We asked Sandra for help. She was the first person we went to, and she refused to even speak to me. Then Deacon almost killed Roman and kidnapped Allie. If she had just cooperated in the first place, none of this would have happened. Now she's suddenly willing to help. It doesn't feel right."

"You think she has ulterior motives?" Lydia asked.

"I don't think she's helping us out of the goodness of her heart, that's for damn sure."

Moments later we pulled into Sandra's bar and I felt the familiar chill down my spine. Roman was already here. Lydia pulled her car around back, parking in the grass where it couldn't be seen from the road. We stepped out of the car, careful not to step on the rubble on the ground. We ducked under the police tape and entered through the back door.

The bar was still in ruins. Obviously, no one had returned since Deacon's attack. Roman and Sandra were the only ones there. Sandra sat in a chair, leaning against one of the few tables that hadn't been destroyed. Her hands were still wrapped and her face was still badly bruised. She had no business being out of bed. Roman moved about the room, finding surviving chairs and setting them up at the table where Sandra sat. Lydia took a seat at the bar.

"Who else is coming?" I asked. There was no need for anyone to answer. Cassie walked through the door. She walked right past me without even a glance. She was obviously bitter about my fight with Mallory. Isaac and Mallory followed her. My eyes bored into Mallory, remaining there even as she walked past. I could feel anger bubble in my chest. Just as I started to take a step her way to do something really stupid, a hand grabbed my wrist. A cool breeze rushed up my arm, always more powerful with direct contact. Immediately the anger diffused and my head cleared. I turned toward the source of the hand.

"Don't." Roman's voice was low enough that only I could

hear, but his tone was sharp. Slowly, my arm relaxed and the anger seeped out of me. I opened my mouth to talk, to apologize for not telling him about Evan, but before a word came out, he released my arm and joined the others. Exhaling loudly, I followed him so the meeting could begin.

Anticipation hung heavy in the air. The lights were off. Only a few small candles lit the room. We didn't want anyone from the outside to see that people were in the bar. It was still an active crime scene. I noticed one candle had lost its light. Quickly, I flicked my hand, throwing a small flame at the candle. It lit up brightly.

Most of the group had stationed themselves at the table; Sandra on the very end. Still too amped-up to sit, I perched atop the bar, near Lydia. I kicked my feet restlessly. No one seemed to know what to say and the silence was starting to make me itchy.

Sandra finally spoke. "Why don't you begin by telling me what you do know."

Roman took over. "Eighteen years ago, Kyndal's mother, Sofia, stole *The Book of Breathings*. Through her journals, Kyndal has deduced that she hid the book rather than keep it with her. We tracked it down to a lake inside the Allegheny. We went to the lake yesterday, but encountered what appeared to be some sort of barrier. None of us were able to pass the threshold of the water. It was like some sort of invisible wall."

Sandra smiled knowingly. "It was a boundary spell. One

that came from *The Book of Breathings.*"

"No Kindred has practiced magic in centuries," Cassie threw in. "We don't even teach it anymore."

"You are correct," Sandra said, "except for a very particular exception: The Guard."

"Wait," Cassie interrupted again, "you're saying that her mother—" she pointed to me, "was in the Guard?"

"What's the Guard?" I asked. Everyone ignored me.

"That's correct," Sandra said to Cassie.

"Wow," Isaac said, his voice filled with wonderment. My eyes jumped from Isaac to Cassie to Roman. All three wore the same awestruck look. They were frozen, staring at Sandra. I looked at Lydia. She shared my confused look.

Everyone seemed to have forgotten we existed. "Guys!" Lydia finally yelled, waving her arms back and forth. Finally, they turned our way. "Remember us? Brand new baby Kindred and a run-of-the-mill, non-magical human over here. We have no frickin' clue what you're talking about."

Cassie answered. "According to the stories, the Guard was an elite group of Kindred. The original four were hand chosen by The Thrice Great Hermes, endowed with a special set of gifts to help protect our people. Warriors so well attuned to each other they could sense each other's presence, communicate telepathically, sometimes even share their powers."

Damn.

My eyes cut quickly to Roman at the mention of the Guard's abilities, but he was staring straight ahead. However, the hard lock of his jaw gave away the fact that he heard what she said and made the same connection I did. I returned to Sandra. "How do you know my mother was in the Guard?"

She gave me a ghastly smile. "Because I was in it with her." The whole room went still. This was obviously news to everyone. "Through the generations, the power of the Guard had become diluted. While it is true we were stronger together, for the most part, we were simply a group of highly trained fighters, tasked with the protection of an ancient artifact."

"*The Book of Breathings*," I filled in.

"Yes," she replied. "When you are a Guard member, it is not a part-time career. It is a lifelong commitment, and as you know, our lives can be very long. Sofia and I, as well as two others, protected the book for over seventy years. You see, the Kindred believed it was ill advised to keep the book in one location, lest the wraiths discover its whereabouts and try to steal it from us. So the book always traveled with the Guard. We moved often. Eighteen years ago, we came to Marienville. Then, everything changed."

"Why?" I asked.

Sandra's face scrunched up as if she smelled something sour. "Sofia met a boy. A mortal, of all things." My heart ached at the mention of my father.

I interrupted her story. "I don't understand the problem."

Roman answered. "Guard members take a vow of celibacy when they begin their watch."

Oh.

My very existence showed how well my mother followed that rule.

"To say the rest of us disapproved of her relationship with the boy would be an understatement." I couldn't help but notice how she never called my father by name. He was always the boy. "We tried to explain to her what would happen if the Council found out about them, but she didn't care. Instead, she grew distant from the rest of the Guard, began questioning Kindred law. One day she just quit. Stopped hunting wraiths, stopped reporting in to the Council. They took notice."

Sandra paused and took a drink of the water in front of her. "What happened next?" Isaac asked. By the look on his face, I could tell he was completely enthralled by the story, but not in the same way as me. His interest came from the forbidden love story and promise of consequences. He didn't care that these were my parents we were talking about.

"As the regional Nomarch, Ezekiel was tasked with arresting Sofia and bringing her before the Council. It almost killed him to do it." She looked at me. "Ezekiel and your mother were very good friends. Unable to do it himself, he sent a lieutenant—Xavier. When he showed up where we were staying, she put up a fight and managed to escape."

Isaac snorted. "She defeated Xavier. How embarrassing."

Sandra leveled him with an even stare. "The Guard are the most skilled warriors in the world. There isn't a single Kindred that can stand before us and prevail. You would do well to remember that." She paused a moment longer to stare at a now stone-faced Isaac. It took everything I had not to giggle. I loved watching Isaac get put in his place. "But as I was saying, it wasn't until after Sofia escaped that we realized she had taken the book with her."

"That's why he's so adamant we find the book," I said. "He blames himself for it disappearing in the first place."

Sandra nodded.

Lydia broke her silence. "What happened to the other Guard members?"

"We were put on trial for treason in front of the Council. The consequences were severe. I repented and was allowed to keep my brand. Others were not as lucky."

Her words hung heavy in the air. I knew very little of Kindred law, but even I thought that sounded harsh. My mother seemed to have a knack for leaving a mess for others to clean up. I tried to process all this information, but something kept nagging at me.

"Why did my mom take the book? How did that benefit her?"

Sandra shrugged. "I don't know for sure. I never found her

to ask. The only answer I could come up with was leverage."

I wrinkled my brow in confusion.

Roman explained. "If the Council ever caught up with your mother, she would have been executed as a traitor and a deserter. Knowing the location of the book was the only thing that would have kept her alive."

Cassie spoke up. "How does any of this help us now?"

Good question.

"You say the lake you found was protected by a boundary spell. I know how to break it."

"How?" Roman asked.

Sandra stood. "Follow me."

She led us through the back offices. We passed the kitchen which was completely destroyed from the attack and entered the private office I had found her in before. Without a second glance, she walked past the chair she had been tied to and stopped at her desk. "Isaac, move this off the rug." He did as he was told. "Roman, lift the carpet." Roman pulled the rug back, revealing a trap door. "Open it." I could see the top of a staircase, but after that, nothing but blackness. Everyone stared at Sandra in astonishment. "Alright everyone, in you go," she said.

"You're joking, right?" I asked sarcastically. No way was I walking down that staircase.

"Do you want my help or not?" she challenged.

Cassie stepped up to the edge of the staircase. She took one hesitant step before committing but then continued her descent. When no one heard screams, we followed, one-by-one. I made sure Lydia went before me. As worried as I was about what was at the bottom of the steps, I was more concerned about leaving Lydia alone with Sandra. My feet finally reached the bottom. Sandra was immediately behind me. She whispered in a language I didn't recognize and I heard the stairs retreat into the ceiling. It was now completely black. Too dark even for my enhanced vision. I turned toward where I thought she was standing.

"What did you just do?" I accused. She whispered again in the same language. One by one, torches came to life, each holding an eerie blue flame. The room lit up. The walls were covered in symbols. Some I recognized as zodiac signs, others were foreign to me. Shadows danced over the walls. I walked over to one of the strange torches and reached toward it. The blue flames danced along my fingers, but unlike real fire, this felt cool to my skin.

"What is this place?" I whispered. Sandra shuffled past me, placing her hand on my shoulder momentarily. I turned and watched as she went to the opposite wall. There was a shelf and table there I hadn't initially noticed.

"Every member of the Guard has a specific job," she began. "I was the Scribe. I spent many years studying our texts and memorizing them in order to teach others our practices. I was in charge of learning healing practices and training techniques, but primarily, I studied magical incantations."

She reached out and carefully grabbed a large book. Her bandaged hands made her movements awkward, but she managed. *The Book of Breathings* disappearing was devastating to our people. Part of the reason the Council pardoned me was due to how familiar I was with the text. If they executed me, they had no one left that knew what the book contained." She turned the book toward us. "What they didn't know, was that I'd been recreating the book on my own."

Cassie jumped forward. "You rewrote the book?" She ran her fingers over the spine. "That's amazing."

"It's incomplete," Sandra answered. "Everything is written from memory. Many of the spells in here are intricate. Mistake one detail or ingredient, and there could be consequences."

Roman spoke up. "Do you have the spell we need?"

"Yes," she said smiling. "I believe so." She opened the book. "It's deceptively simple. There are two ingredients. One—a major celestial event."

Cassie piped up, "There's a full lunar eclipse in two days."

How the hell does she know that? Does she have an almanac for a brain?

"And two," Sandra continued. "Blood. Cardinal blood, specifically. One to represent each of the elements."

"Between you, Kyndal, and me, three of the four are right in this room," Roman said.

"What's the fourth?" Lydia asked.

Roman responded. "Capricorn."

My eyebrows shot up. "Ezekiel is a Capricorn. He'll help."

Sandra and Roman made eye contact. It was brief, but I caught it. They were hiding something.

"I'll speak to him," Roman said. I couldn't tell if he was talking to me or Sandra.

"Do it quickly, son," Sandra replied. "We are running out of time."

/|\

The group filed out one by one, including Lydia. I stayed behind, waiting for Roman on the back porch. Once he had Sandra settled in Isaac's car, he joined me.

"So." I crossed my arms and jumped up on the porch railing. "Sandra is pretty good at keeping secrets, huh?"

He turned my direction, his eyes ablaze. "Speaking of secrets, did you ever plan on telling me about the fight at school?"

I cringed slightly at his tone. I knew this fight was coming. "Eventually," I answered slowly.

"Eventually?" he huffed back at me. "Once someone else mentioned it? You had the perfect opportunity to tell me the other night, and you didn't. I thought we agreed on no more secrets." He was pissed. It made me defensive. I jumped off the railing.

"I thought we did too. So tell me Roman, how exactly did you get Sandra to agree to help us? What did you have to promise her in return?"

Silence.

"Exactly," I accused. "So don't get pissed at me for keeping secrets when you're doing the same thing."

He ignored my accusation. "I understand you are going to get into fights, it comes with the territory. But you can't go looking for them. Especially without me there to back you up."

I gaped at him. "I don't need you to protect me. I can take care of myself just fine, thank you."

He let out a frustrated growl, running his hands through his hair. "You are the most frustrating person I know."

"Right back at ya," I replied, crossing my arms.

It was silent for a long moment. Both of us were being stubborn, refusing to talk. Finally, he broke. "Her freedom," he whispered.

"What?" I said, annoyed.

He looked at me with considerably kinder eyes. "I promised Sandra I would get Ezekiel to lift her sentence and reinstate her powers."

"How do you plan to do that?"

"I don't know," he admitted. "The only thing Ezekiel wants more than to keep the book out of wraith hands is for you to read that spell. We just need to convince him that can't happen without Sandra."

"I don't trust her."

"She raised me," he replied, offended.

I did my best to ignore the hurt in his voice. "She refused to help us when we needed her. If she had, Allie never would have been taken. This is all her fault."

"She isn't the only one who has kept information to herself," he challenged.

"I had to do something! Evan knows where Deacon is keeping my aunt. I couldn't just let him walk away. And it worked. He gave me the clue I needed to find the lake."

Roman's shoulders dropped. "I didn't know it was Evan."

My jaw tightened. "Yeah, well it was."

"That couldn't have been easy." Roman knew how difficult Evan's death was for me. The guilt of it nearly kept us apart.

I popped my knuckles, looking anywhere but at him. "I had him beat. I had my dagger at his throat—but I couldn't *do it*."

"It's not really him. The Evan you knew is dead. I know this wraith has his memories, but he's just a sick perversion of the boy you knew."

I shook my head. "Doesn't make it any easier. I couldn't kill him. Again."

"Death would be a kindness," Roman replied.

I'm not so sure.

24

I was staring at a now all too familiar view. Ezekiel's office door. Roman and I were waiting to speak with him. Again.

"This bureaucratic red tape is really starting to get annoying," I whispered to Roman.

"Kindred work on a chain of command. Besides, we need his help," he whispered back.

Just then, the door opened. Xavier stood there. He nodded at Roman and completely ignored me.

"Come in, you two," Ezekiel beckoned. We entered the office. I expected Roman to sit as he had every other time, but instead he stayed standing at the back of the room. I did the same.

I skipped past Ezekiel and watched Xavier take up his post behind the desk. *So this was the man tasked with arresting my mother?* His failure allowed mom to get away with the book. No wonder he had such a huge chip on his shoulder.

Roman nudged my shoulder. "What?" I asked him.

"Ezekiel asked you a question." I looked at Ezekiel. "Excuse me, sir. What did you say?"

He smiled at me. "I asked if Sandra was helpful."

"Yes, sir. Why didn't you mention before that my mother and Sandra were in the Guard?"

He smiled at me again. "You were so new to our world I didn't want to overwhelm you with the sordid story of your mother's past. As you've learned, it is a rather upsetting one. It was a difficult time for all of us. No need to relive it unless necessary."

Roman spoke up. "Sandra says the reversal spell requires a celestial event. There is an eclipse tomorrow night. The moon will be completely covered at exactly 10:12 p.m. That's when we start the spell. You sir, Kyndal, myself, and Sandra."

"Sandra will not be a part of this. She is banned from using her powers." His tone was firm. It said, *I mean it—don't push me.*

But Roman pushed.

"Sandra *will* be a part of this. Her power as a Cancer and intimate knowledge of the book is imperative to breaking the spell. You will give her access to her powers so she may heal herself, and then, after it's over, you will lift her banishment and give her full use of her powers again."

Xavier interjected, "Why would he agree to such a

ludicrous demand?"

Roman ignored him. "Sir, you are a good man, and you want that manifestation spell to bring strength to our fire users. You don't get that without us. And you don't get us without Sandra."

After a long pause, Ezekiel nodded his assent. "So be it. Set it up. We have a little over 24 hours."

Roman turned to leave, but I paused at the door. "Sir?"

Ezekiel looked at me. "What is it, Kyndal?"

"You didn't mention what we'll do once we get the book. You do plan to trade it for Allie, don't you?" I held my heart in my throat. I didn't know what I'd do if Ezekiel refused to save Allie.

"That shouldn't be necessary," he replied.

"Sir?" Roman asked. He turned back around.

"While you were at *Sandra's* last night, Xavier captured one of Deacon's wraiths. He interrogated him and learned the location of their den. The intel was corroborated by the wraith previously in our custody. They've been holding her in a cave underneath Hector's Falls."

"With all due respect to Xavier," Roman said, "I'd like to interrogate the prisoner myself. I know this area better than anyone. Where is he being held?"

"I'm afraid that won't be possible," Ezekiel responded. "The prisoner was executed once he was no longer needed.

The team leaves tonight. I suggest you both get ready."

I stepped back in surprise. "You're letting me go?"

Ezekiel smiled at me. "You've shown great promise, Kyndal. And she is your aunt after all. It only seems fair you take part in her rescue."

"Thank you, sir."

"I know you'll make me proud."

/|\

We immediately returned to Roman's house to prepare. I slipped into black pants and a matching shirt. Roman was dressed similarly, but he had tucked a second dagger into a hidden scabbard in his boot. We would need to blend into the forest tonight. The element of surprise was our best bet for rescuing Allie. We couldn't be seen. I stood in Roman's bathroom, tying my hair into a tight ponytail. Out of the corner of my eye, I saw Roman moving through his room. I didn't know when we would be alone again so I brought up something that had been bothering me. "I want to talk to you about the Guard."

"What about them?" Roman asked, sitting on the edge of his bed and lacing up his boots. I could tell he was only partly paying attention.

"Cassie said they had special powers. That they could sense each other. Do you think that sounds like the connection between us?"

I officially had his attention. He stood up and walked over to me. He looked at me in the mirror. "I may have noticed some similarities."

"We're like them. Do you think it means something?" I asked.

He reached up and grabbed my dagger off the sink. He stood behind me, securing it to my waist. He hands lingered on my hips. "We're only partly like them. According to the stories, the Guard could also speak telepathically and share powers. We can't do either of those things."

I spun around to face him but stayed in his embrace. "But I can tell when you're near me. Sense when you're hurt."

"I don't know, Kyndal. It could have something to do with your mom being a part of the Guard. Maybe you inherited some of her gifts. Maybe it's because you're a Descendant. You're the only one of your kind. No one really knows what you're capable of yet. Or, one thing could have nothing to do with the other."

"Well, that's helpful," I said sarcastically.

He paused, smiling, amused as ever by my smart mouth. He looked me up and down. "I want to take you on a date."

Whoa. Talk about a topic change.

"Seriously?" I asked. "If you haven't noticed, our schedules are pretty full. Finding ancient artifacts, fighting wraiths, saving innocents."

He chuckled again and leaned over, placing tiny butterfly

kisses on my neck. "Later," he said. "when all this is over, I'll take you out. Our first date."

"What about *Sandra's*?" I asked.

He shook his head. "That hardly counts. I was too busy trying to figure out how I was going to explain the Kindred to you."

"Which you didn't," I interrupted.

"And you were too busy trying to pump me for information. This time we'll do it right. Sound good?"

I smiled. "Sounds perfect."

/|\

The hunting party gathered outside. In addition to Roman and me, Cassie, Mallory, Darius, Xavier, Isaac, and four others were there. It didn't escape me that Mallory and Isaac stood on the opposite side of the group as me. Every now and then one of them would look up and send a death glare my way. I rolled my eyes. I sent a quick text to Lydia letting her know I was going to get Allie. I promised to text her when we were back and I had her settled. I put my phone in my pocket before joining the others at a table. They had a map laid out.

Xavier stood at the front. He seemed to be running point. "Hector's Falls is a several-mile run. We follow the highlighted route and we stay as a group. When we reach the Falls, our water users will be our first line of offense. We need to get in quietly. Cassie and Darius—you two need to keep us from being heard. There's no telling how many wraiths could be hiding in there. As soon as someone gets eyes on the package, we get her out. As soon as she's extracted, we move out. Let's keep this clean."

Everyone nodded. I looked over to Roman. He winked at me. Above him I saw Ezekiel standing on the porch. He was dressed in similar fighting gear as us. *Strange, I didn't think he was going with us.* Roman touched my arm. His eyes were yellow, already drawing from the elements. "You ready?"

I dug into my power. I pulled from the trees, the earth under my feet, even the everlasting torch. My senses sharpened. I looked back at him with blazing red eyes. "Let's do this."

We moved quickly. Xavier led. This was the first time I had seen him outside the sparring ring. He was completely silent, a surprising fact for a man his size. Roman and I stayed toward the back of the group. We moved silently through the forest until finally we could hear water. We had passed several rivers and streams, but this sound was different. I could hear the water rushing over the rocks and hit the ground below. My shoes were wet as we stood in the pool before the caves. I could just barely make out the entrance behind Hector's Falls. It was well hidden behind the water, but we were just close enough to see it. I was surprised Xavier wanted to stop so close to the entrance. We could be easily spotted out here.

Xavier turned and whispered to us. "Water users—you're up first. Once you've made an opening, the rest of us will push through."

Cassie and Darius stepped up. Darius placed his hands in the pool of water we stood in while Cassie raised both arms. The waterfall split in half, revealing the entrance of the cave. The group took a step forward. That was when I noticed my steps no longer sloshed when I moved. Darius had parted the water so that we now moved soundlessly into the cave. Mallory was the first one in. Roman and I followed. Xavier and the others came next with Cassie and Darius at the end, closing up the waterfall behind us. The cave was completely dark. I called forth my power, creating a small fireball in my hand. I stood next to Mallory, using my hand as a torch. She glared at me, but allowed me to stay. We walked through the cave quietly. There was no sign of Allie and no sign of wraiths, either.

"Something isn't right," I whispered to Roman. "Shouldn't we see something by now?"

He nodded. Suddenly, we heard a sound to the right. I whipped that direction. Holding out my hand, I saw that the cave forked into two smaller tunnels. We split into two groups. Mallory and Cassie led half the group down the left fork. Isaac went with them, lighting their way. Roman and I took the right. We walked for a while before I heard the sound again, this time much closer. It sounded like someone groaning in pain.

Allie.

Without thinking, I ran ahead. I could feel Roman following me. We had almost reached the end of the tunnel.

I could see pink flowers hanging from the ceiling. I had just stepped into the cavern when a hand snuck out from the shadows and whipped me across the face. I flew into the opposite wall, hitting my head. I heard a crunch as I landed. The fire in my hand went out. Shrouded in darkness, I could hear the sounds of battle. I recovered, calling on my power in full force. Both hands lit up. The light revealed a gruesome scene. I looked down and had to swallow a scream. I had landed on a pile of desiccated bodies. I scrambled to my feet, trying my hardest to ignore the snapping of bones as I escaped the mass of wraith victims. Once free, I saw Roman and the others were surrounded by wraiths, fighting for their lives. Acting on instinct, I reached out with my right hand, lighting the nearest wraiths on fire. They fell easily, disintegrating into grey dust. I pulled out my dagger and joined the fight. Roman and I worked together, fighting off the wraiths that had cornered us, until we finally made it back into the tunnel. We ran full speed back to the central cavern. I could see outside; the moon provided just enough light. Near the entrance, we found the others locked in a similar fight. We wasted no time joining the battle.

Somewhere in the chaos, I lost track of Roman. I dusted a wraith and turned to find him. Distracted, I was hit with a backhand like a hammer and flew several feet into the air. I landed in a heap of limbs on the hard ground. I took the brunt of the fall on my right shoulder. I heard something pop. I tried to push myself up, but at the slightest weight, I cried out in pain. My shoulder was most likely dislocated. Gritting my teeth, I turned onto my back and sat up. I got a swift kick to the face for my trouble. My head snapped back to the ground. "Stupid girl," I heard through the ringing in my ears. I looked up, expecting to see a wraith, maybe Deacon there to deliver my death, but instead I was shocked when I saw Xavier looking down at me. His face was twisted in a snarl.

"Xavier?" I gasped out through the pain. "What are you doing?"

He laughed, and the sound was off somehow. "I told you this would happen. I told you that going after Deacon was a bad idea. That it would get us all killed. But you just couldn't fall in line. Just like your *bitch* of a mother." He knelt down, grabbing me by my hair and forcing me to sit up. My shoulder exploded in pain and starbursts obscured my vision.

"I don't—I don't understand," I managed to say. Each breath I took shot more pain into my shoulder.

"You will," he growled. "Very soon." Then he hit me once more and the world went black.

25

When I came to, I was lying on a stiff, wooden floor. My hands were bound in rope. I looked around, but nothing seemed familiar. I knew I was in a house of some sort. An old one, considering the walls were half-torn apart. I couldn't tell what floor I was on. The room had no windows. Someone grabbed my injured arm and dragged me to my feet. I looked over to see a wraith. He smiled at me with his serrated teeth. He pushed me forward until I come to a stop right before Xavier and Deacon. They were flanked on either side by two more wraiths. Including the one clutching my arm, that was a grand total of five bad guys. No way I could fight them all and get out alive.

"Ah, Kyndal! Thank you for joining us," Deacon said. He sounded like I just came by for dinner. "Sorry about that little bump on the head. Xavier can get carried away."

"What the hell is going on?" I asked. Neither of them answered me. I strained against my captor's hand, but he squeezed and I grimaced in pain. "Xavier, what are you doing with him?" I pleaded, but it wasn't him who answered.

"Ushering in a new era." I whipped my head to the side just as Ezekiel walked into the room. He was dressed in the same fighting gear I saw him in earlier. "Too long the Kindred have had to live in secret, fighting the never-ending battle against evil. Never getting to show who we are, what we can truly do. But we are going to change all of that." He smiled at me and it was like I was seeing him for the first time. Before, he always looked so polished, refined. I thought his clipped attitude was formality, the effect of being on this planet for centuries. When in reality—it was the effort of holding back his true self. And his true self was bat-shit crazy.

"Ezekiel, I don't understand." I couldn't seem to wrap my head around what was happening. *Why were Ezekiel and Xavier with Deacon?*

"You know; your mother never could understand either. That day she came to me and explained what had happened. Told me about her *condition.* I bet you didn't know she told me, did you? That's how much she trusted me. She broke the law, knowing full-well Guard members couldn't have families—and still, she told me." He ran his hand through his hair, pulling loose his ponytail, shaking free his wild locks. I shook my head, trying to clear the cobwebs. That last hit from Xavier had some lingering effects. *Why is Ezekiel talking about my mom? What does he mean by her condition?* Then it hit me. Ezekiel could see the moment I understood. "That's right, Kyndal. I knew your mother was pregnant, long before anyone else did.

Rather than persecute her, I wanted to help her. Protect her. Very few of us knew about the legend of the Descendants and what your kind would be able to do, and here we were, with an opportunity dropped right into our laps. But she just refused to *understand*." It was at this point I saw how truly unhinged Ezekiel was.

"My mother wasn't a traitor, was she? It's *you*."

Ezekiel's eyes grew wide with maniacal glee. "Ah, but she was a traitor. She betrayed her people the moment she started a relationship with that *boy*. Through my mercy, she would have been spared. But she was so stubborn. She refused to see reason and I was left with no other choice but to eliminate her." I couldn't help it, I gasped. "Don't worry," he said, his voice sickeningly sweet. "I always planned to keep you. Raise you in our world until you were ready to control your powers."

"But you didn't get her," I added, raising my head in pride for my mother. "She was better than your lap dog." I nodded toward Xavier. He reached out and hit me. I rolled my jaw around. *That hurt.* I spit blood at his feet. "I can see why you were so easy to beat." He moved to hit me again, but Ezekiel raised a hand and he backed away. "Good doggy," I jeered.

Ezekiel's lips curled into a sneer. "She may have evaded me temporarily, but in the end, I found her. Terrible thing that car accident. Took out your entire family. If your mother hadn't run in the first place, the lives of your family could have been spared. Of course your brother never would have existed, but there is a difference between dying and never being born. What a waste. Their blood is on her hands."

My knees completely gave out and I crumbled to the ground. I was suddenly back to that day six months ago, when everything was ripped from me. *I'm driving the car, listening to my father and brother argue in the back. Mom laughs in the passenger seat and I take my eyes off the road for just a moment to smile at her. When I look back, something is in the middle of the road.* Until now I couldn't remember what it was. Now I saw it clear as day.

A man stood in the road. He wore an old, black cloak, the hood up. Between that and the rain, I couldn't see his face, but I remembered one startling detail—his eyes were bright green. So bright, it was as if they glowed from beneath the hood. He raised his hands up, then slammed them onto the road. As if lightning had struck, the road crumpled right before my eyes, breaking apart in huge pieces. I slammed on the brakes. Mom reached for the wheel and the car swerved. It flipped, landing us on top of the broken road. My mom screamed for us to wake up. When I finally came to, I could see two sets of feet approaching the car. Suddenly, the rear of the car caught on fire. I don't know how I didn't figure it out until now.

My family didn't die in an accident. They were murdered. By Ezekiel.

My body crumpled as I openly sobbed. Losing loved ones isn't easy no matter how they die, but there was something different about knowing they were murdered. Knowing they were purposefully taken away as a part of someone's sadistic plan. Ezekiel said he wanted to keep me, raise me as his own, and when my mother took that from him, he tracked her down, killed her, and took me anyway.

I lifted my head just enough to see Ezekiel. My voice was hoarse, my throat thick with grief. "There was never any spell, was there?" I asked, realizing just how much I had been played for a fool.

He smiled a wide, toothy grin. "There is a spell. One that will bring great power to the Kindred. Once we break that boundary, you're going to help me get it."

"The others will never help you," I threatened.

Ezekiel just smiled at me. "Oh, my dear. They will help. I've already sent word to Roman. He will meet us at the lake tomorrow night to complete the reversal spell. And if he doesn't, I'll kill you."

"You can't kill me. You'll never get the book."

"I thought you might say that." Just then two other wraiths walked in. One was Evan. Between them, I saw her—being dragged like an unconscious ragdoll. A cry escaped my lips. I could immediately tell she'd been fed on. Her skin was pulled taut over her cheekbones. Her arms and legs lacked their usual muscular definition. Her normally well-kept hair was dirty and tangled. She was still wearing her work uniform, now filthy and torn. Evan dumped her to the ground roughly, a mere two feet from me. My power pricked in anger and I lunged forward, immediately drawn to her despite the obvious threat around me. I finally reached her. "Allie. Allie, wake up." She gave no response, but I saw the shallow rise and fall of her chest. She was alive.

I looked up at Evan who stood there emotionless. Overcome with fury, my hands heated up. I focused on the energy, pulling from the few natural elements around me. There was a pile of dirt in the corner, a half-empty bottle of water in the doorway. I drew them to me. It was just enough to burn through some of the rope that held my hands. I snapped the rest of the rope, jumped up, and lunged at Evan. I grabbed him by the throat and pushed him into the wall. I turned and stared at Ezekiel. "Let us both go. NOW!"

Ezekiel looked back at me impassively. "You can kill him if you like." I squeezed Evan's neck tighter. His eyes bugged out in fear. "But—" Ezekiel continued, "there's no need to be difficult. Just take me to the lake and I will let your aunt live. Refuse, and I will let Deacon drain her dry."

I looked down at my aunt where she laid broken and beaten on the ground. Deacon now stood over her. "Promise me she lives," I spit out through gritted teeth.

"You have my word," he responded.

"Swear it!" I yelled.

"Take me to the lake, complete the spell, and your aunt will live. I swear it."

I released Evan's throat and took a step back. "Then you have a deal."

/|\

Ezekiel, Deacon, and Xavier left the room. Evan posted himself as guard at the doorway. They left Allie in the room with me. I guess they figured I was less likely to try and escape if she was with me. My hands were still unbound, so I reached under Allie's arms and dragged her into my lap. I leaned against the back wall for support, keeping Evan in my eyesight. I checked Allie for wounds. She had a large bruise on her forehead. Her wrists were circled in red, most likely from being bound like I was. Beyond that, she had no other outward injuries. I knew that didn't mean she wasn't hurt. The tell-tale signs of feeding were there. There was no telling how many times they had fed from her in the time they kept her prisoner.

There was no way to tell time in that room. They had found my phone and stolen it before I woke up. Sometime after they left us alone, Allie began to move. Her arm twitched first, but her eyes stayed closed. I thought she was having a bad dream until her eyes fluttered open. She looked around the room, her gaze unfocused and bleary, until finally, it landed on me.

"Kyndal?" she whispered. Her voice was raspy. "What's going on?" She started to sit up. I supported her until we sat eye-to-eye. "You're hurt." I knew the side of my face was bloody, but I didn't care about myself. I reached over and wrapped her in a soft hug.

"I thought I lost you," I said through tears. I noticed Evan turn his head and glance at us.

Allie pulled away. Her voice was frantic. "Kyndal, you need to get out of here. These men are dangerous. There's something strange about them."

I put my hands on both her shoulders. "I know, Allie," I said soothingly. "I know." She looked back at me scared and confused. "It's hard to explain, but I'm going to get us out of this. You just have to trust me. When those men come back, I have to go with them. Don't try to stop it. You'll only end up getting hurt."

She shook her head wildly. "I don't understand what's going on."

My eyes welled up. "I know you don't. I'm so sorry, Allie. This is all my fault. I've lied to you about so much, but I promise if we—when we make it out of this, I'll explain everything to you."

She searched my face. She was frightened, but she nodded anyway. "Alright."

I heard footsteps coming down the hall. I looked up as Ezekiel and Deacon walked in. Ezekiel turned to Evan. "Take them both."

"What? No!" I screamed. I tried my hardest to put myself between Allie and Evan, but I was too weak. He pulled me up and threw me toward Deacon, then grabbed Allie. "This wasn't part of the deal! You swore!"

Ezekiel stared at me. "I promised you her life. Nothing more. She will accompany us to remind you of why you're doing this. And to keep you from crossing me."

/|\

They dragged Allie and me outside. I wasn't surprised when I found we were at Ezekiel's old farmhouse. It made sense. It was secluded, presumably abandoned, and no one knew it existed. From there we moved slowly toward the lake. Ezekiel kept pushing me to move faster, but I refused. Allie was struggling from the effort and I didn't want to hurt her more than necessary. Eventually though, we broke through the trees and I found myself standing on the water's edge for the third time. The eclipse had started and the full moon was about three quarters of the way covered. The remaining moonlight reflected off the water, just enough to make the center island visible. Ezekiel stepped up to the threshold of the lake and raised his hand tentatively. At the last second he pulled back.

"Coward," Evan cackled before reaching out on his own. The second his hand hit the barrier, his skin began to sizzle. He let out an inhuman growl before pulling his burning hand back. "Son of a—did it do that to you?" he asked, looking at me.

I furrowed my brow and shook my head. "It must not like you."

Just then, my spine tingled and a refreshing breeze surrounded me. Roman was here. Mere seconds later, he and Sandra entered the meadow. Our eyes instantly locked and my heart jumped. As if against his will, he ran toward me. He was cut off by Evan and Xavier. He shoved them both, but they didn't let him pass.

Ezekiel surprised me when he spoke. "Let him through."

Roman glared at them. He shoved his shoulder into Xavier as he pushed past him to get to me. When he reached me, his hands immediately dug into my hair and his lips slammed against mine. It was the first time he'd kissed me in front of other people. He only pulled back the smallest fraction. "I know you're hurt."

"I'll be fine," I whispered. "We have to help him, Roman."

"We don't have to do shit," he growled.

I shook my head. "If we don't, he'll kill Allie. This is the only way."

"If you are quite finished," Ezekiel interrupted, "it's 9:55."

Roman's muscles tensed and I didn't need the connection to know he was pissed. If I didn't defuse this fast, there was going to be bloodshed before we even had a chance to reach the book.

Sandra stepped up. The difference in her was obvious. The wounds on her face were completely healed. Her hands were wrapped like a fighter's. She stood up straight, a fire in her eyes I hadn't seen before. I mustered a grin. "You look better."

"Yes. It feels good to be in touch with nature again."

"What do we do?" I asked.

"The four of us will position ourselves at the four cardinal points around the water. Libra—North, Aries—South,

Capricorn—East, and Cancer—West. When the moon is completely covered, cut your hand with your dagger and place it on the barrier."

"Then what?"

"And then wait," she said, her eyes fierce.

"What do I do?" Evan asked. Crazy—he actually sounded hurt. Like he was being left out of the fun.

"Stay out of the way," I told him sharply. "And if anything happens to Allie," I stepped into his personal space, "I will kill you. This time I'll make sure it sticks."

"Places," Ezekiel said. I walked up to him and held out my hand.

"My dagger." Every ounce of my words dripped with disdain. He handed it over reluctantly.

I took one more look at Allie before moving into position. Mine was on the shore, Roman across from me. I couldn't see him in what little light was left, but I could feel him. I was uncomfortable with him so far away. To my right, his adoptive father, the man who killed my family. To my left, his adoptive mother. The alarm on a phone beeped. "10:12," Xavier said from behind me. I looked up. The last of the moon disappeared, as if it were hiding from what came next. I held my dagger above my left hand. I brought the tip down slowly across my palm, careful to draw blood without cutting too deep.

I closed my eyes, lifted my now bloodied hand, and

reached toward the barrier. I spread my fingers and placed my hand against the invisible wall. At first nothing happened, but then Sandra added her hand and I felt a slight jolt of electricity jump through my fingertips. I opened my eyes. A faint orange cord ran around the boundary of the lake, connecting me to Sandra. Ezekiel added his hand next. The power increased and the cord reached from me to him. My hand heated up, my power was being drawn into the connection. It was intense, even somewhat painful. I could sense the moment Roman added his hand to the barrier. The light of the cord intensified, eager to connect him to our circle. When the cord reached him, the power rushing through my hand doubled. Its intensity was more than anything I'd ever felt before. I let out a scream. The cord widened, its light reaching for the sky and earth simultaneously. The wind started to whip and the ground began to shake.

"Hang on!" Sandra yelled.

I could just make out the island through the now illuminated barrier. It was rumbling, like it did in my dream so many weeks ago. Soon, the edges began to break off, dropping into the water. We didn't have much time. The cord reached the ground. The light pulsed until I had to close my eyes to keep from being blinded. Suddenly, a shockwave of energy burst out from the barrier, throwing us all back several feet. I hit my head and was momentarily disoriented. When I came to, I was amazed at what I saw. The ground was still, the wind had stopped, and where the lake used to be was now a dried-up valley. In the middle of the valley was a single object. It was an oversized book emitting a faint orange glow.

The Book of Breathings.

26

Everything happened at once. Ezekiel and Roman broke, both running toward the book. I was shocked when Roman didn't stop at the book, but instead leapt over it. I realized he was running toward me. Moving full speed, he pulled his dagger and threw it directly at my head. I didn't even have time to scream. I dropped to my knees. I heard a grunt behind me and I turned in just enough time to see a wraith turn to dust. Past where the wraith had been, I saw movement in the trees. Wraiths came barreling out of the brush, headed straight for me. More than I had ever seen before. There must have been dozens. I dug my fingers into the earth, demanding it give me strength. I felt my power surge forth. Through the connection, I could feel Roman getting closer. He wouldn't reach me before the wraiths. Even without him at my side, I still knew what to do.

I kept my hands in the soil, pulling on as much power as I could without releasing it. I waited until just the right moment. I felt the wind whip around me.

"Now!" Roman shouted.

I lifted my hands out of the dirt, throwing them both toward the onslaught of wraiths. At the same time, a huge gust of wind came from behind. My hair flew forward into my face. The wind grabbed the flames, hurling them toward the approaching enemy. Rather than one fireball, the combination of Roman and my powers turned my hands into flame throwers. One by one, the wraiths went down, until I could no longer hold onto the power. Just as my flames went out, Roman reached me. He knelt down to my level. "You alright?" he asked.

I nodded. "More wraiths are coming. We need to get Allie out of here." We stood together and turned toward where she had been left in a heap on the ground. The wraiths had regrouped and were waiting.

"Look out!" I shouted. Roman turned just in time to block the blow. It was Evan. I felt a pulse in the air and suddenly Evan was pushed back several yards. He landed gracefully on his feet. Roman turned and looked at me. "I've got this. Get Allie to safety." I didn't want to leave him, but I had no choice. I turned away from him and toward the enemy.

I held my dagger in my right hand, a fireball in my left. Three wraiths stood between me and my aunt. I marched straight to the first one. I fought hard and managed what I knew was a killing blow, but I didn't pause to watch it turn to dust. The second one met the same fate. Before I reached the third, I chanced a look at where Evan and Roman were locked in deadly combat. I could feel through the connection that Roman was trying to move in for the kill.

He was worried about me and wanted to make quick work of Evan so he could help me. I didn't want to be his weakness. I charged the last wraith. I kicked and slashed at it, using every ounce of energy I had. This one was different than the others. He was patient, deliberate in his attack. I cut his arm, but all that did was piss him off. He hissed at me, knelt down, and grabbed a handful of dirt. He threw it directly in my face. Temporarily blinded, I lashed out with the dagger. He blocked the move and grabbed my arm. I screamed as his teeth came down around my forearm, ripping through my flesh. I could feel the blood gush over my arm.

I heard a quick, guttural sound followed by the unmistakable feel of wraith ash on my skin. I opened my eyes expecting to see Roman, but instead was shocked to be face-to-face with Mallory.

She didn't say anything. She just turned and ran into the action. The moon had fully emerged from its temporary darkness, lighting up the battlefield. And that's exactly what it was—a battle. The wraith numbers had grown, but so had ours. There were more Kindred than I had ever seen before. I didn't know where they all came from. I could pick out Mallory, Cassie, Darius, and surprisingly, Isaac. He had jumped in to help Roman. Once Evan saw he was outnumbered, he ran; actually turned tail, and ran. Across the valley, Sandra was fighting, too. I watched in amazement. She was spectacular, cutting down every wraith in her path. She was headed directly for the middle of the valley, where Ezekiel stood, surrounded by a wall of wraiths.

Isaac, Cassie, and Roman reached me.

"Help me get her up," I said to them, nodding to Allie. Cassie immediately grabbed one side, Isaac took the other, while Roman stood watch. Allie tried her best to help, but she was too weak to do much. "Get her back to the compound. I'll join you soon."

Roman's head whipped back to look at me. "What are you doing? You should go with her."

I looked at him square in the eye. "No. I'm not leaving."

"Who gives a shit about the book, Kyndal? You need to run." His voice was firm. It was the voice of a leader. He was used to people doing what he told them to do. *Too bad I've always had an issue with authority.*

"It's not about the book," I said, challenging him. "He killed them, Rome. My mom, Dad, Chase. He killed all of them." Roman stared at me, his gaze unwavering. I could tell he had half a mind to drag me out of there himself. I grabbed his arm, using the connection to show him exactly how determined I was to stay and fight. "I'm not going anywhere."

He held my eyes for a moment longer, then turned and looked at Cassie and Isaac. "Get Allie to safety. We'll meet you later." Cassie grit her teeth. It wasn't in her to run away, but it also wasn't in her to disobey a direct order. She and Isaac turned toward the forest and ran.

I looked back at Roman. Before I could react, he kissed me. The kiss was brief, but it was fierce and full of all the things we hadn't had the chance to say to each other yet. "Stay close to me," he growled. I nodded, my red eyes reflecting in his gold. Then we went off to battle.

We fought until time lost its meaning. We started out back to back, taking down every wraith in our way, slowly cutting a path to Ezekiel. I didn't stop to think—I just took on one wraith after the other. Any that were left, Roman took care of. I killed some with fire, but mostly I used the dagger. The dagger took longer, but it also took less energy. The numbers had dwindled on both sides. I'd stepped over multiple Kindred during the fight. I didn't have time to stop and see if any of them were alive. I just kept fighting.

Sandra and I broke through the wall of wraiths at the same time. I knew we were both going for Ezekiel, but she was faster than I was. His head was down. He stared at the book and I could see his lips moving like he was reading out loud. Sandra raised her dagger, intent on stabbing him right in the heart. She never made it to him. Xavier stepped up, backhanding her across the face. He hit her with so much force, she went flying several feet away. Ezekiel never looked up. He just kept reading. I had almost reached him when the book started to glow. The color was soft at first, a light yellow. Then the color intensified, changing to orange, then a bright red. A burst of light jumped from the open pages, pulsing through the valley, knocking everyone down, wraith and Kindred alike. I flew through the air, landing on a remaining piece of the island. My head smacked against it and my vision blurred. I tried to stand, but every time I did, I fell to my knees. My vision became cloudier. I tried my hardest to fight it. I tried to make it to where I could see Roman laying on the ground not five feet from me, but I couldn't. Finally, I crawled until I couldn't move anymore. I laid my head down and closed my eyes.

When I woke up, I was lying at Ezekiel's feet. Next to him was the book, sitting atop a makeshift podium created from part of the island. Just on the other side of the book was Roman. He was unconscious on the ground, lying on his left side. His shirt was torn and soaked in blood. I could see a gash across his right ribs. It didn't look deep, but for some reason, it bothered me.

Xavier and Deacon stood behind Ezekiel, along with three other wraiths. When I looked behind me, I could see Sandra, Darius, and Mallory several feet away, staring at us. Sandra's hands were up and she looked like she was pushing at something invisible. I yelled to them. I saw Sandra's mouth move in response, but I heard no sound.

"You won't be able to hear them." I turned and glared at Ezekiel.

"Why not?" I asked. "What did you do to them?"

He walked over to the book and placed his hands on it, lovingly. "Boundary spell," he explained. "Not as powerful or long-lasting like your mother's was, but I was in a hurry. This one only lasts a couple of minutes. Anyway, it will do." He clapped his hands together. "Shall we begin?"

He nodded to the wraith standing closest to me. He ripped me to my feet, taking no mind of my injuries, and forced me to stand across from Ezekiel. *The Book of Breathings* was the only thing separating us. I caught a brief glimpse of Roman, but he was still passed out cold on the ground, bleeding. I tried to reach him through our connection but nothing happened. I pushed my power toward him, and again, nothing. I could see his chest moving lightly, so I knew he was alive. *Why can't I feel him?*

"Your hand please, Kyndal." I turned to see Ezekiel holding his hand out expectantly. His hair was still down and wild. I guess he was no longer pretending to be the well-polished leader everyone thought he was. His false manners were infuriating. I stared at his hand, but made no move to give him mine. No way was I making this easy for him. Suddenly, Xavier lashed out, hitting me across the face. Again.

I turned and glared at him. My power surged up. "Do that again and it will be the last decision you make on this earth." He smiled in return, taunting me.

"There is no need for such violence," Ezekiel said, admonishing Xavier as well as me. "Kyndal, please remember, while I do not wish you any harm, there are ways of making you cooperate."

"Go to hell," I spit at him. Ezekiel's eyes glazed over, all thought of false civility gone.

"Deacon," he said. I tensed, expecting Deacon to hit me, but instead he moved away from me and toward Roman. He reached down and grabbed Roman's limp body by the throat, the other hand coming to rest over his heart. I knew exactly what was going to happen next.

"No, no. Deacon don't," I said frantically. I turned to Ezekiel. "I'll help you. Just don't hurt him." I thrust my hand out to Ezekiel, hoping that would satisfy him, while simultaneously looking back at where Deacon still hovered over Roman. It wasn't until I felt the slashing of a blade against my wrist that Deacon pulled away, dumping Roman back on the ground.

I sucked in a breath at the sudden pain. Ezekiel was holding my wrist over a cup, letting the blood drain into it. I expected the wound to heal, but it didn't. "Funny thing about the spells in this book," he began. "They almost always require blood. I suppose that's why the Council banned their practice centuries ago. People started to get a little overzealous in their sacrifices."

I grimaced through the pain. "This isn't extreme?"

He looked up at me, his eyes completely serious. "No. This is the future of our race. The Kindred were always wasting their talents on hunting down the wraiths, when in reality, we should be working together. I will create a new race, one that will usher in a new beginning with the Kindred at the helm." When the cup was about halfway full, he released my wrist. I instantly pulled it back, pressing it against my stomach, trying to add some compression and stop the bleeding. Then I watched in disgust as he brought the cup to his lips and took a drink.

Gross.

He lowered the cup down from his lips and handed it over to Xavier, who also drank and then moved toward Roman.

Deacon held him up while Xavier force fed him. I expected him to come to me next, but they both returned to Ezekiel's side. Apparently I had enough of my blood in me.

Ezekiel turned to the book and started to read. He spoke in the same language I'd heard Sandra speak in her cellar. The words sounded dark and twisted. They spoke of death. Ezekiel paused, turning to Xavier and handing him a blade. I briefly noticed it was not a true Kindred dagger, just a simple knife. Xavier brought the blade down hard, directly over his brand. Then he turned and stabbed the wraith behind him in the gut. The body instantly dropped. But only a true blade can kill a wraith. Any other knife just kills the body and leaves the wraith intact. I had no choice but to watch with sick fascination as a dark ink began to pour from the mouth of the dead host. It slithered along the ground, slowly inching its way toward Xavier. When it reached him, it crawled over his feet and up his body until it reached his face. Then, it creeped even farther, diving into Xavier's mouth. The veins on his face darkened and his eyes turned bloodshot. Xavier was possessed.

I understood what Xavier meant at the cave about wasting the Kindred and needing more to join our ranks. Ezekiel was building an army. When all the veins had faded from Xavier and he looked like himself again, Deacon spoke. "Did it work?"

Without hesitation, Ezekiel lashed out and struck Xavier with a blade, this time one I recognized. It was my Kindred blade. Xavier grimaced at the contact, but otherwise didn't react. A cut like that would have made a wraith, well any *normal* wraith, scream in pain. But Xavier didn't move. He just watched as his arm quickly healed itself.

Ezekiel let out an excited cackle. "And the rest?" he asked. Xavier reached in his pocket and flicked open his lighter. As I've seen him do before, he grabbed ahold of the flame and held it in his hand without hesitation. "Perfect," Ezekiel purred. I couldn't believe what I was seeing. I stepped back, disgusted. Wraiths had never been able to control the elements. Xavier shouldn't be able to contact his powers. When a Kindred loses their brand, they lose touch with their powers. They lose touch with nature.

Ezekiel turned to me, "You see, Kyndal. A typical possession leaves the host dead. But your blood lets the wraith bond with the host, allowing them to maintain their consciousness. Xavier is very much alive. He is transformed. Stronger!" His eyes were wide with maniacal pleasure.

That's when I figured it out—why I couldn't reach Roman through our connection. Why his injury had me so concerned, even though it was superficial. They disfigured his brand. They were going to turn him into a twisted wraith/Kindred hybrid just like they did Xavier. And then they would do the same to me.

Ezekiel began to read the spell again. I looked around frantically. I knew the others were no help to me, not as long as that boundary spell was up. If I was going to make a move, it had to be soon. I didn't know how I was going to save both Roman and myself, but I had to try something. Suddenly, my eyes landed on something shiny sticking up from Roman's boot. His extra dagger, forgotten. I glanced at my captors. They were all focused on the book as Ezekiel read. No one was paying attention to me. I just had to wait for the right moment to strike. Just as Ezekiel neared the end of his chant, Deacon turned to stab the wraith. I waited until his back was completely to me. I didn't think, I just acted. I tucked my arm and rolled forward, toward Roman. I grabbed the dagger from his boot and flung it toward the closest wraith, the one Deacon was nearing. My aim was off, and instead of hitting the wraith, I hit Deacon in the arm.

Deacon let out a terrifying, inhuman screech. He turned my way, but not before cutting open the wraith before him. I watched the body drop behind him. Deacon stalked toward me, the inky shadow of the dead wraith following him, searching for Roman. I turned quickly to Roman and shook him violently. "Roman, wake up." He didn't respond. "Dammit, Roman!" I yelled. "You are not allowed to die on me!" I hit his chest in between each word. On the final hit, I put all the power into it I could muster. A jolt of energy passed from me to him. I looked back at Deacon. He was almost on us. His knife, Roman's knife, was raised above his head. I knew then he was going to kill me. I braced myself for his attack. I was injured and weaponless. There was no way I could beat him. I closed my eyes and sent out a silent apology to Roman for failing him. I expected to feel the fire of Deacon's blade, but it never came. Instead I heard the unexpected sounds of metal hitting metal. I opened my eyes to see Sandra between Deacon and me, her blade crossed with his.

"Get him out of here," Sandra said to me between gritted teeth.

Past her, Darius had jumped in front of Ezekiel, and Mallory was fighting the newly upgraded Xavier. Underneath me, Roman groaned in pain and his eyes opened. "Good!" I yelled. "Look at me, Rome." His eyes searched wildly before landing on me. "We have to get out of here, but I'm going to need your help. Can you stand?" He nodded and moved slowly to his feet. I put his arm around me, trying my best to support his weight. We moved toward the trees slowly. Suddenly, a wall of fire burst to life just a few steps in front of us. Xavier did not want us to escape. I readjusted my hold on Roman as we moved around the fire. The flames wouldn't hurt me, but Roman was not fireproof.

"Something—something feels wrong," he said. "I feel weak. I'm not healing." I knew it was because they had disfigured his brand. He'd lost his connection to nature, to his ability to heal, but I didn't tell him that yet. I couldn't.

"Just keep moving," I said. I looked behind us. The wraith, an inky shadow, was trailing behind us, still seeking out Roman. I pushed us faster. We reached the edges of the trees.

We're going to make it.

Out of nowhere, something whipped around my waist and I was yanked backward. Roman was pulled from my grasp. Without me there to support him, he stumbled to the ground. I hit the ground several feet back, face first. Pain shot up my arm. I laid on the ground, groaning. I picked my head up slightly and reached down, trying to figure out what was wrapped around my waist. I growled in frustration when I realized they were tree branches.

Ezekiel.

Sure enough, I looked up and he stood before me. Behind him was Roman and the shadow of the wraith inching even closer. If I didn't do something quickly, it would be too late. I reached out my hand, fingers stretched along the ground. I dug deep, past all the pain, trying to summon my power. I felt the power stir in my stomach. It traveled up to my shoulder, then down my arm. The heat finally reached my fingertips. I prepared to release it, to burn the wraith away from Roman, but I never got the chance. Ezekiel slammed his boot down on my hand. I heard the bones crunch and I screamed in pain. Ezekiel pivoted his foot, grinding the already broken bones into pieces. I looked toward Roman. The wraith had reached him, crawling slowly up his body even as he tried to escape. He was too weak. Without his powers he had no way of protecting himself. As the shadow reached his face, I let out a fierce scream. "No!" I yelled, with every ounce of my being. The fire behind me intensified in response, climbing higher and racing toward me, eager to do my bidding. I willed the flames toward Ezekiel. This man betrayed me, *killed my family,* and now was taking Roman from me.

I wanted him dead.

The fire raced over me, headed straight for Ezekiel. I could feel the flames lick at my back. My clothes were scorched, but my skin was untouched. Ezekiel backed up quickly, releasing my broken hand. The flames chased him further into the tree line. With a flick of his hand, the branches from the trees moved unnaturally, releasing from around my waist, pulling themselves together to block Ezekiel from a fiery death. I pushed the flames harder, but they found no gaps in Ezekiel's wall. For as angry as I was, he was centuries older and stronger than me. I couldn't hold it any longer. I lost control of the flames. They still crackled around me, angry and violent, but they no longer did my bidding. I struggled to sit up, cradling my broken hand close. I never took my eyes off the enemy in front of me. I heard rustling at his feet and then he was no longer the only person staring back at me. Roman was standing there, his eyes a luminous gold. Hope stirred in my chest. *He's alive.* I reached out to him through our connection, but instead of a cool breeze bringing clarity and peace, I felt only icy coldness. My heart cracked and hope vanished. Roman's veins darkened and his golden eyes were surrounded by bloodshot red. He smiled at me, his teeth serrated and sharp.

Roman was a wraith.

I tried to stagger to my feet, but failed miserably. I fell again, breathing heavily, using every ounce of strength to stay conscious. The last thing I saw before everything went black was Ezekiel placing his hand on Roman's shoulder and the two of them turning as one, disappearing into the darkness of the forest.

Epilogue

The first thing I registered was the warmth beside me. My face unconsciously leaned toward it, seeking its strength. I opened my eyes slowly. It took them a moment to adjust to my surroundings. I was lying in a bed. Three candles were lit on the table next to me. Beyond them was an unfamiliar room. I sat up, grimacing in pain at the effort. My head pounded. I reached for the covers, surprised to find that my left hand was in a cast. I pushed the blankets back with my good hand and shuffled my legs off the edge of the bed. Just as I mustered the strength to stand, the door to the room opened.

Lydia walked through. Her arms were full of fresh blankets. She looked different. Her hair was dirty and thrown into a ponytail. She wore sweatpants and a loose shirt. We made eye contact and I couldn't help but notice the dark circles shadowing her cheekbones. Her mouth dropped open. "You're awake."

I tried again to stand, but my legs buckled and I fell back onto the bed. Lydia dropped the blankets on the ground and ran over to me. "Don't get up. You're still weak. I'll go get Cassie, tell her you're awake." She moved back toward the door, but I reached out and grabbed her arm.

"Don't leave. Not yet." She sat down next to me. "Tell me."

"Tell you what?" she asked gently.

My head was still pounding and my brain was fuzzy. I was struggling to put everything together. When I spoke, my voice was hoarse. "How long have I been out?"

"Three days," she replied. "Your hand is crushed, broken in several places. Cassie put a cast on it while you were asleep. She says you lost a lot of blood and she thinks you have at least two broken ribs. It was hard to tell with you asleep."

I nodded. "Allie?"

"She's here. Cassie and Sandra are taking care of her."

"She should be in the hospital."

Lydia shook her head. "Sandra says we can't risk it. If she goes to the hospital, the Sheriff will want to question her. That can't happen until we're sure she won't say anything."

I pursed my lips. I understood what she was saying, but I still didn't like it. I sat there silently, focusing on breathing past the pain. When I didn't say anything, Lydia broke the silence, answering the question I had been too scared to ask.

"The book is here. Sandra is keeping a close eye on it. Deacon was killed and so was Xavier. No one has seen Ezekiel or—" she broke off, clearing her throat, "or his men since the battle."

I took a deep breath, this time relishing the pain in my lungs as a distraction. I sat up, looking around the room. My eyes settled on the windowsill and my entire body froze.

"What are those?"

Lydia followed my gaze. "I don't know," she replied, confused. "They weren't here when I left earlier."

My eyes never moving, I stood and turned toward the window, ignoring Lydia when she tried to help me up. I walked on shaky legs until I held them in my hand. A vase full of wild pink flowers.

"What are they?" Lydia asked.

"Wild Bleeding Heart," I muttered.

I picked the card out and turned it over. On it were written two lines in an elegant script.

Our future begins now.
I look forward to seeing you soon.

Acknowledgements

House of Aries is the first book I've ever written; and believe me when I say it took a village to bring it to life. Thank you to Gabby Tanner, my dear friend. Thank you for your diligence reading and editing those early drafts, not to mention dealing with all my texts about the smallest of details. Next, Traci Osborn. You are truly my fairy godmother. *House of Aries* would not exist as it does today without you. To Thea Rademacher and Nathan Fredrickson, my team at Flint Hills Publishing, I knew we were going to work well together since our first meeting. I truly enjoy working with you both. You have helped me make this book so much more than I ever could have dreamed. Finally, to you, the reader. There is no *House of Aries* without you. All of this is for you.

About the Author

Whitney Estenson was born and raised in Topeka, Kansas. The daughter of two teachers, she spent her summers swimming at the pool. Through the years she played several sports, including softball, basketball, volleyball, and running track. While traveling to the next tournament, an hour or several states away, Whitney always brought a book. It was on these long trips that she developed a love of supernatural and fantasy stories.

After high school, Whitney attended Washburn University, graduating with a Bachelor of Arts in English Education in 2009. That summer, she married her husband Josh in a seven-minute ceremony on a Jamaican beach. When she returned, she began her teaching career and has been teaching middle school ever since. In 2012, she received a Master of Science in Educational Technology from Pittsburg State University. In 2014, Whitney and Josh welcomed their daughter Avery.

Follow Whitney on Facebook: The Ascendant Series by Whitney Estenson,
Instagram: the_ascendant_series,
and her website: theascendantseries.com

A GIFT FOR YOU ~

The first two chapters of Book II in
The Ascendant Series:

HOUSE OF TAURUS

Available on Amazon and wherever books are sold.

"Everything is Dual; everything has poles; everything has its pair of opposites; like and unlike are the same, opposites are identical in nature, but different in degree."

Hermes Trismegistus

1

The forest is quietest in the early hours of the morning.

Most people think it's quiet at night, but that's not true. When the sky has turned black, and the only light piercing the sky comes from the stars and moon, the forest is alive. The animals that spent their day hiding away come out, the joint chorus of their voices creating a cacophony of life. Eventually though, the horizon breaks, and the soft colors of pink and orange bleed through the trees, chasing the animals back into their homes. These few precious hours, while the forest is at its stillest, are my favorite.

I ran through the well-worn trail behind my house as it twisted and turned, skipping over fallen limbs and other obstacles without a second thought. The trees whizzed by me in a wall of green, their thick arms melding together, as each reached for more room to grow in the already dense forest. I never would have guessed, even just a few months ago, that I would ever be this familiar with such a wild landscape. I was born and raised in Dayton, Texas. The climate there was dry, sandy, and hot. Ridiculously hot. Like, fry an egg on the sidewalk, hot. The trees outside my home were built to survive without a constant source of water, the exact opposite of the lush vegetation of the Allegheny.

I reached the end of the trail, but instead of stopping or turning around, I took a sharp turn into the trees. I slipped in and out of the black cherry trees, finding my footing with ease even though it was darker here than on the trail. The forest had grown more dense and the rays of early morning sun were just beginning to peek in. I'd taken this route so many times, I could've done it blindfolded. I came to a rock formation, several large boulders stacked on top of one another. Rather than climb over like I usually did, I ran around, through the small creek. My shoes sloshed in the water, the creek deeper than normal due to recent rain. I could see the end of the tree line and I slowed to a walk. It wasn't until I reached the edge that I finally stopped. The sun was shining fully in the open space ahead of me, which only made what I was looking at more eerie. The first time

I came here, the trees were rimmed in a beautiful meadow full of different colored wildflowers, like something out of a dream. In the center had been a still lake, with only a low-lying island breaking its surface. None of that was left. The water was gone, the flowers—dead. The remaining valley was barren, scorched earth, like the negative of a photograph.

To the average hiker, the area would have been an anomaly. A gigantic dead spot in the middle of the forest. Maybe they would think the ground had been contaminated or a wildfire had cleared the area—I didn't know. Only those like me, The Kindred, would know different.

Several months ago, I moved to Marienville, Pennsylvania against my will. My family had been killed in what I believed to be an accidental car crash. I was still a minor, so I was forced to move in with my aunt Alessandra; my only living relative. Moving here put me right smack in the middle of a supernatural war I had unknowingly been involved in my entire life. My mother had been a Kindred for decades (I'm not sure how many decades, actually). She fled the Kindred with my father when she was pregnant with me to escape Ezekiel, a powerful Kindred elder who wanted to use me to create his evil army of Kindred/wraith hybrids. My mom had successfully stayed hidden for almost 18 years, until Ezekiel found us and killed my entire family, activating my dormant powers. When I came here, I knew nothing about my heritage or Ezekiel's nefarious motives. In fact, no one did. All of the Kindred believed Ezekiel to be an honest, trustworthy leader of our people. He used that faith to deceive me into believing my mother was a traitor. He tricked me into finding *The Book of Breathings*, my people's most powerful artifact. It held a series of incantations, that when read correctly, allowed us to perform magic. Once I discovered the book, Ezekiel turned on us, using it and my blood to create the first of his new army.

That was what brought me back to the ruined lake. It was here that Ezekiel revealed his true intentions and robbed me of one of the few important people I had left. The haunting images of what happened that night kept me awake, drawing me here to relive the mistakes I made and the price those closest to me paid.

I walked to the center of the dried lake and laid down on my back, closing my eyes. The sun had finally crest the trees, chasing away the remainder of the morning chill. I felt the warmth on my skin, but it fell flat, its rays only serving to dry out my shoes. All Kindred possess powers in one of the elements, and as an Aries, my element was fire. More than that, I was a Descendant, the last in a long line that could be traced back to the first Aries. Fire lived inside me, keeping the cold at bay. But my powers could only chase away the physical, they could do nothing to touch the cold that lived inside me. The cold that came from *him*.

It'd been two weeks since I had seen him. Last time I saw him, his eyes, the beautiful eyes that I loved so much, had been frozen and unwelcoming, rimmed in red and shadowed by the darkened veins of his new state. The bond that had connected us to each other, the one that always brought me comfort and strength, had twisted into something dark that now put a block of ice in the pit of my stomach. Ezekiel had taken him from me. To everyone else, he was dead. But they hadn't seen him leave. They hadn't seen him turn into the very thing we were created to kill. I wished he was dead. Instead, he was the enemy.

I laid there for a short time longer before I knew I had to leave. The forest would soon be full of more than just animals, as hikers, kayakers, and wildlife enthusiasts would join them. It was harder to run in the forest when people were awake. Animals don't care to notice when I run at inhuman speed, but people do. And today, I don't want to hold back. I opened my powers up fully to the elements in the forest, hoping that they could fill the void left in me. I knew the path ahead would not be easy, so I did my best to be prepared. When I left, I didn't go the way I came. Instead, I headed the opposite direction, toward town.

In no time, I crossed the expanse of the forest and reached the outer edges of Marienville. I slowed down a little, but not much since my destination was close. I only stopped when I saw the small wooden building sitting just on the other side of the trees. Sandra's bar sat on the outskirts of town. A small, rundown building on a good day, it now was in damn near ruins—the aftermath of the recent battle between the Kindred and wraiths. The owner of the bar, Sandra, was Kindred like me and a Cancer sign. She spent the last two decades as a ward of the Kindred for her role in helping my mom steal *The Book of Breathings*. Her powers had only recently been reinstated. With Ezekiel's betrayal and subsequent disappearance, Sandra was the oldest living Kindred among us, so she resumed leadership. That was until the Council showed up and resumed control; which could be any day now.

I walked across the open area and onto the back porch, doing my best not to think about the first time I had been there. It was our first date, even though *he* had since claimed it didn't count. We had barely known each other but were drawn together even then. I stepped carefully over the debris that now dominated the space, only glancing slightly at the railing where we shared our first kiss, before finally stepping inside. The back door was completely missing, complements of my fire power. Deacon, a wraith, had taken Sandra and *him* captive inside the bar. I, along with several others, had staged a rescue. We had barely gotten there in time. Sandra had been tortured, while *he* had been stabbed and left for dead, bleeding on the floor.

Inside the bar, the senses that had been dull outside roared to life. The smell of fresh wood and paint dominated the space, my extra sensitive senses a bit overwhelmed. From somewhere in the back offices, a table saw screamed. Before I got a chance to really take in the scene, someone noticed me.

"Davenport!" Isaac yelled from where he was holding a beam up to the ceiling. His large, dark arms were taut with exertion from holding them above his head. Sandra was next to him, standing on a ladder and nailing the beam in. She turned my way and sent me a sad smile. "Lydia told me she didn't think you were coming," Isaac continued.

I shrugged.

Suddenly, the front door, which was really just a temporary piece of plywood, opened.

Sunlight poured in, broken only by the silhouette of the tiny blonde standing in the doorway. "Kyndal!" Lydia shouted, a smile on her face. She entered, donuts and coffee in hand, "I thought you weren't coming."

"Figured you guys could use the help," I replied.

She placed the sugar and caffeinated goodies on one of the few tables that hadn't been destroyed and came over to give me a hug. I did my best to return the gesture but the effort fell short. She pulled away from me smiling, doing her best to hide the glint of pain in her eyes at my cold response. "Well, we are so excited you're here."

I gave her the best smile I could muster. "How can I help?" I asked.

Isaac walked over to the table, grabbed a donut, almost shoving the whole thing in his mouth at once. He stood directly next to Lydia. She looked up at him quickly, shyly, before averting her eyes. "Mallory and Darius are in the back office, cutting new beams for the ceiling," Isaac explained between bites. "You could go help them if you want." I looked back toward the office and cringed. While I didn't mind Darius, Mallory and I weren't exactly the best of friends. It wasn't too long ago since we had been duking it out after I accused her of being a hateful bitch.

"Is Cassie there too?" I asked. Usually when Mallory's girlfriend Cassie was with her she was easier to handle. Lydia shook her head no. I sighed, "Then I think I'll pass."

From the back room, I heard Mallory yell, "I can hear you!"

I rolled my eyes. "I'll start out back on the porch."

"I'll go with you," Lydia said. She grabbed a coffee before following me back out through the broken door.

Lydia propped herself up on the railing of the back porch, taking a swig of her coffee. I instantly got to work. The porch was covered in broken pieces of the back door and discarded trash from inside the bar. I gathered together as much as I could carry and walked it over to the dumpster on the side of the bar. I continued until the porch was almost completely clear. Lydia sat and watched the whole time, her eyes on me. I finally threw the last load in the dumpster and winced when a bolt of pain shot through my hand. I walked back to the porch, rubbing my left hand, trying to make the pain go away.

"It hasn't healed, has it?" Lydia asked from her perch. I ignored her and grabbed a broom to sweep away the dust. This wasn't something I wanted to talk about, especially with a bar full of Kindred with supernatural hearing just on the other side of the nonexistent door. I heard Lydia jump down from the railing and walk over to me. I stopped working and turned to face her.

"It's fine," I said quietly. "It will heal, it's just taking a little longer."

She reached down and grabbed my injured hand. She pushed in different spots, looking for any signs of pain on my face. I did my best to keep my expression neutral but I couldn't help but suck in my breath when she pressed just below my thumb. "Why aren't you still wearing your cast?" she asked, concerned.

I took my hand back. "It'll be fine," I repeated. I looked up at her. "Really, Lydia, I'm okay. I promise." I felt guilty for lying to her. The truth was, I'd been in pain ever since Ezekiel broke my hand. I had been trying to save *him*. He was being chased by a wraith trying to possess him. I was beaten and injured on the ground, too weak to stop it personally, so I threw my hand out, trying to burn the wraith away when Ezekiel stomped on it, grinding the bones to pieces. My enhanced healing should have fixed it by now, but for reasons I didn't understand, it wasn't working. Maybe I didn't want it to. Maybe I thought it would make me forget what happened that night and forget the price people paid for me, and that was something I could never let happen.

Lydia interrupted my memory. "You should at least have Cassie look at it. If you're not healing, maybe she can help you figure out why."

"No," I answered quickly. "She can't know. None of them can. Promise me you won't tell anyone, Lydia." I stared at her, begging and pleading. I could see she was torn between doing what she thought was best for me and agreeing to what I was asking. I felt horrible doing this to her, but I didn't need anyone thinking I was hurt. If they thought I was injured, they wouldn't let me go after *him*. As I waited for her response, Sandra called my name from inside the bar.

"Swear it," I pushed her.

She grimaced. "Fine, I promise." She pointed her finger at me. "But this is against my better judgement. If you're not better soon, I will tell Cassie."

I gave her a brief hug. "Thank you." I held the broom out to her. "Now, do some work. Sandra wants to see me."

I found her in her office. She was rifling through the desk, ripping open drawers and throwing papers on the top of the desk. I walked past the table saw Mallory and Darius had been using. I could hear them in the main bar area, laughing with Isaac. To my left was the rug that covered the trap door to Sandra's secret basement. I had only been down there once, when Sandra revealed her history as a member of the Guard. She, along with my mother and two others, had made up the Guard for over 70 years. Their primary job was to protect *The Book of Breathings*. Sandra was the Guard's Scribe. She had studied it for decades, learning the intricacies of the incantations the book held. Performing the incantations correctly was no easy task. Mistake any detail and the consequences could be deadly. When my mother stole the book before I was born, Sandra began rewriting it from memory. Although incomplete, her reproduced copy of the book had been invaluable in recovering the real *Book of Breathings*. Both works were hidden there now, spelled shut under a door only Sandra could unlock.

"You wanted to see me?" I asked Sandra, interrupting her rummaging.

She looked up at me. Her dirty blonde hair was pulled back into a messy bun. Her caramel eyes were distant. Most people would think she was aloof, but I knew different. I knew her closed off look was a type of armor. More than anyone else, Sandra and I felt the weight of recent events. She had spent almost the last twenty years as a ward of the Kindred, forbidden from using her elemental magic; a punishment she blamed on my mother. We knew now it wasn't my mother that was the traitor, but rather Ezekiel. He not only allowed Sandra to be unjustly punished, he took my entire family from me, and he took *him* from both of us.

Sandra had gained her power back only a few weeks ago, but I could already see the impact it had made. She stood taller, her eyes were more alert, even her face had begun to smooth out, eliminating the few natural wrinkles that had appeared. Kindred could use nature to heal themselves, even to the point of halting the aging process. These small changes in Sandra indicated exactly how in tune she was with the elements.

She shuffled through the papers on the desk, grabbing one and handing it to me. "This came today."

I took the paper from her, noticing it's heavy weight as well as the old school wax seal on the edges, showing the brand of the Kindred. "What is this?" I asked.

"The Council is sending an emissary to Marienville. Word of Ezekiel's betrayal has spread all the way to Awen. They're coming to do damage control."

"What's Awen?" I had never heard of it.

She looked at me sideways. "It's the name of our island. You didn't know that?"

I looked down, embarrassed. There was a lot about being Kindred I didn't know. I'd never had the chance to learn. I'd been too busy fighting for my life. I read over the letter quickly. "It doesn't say when the emissary will arrive."

"I know," Sandra replied, thankfully allowing me to change the subject. "But it will be sooner rather than later. They will want to take control of the situation quickly. They'll want *The Book of Breathings*."

I looked up at her. "The book? They can just take it?"

"Technically, it belongs to all Kindred. Without a Guard to protect it, it makes the most sense that the Council would assume possession of it."

"You're just going to let them take it? What about everything we went through to get it? What about—" I couldn't finish the sentence. I couldn't say his name.

"I know exactly what was sacrificed to get this book." Sandra's voice was rough, although from anger or grief, I couldn't tell. She took a deep breath, pulling herself together. "Roman was my son. Maybe not by blood, but he was *mine*. I will never forget him and I will not hand over what he sacrificed his life to retrieve."

I took a shaky breath. That was the first time I had heard his name in days. Everyone always took special care to not say it around me, afraid of how I would react. It shook through me, rattling me to the bone. "But he's not dead."

Her eyes welled with tears. "Roman as we knew him is gone. That thing wearing his face is not him. The only thing we can do now is honor him by protecting the book."

I nodded. "What do we do?"

"When the emissary arrives, it's important that we have our story straight. The closer we are to the truth, the better, but we must all be on the same page. Now, I've already spoken with the others, and they've agreed; we say nothing of Descendants, Kindred/wraith hybrids, or how they got that way."

"You're asking me to break the law. What if we need the Council to help find Ezekiel?"

"The Council labeled your mother a traitor, stripped me of my power, and had a homicidal maniac within its midst for decades and didn't notice. I think we're better on our own."

I nodded. She had a point. "Anything else?" I asked.

"As long as the Council has a presence here, no humans are allowed at the compound."

"I'll tell Lydia. She won't be happy about it, but I'll convince her it's for the best."

She nodded curtly. "What about your Aunt Alessandra? Will she be a problem?"

I shook my head and shrugged. "She's barely spoken to me since recovering from her capture. She doesn't seem to want anything to do with the Kindred, so I can't imagine her popping by while the emissary is here."

"Good."

2

When I got home, I was surprised to see Allie's car missing from the driveway. She hadn't left the house in days. In fact, she had barely left her room, not that I blamed her. She had been Ezekiel's prisoner for weeks. During that time, several wraiths had fed from her, consuming pieces of her life source in order to keep their own stolen bodies charged. That type of thing took a toll on anyone. When wraiths had fed on me, it was several days before I recovered. That wasn't the only reason she had hidden away. Before she had been taken, Allie knew nothing about the supernatural part of my life. Her rude introduction to the eternal war between Kindred and wraiths left her with a lot of unanswered questions. I had tried several times to talk to her, but she always stopped me before I even got a word out. She wasn't ready. I didn't know if she ever would be.

Once inside, I went right upstairs to Allie's room. It was empty. The bed was neatly made and the clothes that had been piling up in the corner were gone. I went back downstairs, looking for an indication of where she might be. She used to leave me notes when she left, but I didn't see one now. I started to panic, thinking back to the last time I had come home to find her gone. Deacon had taken her, delivered her to Ezekiel to use as ransom for the book. I ran to the front door and ripped it open, intent on searching the entire town until I found her. I made it two steps onto the porch before I ran smack into someone.

"Ow!" Allie yelled. She stumbled back. Using my quick reflexes, I reached out and steadied her.

"Sorry," I said quickly.

"What are you doing?" she asked.

"You weren't here. I was worried."

"I'm fine," she replied. She stepped around me, into the house. I followed her in, down the hall, and into the kitchen.

"Where'd you go?" I asked.

Allie reached into the fridge and grabbed a bottle of water before sitting down at the kitchen table. She let out a deep breath before looking up at me. "The Sheriff's station."

My heart dropped into my stomach. Sheriff Christensen knew nothing about the supernatural war waging in his town but he definitely knew something was going on. He arrested me not that long ago regarding the deaths of several locals, all of which were wraith kills. He also thought I had something to do with the deaths of my parents and brother. When Allie went missing, he accused me of having something to do with it. Needless to say, we weren't friends.

"What—what—" I stuttered. "What were you doing there?"

"Giving him my statement." She took a swig of her water. I rushed around the island to sit across from her.

"Allie, what did you tell him?"

"The truth," she replied adamantly. "At least what I can remember. I was attacked while at Allegheny Explorers. I was kidnapped and held prisoner by several men who tortured me until finally I was able to escape."

"Is that really all you remember?" I asked. So much more had happened to her, could she really not remember anything else?

"I don't know what happened exactly. What I do know is that I want my life back, and that starts today. The Sheriff is opening a full investigation into finding my kidnappers so I can finally get some normalcy back."

"How does the Sheriff plan on finding your kidnappers?"

"I know what they looked like. One was Deacon, that asshole that came to Allegheny Explorers pretending to want to hire me for an expedition. Another one had long hair, pulled into a ponytail, and the last one was younger, with hair so blonde it was almost white."

I gritted my teeth. She had described Ezekiel and Evan. If Sheriff Christensen went after either of them, he would lose. He had no idea what he was up against. Not to mention, going after Ezekiel not only meant dealing with him, but with Roman, who was nearly indestructible. Human made weapons would do nothing to hurt him, only Kindred daggers worked on a hybrid.

"You have to change your statement."

She lowered her eyes at me. "I absolutely won't."

I took a deep breath in. Every other time I brought this up, she'd shot me down. But this time, we had to talk about it. "Allie, you know there is more going on here than Sheriff Christensen can handle. If he pursues this case, it will end badly."

"I don't know what you would like me to do, Kyndal. It's his job to handle things like this."

"No," I argued. "It's my job. And the other Kindred." She started to squirm in her chair, a tell-tale sign that she was going to bolt. I reached out and grabbed her hand softly. Her eyes jumped up to mine. "We have to talk about this." She held my eyes for a while before finally sitting back in her chair. She crossed her arms across her chest. It was a stubborn move, one that reminded me so much of my dad, I almost smiled.

"What if I don't want to know?"

"I used to feel the same way. I tried running from all of this and pretending like it never happened. Guess what? It didn't matter. It all caught up to me anyway. Denying what was going on didn't make it any less real, it just put people in danger. It got them killed. It got you kidnapped. I understand if you don't want to know all the gory details, but you can't live in the dark anymore."

Allie closed her eyes and took a deep breath through her nose. "Okay." She opened her eyes. "Tell me. Tell me everything."

We sat at the table for hours, long into the evening. I told her about my mom, and the real reason she left town, and why my dad followed her. I told her about Ezekiel causing the crash that killed my family and about how he had lied to me and used me for his own purposes. I explained Evan's death and subsequent rebirth as a wraith. I even told her about Roman and what he turned into. She asked a lot of questions, which I answered the best I could. By the end of it all, we were both crying. Just like me, the supernatural had stolen a lot from Allie. It was difficult to accept.

When our tears had dried and there were no more secrets between us, we both retreated to different parts of the house. I think we needed our space to process everything. Allie headed upstairs and back into her room. I went outside and laid down on one of our patio loungers. I stared up at the sky, watching the stars as they emerged from the darkening sky. Eventually, I closed my eyes and fell asleep.

I'm in the desert. The sun is beating down on my face and the wind whips the sand over my skin, biting at it with each passing gust. I stand up, brushing the sand off me and look around. To my left, the land is flat and I can see for what seems like miles. To my right is a large sandy hill, beyond it I think I hear voices. I turn to the right and begin the trek up the hill. My feet are unsteady and I sink into the sand, but eventually I make it to the top. Once there, I'm looking down at a village. It's small, partially destroyed, but it's definitely a settlement of some sort. I must have been mistaken earlier, because there doesn't seem to be anyone here. I start to walk down the hill. Just as I reach the bottom, a group of three people slip around the side of a house. They stop just short of the door and lean against the wall. Each of them is dressed oddly in loose pants and long tunics. Their faces are covered, but I can see their eyes and they are glowing. **Kindred.** *Simultaneously, without a single word spoken, all three reach behind their backs and pull out a dagger. Just then, the door of the house bursts open from the inside. Wraiths pour out, immediately attacking the outnumbered Kindred. My instincts kick in and I run to help. I reach for where I keep my dagger, but it's not there. When I reach the first wraith, I strike out with my broken hand. It connects and I feel no pain. Emboldened, I take on the next wraith. Around me, the other Kindred are fighting too. After delivering a perfect spin kick to the stomach of a wraith, I end up face-to-face with another Kindred. His eyes are red, he is a fire sign like*

me. He gives me a confused look and says something in a language I don't understand. When I don't respond, he repeats himself, this time louder. "I don't know what you're saying," I tell him. He growls, clearly frustrated. Before I know it, he cocks his arm back and hits me square in the face, knocking me out cold.

I woke up back on my patio. I sat straight up, breathing heavily. The sky had grown darker. It must have been the middle of the night. My hand instantly went to my face where the man in my dream had punched me. The second my fingers touched my lip, I cringed. It was tender. I pulled my fingers away and found blood on them. I plopped back on the lounger. *Why do my dreams always leave a mark?* This was not the first time my dreams leaked into reality. I was branded in a dream, and when I first got my powers, before I really had control over them, I use to dream about using them and would wake up with my sheets on fire.

"This is not normal!" I yelled out into the open. My voice echoed off the trees, scaring the chirping insects of the forest into silence. I laid there for a moment before I realized I never heard the sounds of the forest return. My right hand reached out, searching for the dagger I put on the small table next to me before I had fallen asleep. I scanned the darkness, looking for any sign of movement. I pulled a small amount of power from nature to enhance my vision. I caught movement to my right. Just on the edge of the trees, a man was there. I leapt up, landing off the porch. He took off into the forest. He moved quickly, darting in and out of the trees with ease, even though there was only moonlight. He was fast. Too fast for a human.

Wraith.

I took off into the forest after the intruder. I chased him through the trees and over a low-running creek. The more we ran, the farther it got from me. I knew if I kept this up much longer, it would get away. Then, suddenly, he disappeared. I skidded to a halt, looking in every direction. No matter where I looked, I didn't see him. I froze, using my superior senses to search for any clue to where it went. A tree branch snapped above me. I looked up, just in time to see the wraith jump out of the tree. It landed directly on me, knocking me to the ground. I scrambled to my feet and turned to face my enemy, dagger in hand. His eyes were bloodshot and the veins in his face twisted it into something straight out of my nightmares. He growled at me, baring his long, serrated teeth. "Kindred," he spat.

I smiled at him in return. Most Kindred could only wield their element, not create it, but I was special. I conjured fire from nowhere, pushing it toward my hand, molding it into a fireball. My hand lit up the dark, a living flame sitting in my palm. I threw it at the wraith. He dodged, rolling just out of reach. I formed another fireball and launched it at his retreating form. It glanced off a tree, leaving tiny embers in the bark. I dug into my power again, pulling it forward. My palm heated, but when I looked down, expecting to see fire, all I saw was a faint glow emitting from my fingertips. I pushed my power farther, but still no fire came. I heard the wraith cackle.

"Seems someone ran out of gas." I snapped my head up, but the wraith was gone again. Suddenly, a fist flew out, cracking against my jaw. My head whipped to the side but I managed to maintain my balance. I lashed out with my dagger but came up empty. The wraith attacked again. This time I blocked it. Finally gaining my bearings, I took the fight to him. I kicked out, my foot landing solidly in his stomach. The wraith folded over and I delivered a left hook. The second my fist connected with his cheekbone, my hand exploded in pain. I screamed and instinctively tucked my hand against my body to protect it.

With my powers not working, and my hand possibly broken again, I knew I had to end the fight quickly. Before I knew it, the wraith lunged, tackling me to the ground. My dagger dropped from my hand. He sat on top of me, pinning me to the forest floor. My legs and arms immobilized, I did the only thing I could. I headbutted him. He fell back, and I was able to escape from under him. I crawled away, grabbing my dagger with my uninjured hand. Clutching it as hard as I could, I leapt back toward where the wraith laid on the ground. I drove the dagger through him, to the hilt. A brief look of surprise crossed his face until he disintegrated into nothing but ash.

I let out a sigh of relief as I plopped back against the ground, cradling my injured hand against my chest. That one had been close. For reasons I didn't understand, my powers were on the fritz. First, I didn't heal the way I should, and now I couldn't reach my fire power.

What is happening to me?

Made in the USA
Columbia, SC
13 August 2017